...

KAROLINA'S
TWINS

...

. . .

KAROLINA'S TWINS

Ronald H. Balson

St. Martin's Paperbacks

This is a work of fiction. All of the characters, organizations, and events portrayed in this novel are either products of the author's imagination or are used fictitiously.

Published in the United States by St. Martin's Paperbacks, an imprint of St. Martin's Publishing Group.

KAROLINA'S TWINS

Copyright © 2016 by Ronald H. Balson.

For information, address St. Martin's Publishing Group, 120 Broadway, New York, NY 10271.

www.stmartins.com

Library of Congress Catalog Card Number: 2016007229

ISBN: 978-1-250-23620-3

Our books may be purchased in bulk for promotional, educational, or business use. Please contact your local bookseller or the Macmillan Corporate and Premium Sales Department at 1-800-221-7945, ext. 5442, or by email at MacmillanSpecialMarkets@macmillan.com.

Printed in the United States of America

St. Martin's Griffin edition / August 2017
St. Martin's Paperbacks edition / November 2019

10   9   8   7   6   5   4   3   2   1

In blessed memory of Fay Scharf Waldman,
the remarkable, courageous woman
who inspired this story.
And to my wife, Monica, who inspires
me every day.

ONE

...

THE STENCILED WRITING ON the frosted glass door simply read INVESTIGATIONS. On the second floor of a vintage walk-up on Chicago's near north side, a broad-shouldered man in a Derry rugby shirt unwrapped a sandwich and opened the *Chicago Tribune* to the sports page. His hair, just a little thinner this year with tinges of gray sneaking in, was cut short. His ruddy face evidenced the wear of twenty years in his business.

Just as he took a healthy bite of his sandwich, the phone rang. "Damn," he mumbled.

"Liam Taggart," he said, as he swallowed.

"My name is Lena Woodward." Her voice was thin and sounded elderly. "Is this the private detective?"

"Yes, ma'am, it is. How can I help you?"

"I'd like to schedule an appointment."

"Can I ask what you have in mind, Miss Woodward?"

"It's Mrs. Woodward. I'd like you to help me find someone. Actually, two people."

"Are these people related to you?"

There was a pause on the line. "No. May I have an

appointment, please? I'll tell you all about it when I see you."

"Well, I have time this afternoon. Do you want to come in today?"

"Tomorrow morning would be better," she said, "but I need to meet with you and Ms. Lockhart. Both of you."

"Catherine's a lawyer, she doesn't find people. Does this involve a court case?"

"No."

"Well, let me make a suggestion: we'll meet tomorrow and if you have legal needs, we can always talk to Catherine later."

"Respectfully, I must insist upon her presence, Mr. Taggart. Would you see if she's available, as well?"

"Mrs. Woodward, she's a busy lawyer and she has a busy morning court call. Her time is very expensive . . ."

"Then three o'clock tomorrow afternoon, and please don't patronize me, Mr. Taggart, I know what legal costs are. I have the money to cover each of your fees if I choose to engage you."

"Could you give me just a little more information, just a hint? Why are you trying to find these people? Who are they to you? Are they in the Chicago area?" There was another pause. "Mrs. Woodward?"

"I'll tell you all about it tomorrow. Three o'clock?"

Liam sighed. "I don't have Catherine's calendar, but I'll see if she's available. May I have a number where I can reach you?"

After jotting down the information, he ended the call and sat for a moment contemplating why this woman thought it was necessary to involve Catherine in a simple skiptrace. He shrugged and made the call.

"Law offices of Catherine Lockhart."

"Gladys, what's Cat doing tomorrow afternoon at three?"

"Preparing for a hearing on Monday morning."

"Okay, would you pencil me in the book for three o'clock? We'll be meeting with a woman named Lena Woodward."

"What's it about?"

"I don't know."

IN A THREE-STORY BROWNSTONE on West Belden Ave., two blocks west of Chicago's Lincoln Park, Liam sat at the kitchen table, drinking a Guinness, staring at his computer and waiting for his wife. Two subjects occupied his thoughts: the mysterious call from Lena Woodward earlier that afternoon and his lack of a strong running back in advance of his weekly fantasy show-down with his cousin. The door opened and Catherine Lockhart-Taggart entered carrying a box of documents.

"Working tonight?" Liam said.

"I have a TRO set for Monday morning, for which I'm unprepared, and then somebody I know told Gladys to schedule an appointment for tomorrow at three, taking away my entire afternoon."

Liam took the box from Catherine and placed it on the dining room table. "She was very insistent. She bullied me."

Catherine slipped her heels off, hung her raincoat on the hook, walked to the refrigerator, and poured herself a glass of cold milk. "What does this woman want? Why are you two coming to my office?"

Liam shook his head and shrugged his shoulders. "Because she wants to see us."

"For what?"

"I think she wants us to find two people."

"What two people?"

"No idea."

"Liam, honestly, sometimes you do the goofiest things. Why didn't you ask her?"

"I did. She wouldn't tell me. She's very bossy."

"Oh hell, Liam, she's probably a kook. She won't even show up."

He shook his head. "Nope. Not a kook. She'll show."

"And you know this because . . ."

"It's me Irish intuition."

Catherine started to spread her papers out on the table. "Then your intuition should tell you that you're in charge of dinner tonight."

LIAM LOVED CHATTING WITH Catherine's secretary, a fiery Latin from Chicago's Pilsen neighborhood, who ran Cat's office tighter than Patton ran the Third. "How many paper clips did Cat use this week?" Liam teased.

"You think I don't know?" Gladys said with her hands on her hips.

Just then the door opened and a tall woman in a camel coat, knitted scarf and soft brown pillbox hat entered the office. Her gait was a bit unsteady and she needed the assistance of a shiny black cane. She smiled at Liam. "I presume you are Mr. Taggart?" She extended her hand. "I'm Lena."

"It's very nice to meet you, Lena. This is Gladys, Catherine's security force. I think Catherine is waiting for us."

Gladys took Lena's coat and escorted them back to Catherine's office. Lena appeared to be well into her eighties. She stood straight and poised, smartly dressed in a gray two-piece suit, a silk designer scarf and a pearl lattice barrette, which was clipped neatly to the right side of her styled silver hair. After the introductions, Lena came straight to the point. "I'd like to hire you both. I need to find out what happened to two children."

"Like I told you on the phone," Liam said. "Catherine doesn't find children. That's my stock-in-trade."

Lena nodded with a knowing smile. "I didn't come here by accident. I was a very close friend to Ben Solomon. Eight years ago you guided him through the final pursuit of his life—the quest to bring Hauptscharführer Otto Piatek to justice. Adele Silver and I sat with him almost every night during those trying times. I'm aware of what the two of you can do when you put your minds to it. I've seen it and I want to hire the team. I can pay for it."

"It's not a matter of money, Mrs. Woodward," Catherine said. "Ben needed a trial lawyer and I met that requirement. Ben also needed an investigator and that's where Liam came in. Ben's situation was unique. I'm sure it was quite different from yours."

Lena was unfazed. She continued to smile. "Different in some respects, but there are probably more similarities than disparities. Nevertheless, the project will require tireless efforts and a creative approach. According to Ben, it's the magical combination of your two minds that distinguishes you. He said he'd never seen anything like the way you two work together." She punctuated her declaration with her index finger. "I want the package."

"What do you want us to do, Lena?" Catherine said in a more resigned tone.

"I told you. I want you to find two children."

"Are they your children?"

Lena shook her head. "They aren't mine. But I made a promise to a very special person and I intend to keep it."

Catherine swiveled to her credenza and pushed the button on her phone. "Gladys, would you please put on a pot of coffee and hold my calls."

TWO

• • •

I SUPPOSE I SHOULD start out at the beginning and tell you how I came to know these children. I was born Lena Scheinman in the town of Chrzanów, Poland, southwest of Kraków, in the province of Silesia, in 1924. When I entered my teenage years—"

Catherine held up her hand. "Chrzanów. Is that anywhere near Zamosc?"

"No, that was Ben's town. Although spelled Chrzanów, the town is pronounced *Shah-nov*. It's on the other side of Poland, near the Czech border."

Catherine looked at Liam. "I think we've been down this road before. Will this assignment involve us in something that happened during the Holocaust? Is that why you sought us out? Because of Ben Solomon? I mean, his case was certainly about the Holocaust, but it didn't make us experts in the field of wartime Poland."

Lena raised her eyebrows. "I came to you because of your talents and, I admit, also because of Ben. He was your greatest fan. And I was his. Maybe because we were both survivors, maybe because we both went through hell in wartime Poland—as I told you, there are similarities—Ben and I had a special bond. I sought you out because I must find out what happened to two children and I think you are the ones to help me."

"I apologize for the way my question was framed. I just wanted you to know that if you need an expert on Poland or World War II, you could do a lot better than Liam and me. We were able to help Ben find and prosecute Otto Piatek, but Ben was the source of all wartime information."

"I understand, but I know I've come to the right people and I beg you to hear me out."

"Of course." Catherine turned and picked up a yellow pad. "First, let's get a little background. Are these two children related to you in some way?"

Lena shook her head. "No. They were Karolina's. They're twins."

Liam leaned forward, his elbows on the table "What are their names, Lena?"

She shook her head again. "Today? I wouldn't know. Many years ago they were Rachel and Leah."

Catherine glanced at Liam and then back to Lena. "Who is Karolina?"

"She was my dear, dear friend. She saved my life, but in the end I could not save hers." The memory made Lena pause. She blinked away a tear and brushed it aside with the back of her fingers. Finally, in a whispered tone she said, "I beg you to help me fulfill my promise. Please find Karolina's two little girls."

Catherine reached for a box of tissues and set it on the desk. "Where did Karolina live?"

Lena lowered her eyes. "In Chrzanów, near me. Many times with me."

Catherine again glanced at Liam, but he only shrugged.

"I suppose these twins were born during World War II? In Poland?"

Lena nodded.

"Lena, that's seventy years ago."

"I know. That's how long I've carried this burden. And soon, like my husband used to say, my membership card in the human race is due to expire. Two years ago, a month or two before Adele died, cancer took my husband from me. I lost my two dearest friends within sixty days. After their deaths, life had one purpose for me: my promise to Karolina.

"Over the years, my husband was very good with his business and his investments. Just before he died, he said, 'Lena, we have the money, keep your promise to Karolina. Put your soul to rest.' So, after a while I dove into it, made some inquiries, even flew back to Poland. But Chrzanów has changed. My inquiries went nowhere. I failed to generate any momentum. I really didn't know where to start. I finally came to the conclusion that if I were going to succeed in finding these girls, I would need professional help."

"And you came to us because of Ben?"

"As I said, Ben, Adele and I were very close. Ben told me that if I was ever going to seek out these children, I should come to you and Liam. He said you were a good listener, and if anybody could do it, you could do it. He constantly raved about you, Catherine. How patient and understanding you were."

"I'm honored, thank you. Ben was also very special to me."

"Where was the last place these children were seen?" Liam said.

"I wish I could give you the precise location or even the name of a town, but I can't. I know the general region, at least the way it was in 1943, but it's probably too imprecise."

Liam shook his head. "I have to be honest with you, Lena. I don't know if it's possible to help you. I'm pretty good at locating people, but I need a starting point." He counted on his fingers, "One, we don't know their names. Two, we don't know where they live. Three, we don't know where they were last seen. Four, we don't know what they presently look like and we don't even know if they're still alive. I'm afraid you'd be throwing your savings away on a wild-goose chase."

Lena remained unfazed. Her countenance was resolute and she pointed her chin. "We'll find them, I know we will. With your expert help." She gave a sharp, definitive nod. "We'll find them."

"Maybe it would help if you tell us a little bit about Karolina and why you're so invested in finding her children. Maybe after all these years they're doing just fine and don't need your assistance."

"That's not the point. There's information they need to know and I need to tell them."

Catherine picked up her pen. "Well, there's information I need to know as well before I can agree to get involved. I'm not going to accept your money if I don't have confidence that Liam and I can do something for you."

"Understood and agreed."

"All right, let's get started. Tell me about Karolina. Everything you remember."

"You'll listen? Keep an open mind?"

Catherine smiled. "Yes, I will."

"Thank you. Thank you so much." She took a sip of coffee, crossed her legs, smoothed her skirt and began. "I first met Karolina on the day she pushed my brother home from school."

Catherine furrowed her brow. "Pushed him?"

"My brother was seven and needed a wheelchair. When Milosz was four, he was stricken with childhood polio. My father took him to a doctor in Kraków who attended to him night and day. Back in the thirties, Milosz was a miracle child—he beat the disease. But it left him with severely withered legs and an inability to walk. A disability, to be sure, but not one that ever minimized Milosz. He couldn't play outside with the other boys, so the Muses compensated him with gifts of music, art and poetry."

"At age seven?"

"Absolutely. He could delight you with his talents—he played the violin. I'm sorry you never got the chance to hear him play. Or see his drawings. Or hear him recite his poetry. Even at seven years old."

Lena smiled at the memory. "Milosz could infect you with his joie de vivre. Though physically hampered, he never considered himself unlucky and a smile never left his face. He had nothing but kind words to say. Everyone adored him. Simply said, he loved life.

"Anyway, because of Milosz's disability, someone had to take him to and from school every day. Usually that person was Magda—she was our live-in nanny and housekeeper. Really, she was much more. She was part of our family and a great influence in my young life. She would take Milosz to and from the elementary school in his wheelchair—which Milosz referred to as his 'Maserati.'"

"Was the school far?" Catherine said. "I'm trying to get a sense of your town."

"Maybe seven, eight blocks. Nothing was too far in Chrzanów. There was a central market square and the town blossomed out from there. Cars were rare in Chrzanów. My family didn't own a car, even though we were quite comfortable. Everybody walked. If you needed to go farther than a good walk, you took a horse and buggy. We had a carriage. It was a fancy buggy.

"In those days, Chrzanów had about twenty-five thousand residents. Forty percent of the town was Jewish and the remainder was Catholic. The immediate area around Chrzanów was hilly and thick with forests. Beyond the perimeter, the countryside was a patchwork of farms, lumber mills and mining operations, especially coal. Kraków, Poland's second largest city, was forty-five kilometers to the east.

"My mother's family owned a store on the edge of the main square that sold building materials and farm provisions. It had been in her family for years. My mother, Hannah Scheinman, worked in the store several days a week. My father, Jacob Scheinman, worked there as well. With both my parents working, Magda not only took care of the house, she took care of Milosz and me.

"The day I met Karolina, it was raining. Magda had gone out of town to visit her mother. My father was supposed to pick up Milosz, but he got tied up at the store and couldn't break away. He asked the school's headmistress to have someone help me bring Milosz home. Karolina was chosen.

"Our home was three blocks off the market square—a two-story, stone house with a gabled roof and a small attic. I mention the attic because it would soon become the centerpiece of my existence. When Karolina brought Milosz home, she hung around for a while. As young girls will do, we had a snack and gossiped away the afternoon. Soon my mother arrived and insisted that Karolina stay for dinner. I was twelve at the time. Milosz was seven. Karolina was thirteen.

"I had seen Karolina at school, but she was a year ahead of me. She was also very popular. Even then, as a young teen, she was exquisite and she grew more beautiful with each passing year. She was strong, athletic and vivacious. She had dark, curly hair and big expressive eyes. Coy, flirtatious, smart, bold and very sure of herself, the boys flocked to her.

"I didn't know at the time, but her confidence was a charade, an appearance that she wore like an overcoat. Inside she was unhappy and insecure. Her father, Mariusz Neuman, was a withdrawn, severe man, always worried about his business. He had little patience for Karolina's gaiety. His business was struggling, especially in the 1930s. So, Karolina started spending a lot of time at our house.

"Karolina became an adjunct member of our family. We all loved her and she loved us, but I think she loved Milosz the most. She would sit and listen to him play even when he was just practicing his scales." Lena shrugged. "Or perhaps it was my mother's kreplach soup. Anyway, Karolina practically lived at our house."

"Was Karolina Jewish as well?"

Lena nodded. "At the time, Karolina and I attended Chrzanów's public school. Our new friendship opened a large social circle for me. She took me under her wing and brought me into the popular crowd. It was so easy being around Karolina. I grew to love the Chrzanów elementary school, but my time there came to an end in 1938, when I was ready for high school.

"Partly because I was a good student and partly because we were a privileged family, when I was fourteen my parents sent me to attend the Gymnasium in Kraków."

"The gymnasium?" Liam said.

Lena smiled. "Although it was called the Gymnasium, it wasn't a gym, it was a private secondary school where gen-ed courses were taught in Polish, and Jewish studies were taught in Hebrew.

"I didn't want to go there. I wanted to stay in Chrzanów. That's where all my friends were. I wanted to go to high school with Karolina. I protested, but I never had a chance in that battle. My Jewish studies were compulsory and my parents were able to enroll me in a prestigious high school, so that's where I went.

"I'm sure you know, before the war, Poland had three million Jews, more than any other country in Europe. Ten percent of Poland's population was Jewish, and my parents were observant—they took their religion seriously. Anyway, I would travel to and from Kraków every day on the train. The Chrzanów station was six blocks from my house. However, thanks to the Germans, I only attended for the one year."

"One year?"

Lena shrugged. "The war."

"So was life comfortable in Chrzanów before the war?"

Lena tipped her head from side to side. "For *my* family, yes. But not for all. My parents' store was very profitable and served customers from the neighboring Silesian towns. And my father was a decorated war hero. He held the rank of captain—three stars—in the army of the Austro-Hungarian Empire. In World War I, he fought alongside German troops."

"Alongside the Germans as a Jewish captain. How unusual," Liam said.

"No, not unusual at all. No religious distinction was made during World War I. The Jews of Germany and the Austro-Hungarian Empire fought together in the armies of the Central Powers as enlisted men and as officers. One hundred thousand Jews fought in the German army, often holding high ranks, and twelve thousand lost their lives. The empire had always welcomed Jews, and Jewish society flourished. We were doctors, lawyers, judges, scientists. The same throughout Germany.

"After the First World War, my father enjoyed a certain

status and prestige because of his rank and service. Everyone called him 'The Captain.' I wouldn't say we were wealthy, but we were comfortable. Still, in the 1930s Poland suffered from the Depression, and Chrzanów's economy suffered. Our store continued to sell provisions to the farmers, but oftentimes on credit, which we knew would never be repaid.

"Karolina's family fared much worse during the Depression. Her father was a tailor. In the early 1930s his business did okay, probably because it was cheaper to have clothes repaired than to buy new ones. He was often so busy that Karolina would help him on Sundays and after school. She became a proficient seamstress as a teen. Come 1937, in the depth of the Depression, people had no money, even for repairs, and stopped going to the tailor. Karolina's father had to close his shop. He went off to Warsaw, where his brother had a butcher shop, only returning once a month. Karolina and her mother stayed behind.

"When her father left, Karolina's mother began to drink. Those times that I stopped by Karolina's, her mother was always in some state of inebriation. Her speech was slurred, her balance unsteady. It was an embarrassment to Karolina and because of that, I rarely visited.

"Karolina had a dog, a white French poodle with pink paws that she loved with all her heart. She got it when she was in the eighth grade. Karolina and I were coming home from school one day and we passed a yard where a boy was giving away puppies. 'My mom won't let me keep them all,' he said, pointing to a box with nine little white dogs. 'If you want one, you could have one.' At first, Karolina's father wouldn't let her keep it, but seeing her so disheartened, he relented, providing she took care of it and worked to buy the dog food.

"Because it was a French poodle, Karolina named her

Madeleine. With her father and mother essentially in absentia, Madeleine was Karolina's anchor. In her almost daily visits to our home, Madeleine would tag along. At first my parents weren't thrilled, but Milosz loved that dog, and Madeleine loved Milosz. He would sit on the floor and play with Madeleine and giggle so hard it would make all of us laugh. Milosz even taught her tricks. So, Madeleine became another member of our family.

"My father had three brothers. One lived in Warsaw, one in Kraków and one in Berlin. They were all successful. My father traveled to Berlin quite often on business or to spend time with his oldest brother. He took me there twice. I don't remember much about Berlin except my Uncle Samuel had a very large house with a beautiful garden.

"I do remember in 1933 my father returned from Berlin to tell us that the Hitlerites were burning Jewish books in bonfires. I was only eight years old and I asked him, 'Why would they burn Jewish books? If they didn't like them they didn't have to read them.' He told me that was a very good point.

"As Germany descended into abomination, he traveled less and less to Berlin, and only when absolutely necessary for business. Two years later, in December 1935, he told us that Uncle Samuel was moving to America. The Nuremberg Laws had stripped Jews of their professional licenses and my uncle was a respected pediatrician and a professor at the medical school. The Nuremberg Laws forbade him from treating anyone but Jewish children and prohibited him from teaching at the school. He wisely decided it was time to leave and he left for New York.

"Finally, in 1938, my father made his last trip to Berlin. It was two weeks before Kristallnacht. About that time we started to feel tensions forming in Chrzanów's once-tolerant society. Nazi propaganda filtered into Poland and anti-Semitism was gaining a foothold throughout the country. When commuting to the Gymnasium, I remember people on the train pointing at us, holding their noses and chanting, 'I smell garlic.'

"Because Chrzanów was close to the German and Czechoslovakian borders, refugees fleeing Silesia and parts of Germany would come through Chrzanów on their way east, wheeling their worldly belongings in carts and wagons. Before the war began, Jews were free to emigrate from Germany under the condition that they leave most of their belongings behind and pay a stiff emigration tax. From these refugees we would hear about Germany's persecution.

"As the war approached and the German rhetoric heightened, our town became keenly aware of the impending storm clouds. Polish troops were bivouacked in our area. In fact, they were stationed in the redbrick army barracks at the fort in Oświęcim, twenty kilometers down the road. I don't have to tell you, those were the very same barracks that would later hold thousands of Jewish prisoners when the name was changed to Auschwitz. My father was no fool. He anticipated the worst. It was time for us to leave.

"I remember the night in December 1938 when my father sat the family down at the dining room table and said, 'Hannah, the Nazis are coming, make no mistake. They took over Austria in March, they annexed half of Czechoslovakia in September and they'll be here whenever they feel like it. There'll be no stopping them. And they've made their intentions for our people well known. Last month, on Kristallnacht, the Nazis destroyed a thousand synagogues and thousands of Jewish businesses throughout Germany, Austria, East Prussia and the Sudetenland. Thirty thousand Jews were arrested and most of them were sent to the Buchenwald prison.

Germany will only release them if they can prove they have the means to emigrate.

"'They want us out of Europe, Hannah. Not just Germany, but all of Europe. All of us. Men like me, respected Jewish officers in the German army who served their country with distinction, have been stripped of our rank and even citizenship. We need to face facts. We can't stay here in Chrzanów. I'm going to make the arrangements.'"

"Did your mother object?"

Lena smiled. "She protested gently. Times were different then. He was the head of the family. If the father made plans, then the family followed. My mother's family had lived in the region for generations. They'd founded the provisions store eighty years earlier. It was hard for her to leave. How could she ever live somewhere else?

"'Where do we go?' she said. 'America, like Samuel? He ended up in Chicago. They have gangsters there, Jacob. Al Capone. I don't think I'd like that. It's too dangerous for the children.'

"My father chuckled. 'Al Capone's in jail.'

"'It's still too dangerous in Chicago. They have other gangsters.'

"'I'm not thinking about Chicago, Hannah. I want to move us to Paris. They have a very solid Jewish community, two hundred fifty thousand. I know prominent people there. There's a grocery store I can buy, I've contacted the owner. We can sell the house and the provisions store and use the money to move to France.'

"I was distraught, of course. Devastated was more like it. Fifteen years old, and like my mother, Poland was all I knew. I certainly didn't want to live in Paris. Or Chicago. I didn't speak a word of French or English. German was my second language. It was taught in all the schools.

"Most of all, I didn't want to leave Karolina or any of my friends. By then, Karolina and I had become very close. I'd be lost without her. With Karolina, I was part of a larger, more dynamic group. Our crowd was so much fun, and I was included because of Karolina. We were the best of friends. Inseparable. I'd be a nobody in Paris.

"One afternoon, my father took me for a soda. Just the two of us. 'I know this is going to be hard on you, Lena. And it will be even harder for Milosz. But I have to do what's best for us, and staying in Chrzanów is too dangerous. I found a lovely apartment for us in Paris—in the 12th Arrondissement, just south of the Jardin du Luxembourg. I promise you will find it enchanting. I found a store for sale that we can buy. In time, if things get better in Chrzanów, we can always return. But you may grow fond of Paris.'

"'What about Magda?' I said.

"He shook his head. 'I'm afraid we'll have to leave Magda here. Truth is, I can barely afford to keep her as it is, but I haven't had the heart to let her go.'

"'What about Karolina?'

"'I'm sorry, but you'll make new friends and maybe someday Karolina can visit.' That was totally unacceptable to me and I ran home to my room. He came up a few minutes later and sat on my bed. 'I'm sorry to make you sad, but I have to do what's best for all of us. Please try to understand.'

"'Can Karolina come and live with us in Paris?'

"'Well, I doubt her parents would approve.'

"'They don't care. Her father is mean to her and lives in Warsaw most of the time. Her mother is drunk all the time. What if they say it's okay?'

"To my surprise, he nodded his head. 'If her parents will give her permission, I'll take her with us. Don't say anything yet. Before we can leave Chrzanów, I have to sell the store and the house. It could take a while. When I get an offer, and I know for certain that we'll be going, then you can tell Karolina and see if her parents will let her come along.' I hugged him to death. What a great father.

"There weren't many who could afford to buy a house and a store during the Depression. Our store was quite profitable and thus pricey for a small-town business. But by February 1939, my father had obtained a signed contract from a Warsaw investment group and we were packing to move."

"And Karolina?"

"Of course I had already spilled the news to Karolina right after my father and I had our talk, but she hadn't asked her parents yet. She went home that night and asked her mother, who, shockingly, approved. But when her father came home that weekend, he put his foot down. 'No way,' he said. 'It's all crap, this war hysteria. Just a bunch of German blowhards. The Scheinmans are Polish. They're not going to like those stuck-up Parisians, Karolina. They'll be back soon. Things will be better then.'

"Karolina was heartbroken. *We* were heartbroken. She was part of our family. My mother called us the Two *L*s—Lena and Lina. I was losing my best friend. Karolina kept begging her father. All around us, our social circles were disintegrating. Families were making plans to move. Some just packed up and headed east to Ukraine or Romania. Some went south to Slovakia. Every day another one of our friends would say good-bye. But Karolina's father wouldn't change his mind.

"Of course, as he pointed out, not *every* family was moving. Some were in denial and foolishly believed in Poland's military defenses or the alliances with Britain and France. Some had no money and no way to leave.

Karolina's father had decided his family would stay in Chrzanów. He was saving his money in Warsaw and he intended to come back and reopen his tailor shop.

"I cried. Milosz cried. I didn't know who he'd miss more: Karolina or Madeleine. But Karolina and I made a secret pact. As soon as I was settled in Paris, she was going to run away, take a train and join us. I was going to send her the money. Milosz overheard us and threatened to tell our parents if she didn't promise to bring Madeleine, but I don't think that thought ever entered her mind. She wouldn't go anywhere without her dog."

"But your family never did move to Paris, did they?"

Lena slowly shook her head. "Sadly, no. The buyers, the Warsaw consortium, couldn't raise the money. Because of the Depression and the impending threats from Germany, the bank wouldn't consummate the loan. The buyers begged us for time to raise the money and pleaded with my father not to sell to someone else. But there was no one else. It was now June 1939. My father couldn't move without the sale proceeds. So we waited. And hoped.

"On September 1, 1939, Germany invaded Poland. Seventy thousand Poles were killed and almost seven hundred thousand were taken into custody. At six A.M., Stukas strafed the nearby railroad station. We heard radio broadcasts of German bombings and we knew that our plans to move were off the table. In retrospect, it probably wouldn't have mattered if we had moved to Paris. Hitler invaded France the following May, and Paris fell on June fourteenth. I doubt our fate would have been much different in Paris. Anyway, three days later, on September fourth, German trucks rolled into Chrzanów and soldiers occupied our town without a fight.

"The Nazis settled in like the deep winter snow and just as cold. And they never left. Their numbers seemed to increase every day. The SS and Gestapo didn't arrive until a little later, but the German army was bad enough. The first thing they did was to take prisoners. Men only. They arrested Jews and non-Jews alike.

"Soldiers came into the store in the late afternoon and pulled my father out from behind the register. The more prominent you were, the more likely you'd be taken. If you hesitated, they shot you. One older man named Chaim, who was hard of hearing, failed to immediately follow a command to halt and was shot dead in the middle of the street.

"The Germans locked the Jewish men in the synagogue and the Catholic men in the church. The overflow was locked in the city administration building. They roughed people up and interrogated them, but there were no mass executions. They just kept everyone prisoner overnight. The next day they announced their new rules and let all the prisoners go home. The message was clear: we are in charge and we can do whatever we want. Don't buck the order. Follow the rules. Then you will live.

"The Nazis set up their command post at city hall and demanded a census. I'm certain you heard the same story from Ben. They wrote down the names of everyone in town, every member of the family, and where they lived. At that time they didn't ask if you were Jewish, or a Communist, or a Roma. That all came later. Their immediate goal was to drive home a point—they were superior, we were inferior and they had a license to be cruel. They could and did act without constraint—legal, moral or otherwise.

"The Germans posted lists of their new rules all over town. All stores were required to stay open every day, even on the Sabbath. No one was permitted to leave town without a permit. Permits were not issued. A curfew was established at sundown for all residents. Anyone out after curfew was subject to summary execution. All radios were to be turned in immediately. Anyone caught with a radio would be executed. Our radio was a large console model. We carried it to the curb, and they came by and demolished it with a sledgehammer. Then we cleaned up the mess. On September fourteenth, Erev Rosh Hashanah, uniformed soldiers surrounded the synagogues and ordered them shut.

"Ration coupon cards were issued to Jews and non-Jews alike. Of course, that didn't mean there was food to buy. From the moment the Germans rolled into town, there was a severe food shortage—they took it all. They cleaned out the shelves at the markets and the bakeries. They requisitioned most of the production of the surrounding farms. Lines for food formed early at the butcher shop, the bakery, the grocery store. A long wait at the butcher, if successful, might yield six ounces of some portion of a cow or maybe nothing.

"Polish signs on public buildings were taken down and replaced with German signs. Street names were changed from Polish to German and renamed for German heroes or replaced by the German phonetic name. In 1941, they changed the name of our town from Chrzanów to Krenau.

"Those were the written rules. The unwritten rules were driven home by experience. Get off the sidewalk if you see a German coming. You better not be in his way, even if it means stepping into a puddle. If a man walks in public with a yarmulke on, a Nazi is sure to take it off and force the man use it to polish his jackboots. And don't make eye contact. It's considered provocative. For girls, we knew to go out in groups or not at all. Even in the hot weather, girls were smart to cover up.

"The city became red and black with Nazi flags. They were hung from all the city buildings. Swastikas were everywhere. And so were the Germans. On every block, at every corner. I know that Ben must have told you all about the horrors of life during the occupation."

Catherine nodded. "Yes, I'm afraid he did."

"The Germans levied a tax upon the Jews. The professed purpose was to pay for the German administration of our town. After all, how could the Nazis be expected to pay for their own conquest? Obviously, the real object was to impoverish the Jews. To that end, Jewish men were conscripted and ordered to go door-to-door to collect the taxes in paper bags. Woe be to the family that did not pay.

"Within months Germany annexed Chrzanów and the Polish towns to our west—Chełmek, Trzebinia, Libiąż. We were now located inside Germany and were no longer part of the Republic of Poland, but of course we were not German citizens. We were Jews and Jews cannot be citizens. Krenau was now a German town. Poles in our town who could prove some German origin or ethnicity, the *Volksdeutsche*, could become Germanized, and thus privileged.

"I'm sorry to say that many of the *Volksdeutsche* took to it like a duck to water. They immediately became superior to us and would enthusiastically shoot their arms up in a *Seig Heil* salute to the German soldiers. The *Volksdeutsche* strived to ingratiate themselves and would point out Jews to the Gestapo. They would gleefully run to report any infraction of the rules. I remember Mrs. Czeskowicz, an unassertive, spineless widow who became Germanized, running full speed to find a German soldier to report little Tomas Resky for walking through the park."

Catherine wrinkled her brow in a confused look.

"He was a Jewish boy and Jews were prohibited from using public parks. Mrs. Czeskowicz caught him cutting through the park on his way home and turned him in.

He was only twelve, but that didn't stop the Nazis from giving him a beating. And Mrs. Czeskowicz stayed to watch.

"Our currency, Polish zlotys, was officially abolished and could no longer be used in any stores. The new currency was the German mark. We were allowed to exchange zlotys for German marks—two zlotys would get you one mark, though it was counterproductive to make the exchange, because you would be telling the Germans that you had money and they'd come and get it.

"I was fifteen in 1939. For my friends and me, we viewed the occupation through a teenager's eyes—how did it affect our lives? How much were our social and educational lives disrupted? As I already told you, the first thing that happened to me was the change in my education—the Gymnasium was closed. Not that it would have mattered if it stayed open—taking the train to Kraków was out of the question. Passage on the trains was forbidden without a passport.

"My father immediately enrolled me in the Chrzanów public high school. To tell you the truth, at the time, it didn't seem so bad. I was reunited with Karolina and most of my friends. My social group was back in business. Unfortunately, that only lasted until October 30, 1939. That was the day all secondary schools in Poland were closed. Our high school was requisitioned by the Germans to serve as an arms depot. All of the maps, equipment, books—the entire library of over six thousand volumes—were destroyed by the Germans.

"The grade schools were still open, but after they took the Jewish census, all Jewish students were barred from attending. Jews in Chrzanów were identified and issued white armbands with blue stars to wear on our left arms. How did they know who were Jews? Because, as I mentioned, there were Poles who, in an attempt to curry the favor of the Germans, would take them around town, pointing and yelling 'Jude.'

"Germans issued new regulations for Polish education. Reichsführer Heinrich Himmler, who you may remember as the architect of the Holocaust, set the new rules. Since the non-Jewish Poles were destined to become subservient slave labor for the Germans in the General Government, there was no need to waste time and money educating them. Himmler said Poles should learn only simple arithmetic, up to five hundred, and the writing of one's name. He said, 'I don't think reading is necessary.'

"I remember the winter morning they closed the grade school to the Jewish children. I had taken Milosz to school and when we arrived, we saw German soldiers standing shoulder to shoulder at the schoolhouse door, their rifles pointed at the children. They had lists of the students. One of the soldiers with a clipboard addressed us. 'What is your name?'

"'Milosz Scheinman,' I responded. He looked at his list and checked off his name. 'Take him home. He is a Jew. He is terminated from the school. Do not bring him back or your parents will be arrested.'

"In response to the school closures, our Jewish community established classes at the synagogue, but that didn't last either. Harassment of students coming to and from school was so pervasive, the classes had to be abandoned. So, Karolina and I ended up studying at home with books my father obtained. My mother was a tough teacher. She made sure we kept regular school hours and did our homework.

"She also enforced the curfew hours, which, of all the restrictions, were the toughest for me because it meant alienation from my friends. She was insistent. 'The Germans would like nothing better than to arrest and abuse young girls. Stay off the streets unless absolutely necessary, and never after curfew.' But we were teenagers and when did teenagers ever listen to their parents?

"As the days grew shorter, the opportunities to socialize became fewer and more difficult for us. Curfew would begin as early as four-thirty. One evening, just after I had turned fifteen, I snuck out the back door, met Karolina and went to Freda's house. There we joined all our friends in her basement for a wild party. There was music from a phonograph, lots of boys and even beer." Lena bit her bottom lip in a mischievous gesture. "That was a bad mistake on my part. When I came home, my mother was furious.

"'Where have you been? Are you crazy? Do you know that people are being shot for violating curfew?'

"Because I was emboldened by a glass or two of beer, when my mother scolded me, I shrugged my shoulders and smiled with an air of disobedience, which enraged my mother. She hauled off and slapped me across my face as hard as she could. The only time in my life. And she grounded me for a month. No going out, and Karolina could not come over. Except for dinner and chores, I had to stay in my room. She ultimately relented on Karolina because she felt sorry for her, but she kept us apart for the month.

"In the spring of 1940, I came downstairs to see my father and some other men talking in our living room. They said something about a large prison camp being built just southwest of town. One of the men said the Nazis were requisitioning workers to expand the former Polish army camp at Oświęcim. By then, the name had been changed to Auschwitz, which is the German pronunciation for Oświęcim.

"When the men left, I asked my father about it. He thought deeply for a few moments, and then said, 'You're old enough and you'll know soon enough. Come with me.' He took me into his study and shut the door.

"'Lena, what I'm about to tell you is private information, just between you and me, not to be repeated to anyone. Do we agree?'

"I nodded calmly, but his demeanor was frightening me.

"'Those men who met with me, do you know them?'

"I shook my head. 'Only Mr. Osteen, the math teacher.'

"'Good,' he said. 'Forget they were ever here. Do not tell anyone that I met with those men. There may be more meetings in our home, or I may have to leave to go to meetings, and you are never to tell anyone about any of it. Do you understand? Do I have your promise?'

"I nodded. 'I promise.' On the one hand I was scared, but on the other hand I was proud to be taken into my father's confidence. 'I heard someone talk about working at a prison camp at Oświęcim,' I confessed in a whisper.

"My father cursed under his breath. 'Lena, if you haven't already, you will see German soldiers grabbing men from our town, supposedly for work details. They send them away for a day, sometimes several days. We know that some of them are sent to Oświęcim where the Germans are building a very large prisoner-of-war camp to house thousands of Poles.'

"'Will they take you for work detail?'

"'I hope not, but who knows? They might. Most of the men come home at night.'

"'But not all?'

"'Not all.'

"'Why were you and the other men talking about it?'

"He smiled and patted me on the head. 'You know more than you should. Now remember, this is our secret. Not a word to anyone.'"

"So your dad knew about Auschwitz from the beginning?" Catherine said.

"Well, the prison at Auschwitz was never a secret. People would work at the camp and come back to Chrzanów. They would talk about what they had done. At that time, Auschwitz didn't have gas chambers, crematoriums or mass extermination sites, it was a barbed-wire-encircled prison camp. In June 1940, the camp became operational. It housed Polish prisoners of war—soldiers, dissidents and the intelligentsia—who were transported from other jails and prisons that were overflowing. They were kept in cellblocks. Block 11 was a notorious building used by the Gestapo for torture.

"Actually, from the onset, Auschwitz was a place of abuse and summary executions. It was enlarged the following March to hold thirty thousand prisoners. I didn't know in 1940 why my father and the others were meeting to discuss Auschwitz, although I had my suspicions. I only surmised that my father was part of an informal resistance group.

"Later that year, the Germans began to requisition houses all over town. They gave notice, usually not more than a few days, that the Reich was taking possession of the house. Families were forced to vacate and relocate to other living quarters. The house was then handed over to Wehrmacht officers, SS, Gestapo or Polish collaborators. We knew it wouldn't be long until they expropriated our home as well. It was one of the nicer ones in town and centrally located."

"Where were displaced people supposed to go?" Catherine asked. "Had the Germans established alternative quarters for Chrzanów? A Jewish ghetto?"

"Hmph. What did the Germans care? Nothing had been established as of that time. There was a ghetto, but it was de facto. Chrzanów's displaced Jews started to congregate in the northeast section. The buildings were old—both commercial and residential—many were vacant, and rooms were available for small amounts of money. Or no money. Squatting became an accepted form of tenancy. So the northeast area became the unofficial Chrzanów ghetto. Later, it became the designated, mandatory Jewish ghetto. But, for whatever reason, our house wasn't taken until several months later.

"Almost every day I'd see a family pushing a cart or a wagon up the residential streets toward the ghetto. The carts were overloaded with as many of their belongings as they could fit in or on the cart, usually bundled up in blankets and sheets and tied together. Clothes, shoes, bedding, pots and pans. Children would walk alongside the carts with suitcases. They took whatever they could, because they knew they could not return to their home. Sometimes they took pieces of furniture and piled them on top of the cart, but more often, if the Germans were requisitioning a home, they'd require the owners to leave their furnishings behind.

"As 1941 began, the Germans really tightened the vise. They declared that most of the stores were *Für Juden verboten,* off-limits to Jews. Our store was forfeited to a German owner, though my father was appointed to run it for a small stipend. Jewish ration cards were no longer valid to purchase clothes.

"Food became scarce, not because we couldn't afford it—my father had stashed away a bit of cash and jewelry—but because it simply wasn't available. Each month, the Nazis issued the family a *Lebbensmittel-karte.* Food card. The card was divided into sections. Each coupon was dated and designated with what you could buy on that day. For example, in the month of November there were fifteen bread coupons. You could stand in line for bread every other day. If the bakery still had bread. There were only four coupons on the card for meat. Only four for marmalade. Only four days on which you could buy sugar, if you got there early and if the store still had it in stock. So if the store was out of sugar, you had to wait until next week, when the next coupon would be valid.

"Our food cards bore a Jewish star in the middle and read '*Für Juden*.' They had to be signed by the family and were not transferable. If a card was lost, there was no replacement.

"At first, Magda would go to the stores and stand in line for our rations, but soon the Germans forbade her from working for us or from standing in line with our card. Since Christians were not allowed to work for Jews, Magda had to leave our house. It broke our hearts and hers as well. She was like a second mother to us.

"As difficult as the Germans had made our lives, another crushing, heartbreaking event occurred that November. I was home reading when Karolina burst into the house in a state of hysteria. 'Madeleine,' she wailed. 'They want to take my Madeleine.' My mother nodded. She had heard the news. Jews were ordered to turn in all pets. We were given two days.

"Karolina was inconsolable. She sat with Madeleine, hugging her and kissing her. 'I won't give them Madeleine. I'll run away. They're not going to take my dog. She's my baby.' My mother put her comforting arms around her. She knew that in Karolina's world, with a drunken mother and an absent father, the love of that dog was all she had.

"'You can't run away, there's no place to go,' my mother said gently. 'Let me talk to the Captain. Maybe he'll have an idea.' Karolina nodded and sat rocking with her dog, sobbing continuously until my father came home.

"He pulled up a chair, leaned over with his elbows on his knees and listened. He knew how important Madeleine was to Karolina. And to Milosz. He also knew there were times to make a stand and times to give in.

"'Let me talk to a couple of farmers,' he said. 'They might take Madeleine for a while until the Germans leave. Would that be all right?' Karolina threw her arms around my father's neck, thanking him profusely.

"But he couldn't do it. None of the families wanted to risk violating a Nazi order just to save a dog. Sadly, he told Karolina that he'd had no success. She'd have to give up Madeleine. He said he'd accompany her to the town square the next day.

"She stood defiantly. Her eyes were wide with anger. I'd never seen her like that. 'I will not give my dog to the Nazis. She's my dog. She's a sweet little dog, she never hurt anybody. Why do they want to take her? I won't let them. They can't have her. I'm going to disobey that evil order. They can kill me if they want to, and we'll die together.'

"My father shook his head. 'I can't let you do that. You're too precious to us.'

"'But they'll kill Madeleine. For no reason.'

"'Yes, I'm afraid they will,' he answered softly. 'We've had to give up many of our beloved possessions. But they're possessions. Remember this—our lives are more valuable than any possession. We must preserve our lives and the lives of our family. They can have our possessions, they cannot have our lives. We can give up a radio, a fur coat, even a beloved pet, as long as we protect our family. And you, Karolina, are family to us.'

"'I won't let them. I'll take her to the country, to the edge of town, to wherever I can and let her loose.'

"Again, my father shook his head. 'She won't survive on her own. She's domesticated. She'll just lie down and wait for you to come back and feed her. It might be more merciful to give her to the Germans.'

"Karolina stomped her foot. 'You don't know that. She might survive. Someone might find her and love her. She could find things to eat. Maybe a bird, maybe a mouse. I'd just as soon throw her in a field as let the Nazis kill her.'

"In a surprise move, my father said, 'You're right. Someone might find her. But you can't be the one to take her, she'll just follow you home. I'll take her.'

"'Really? You wouldn't lie to me?'

"My father took her in his arms and said, 'Karolina, I would never lie to you. I'll take Madeleine to the edge of town tonight, into the country as far as I can, and we'll let God take care of her from there.'

"And that's what happened. That night, my father put the leash on Madeleine, and Karolina said good-bye to her.

"'You find a nice family,' she said, kneeling on the floor, hugging Madeleine, Madeleine licking her face. 'Another family will love you and treat you well. You're tough, Madeleine, you'll make it. After the Germans leave, I'll find you, wherever you are. I'll come back and find you, I promise.' With that, my father left the house and did not return for several hours.

"Karolina wailed from the bottom of her soul. My mother rocked with her. We all wept with her. Taking a pet from a child could serve no purpose other than to impose heartless cruelty. Little did we know of the cruelty that was to come.

"New rules came down every day and more restrictions were imposed. Still, we survived. We adapted. We would wait it out. We held tight to the belief that soon the world would crush the Germans and they would leave. But that all changed for us in 1941.

"Throughout the occupation, my father had been outwardly compliant with the German standing orders, while secretly continuing to meet with his resistance group. It was dangerous to be a dissident. It was a standing invitation to an execution. Any talk of insubordination was punishable by death, and rewards were given to Polish informants. Yet, Polish partisans were passionate people. Do not think all Jews were lambs to the slaughter. There were cells—covert meetings in basements where plans to disrupt the Germans were discussed. My father was a respected army officer and his contributions were valued.

"In Chrzanów, however, the web of secrecy was too porous. Ultimately, the Germans, with their slinking intelligence units and frightened collaborators, uncovered groups of dissenters and the Nazis quickly apprehended them, one by one. Many times they were taken to the town square and publicly hanged from wooden gallows. Other times they were sent away to unknown destinations. My father had friends in town, Jews and non-Jews alike. And so, when his time came, he received a warning note—the Nazis were on their way to pick him up.

"It was early afternoon. March 12, 1941—the precise date has been permanently etched in my memory. My father rushed into the house, pulled me aside and said, 'I've been told the Germans will be here later today. They're coming here to question me. They may take me down to headquarters and then let me go. In a worst-case scenario, they may not let me come home. I could be sent to a prison camp. You should be prepared for that.'

"'Why?' I said. Suddenly I was shaking, my lips were quivering, my eyes were starting to fill. 'Why would they take you?'

"'Rumor? Innuendo? A traitor among us? I don't believe they have any evidence of wrongdoing, but that's never stopped the Nazis. I don't think they'll bother the rest of our family, but they might. They may want to take us all in for questioning. Just remember, you don't know anything and you never saw anybody.'

"'Daddy,' I cried.

"'Lena, they may just be coming to tell us that we have to move from our house. They're telling people all over Chrzanów. I don't know. No one knows. That's why everyone's constantly afraid, because they're unpredictable. Like a coiled snake.'

"He put his hands on my shoulders. 'They might just want to relocate our family. But I can't be sure. It could be worse.' He handed me an envelope full of money. 'You're young and strong and healthy. When they come, I don't want you anywhere near us. Go upstairs into the attic and shut the trapdoor. Do not use the ladder. Do not make a sound. If they're here to take the family, you stay up there. Even if they shout. Do not come down until you're sure it's safe. Maybe late at night. Maybe not even until tomorrow.

"'They know who's in our family and they might search for you. When it's safe to come down, go directly to the Tarnowskis' farm, out Slaska Street, west of town. About ten kilometers. I've made arrangements with the Tarnowskis. They'll take you in and hide you.'"

"So, your father thought the whole family might be arrested and sent to a camp?" Catherine said.

"Or worse. But by 1941, it was also possible for me to get sent to a labor camp, independent of my father's activities. By then, the Nazis had been demanding young men and women to send to slave labor camps. There were whole industries staffed by Jewish slave labor. Being seventeen, I was old enough to be chosen.

"Demands for Jewish workers were generally filled through the Judenrat. We were required to check the board every day. If the Judenrat posted your name for work, you had to appear at the given time and place, most often the town square, first thing in the morning. If you didn't show up, the Nazis would search for you. If they found you, they'd kill you. Then they'd take five other members of your family. If they didn't find you, they'd grab twenty other people at random. There was no mercy. No pleading.

"A few weeks before, the Nazis had rolled through town, screaming through their megaphones, '*Alle Juden auf den Marktplatz. Schnell. Macht schnell.*' Thousands of us, men, women and children, gathered in the rain in the market square. In the middle, wooden gallows had been constructed. Four Jewish men stood on stools, yarmulkes on their heads, ropes around their necks, their hands tied behind their backs, waiting to die. They softly chanted the *Shema,* which was fine with the Nazis. People that chanted the *Shema* died, and everyone should know that it doesn't matter what you chant, you will still die. They stood that way for two hours. Then an SS commandant strode to the center and raised his megaphone.

"'These men have been tried and convicted of willfully violating the law.' He turned to the men and pointed. 'This one gave money to a Polish woman to buy him fruit in blatant violation of the ration laws. Verboten! This one was found listening to a radio hidden in his basement. Verboten! This one was convicted of plotting insurrection against the Reich. This one refused to report for work.'

"Then he turned to face the crowd. 'Do not think our rules are mere suggestions. They are mandatory! They are to be obeyed without question. We told you violations would be dealt with harshly. Now you will all witness what happens when you choose to violate the law.' He raised his arm and walked away. One by one, the stools were kicked out from under the prisoners."

"And you saw it happen?" Liam said.

Lena nodded. "That, I did. And heard it. And felt it."

"How awful," Catherine said, and placed her hand over her mouth.

"Seven more were hung in the same fashion in 1942. Although I have not seen it, a monument to the seven martyrs has now been erected in Chrzanów.

"When my father gave me my instructions to hide in the attic and go to the Tarnowskis, I protested and I cried. I didn't want my family going anywhere without me. I didn't know the Tarnowskis. I'd seen them in town, but only on occasion. Mr. Tarnowski was a gruff old man. He frightened me. They were not Jewish, nor did they have any young children. I knew that the store had carried their account for months when they couldn't pay. I could well imagine that this was their way of paying my father for their overdue loan, but I was wrong. I later learned that it wasn't a monetary obligation to them. They were Righteous Gentiles, and they made that offer to my father out of the goodness of their hearts.

"'What about Milosz?' I said to my father. 'Will he stay with me in the attic?'

"He shook his head. 'No.'

"'I can take care of him,' I protested. 'He can hide with me.' My father brushed away a tear, cupped my face and kissed me on the forehead. 'My angel, always looking out for your little brother. But Milosz cannot climb up into the attic and he cannot make his way to the Tarnowskis. He will stay with your mother.'

"'I can lift him into the attic, I can push his Maserati to the Tarnowskis. I'm strong. We can make it, I promise.'

"My father's eyes glistened and he hugged me so firmly I thought he'd squeeze the air out of me. 'I am so blessed to have such a wonderful family. Milosz cannot make it in or out of the attic, and you cannot push his

Maserati into the countryside. It would only mean that the two of you would be caught.'

"He smiled so gently. 'It may be that the Germans only want to talk to me. They may not disturb your mother or Milosz. But if they do, if they decide to take them somewhere, I have made arrangements for you to be safe. Hide. Then go to the Tarnowskis, and may God be with you.'

"No sooner had he finished his sentence than we heard the squeal of tires outside the house. 'Go!' he commanded, and I scrambled into the attic."

THREE

...

LIKE MULTIPLE BLOWS OF a hammer, a rifle
stock pounded on the front door, reverberating
throughout my house. I shivered in the seclusion
of the attic while I heard repeated shouts of *'Öffnen Sie
die Tür,'* meaning 'Open the door!' My father called out,
'Just a minute, I'm coming, I'm coming, don't break my
door.'

"The banging didn't stop, and neither did the shouts.
Finally, I heard the door open and the sound of jackboots
clacking across the floor of the foyer. A stern command
followed: *'Herr Scheinman, folgen Sie uns,'* meaning,
'You are to come with us.' 'Why?' my father answered.
'What do you want of me?'

"'*Mitkomen!*' the German snapped, 'Come along.' There
was a pause, and then my mother said, 'He's an officer. He
fought in the war. He fought for you. Veterans are not supposed to be arrested. Show them your medals, Jacob.'

"'We know who he is, madam.'

"Something was said that I didn't hear, and then, 'All
right, all right, I'll come. Hannah, you wait here. I'll be
home in a little while.'

"'*Nein. Nein. Alle,*' the German said. 'All of you.' My

father replied, 'What do you want with my family? I'm the one you want to question. There's no need for them to come.'

"'*Ich sagte, Alle!*' the German shouted. 'I said, all of you! I have my orders. You are being relocated.'

"'But our things,' my mother said. 'I need to pack them. You didn't give us any notice. The other families got at least a week's notice.'

"There was silence again. Then I heard my mother. 'No, please, sir. Please give me a few minutes to gather some clothes and a few items.'

"'You may come back, maybe tomorrow,' he answered slowly.

"'Let's be honest,' my father said. 'You're not going to let us come back here. Let us pack our things.'

"'*Das ist genug*—that's enough!' he said. '*Wir gehen*—we're going.'

"Silence again. Then I heard my mother cry. 'Stop. You're hurting my arm.'

"'Leave her alone,' my father said, and I heard him grunt as he must have been punched or knocked to the floor. And then there was another plea from my mother. 'Stop. He needs his wheelchair. He cannot walk.'

"'Then he will have to crawl,' the German said. 'We're going and there is no room for a wheelchair.'"

"'She told you he can't walk,' my father said angrily. 'What's the matter with you?'

"Milosz cried out, and I heard my mother scream, 'Stop pulling on him! He's a child.'

"'I told you, no chair. He will walk or he will die.'

"'I'll carry him, I'll carry him. Let him be,' my father said. 'Don't cry, my little Milosz.'

"'Where is the rest of your family? The girl?'

"'Not here. My daughter's at school in Lublin. She doesn't live here.'

"Ha! Do you Jews ever tell the truth? All the Jewish schools and all the high schools are closed.' He then barked commands to others, instructing them to search the house. I heard soldiers walking and opening doors. I heard their boots on the stairs and I was sure they were coming for me. They would find me and pull me from the attic and God knows what they'd do to me for hiding. I sat very still, breathing as shallowly as possible. They opened the closet door and rustled through the clothing, barely two feet below me. And then they moved on. '*Nichts,*' they finally reported. '*Hier ist niemand*—there's nobody here.'

"The whole scene seemed to take an eternity, but in minutes they were all gone—the Germans, my mother, my father and Milosz." Lena took an embroidered handkerchief from her purse and blotted her eyes.

"I'm so sorry," Catherine said.

Lena nodded. 'It was a long time ago, but still . . .'

"They were right below you, searching the closet, and they didn't see the attic door?" Liam said.

"Our attic was very small, not a real attic, just a space above the second floor, so small you couldn't stand erect. It didn't have a trapdoor, just a three-foot panel in the ceiling of my mother's closet. Just a piece of painted plywood you could push up and move aside. Unless you knew the opening was there, you wouldn't guess there was an attic. Certainly not one that could accommodate a person. And it was further hidden by my mother's hatboxes that sat on the top shelf, blocking the panel."

"How did you get up there without a ladder?" Liam said.

"There were closet shelves that held her shoes and handbags. It was easy—hang onto the rod and climb up the shelves. I'd done it many times. For a child, it was a ladder to a secret hiding place.

"By nightfall my family had not returned and I suspected my father was right, they would not be coming back. Of course, I didn't know what had happened to them and I tried to keep a positive attitude. I think if I'd allowed myself to believe they'd been sent away or killed, I would have panicked. I held fast to the belief that we'd all be reunited soon. That was the only way I could keep it all together.

"I remember that first night alone. I curled up, but I couldn't sleep. I cried most of the night. I was so frightened of being left alone, frightened of the men who took my family, and frightened of an uncertain future. In the morning, I lay there listening to the silence. Eerie, for my house was never without sounds. Simple everyday sounds—footsteps in the hall, a pot on the stove, a shower running, Milosz practicing his scales, the creak of a door—the sounds of a house that was alive. But this day, except for the wind rattling the windows and a squirrel on the roof, the house was dead quiet.

"I was hungry and thirsty, but afraid to come down. I decided to wait until it was dark again. It was March and the sun didn't set until after six. By then I was starving and I had to use the bathroom. I quietly removed the attic panel and, in my bare feet, lowered myself to the closet floor.

"No lights had been left on and the house was pitch black. I walked down the stairs, my back against the staircase wall so I wouldn't be seen through the front window. I stopped first in the bathroom and then headed to the kitchen. The living room shades were up and I was scared that someone outside would see me, so I crawled through the room on my hands and knees.

"In the middle of the floor I came upon Milosz's Maserati. It was bent and broken, one of those bastards must have stomped on it. One of Milosz's shoes lay on the floor. That hit me like a punch in the stomach. They had yanked him out of the house with only one shoe. Poor little, gentle Milosz. I sat there and cried. Why would people do this?" She looked at Catherine. "Seventy years and I still don't have an answer."

"No one does," Catherine said.

"I wanted so badly to run out the door and catch up to my family, wherever they were. But . . ." Lena shrugged and shook her head. She wiped away a tear. "Finally, I crawled into the kitchen and found a piece of leftover chicken and some milk in the refrigerator. I sat on the floor and ate my dinner. Actually, I wolfed it all down because I was deathly afraid that someone would walk in at any minute. Then I packed some food and a jar filled with milk, put them in a bag and brought them up to the attic, like a squirrel hoarding acorns.

"There were no windows in my attic, but there was a tiny aperture, a split in the wood, maybe a half-inch, just below the very top. I could see the moon for a few minutes each night. With my eye up against the seam, I could see the stars. I talked to the stars. I asked them where my family was. I asked them when I should try to make my way to the Tarnowskis." Lena sat back and smiled. "They never gave me very good advice.

"I ventured back down the next night and the nights after that. I grew bolder. I no longer crawled. I stopped caring whether anyone could hear the toilet flush, even though I'd only flush in the middle of the night."

"You didn't go directly to the Tarnowskis?" Catherine said. "I thought you were instructed to go directly there."

"I was, but I was more frightened of leaving than I was of staying put. Things were settling into a routine. I began to think that maybe I would be safer just living in the attic until the war was over and my parents came home.

"The attic became my little corner of the world. I

decorated it. I brought up sheets, a pillow and a coverlet. Two dolls I had owned since I was five sat by my pillow. With a candle, I would read my favorite books. It's a funny thing—at first the loneliness is insufferable, but after a while, you find that your mind is very good company. Your thoughts become conversations. My solitary existence became manageable. Even enjoyable at times."

"That didn't sound like a workable solution," Catherine said. "Sooner or later you would have to come out."

"Of course. But I was seventeen. And I missed Karolina. I thought about her a lot. What if she came by the house, how would I know? I certainly couldn't answer the door. I imagined the two of us getting together somehow and hiding from the Germans. I contrived scenarios. The two of us could run away, make it into the countryside. Find our way down to the mountains." Lena shrugged. "I had a lot of time to think."

"By the end of the week, I ran out of food. I had already run out of milk. I had water, I could do without milk. But food? That was another story. Other than a few cans of pickled preserves, there was nothing left in the house. I had devoured the contents of the refrigerator, the cupboards, the boxes of cereal and all the canned goods. There was no avoiding the obvious—I would have to leave for the Tarnowskis or go to the store.

"I conferred with the stars that night. The grocery stores were open only during the day and walking the streets in broad daylight was dangerous for me. What time would be best? Should I walk the streets when they were busy? Would I be invisible in a crowd? Or is it better when fewer people are on the street? Would there be less chance of recognition?

"I wondered, since the Nazis came for my family, have they come for others as well? What remains of the Jews in our neighborhood? Have they come for Karolina? Are the Germans watching my house? Patrolling? They had laughed when my father said I was in Lublin. Are they now looking for me? Am I better off abandoning my safe hiding place and making a mad dash for the Tarnowskis?

"I struggled with those questions all night and decided the devil you know is better than the devil you don't. I would stay and replenish the pantry. My father had given me money, so he must have intended it to be used. I weighed the options and decided the risk of a short walk was preferable to moving in with the Tarnowskis. I was comfortable in my little corner of the world. Just me and the stars. I could wait it out. Wait for my family to return, wait for something better to happen, wait for . . . I didn't know what. Putting off the decision seemed more agreeable than placing myself at the sufferance of total strangers."

"I understand," Catherine said. She looked at her watch and stood. "Lena, it's getting late. How are you feeling? Do you want to work this evening, or take a break for dinner?"

"I'm taking a long time, aren't I? You want to know about the two girls."

"No, it's okay. A few years ago, our mutual friend chastised me for fixating on the ultimate question. We were sitting at the Chop House and—I'll never forget this—Ben said to Liam, 'Why does she have to be in such a hurry? How can a person understand something when she's only interested in getting to the last paragraph?' I've come to appreciate the value of that admonishment. You can take all the time you want."

"I am getting a little tired and I don't want to take up your evening. Do you suppose we could pick this up tomorrow?"

"Sure. I have a morning court call, but we can start at eleven."

FOUR

...

S O, WHAT DO YOU think?" Catherine said to
Liam, who pulled the car into the lot of Café Sorrento and handed the keys to the valet.

"I think I'm starving."

"I mean about Lena, smart guy."

Liam grinned. "I know what you mean. I think unless
she comes up with some hard facts telling us who they
are and where they lived, it will be impossible to locate
these two girls. If they're still alive after seventy years."

"She must have some basis for believing they're still
alive. She wouldn't come in and use up her savings to locate her friend's children unless she had reason to believe
we'd find them. There must be something else involved."

"Like what?"

"I have no idea."

"First things first," Liam said as the waitress approached the table. "We'll both have the eggplant Parmesan and the house salads. Vinaigrette. And water is
fine for both of us."

"Liam!" Catherine protested. "I hate when you order
for me. I'm a grown-up woman."

"Okay, I'm sorry."

"What would you like, ma'am?" the woman said with a smile, mocking Liam with her raised eyebrows.

Catherine sighed. "I'll have the eggplant Parmesan and a house salad."

"With vinaigrette dressing?" the waitress said.

"That'll be fine."

"Water okay?"

Catherine nodded, and the waitress left to fill the order.

"Why is Lena doing this, Liam? Why is she so driven to find these girls?"

"I'm sure she'll get there if you give her the time. Of course, you could always tell her to cut to the chase."

"Very funny, and I'm not trying to rush her. I'm taking copious notes."

"Good. You never know what piece of information will be important."

"That, and because she deserves it. She's held this story in for seventy years. She's a survivor, Liam. Just like Ben. I'm not going to cut her short. Her narrative may never result in finding these people, but the telling may very well be a catharsis for her, and I'm going to give her that."

Liam leaned over and kissed her. "That's my Cat. That's why I love you."

They clinked their water glasses and Liam added, "I can't join you tomorrow. I have an appointment."

Catherine sighed and closed her eyes. "Isn't that just like Liam. Bring a client to my office with a problem for *us* to work on and then leave it all to good ol' Cat."

"Just tomorrow, Cat. I'll catch up with you."

FIVE

• • •

I DECIDED I'D GO to the store first thing in the morning, when the fewest people would be out and about," Lena said. "I didn't want someone to stop me and ask me where my mother and father were. You know, 'We haven't seen them in the past couple weeks, how are they doing?' Or, 'We heard the Germans came for your family. How come they didn't take you?'

"Even more frightening to me was the prospect that other Jewish families were rounded up and my presence would be reported to the Germans. Nevertheless, those were the risks I had to take if I was going to stay in my attic. I would go shopping first thing in the morning.

"The rain woke me up, like little pebbles dropping on my roof. A March chill had caused a fog to settle in and I could barely see across the street. What a lucky break! Rain meant fewer people on the sidewalks and my face would be hidden by an umbrella. I wore a knit hat pulled down around my ears and I yanked up the collar on my raincoat. I didn't know what to do about my armband. If they had rounded up all the Jews, then my armband was a dead giveaway. If not, if the Jews were still walking on the streets, it was a criminal offense not to wear the armband and I would be arrested. So, I ended up putting it on.

"Rossbaum's Grocery was at the corner of the square, just three blocks away, but I knew Mr. Rossbaum well, and I didn't want him to engage me in conversation. Not that I didn't trust him, he was a sweet old man, but he might gab to others. 'I saw the Captain's daughter this morning. Didn't they take the Captain? How come they didn't take Lena?' Or 'Where's your mother, Lena? Haven't seen her around. If your family's moved, why are you still here?' But in the end, it didn't matter, because Rossbaum's was closed. The store was dark.

"Four blocks farther and down the hill was a larger store, Olenski's, that my mother didn't like. She would tell me, 'Olenski's is overpriced and Mr. Olenski is unfriendly, especially to Jews. Better you should shop at Rossbaum's.' So, I'd never been in Olenski's and he wouldn't know me, and that's where I headed.

"I took out our ration card. I had a coupon for bread, meat and incidentals. Another dilemma. What would Mr. Olenski say? How would he react to the Jewish girl who came into his store? He was behind the counter when I arrived, a tall, crusty man with wisps of white hair. When it was my turn, I handed my card to him and he looked me up and down.

"'What do you want?' he said. I stuttered: some chicken, sausage, beets, bread, marmalade, beans, milk and a carton of eggs.

"'Ha!' he said. 'Are you kidding me? Do you know about rations? Do you see butter or milk on this card? Do you want me to go to jail?'

"I was nervous, shaking, turning my head around to see who else was listening. Then he wrinkled his forehead and said, 'Why aren't you in school today?'

"I didn't want to answer that Jewish children were

banned from the public schools. He probably didn't know. 'I'm sick,' I said.

"'Sick, and your mother sends you out on a day like this?' he said, backing up a step.

"I shrugged. 'She's sick too.'

"He shook his head and looked askance at me. 'I'm sure,' he said. 'Wait here,' and he walked away from the counter.

"By now my stomach was in knots. Though I stood perfectly still, internally my body was moving in every direction. I was panicking. I waited a couple of minutes, getting more nervous by the second. Every muscle in my body was screaming for me to bolt out of the store, but he had my ration card and he knew who I was. Everyone in town knew Captain Scheinman. It suddenly became patently clear why my father had told me to go directly to the Tarnowskis. Danger was lurking around every corner.

"Just as I was about to run out of the store, Mr. Olenski returned. In his left hand he had a grocery bag and in his right, a small, covered pot.

"'Here,' he said, handing me the pot. 'It's warm *zupa grzybowa*—mushroom soup—Mrs. Olenski made it this morning. Go home, get warm and eat the soup.' He smiled, winked and beckoned me closer. 'Milk, cheese and butter are off-limits to Jews.' He smiled and opened the bag for me to see. 'Fuck the Nazis. I put some in the bag and wrapped them in a white paper. But don't ask me for those again. Too risky. Give my regards to his honor, the Captain.'

"I paid him for the groceries, thanked him profusely and started out the door. 'Bring the pot back,' he called after me. 'But not until you're better.'

Catherine smiled. "So he wasn't such a bad guy after all?"

"No, he sure wasn't, and the soup was delicious. Mushrooms are quite the delicacy in Poland. So, restocked, I was ready to hunker down."

"What went through your mind when you saw that Rossbaum's store was closed?" Catherine said.

"I already knew the Nazis were either closing Jewish stores or appropriating them. I also knew that other Jewish families were being displaced and relocated, especially in our neighborhood. Families would disappear; new people would inhabit their homes. I'd often see Jewish families wheeling their belongings down the street, just like the old-time pictures I'd seen in school of Jews escaping the Russian pogroms.

"As bleak as the situation was, I only envisioned internment, roundup, resettlement. What would be the point of ordering Jewish families to pack up their belongings and move if they were just going to be executed? I was sure that all the Jewish families were being grouped in a ghetto. I never suspected Operation Reinhard—the Final Solution, the death camps. What rational person could? An entire industry constructed by the Nazis to commit mass murders on millions of people? No one could conceive of such a demonic objective, certainly not a privileged seventeen-year-old who had been sheltered most of her life.

"Days would come and days would go, and I was becoming more nocturnal. During the night I would eat in the kitchen, clean my clothes, take a bath—all in the dark. I tried to keep the house clean, dusted and in good order. I knew I couldn't build a fire in the fireplace or put coal in the furnace. The Nazis would see the smoke in the chimney. For those cold, raw spring days, I would lie under the blankets with my coat on. But I was getting along okay."

"Pretty adventurous," Catherine said. "Weren't you afraid?"

"Oh, yes. Mostly afraid of the unknown. We didn't have a radio anymore, so I didn't have a clue what was happening in Chrzanów and the rest of the world. But I knew I didn't want to meet up with those Germans who'd burst into our house. Most of all, I was worried about my family. What had the Germans done with them? Where were they?

"And I worried for Karolina. I hadn't seen or heard from her since the Germans came for my family. My house was her safe harbor. Her father was missing, her mother was as good as missing, Madeleine was gone and now her adopted family had vanished. Karolina's mental state was fragile to begin with, now what would become of her? I decided to go see."

"You were going to search for Karolina?" Catherine said.

Lena nodded. "It was only a few blocks away from the square, across the train tracks and through a field. I could make it at night. After my evening chores, about three A.M., I dressed in a black coat and went out the back door. I saw no one on the sidewalks and no traffic on the streets. By this time, the only cars in Chrzanów belonged to the Germans. The tracks ran through town on a raised berm, elevated from the Chrzanów streets, perhaps as high as fifteen feet. I made my way over the tracks, down the embankment and through the field to Karolina's.

"The lights were off in her one-story home. I peered through the kitchen window and walked around the back to Karolina's bedroom window. It wasn't completely closed and I slowly lifted it. There was a man in her bed! He was sleeping, but he felt the breeze and turned on his side. I ducked down and then heard him snore. I slowly peeked again, and looked at this heavyset, baldheaded man. Obviously, the Neumans no longer lived on Drogarz Street. I crawled to the side of the house and dashed off through the field.

"Now I was sure that the Jews were all being collected somewhere, in one area of the town. I knew it was just a matter of time and I would have to leave my house as well. Still, I procrastinated. I felt secure in my attic. So far, so good.

"I visited Mr. Olenski one more time. I returned his pot and he asked how we were. Then he gave me a few items, including a chocolate bar, and whispered to me that I shouldn't come in anymore. His store was now 'verboten' to Juden."

"Well, when you heard that, how did you plan to get food?" Catherine said.

"I still had some food, so I put off my decision. I went back to my routine. But it all came to an abrupt end two weeks later in early April. I was awakened by the sound of people in my house. It was daylight, that much I could tell from the split in the roof. I heard the voices of a woman and two men. They were quite clearly walking around my house and commenting on what they saw. I couldn't get all of the conversation, but I could get enough to know that the woman was planning on re-decorating the living room as soon as she moved in.

"The conversations got louder, and I knew they were coming upstairs. I heard the woman say, 'Someone has to remove all the clothes from these closets. I'm certainly not going through some Jew's clothes.' The man laughed and told her not to worry, they'd be disposed of, just like the Jews. They laughed and walked away. 'And I want all the toilet seats replaced,' she said.

"I made plans to leave that night."

Six

...

FAMILIES WHO WERE LEAVING their homes and moving into the ghetto packed as much of their belongings as they could and loaded up a cart. But I was trying to sneak out of town after curfew and make it out to the Tarnowskis. I could only take what I could fit into a duffel—a few changes of clothes, a half dozen pictures of the family, and Milosz's shoe."

"Milosz's shoe?" Catherine said.

Lena nodded. "That shoe was important to me. It belonged to Milosz, it was a part of him, it fit on his little foot. If I hugged the shoe, I was hugging Milosz. I was so afraid for him and I missed him so dearly. How was he getting along with only one shoe? I told myself that I'd keep it and return it to him when I caught up with the family. I prayed that we'd all be together soon.

"Before I left, I walked around my house for the very last time. I had lived in those rooms my entire life. I said good-bye my parents' room, to Milosz's room, to the living room, where every piece of furniture held a story. I could see the past—birthdays, holidays, my family sitting on the chairs, guests eating at the dining room table set with Mother's fine china, men philosophizing on the problems of the world. How I longed for those days.

"I opened the door to my bedroom and walked around the room, touching all my things—my art, my books, my dolls, my desk, the notes I'd saved from friends. I laid on my bed for the last time, pulled the covers up over my head and bawled like a baby. Finally, I said good-bye to all my things and shut the door on my past.

"When I reached the front door, I bid farewell to all the memories that inhabited this wonderful house and they said good-bye to me. Dressed in my heavy coat and knit hat, carrying a small duffel, armband in my pocket, I left just after midnight.

"The Tarnowskis lived in the country on a dairy farm. I didn't know how far I would have to walk, but I remembered my father giving me the address and telling me to follow Slaska Street. I'd only started up Podwamy when a black Mercedes rolled by with uniformed men in the front seat. I ducked behind a stone gate and waited until it had passed. At the next block, I saw it had stopped and the two Germans were laughing with other soldiers in front of a restaurant. Thank goodness they didn't see me.

"I stayed in the shadows until I hit the square. Bright lights from the restaurants, bars and the gas streetlights lit the popular area like it was lunchtime. There were still pedestrians, even though it was now past midnight, but as you'd imagine, the after-curfew foot traffic consisted only of the Germans and their ladies. Occasionally, a passerby would say something to me, but I tried not to make eye contact and marched on.

"I was rather tall at seventeen and had grown into my woman's shape. Even in my winter coat, I had a nice figure. Don't think me immodest, but back then, I was very attractive. Since it was the early morning hours, many of the men on the street were coming out of taverns and most were intoxicated. Now and again, someone would make a pass at me. After all, what was a young woman doing walking the streets in the early morning hours unless she wanted to proposition a man, or had just left a romantic tryst? That would be the only acceptable excuse for breaking curfew. I kept my armband in my pocket, put my head down and plowed forward.

"I was almost at the edge of the square when a young German soldier walked out of a bar and almost knocked me over. 'Well, hello, sweetie, where are you going?' he slurred. I shook my head and kept walking. He pulled up alongside of me and continued to make overtures. 'Wait, what's the hurry?' His gray uniform blouse was unbuttoned at the neck and he stumbled as he walked step for step with me.

"'Hey, what's wrong with me?' he said with a slur. 'Am I not as handsome as the one you were just with? Look at me. I'm a beautiful German boy of good rural stock and I'm lonesome tonight. Why don't you have a drink with me?' I continued to ignore him and tried to walk around him, but then he grew insistent. 'Hey, don't walk away from me. I'm a German fuckin' soldier. It's after curfew and you're out and about. I could bring you in, you know.' He grabbed at my arms and turned me around. He had a big smile on his face and wild drunken eyes. 'C'mon, give me a little kiss and then I'll go away.'

"'No,' I said firmly, and tried to pull myself out of his grip. 'Leave me alone.' But he was strong. He opened my coat and stuck his hands up my sweater. I pushed him back, and that only made him more determined. He thought the whole thing was funny. He started to kiss me all over my face, and his breath stank of alcohol. It turned my stomach and with that, I gagged, spun around and threw up on the sidewalk. 'Aach,' he said with a sickened look on his face. 'You are disgusting.' He shivered and quickly walked the other way.''

"You can throw up on demand?" Catherine said.

"He didn't see me stick my finger down my throat. I just figured it might work." Lena smiled. "And it did. For the next mile or so, I shook like a leaf. Thankfully, I didn't see another person for the rest of the night.

"I reached the farmlands as the dawn was breaking. What a difference. The pastoral landscape lay in stark contrast to the apocalypse raging in Chrzanów. Rolling golden hills. Fields of sprouting wheat. Fruit orchards flowering in the April sun. Cattle grazing. It was nothing less than a table set with the bounty of Poland's fertile farmland. And a few miles away, our entire town was starving.

"Farther down the country road, the Tarnowski farm came into view. I walked up their path. Chickens were pecking in the yard. That meant eggs, and I was so hungry. I knocked on the front door and Mrs. Tarnowski opened the door a crack. 'Yes?' she said, with an uneasy stare.

"'I'm Lena. Captain Scheinman's daughter.'

"'Oh, child, come in quickly.' She looked around to see if anyone else was in sight.

"'No one followed me.'

"She eyed me up and down, tip-to-toe. I'm sure I looked like somebody who'd just walked twenty miles through the night. She took me by the elbow and led me into the kitchen, where she fixed a breakfast of eggs and biscuits. Food never tasted so good! I hadn't enjoyed a hot breakfast since the day my family was taken. I told Mrs. Tarnowski what I'd been through and asked her if she knew anything about my family.

"'No,' she said. 'I haven't been into the city for a couple of months. It's too dangerous. Willy goes in twice a week to deliver his milk and butter. He tells me that the Jewish families are being relocated one by one. I suppose that's what has happened to your parents as well.'

"'I think I should go to them.'

"Mrs. Tarnowski shrugged. 'If that's what you want, then that's what you should do. But you just came out of the city. You must be tired. Why don't you take a warm bath and I'll make up a bed for you. I promised your father I would keep you until the war was over and I am not a woman who breaks a promise. Lord knows, it's dangerous for me to hide a Jew, so if you are determined to go, I won't stop you.'

"I laid in that warm bathwater pondering what the Lord knows and what he doesn't know. I recalled my religious classes. The tenets of our faith. Our God is an all-knowing and all-powerful God. He knows everything that has been and that will be. Such a concept now seemed improbable. If that were true, why do Nazis inhabit the earth? Aren't they like scorpions, like adders, like the bugs that caused the plague? They seemed to me to be all the same, with no purpose but to spread evil and cause harm. Why would a good and just God allow such evil to roam the earth, and if God can right the ship, why is he asleep at the wheel? Lying in the tub, I rejected my faith. Logic demanded it.

"I tried to clear my mind and think about happier times, about our peaceful life before the Germans invaded. Life in Chrzanów, life with my family, life with my friends. The bathwater seemed to draw all the tension from my body. I looked at myself lying in the tub. I had lost weight. It bothered me that my figure was losing its newfound curves.

"I worried about my family. Where were they? Were they just in another part of Chrzanów? Had they been sent away? Who was the trespasser in Karolina's bed?

Where was my friend living now? I dreamed about joining them all again. There I am, sitting at Shabbat dinner.
I hear Milosz's laughter. Mother's soup is delicious. Our
house is warm and bright. I can feel the joy and all the
love. The next thing I know, Mrs. Tarnowski is tapping
me on my shoulder. 'Lena? Lena? Are you sleeping?'

"She handed me a towel and a clean robe. I helped
her make up a bed in a small storage room that sat at the
end of the second-floor hall. I asked her, 'Does Mr. Tarnowski deliver to the section where the Jews live? When
he comes home, can I ask him if he's seen my family?'

"My question hit a nerve. She shook her head and
punctuated the absurdity of such a question with a 'Ha!'
'Deliver to the Jews? Certainly not. Does he want to get
shot? You think the Jews get deliveries of butter and
milk? It's against the law. These days Jews are fortunate if
they get a loaf of bread. Me, the farmer's wife? I don't get
deliveries of butter and milk. The Nazis, they take it all.
You come from the city, don't you see what's going on?'

"I nodded sadly.

"'Willy delivers to the few customers he has left. The
Nazis take ninety percent of what we produce. They
come out here in their canvas trucks and raid my farm
like a fox raids the henhouse. They don't buy, they just
take, and then they order Willy to deliver it all to them
at their homes. I barely have a pat of butter left in my
house. Child, they've taken over most of the Chrzanów
factories—the lumber mill, the coal mine, the power plant,
the bakery and, of course, the Shop. If your mother's still
in town, that's probably where she is. Working at the
Shop.'

"'What shop?' I asked.

"'*The* Shop. The old garment factory on Rzeka Street.
Now they've tripled the size, with ten times as many
workers, all sewing uniforms and coats for the Germans.

The Jewish women that are still in town are working there. They work for meager wages. But Poles work there as well, because they need a job. They get paid based on how many coats they make. Since the Germans came to town there are lots of jobs. The Germans brag they brought full employment. Ha! Willy says I might have to work there if he loses any more customers. But I won't work for the Germans.'

"She looked around the little storeroom where she'd made my bed. 'I used to keep my linens in here. It's not very large, but it will do for you.' She smiled weakly. I knew my presence made her uncomfortable and she was doing her best. All in all, I was warmed by the hospitality of this hardened farmwoman.

"'Sometimes they come out here, the Nazis, you know, just to check on us. They want to make sure we're not hoarding butter, even though we give them almost everything we have.' She pressed her lips and stood defiant with her hands on her hips. 'Sometimes they even help themselves to our chickens. If they come out here and they see you, you tell them you're Lena Tarnowski. They won't know the difference.'

"I thanked her and told her that I was grateful, but it was patently clear to me that not only was I an imposition, but a ticking time bomb for her family. I decided that I would have to move on when I got the chance. I would not hold her to her promise.

"I awoke from my nap to the sounds of Mr. and Mrs. Tarnowski engaged in an animated conversation. More like an argument. And I heard my name mentioned several times. They were startled when I walked into the kitchen."

"What were they like, Lena?" Catherine asked. "The Tarnowskis?"

"Mrs. Tarnowski was sturdy. A strong farmer's wife.

A lifetime of summers had weathered her skin. Her hair was dark gray, but always neatly combed and frequently accented with a colorful bow. She wore housedresses that hung like draperies. Mr. Tarnowski was a bear. He had broad shoulders, big hands and stood well over six feet. No facial hair. He was always neatly shaven. They were a matched set. Good people.

"When I walked into the kitchen they immediately stopped talking and offered me a cup of milk. It was a little awkward because the three of us knew I was the topic of the morning. I sat down to drink my milk—fresh milk right out of the cow. There's nothing like it." Lena smiled and her eyes brightened. "I still like milk. I drink it every day. But farm-fresh milk is something entirely different. Have you ever had fresh milk on a farm?"

Catherine shook her head.

"It's like drinking ice cream, only better. You should try it sometime. It's good for expectant mothers." She punctuated her imperative with a sharp nod.

Catherine blushed. "Who told you I'm expecting?"

Lena smiled and shrugged. "I don't have to be told."

Catherine quickly looked down at her midsection.

Lena laughed. "It's not there, it's in your face. And in that of your husband."

"How could you possibly . . . ?"

She raised her eyebrows. "My *babcia* always told me there's a little Gypsy in our family." She laughed again.

"Well, I would appreciate it if you wouldn't . . ."

Lena held up her index finger. "Mum's the word."

She chuckled softly and continued with her story. "Sitting around the kitchen table, I told the Tarnowskis, 'Please don't think me ungrateful, but it's probably best for all if I go back into the city. I think it's my place to rejoin my family. I'm sure they'll be with the rest of the Jews somewhere.'

"Mr. Tarnowski shook his head. 'Big mistake. You stay here. You're safe here. The Jews of Chrzanów are not safe. It's true that many have been forced to move into a small area, but the Germans are not done with them. They are enemies of the Germans and we are at war. They will not be permitted to run their little area without interference and abuse. The Jews have no protectors, not anywhere in Europe. They will live so long as the Germans have use for them. And then they will die. When the Jews are gone, the Catholic Poles will be next. The Germans speak of *Lebensraum*, their living space. They intend to expand, to clear out Poland for the German people. We do not kid ourselves. I make plans.' He nodded his head.

"'Shah! Enough,' Mrs. Tarnowski said. 'There'll be no talk of the plans.' Then she turned to me. 'You may come with us when the time is right for us to leave. Until then, we do not speak of any plans.'

"I stayed with the Tarnowskis through the end of the month helping out with the chores whenever I could. I'd never lived on a farm and my ignorance of even the most fundamental farming techniques was a source of constant entertainment for Mr. and Mrs. Tarnowski. We had dinner every night at six and they were in bed by eight. I know they had a son, but he was never home and no mention was ever made of him at the dinner table or anywhere else. I respected those unspoken wishes and never brought it up.

"Finally, after a few weeks, my anxiety got the best of me and I told the Tarnowskis that I had to go back to Chrzanów and find my family. They cautioned me against it, but my need was stronger than my common sense. I would go into town the next morning with Mr. Tarnowski on his delivery route. It was a disastrous decision."

Lena's eyes filled with tears and she paused to take a sip of water. She seemed ready to say something but stopped and shook her head. "This is a good place for me to stop. Do you suppose we could take a break? Pick it up in a few days?"

"Anytime you'd like," Catherine said. "Why don't you call me whenever you'd like to resume?"

Seven

...

A ND THAT'S HOW YOU left it?" Liam said.
Catherine nodded. "I told her she could take all the time she wants—tell me the story at her own pace. These recollections are very hard on her."

"Did she say anything more about the two girls or Karolina?"

"Nothing yet. At this point in her story she doesn't know what happened to Karolina, and there's no mention of any twins."

"I got a call this morning from a man named Arthur Woodward. He says he's Lena's son and he wants us to stay away from his mother."

"She has a son?"

Liam nodded. "He sounded concerned, but irritated. He asked me if his mother was talking to me about a woman named Karolina. I told him I really couldn't say, that any communications between an attorney and her client are privileged and confidential and that I was working for the attorney."

"Perfect," Catherine said. "We can't disclose any information, even if he is her son. Not without her permission."

"Right. And then Arthur said to me, 'Is she repeating those crazy stories about two lost children? Is my mother telling you she wants you to find Karolina's lost children? Can you at least tell me that much?'

"I told him I was sorry but I couldn't tell him anything. I suggested he ask his mother what she'd said. Then he got downright nasty.

"'Look,' he snapped, 'she's a senile, delusional old woman. There's no babies, there's no Karolina. Never was. I don't know what your play is, but I don't want some moneygrubbing lawyer leading her on and making bullshit promises. You're not going to find any missing children. So leave her alone. And I better not find out you're taking any of her money. Do you understand? Am I clear here?' And then he hung up."

"Whoa. What a pleasant fellow," Catherine said. "I know I've only had a couple of days with her, but I don't get the feeling that Lena's senile. To the contrary, her narrative is well structured, organized and detailed. She's articulate. And Liam—she knows I'm pregnant!"

"Maybe she's also very observant."

"I'm not really showing, am I?"

Liam shook his head. "Nah. And I keep a careful watch on all parts Catherine."

"Did you say something to her?"

"I haven't said anything to anybody."

"Lena said she's part Gypsy, so maybe she's got mystical powers." Catherine wiggled her fingers and laughed. "You know, I'm growing to like her. It's like she's my grandmother. And I don't believe she's mentally impaired. I have colleagues at the bar who can't communicate half as well as she does."

"I agree with you. She doesn't appear to be senile or delusional. I get the feeling that Arthur's more concerned about her money than her mental condition. Do you think he's looking forward to a sizable inheritance?"

"I don't know. She lives on East Pearson Street, in one of the vintage buildings. Her wardrobe is exquisite; she wears beautiful clothes. Haven't you noticed?"

Liam shrugged. "I guess I wouldn't know the difference. She always looks dignified. Put together. She's certainly not some dowdy old lady."

"Liam, that's not a very nice thing to say. Still, I bet she drops a pretty penny on Michigan Avenue."

He nodded. "She's a very attractive woman."

"Without letting her know, can you get some background on her? And on Arthur Woodward?"

"Cat, you cut me to the quick. You're talking to the world's greatest investigator. Not to mention the world's greatest . . ."

"Stop. I'm serious. See what you can learn about Lena and her family."

"I will."

"I don't think I'll mention Arthur's call to Lena. Not yet. I'll just go ahead with the interviews like we've been doing."

EIGHT

...

I SLEPT VERY LITTLE the night before I left the
farm. Once again, I was beset with contradictions.
With the Tarnowskis, I was safe and comfortable,
and they were kind to me. Why would I leave? Yet I
missed my family dearly and I wanted to be with them.
If they were in trouble, I wanted to be in trouble with
them. I had to find out what happened."

Lena took a sip of hot tea and set the cup down on
Catherine's desk. Liam sat to the right of the desk and
leaned his chair back on two legs. Catherine continued
to jot down notes on a yellow pad. She hadn't mentioned
Arthur's disturbing phone call earlier that week.

"I knew that returning to Chrzanów would be risky,
that Jews were being detained and taken into custody.
There was talk about transfers to labor camps, but I
chose to believe that my family had been taken because
they were requisitioning my house. My father had said
there was no evidence against him. I was convinced that
my mother, father and Milosz were alive and living in
some apartment in a resettled area of Chrzanów.

"Mr. Tarnowski, who always rose before the sun, was
surprised to come downstairs and see me sitting at the

kitchen table. He saw my duffel on the floor and nodded his understanding. I waited while he milked the cows, did his chores and prepared to leave for town with his daily supply of dairy products. After a hearty breakfast, I said good-bye to Mrs. Tarnowski, who hugged me tightly and begged me to be careful. The evolution of our feelings toward each other over such a short time was not lost on either of us. When I first arrived, she received me as an unwanted obligation. Now, just weeks later, we had developed a bond.

"She had tears in her eyes when I climbed up onto the wagon seat. She held my hand and looked at me with concern. 'Trust no one. If you don't find your family or if things aren't working out, you know you can come right back here. And watch your money.' I nodded and patted the arm of my jacket. A day earlier, Mrs. Tarnowski had convinced me to sew my money into the lining. 'Don't show it to anyone. It will only mean trouble for you.'

"Very few were awake when we clip-clopped into Chrzanów. The streets were empty as we reached the center of town and veered toward the northeast and to a run-down, tired area of apartment buildings and warehouses, where I believed my parents would have joined the displaced Jewish families.

"'I can take you close, but I'd better not stray too far from my usual route,' Mr. Tarnowski said, and no sooner had he finished his sentence than a black sedan honked and motioned for us to pull over. Mr. Tarnowski looked at me and put his finger to his lips.

"A Wehrmacht officer got out of the car and walked slowly to our wagon. He was a tall, good-looking man dressed in his officer's uniform. He wore a peaked cap with its shiny black visor, golden braid and the silver flat-winged eagle, Germany's national symbol, over the green hatband. His long trench coat was open, revealing his olive tunic with padded shoulders, silver buttons, tall black collars and red waistband. His tunic was adorned with badges and medals. The officer was graying at the temples, clearly in his fifties, not one of the brash young soldiers who bullied their way around town.

"'Ah, Herr farmer, so pleasant to see you out and about so early this morning.' He patted our horse on his neck. 'But what are you doing on this side of town? Your products don't get delivered here.'"

"What did he mean by that?" Catherine asked.

"Milk, eggs, cheese—they were under strict ration and only could be purchased in certain stores. As I told you, Jews were not allowed to buy milk and eggs. Although I didn't know it at the time, the area we were approaching had been demarcated by the Germans as the Jewish ghetto."

"So these Nazis stopped you from entering the ghetto?"

Lena nodded. "Only one Nazi, a ranked officer. He spoke politely to Mr. Tarnowski, not rudely as the other Germans I had encountered. Still, he was a German—frightening and not to be trifled with.

"'What have you today, Herr farmer? Do you have a wagonload full of that wonderful cheese?'

"Mr. Tarnowski nodded. '*Ja*, Herr Oberst.'

"'Mmm. I do like that cheese. It reminds me of my childhood in Bavaria. Will we see you at my house today for your usual delivery?'

"Mr. Tarnowski nodded, reached behind him, pulled out a chunk of white cheese and broke off a corner. 'Mmm. So smooth,' the officer said as he took a bite. 'I will see you later, *ja*?'

"'*Ja*.'

"He turned to leave, walked a step and then returned. 'How ill-mannered of me.' He flashed a disingenuous smile. 'I did not offer my salutations to the young lady. Is she your daughter?'

"'*Ja*.'

"The Nazi's smile broadened. 'Ah, Herr farmer, you think you are fooling me. We know you do not have a daughter. We know you have a son, don't we? A son who is presently serving the Reich by building roads on the Eastern Front. No?'

"'*Ja*.' Mr. Tarnowski's lower jaw shook.

"'But alas, Herr farmer, no daughter. Do you know how I know this?'

"Mr. Tarnowski shrugged and shook his head.

"'Because she's not in the census,' he said in a sing-song tone. 'You think we don't know who lives here in this cozy little town?' He looked at me, smiled and nodded. 'You know what I think? I think maybe you are stepping out on your wife, Herr farmer. No?'

"'No, no, Herr Oberst.'

"The officer pointed at me and held out his hand. '*Dokumente, bitte*.'

"I didn't want to show him my papers. I sat perfectly still. Frozen.

"'He is asking for your papers,' Mr. Tarnowski said to me in Polish.

"I shook my head and held out my open hands. 'No papers.'

"'Tsk, tsk,' the Nazi said with a grin. 'Where did you find this girl, Herr farmer?'

"'I was hitchhiking,' I interjected in German. 'He picked me up on Slaska Street. He doesn't know I don't have papers.'

"'Hitchhiking? Is this true, Herr farmer?'

"Mr. Tarnowski lowered his head and nodded. '*Ja*.'

"'Where did you come from and where are you going, little hitchhiker?'

"'I'm from Lublin,' I said nervously. That's what I'd heard my father tell the Nazis in our home. 'I was going to school there.'

"'I do not believe you. The schools have been closed now for more than a year.' The officer looked at Mr. Tarnowski and waggled his finger back and forth. 'You know, Herr farmer, I would be within my rights to shoot you right now for picking up hitchhikers that are probably Jews, isn't that so?'

"Mr. Tarnowski did not answer."

"The officer raised his voice. 'I said, isn't that so?'

"'*Ja,* Herr Oberst,' he said softly. 'That's so.'

"'But then I would miss my weekly deliveries of cheese and butter, wouldn't I?' He chuckled, and I thought for the moment he was going to let us go. But he pointed at me and beckoned with his index finger. 'Come along, little hitchhiker.' I grabbed my duffel and jumped down from the wagon and walked over to his car.

"Addressing Mr. Tarnowski, the officer said, 'You are very fortunate that I am such a softhearted man. Perhaps, as a thank-you for my generosity, you will deliver an extra portion this week? *Ja?*'

"'Oh, *ja,* Herr Oberst.'

"'Now finish your deliveries and no more hitchhikers. I will see that the young Fräulein gets to the train station.'

"The Nazi, several inches taller than me, pointed at my duffel. 'What have we here?' He fished through, saw only my clothes and pictures and gave it back to me. 'Who are you really, young lady?' His tone was civil, but stern. 'What is your name and where do you live?'

"At that point I figured what the hell, and I told him the truth. 'I'm Lena Scheinman and I'm proud to be Captain Jacob Scheinman's daughter. I'm looking for my family. They were grabbed by your soldiers, treated very rudely and taken from our home two months ago.'

"'Well, aren't you the spunky one?'"

Catherine interrupted. "Pretty bold. At seventeen years old, where did you find that courage? How did you keep it all together? I think I would have lost it during that episode."

"I figured it was all over for me anyway. I was going to be sent somewhere and it didn't really matter." Lena refilled her cup of tea. "Truly, I don't know what got into me. The officer then opened the back door to his Mercedes and motioned for me to get in. I slid into the backseat and we drove toward the northeast part of town. Just me and the colonel. The irony was not lost on me. I had just boldly asserted myself before a Wehrmacht colonel and now I was sitting in the backseat of his posh automobile, shined to sparkle like a mirror, with oblong chrome grille in the front and Nazi flags flying from the front fenders. People jumped out of the way as it rolled through town. German soldiers stopped to salute as we drove by. And here was little me, sitting on the soft leather seats by myself being chauffeured by a colonel.

"The colonel took off his cap and laid it on the passenger seat. 'I know your father, Captain Scheinman. I briefly served with him at Galicia. He's a good man, your father, but he's a Jew.'

"'It didn't bother you back then, when Jews were putting their lives on the line for Germany. Now your German soldiers break into our house, rough up my father, mother and my baby brother and arrest them.'

"'You best watch yourself, spunky one. Times have changed. Jews are no longer respected by the Reich.' He shrugged. 'It doesn't matter whether I agree. It's official policy.'

"'Do you know where they took my family?'

"'I don't know.' He tipped his head from side to side. 'If they're still here in Chrzanów, and they're no longer in their house, then they're probably in the northeast section, where the Jews have congregated. Or they may have been transported to any number of places. They're supposed to treat former officers with respect, but it doesn't always happen. Tell me, Lena Scheinman, how did you wind up in Mr. Tarnowski's wagon this morning?'"

Catherine broke in. "You didn't tell him you were living at the Tarnowskis, did you?"

Lena shook her head. "No, I told him I was hitchhiking around town, looking for my parents. The answer made him laugh. 'Ah, little hitchhiker, you're not being truthful,' he said. 'You're protecting Herr farmer. That's courageous of you, but foolish. Lying to German officers will get you killed.' He paused and then he sighed. 'This war is not even two years old and already I am tired of it.' He slowed his car. 'Put on your armband before one of my soldiers stops you and shoots you. And when someone asks for your papers, don't say you don't have any. I'm taking you to the Shop. They need workers. This time, try to behave yourself.'"

"He didn't take you to the train?" Catherine asked.

Lena shook her head. "I got a reprieve. He took me to Rzeka Street, to a large two-story brick building with no windows. It had been a garment factory in earlier days, but I think it had been vacant before the Germans reopened it as the Shop. Two uniformed sentries stood guard at the front door. We parked and Herr Oberst led me to the door.

"In the large, cavernous interior, there were more than five hundred sewing stations. The noise was deafening, whirring away night and day. Hundreds of workers, mostly women, but also men and children, sat silently at their machines. At its peak in 1942, the Shop employed fifteen hundred workers.

"The colonel took me inside and introduced me to David, the young foreman of the business. 'This is Lena Scheinman. She's got a lot of spunk, but I think she'll be a good worker. If she gives you any trouble, there's a transport to Gross-Rosen scheduled for Thursday.'

"'Gross-Rosen? To the textile sub-camp?' David said.

"The colonel nodded. 'They need seamstresses and cotton bailers. I think we're shipping eight hundred from Chrzanów.'

"'You're taking all my workers. I'm down to twelve hundred here. How am I supposed to fill the requisitions?'

"The colonel shrugged. 'I get my orders. I follow them just like you. More Jews are set to arrive here this week. I'll try not to send your workers. But beware, Chrzanów's ghetto is scheduled for demolition next year. Jewish deportations are to continue each month and I'll try to take workers out of the general ghetto population as much as I can. Thursday's group is lucky they're going to Gross-Rosen and not to Auschwitz or Buchenwald.'

"'I don't know how they expect me to keep this plant running.'

"'The Jews will all be deported, one way or another. Anyway, here is a feisty little one.' He gestured toward me. 'I doubt she's done any labor in her life, but she's young and strong. Let me know how it works out.' And he left.

"I stood there with my duffel, taking in the sounds and sights of the Shop."

"And thinking you should have stayed at the Tarnowski farm?" Catherine said.

"Maybe. But I still intended to find my family and Karolina. I actually felt fortunate. I didn't get arrested, I didn't get transported to some prison camp and nobody harmed me. I was standing in a garment factory staring at a good-looking manager. It could have been a lot worse.

"David was Jewish, seven years older than me, and he'd been apprenticed as a tailor. When the Nazis opened the Shop, they found David working in his tailor shop. They brought him over and appointed him as one of the managers. He did such a good job, they promoted him to general manager of the whole operation. By the time I got there, he was running the show, under the Nazis' watchful eyes, of course. It was his job to produce the daily requirements.

"Each day the Nazis would set their quota and David would tell them how many man-hours and bolts of cloth were required. If more people were needed than were already working, they'd send the young German soldiers out into town to round up additional workers. Inside the Shop, other German soldiers would walk around and prod the workers like Egyptian taskmasters. Each little area of the Shop had its own overseer. They railed about, pressuring the workers to increase their production. They screamed threats of deportation to labor camps, although they really had no authority.

"'You are Captain Scheinman's daughter?' David said to me as he walked me to the far end of the building. 'The man who owns the provision store at the edge of the square?'

"'Used to own. The store was taken from us. So was our home. I don't know where they took my father or any member of my family.'

"David nodded his understanding. He was dashing. He had long black hair, flopped to the side in a cavalier manner, like Errol Flynn. His work shirt was rolled up to his biceps and open at the neck. And he had blue eyes.

An Ashkenazi Jew with big blue eyes and thick lips. He was gorgeous.

"'Do you know where my family is?'

"He shook his head. 'I haven't seen your father in months, but then, I don't go outside this building very often. I sleep upstairs in a little office. As long as this place is in business, I'm not on the transport lists.'

"'Is my mother working here? Hannah Scheinman? Have you heard anything about her or my family?'

"He shook his head again and then pointed to an empty station. 'Do you have a sewing machine?'

"'No. I don't know how to sew.'

"By his look, he caught the irony of having the highest ranking Nazi in Chrzanów bring a girl to the Shop who not only didn't own a machine but didn't know how to sew. 'This is quite funny,' he said. 'Apparently, you caught the eye of Colonel Müller. Most people who come here bring their sewing machines and their sewing experience. Girls who don't sew are sent to the labor camps. Or worse. Why didn't your mother teach you how to sew?'

"'I guess she had bigger plans for me. I was going to . . . never mind.'

"'Private school? In Kraków?' He smiled a knowing smile. 'The Gymnasium, perhaps?' He pointed a finger at me. 'I've seen you at the synagogue. And I've seen you in the square.' He gestured with a sweeping motion at the women in the Shop. 'Their mothers all taught them how to sew and they've all brought their own sewing machines from home. The Nazis have confiscated every other sewing machine in Chrzanów and brought them here or shipped them to other work centers. We do not provide our workers with sewing machines. Or sewing lessons. How do you think you will work here?'

"'I don't know, David,' I said with a bit of an attitude. 'This has not been a very good day.'

"He laughed. 'I like you. The colonel's right, you've got spunk.' He turned and started walking. 'Spunk, but no sewing machine. Follow me.'

He brought me past several workers and around a corner. 'Mrs. Klein is sick today. She's sick every day, poor thing. When she works, she only works a few hours a day. I don't know if she'll ever return. I'm covering for her. I've kept her off the transport lists. If you're sitting at her machine, you'll fit in all right.'

"'Thank you,' I said quietly. 'I'm sorry if I was snippy. But I just got pulled off a dairy wagon and placed in the backseat of a Nazi Mercedes driven by a German colonel. He caught me on the streets without my armband.'

"'You got the royal treatment. Oberst Müller came to Chrzanów three months ago. He's in charge of all the German soldiers stationed here, but rumor is that the SS will soon be arriving and then they'll call the shots. Soon after they arrive, they'll be doubling up the deportations. Jewish families will be sent somewhere else.'

"'How do you know these things?'

"David smiled broadly. 'I keep my ears open.'

"I'm talking to him and the whole time I'm thinking, 'God, he's good looking. How come I never noticed him in synagogue?' I asked him, 'Where are they sent, the people that they transport? Maybe my family has gone there.'

"David shook his head. 'Work camps, prisons. I don't know.'

"I stood there with only the clothes I had in my duffel and nowhere to live. 'The Germans have taken my home and I don't have anywhere to sleep. Do you know where I can sleep?'

"David flashed another handsome smile. 'Is that a trick question?'

"I had to laugh. 'Seriously.'

"He shrugged. 'If you have a friend in town, I suggest

you go there. Or, I hear there are still some rooms in the ghetto for a small rental. That's where all the Jews are supposed to go.'

"I sat down in front of the machine, not having the faintest clue what to do. David chuckled. 'I'll send Ilsa over to teach you.'

"A few minutes later David returned with an older woman and an armload of woolen material. She sat next to me and huffed. 'I am Ilsa. I will show you how to sew a coat.' She proceeded, in twenty minutes, to give me a crash course on how to sew an entire wool overcoat. She was an excellent teacher, but I did not hold up my part of the educational process. 'Coats do not have three armholes,' Ilsa said. 'Ach. You can't put buttonholes on the right side and also on the left side.' She was not overly friendly.

"David came by in the afternoon. 'How's she doing?' Ilsa shook her head in exasperation. 'Look.' She held up a sample of my handiwork. 'Just fine if you have three shoulders.' David smiled. 'Keep working, you'll get it.'

"It took a day or two, and several discarded coats, but I finally got the hang of it. That first day I worked a seven-hour shift and was released at six P.M. Before I left, David handed me an identification card showing that I worked at the Shop.

"'On those days when you are coming or going from the Shop, walking through the town, outside the ghetto, or if you're out after curfew, this ID card is your authority to be on the street. The Germans know to leave my workers alone. Still, many are vicious sadists, so you are wise to walk on the other side of the street and avoid confrontation. Be here, sitting at your station, at seven tomorrow.'

"I thanked him and started to leave when he stopped me. 'Did you eat today?'

"'I had breakfast.'

"He asked me to wait and returned with a paper sack. 'Here is food for tonight. It's already too late to buy food from the stores, the ones that are allowed to serve Jews. They sell out early in the day. You'd be wise to visit a store at sunrise, when they first open. Even before that, get in line with your coupons.'

"I thanked him again. I realized that the bag of food was an expression of David's understanding that I was a fish out of water. I was totally unprepared for the life I was about to experience.

"That evening, I walked across town, through the square and into the ghetto. My home, several blocks away, now belonged to the German woman I'd heard bitching while I was in the attic. Karolina's home, the one-story white house with wooden siding across the field, now belonged to some fat slob lying in her bed. I didn't know anyone else I could stay with. I needed to find a room. Besides, if my family was in the ghetto, there was a good chance I could catch up with them."

NINE

...

THE PHONE RANG IN Liam's office and the caller ID told him it was Bolger & Martin, one of the city's largest law firms.

"Mr. Taggart? This is Mike Shirley over at Bolger. We represent Arthur Woodward."

"Ah, yes. Arthur. A very unpleasant fellow. What is it you want with me, Mr. Shirley?"

"Mike. Call me Mike. And can I call you Liam? Let's get this thing off on the right foot. Things will always go more smoothly if we're sociable."

"You might mention that theory to your client, Mike. But, again, how can I help you?"

"I would like to come and meet with you and Ms. Lockhart."

"To what end?"

"Well, it's about Arthur's mother. She hasn't been well. Arthur's concerned about her . . . uh . . . her . . ."

"Estate, Mike. The word you're looking for is estate."

"No, no, not at all. He's concerned about her health. You know, she's eighty-nine years old."

"She looked pretty healthy to me. But, in case you didn't know, Ms. Lockhart's not a doctor."

Shirley's tone changed. "Liam, let's stop playing these games. My client wants me to set up a meeting. We can meet in Ms. Lockhart's office or we can meet in a courtroom. Why don't we try to avoid the latter?"

"Why didn't you call Catherine directly? Why go through me?"

"I'm sorry, I tried. She wasn't in this afternoon and she hasn't returned my call. I figured you could get through to her quicker than I could."

"When do you want to meet?"

"The sooner the better. Arthur is very concerned."

"No doubt. I'll speak to Catherine and I'm sure one of us will get back to you tomorrow."

"That'll be just fine, Liam. Just fine."

CATHERINE ENTERED THE FOYER, brushed a few November snowflakes from her coat and hung it on the coatrack.

"How was your appointment this afternoon?" Liam said. "Did Dr. Epstein tell you it was the most good-lookin'-est baby he ever saw?"

Catherine laughed. "There's not a lot they can see on an ultrasound at this stage, but he said I'm doing fine." She feigned a pout. "I've gained four pounds!"

Liam spread his hands. "Where? No way. Tell him I've paid close attention to every inch, under the most intimate of circumstances, and the mother-to-be has her movie-star figure intact."

Catherine gave him a peck on the cheek. "There was a message that Michael Shirley called me this afternoon about Mrs. Woodward. He wants to schedule a meeting."

"I know. I spoke to him. He represents Arthur. He wants to meet with both of us."

"Liam, there is absolutely nothing wrong with Lena

Woodward. She's sharp as a tack. I wish I had her memory skills."

"Shirley threatened a lawsuit. Said he'd meet us in your office or in court."

"The bastard's going to sue his mother? She hasn't been through enough in her life that she has to face a competency hearing brought by her own son?"

"It's about the money."

"No shit, Liam." Catherine stormed into the kitchen and started to rattle the pots and pans.

"What are you doing, Cat?"

"Making pasta!" she snapped. "So I can gain another four pounds!"

He walked up behind her, put his arms around her and kissed her on the neck. "Come on, put the pots down. Don't let that jerk get under your skin. I'll take you to Sorrento's."

She turned around and looked up into Liam's eyes. "She's such a sweet, courageous woman." She shook her head. "We'll have to meet with him, you know. I don't want him running into court and filing some scathing petition accusing her of dementia."

"You know how this will go. We'll meet with him. It'll get nasty. He'll demand you stop seeing Arthur's mother. You'll refuse. And at that point he'll hand you a petition that he's already drafted and tell you he's going to file it the next day."

Catherine nodded. "Right. And at that moment, I want you to punch him in the face."

Liam smiled. "I love the way you negotiate."

As they walked to the car, Catherine said, 'I've already set up a meeting with Lena for tomorrow at noon and I'm sure it will take the entire afternoon. Tell Shirley we'll meet with him on Thursday."

TEN

...

"LENA, BEFORE WE GET started, I have to advise you that Arthur's attorney has requested a meeting with me."

Lena sat with her hands folded in her lap. Her posture erect. As always, she was smartly dressed, this day in a tweed suit, white blouse and contrasting silk scarf. Her makeup was deftly applied and her hair was fashionably styled.

"He has scolded me for coming here and demanded that I cease seeing you," she replied. "What is your position? Will you meet with his attorney?"

"I'm your lawyer, Lena. I'll do whatever you ask. But I have to tell you, Arthur's hired a very aggressive firm. If I don't meet with Mr. Shirley, he may up the ante."

"What does that mean?"

"I'm not sure. He's intimated that he might petition the court to appoint a guardian."

"A guardian for what? On what basis?"

"I don't know for sure, but I suspect he'll claim that because of your advancing age, you're no longer able to take care of yourself or make decisions concerning your property."

"What nonsense! There's no truth to such a claim."

"I know that. Do you think Arthur would go ahead with it?"

"Arthur is very headstrong. He's a controlling person, especially since my husband died. There's distance between Arthur and me. I don't know what he'd do to maintain control." She paused. "Could he succeed? I'm eighty-nine years old."

"Your age is not determinative. He would need medical proof, from professionals, not just his opinion. Can I ask you a personal question? Do you regularly see any doctors?"

"I see a rheumatologist for my arthritis, I see my cardiologist twice a year and my regular physician twice a year. I also regularly see my dentist— do you want to know that as well?"

"No, I'm sorry but . . ."

"I don't see any psychiatrists or psychologists. I don't see any geriatric specialists." She looked straight into Catherine's eyes. "And I'm not senile. I've got all my wits. I haven't misplaced a single wit."

"I believe you, but if he subpoenaed your medical records, your chart, your doctors' notes, would they reveal any discussions between you and your doctors about forgetfulness or memory problems?"

"When you get to be my age, it's a subject that comes up regularly at checkups. They're supposed to ask you about your mental condition. We talk about it. I've probably said I wish I was younger, but I don't think I've ever said that I was failing."

"That's good."

"I might have said I was forgetful. I can't remember names as well as I used to. Maybe my memory is not as good as it once was. You know, if you keep packing information into your brain for eighty-nine years, it gets pretty full. But I'm not confused, I'm not incompetent."

"I don't think so either."

"Let me ask: at this meeting that Arthur's demanded, what if his aggressive attorney insists that you stop representing me?"

Catherine shook her head. "I don't take my orders from Arthur."

Lena nodded sharply. "Good. Then this subject is closed. There's nothing wrong with me. Shall we continue?"

Catherine smiled, set her notepad on her lap and replied, "By all means."

"I left the Shop and headed for the ghetto to find a place to sleep. My house, Karolina's house—they were confiscated. I had other friends, but they were Jewish as well, and I suspected that their homes had been taken away too. Besides, I didn't feel comfortable showing up at their houses and asking to stay there. David told me that rooms were available in the northeast section, in the Jewish ghetto, so that was where I was going.

"When I left the Shop, it was after curfew and the streets were quiet. I shouldn't say that. They were quiet near the ghetto. People like me, coming home from work with ID cards, we were quiet. We kept to the shadows to avoid the Germans. But in the square it was a different story. The soldiers were a boisterous, pompous lot. I could see them sitting in the restaurants and bars, full plates of food, steins of beer, laughing and joking. No ration cards necessary for them. If they were out and about, and if they encountered a Jew on the street, they were inclined to abuse her for sport.

"As David had warned, many were sadistic. If you were an observant Jewish man, they'd cut off your beard. They'd make you dance on the street to German drinking songs. I saw them force men to lick the dirt off their boots. I saw them force a woman to squat and urinate on her meager groceries. I could go on, Catherine, but you've heard all the stories.

"After work that very first day, on my way to the ghetto, I was stopped by two soldiers and ordered to show my ID. I said to myself, *stay calm*. But I was afraid. They looked me over and asked me where I was going.

"'I'm headed back into the ghetto. I'm coming from work.'

"'What is your address?'

"'I don't have one yet.' My anxiety increased.

"'No address? Where have you been living?'

"'On the streets.'

"That answer was totally unacceptable to him and he shook his head. '*Nein, nein.*' But then his companion said, 'C'mon, Josef, we're late. They're waiting for us at the restaurant. I don't give a shit about this woman.'

"He gave me back my ID, let me go and I breathed a huge sigh of relief. I saw a few more people on my way to the ghetto, mostly women returning from their jobs. I stopped some of them and asked them about the Scheinmans. Has anyone seen them? As I told you, most everyone knew the Captain. He was a well-respected man. But the people I met told me that as far as they knew, he had never arrived in the ghetto. They hadn't seen him, my mother or Milosz.

"I entered a few of the overcrowded apartment buildings looking for a room, but they were all full. The situation in the ghetto was bleak. You can't imagine. In an area where a few hundred poor families had lived, there were now close to ten thousand people. If your family had lived in a two-story house before the war, you now found yourselves crammed into a single living space in a decaying building. Perhaps a ten-by-ten room.

"I went from one building to another. It was getting late. It was also dark and exceptionally cold for an April night. Near the tracks was a four-story brown brick building with two apartments per floor. Each of the apartments now held several families and there was no extra room. I was leaving the building when an elderly man stopped me. 'Do you need something?'

"'I'm looking for a place to sleep. Every room seems to be taken. Do you know of any vacant rooms?'

"'It's almost midnight. You won't find anything tonight. Most people, if they can, have gone to sleep. I have a little room, but you can stay. I'm harmless.' He smiled warmly. 'I'm Yossi.'

"He lived in the basement in a small furnace room. There was a large coal furnace that heated the building, but it wasn't functional. There was no coal. We were in coal mining country, but there were no deliveries to the ghetto. Yossi told me that I could sleep for the night on the extra mat in the corner. I was grateful to take it and I offered him a few reichsmarks, but he refused. I sat down on the mat, opened the bag of food that David had given to me and took out a portion of bread and meat. I was famished. As I unwrapped my dinner, I saw Yossi staring.

"'Hungry?' I said.

"He shrugged, then nodded. I shared my small provisions with him, for which he was tearfully appreciative. I thought, how is this man getting any food? He didn't look strong enough to stand in the ration lines all day. And he certainly wasn't healthy enough to work. I hoped he had a family that was taking care of him. Otherwise, he was going to die in this unheated basement. His coat was threadbare and his shoes were coming apart.

"'Do you know Jacob Scheinman?' I asked him while we ate.

"He nodded. 'I know Jacob. The Captain.' He smiled. His teeth were yellowing and some were missing. I was certain that toothpaste was a luxury that he hadn't seen for a while. 'I knew Jacob when he was a young man and I was a teacher.'

"'He's my father. He was arrested by the Germans along with my mother and little brother. I think they may have relocated here in the ghetto. Have you seen any of them?'

"He shook his head sadly. 'I'm sorry. My walking is limited and my attendance at social functions is minimal. I go to the synagogue if I can get someone to assist me. If not, I stay in my room and read. But I have not run into Jacob.' He held up his gnarled index finger to make a point. 'You should inquire at the Judenrat. They keep the census—they know who's here and they know who's not.'

"'The Judenrat?'

"'It's the Jewish council. Because they're responsible for filling the work details, they know who's living here, who's been sent away, who left on a work detail and who's never returned. They supply the names of workers to the Germans and then post them outside city hall. Every day, you check the list, and if your name's there, you show up in the market square for work. Sometimes you come back at the end of the day, sometimes you don't come back for a week, sometimes you don't come back.'

"His narrative made me shudder. 'And the Judenrat, this Jewish council, willfully supplies the names for the Germans?'

"'You can't blame the members of the Judenrat they don't have a choice. They don't run this show, here. I think they're generally good people, and they try hard. They're our interface with the Nazi command. If it weren't for them, there would be no community organization and no one to communicate with the Nazis. But in truth, I suppose you're right, they're helping the Nazis enforce their edicts. When you inquire about your family at the Judenrat, ask to see Mayer Kapinski.'

"Yossi gave me the address and told me that the best time to catch him was right before lunch. 'They usually meet during the day until just before sunset. They don't want to violate the curfew.'

"I shook my head. 'I can't go during the day. I have to be at the Shop. Could you find a way to make the inquiry for me? If it isn't too much to ask, could you see Mr. Kapinski and ask him about Jacob and Hannah Scheinman and a young disabled boy named Milosz? I could come back here tomorrow night and you could tell me.'

"He patted me on the top of my head. 'Of course. Of course. Come back tomorrow and I will tell you if I have learned something. And you may stay in the corner of my basement for as long as you like.' He looked at the corner and laughed. 'Or until you find a place to sleep that you don't have to share with the mice. Be careful.'

"I thanked him profusely, put my duffel under my head for a pillow and passed out.

"The next morning I awoke with a sharp poke in my side. Yossi was standing over me. The room was dark, but there was a slice of bright light coming from the stairway. 'You'd better get going,' he said. 'The sun's up and you can't be late to the Shop. They will penalize you for late arrival.'

"'Is there a place to wash up?'

"He shook his head. 'Down the street at the fountain. There's no running water in this building. Only the fountain.'

"I returned to the Shop and took my place at the sewing machine just before seven. Bolts of cloth were brought to my station and I commenced work. At noon, there was a break and portions of bread, cheese and a small piece of sausage were distributed. I was ravenous. I introduced myself to the young woman next to me. Her name was Marcja. A thin, little girl with stringy blond hair and high cheekbones. She had come from the town of Trzebinia, five kilometers away. I knew the town; there was a train station there.

"On the first day of the war, the Germans had bombed Trzebinia, destroying the train station and much of the town. She told me that most of her family had scattered—some to Russia and some to the north—but her mother stayed in Trzebinia. Marcja came to Chrzanów to find work. She walked to and from Trzebinia each Sunday, even through the snowstorms. During the week she shared a room in the ghetto.

"'I've lost track of my family,' I said. 'They were taken from my home. I was hoping that my mother was working here, but David said he hasn't seen her.'

"'People are taken from their homes, people are snatched off the street, people are even grabbed from the Shop,' Marcja said. 'I've heard there are labor camps being set up all over Poland and Germany, where these people are sent. They don't come home. That's where your family might be.'

"Marcja was a fountain of information about the Shop and day-to-day life, which she was happy to share. She told me that we were given three bathroom breaks a day, ten minutes only, and the women's lavatory was the best way to wash your body, even though the water was ice cold. She also told me about the few stores that were open early in the morning, before sunrise, where the lines were short and where you might be more successful with your food card.

"The day ended and I hurried back to Yossi to learn the news about my family. He gently put his hand on my shoulder. 'Ethel Goodman helped me to the synagogue and I talked to Kapinski.' He nodded at me. 'Good news! Kapinski said he knows about your family. He wants to see you in person and tell you himself.'

"'That's wonderful, but how can I see him? My work hours won't let me go during the day.'

"'Kapinski knows that. He says he will see you tonight. Ten o'clock. He will meet you in the old synagogue on Górski Street.' He smiled broadly, proud that he was able to help me. 'Kapinski. He has the information.'

"I was beside myself. Kapinski knew where my family was. I thanked Yossi, I hugged him and I shared my provisions with him. Just before ten, I left for the old synagogue.

"The streets in the ghetto were dark. Streetlamps were either nonexistent or inoperative. No one filled the gas lamps. Electricity was a sometimes thing. I arrived at the synagogue and opened the heavy door. The halls were pitch black and silent. In the sanctuary, a few candles were lit and along with the ner tamid, they cast a dim glow. I didn't see anyone and walked down the aisle toward the bimah.

"'I'm here,' Mr. Kapinski said quietly from behind. I turned and saw a tall man with a full gray beard sitting in the middle row. He wore a dark suit jacket over a badly worn white shirt. He patted the seat next to him and gestured for me to sit. Other than the two of us, the synagogue was empty.

"'Thank you for meeting me. Yossi tells me that you were able to learn about my family.'

"He nodded, but solemnly. 'I don't know how much you know about your father. A genuine Polish patriot.'

"'Oh, I know. He's a war hero. He fought very bravely.'

"Mr. Kapinski shook his head. 'I'm not talking about the Great War. I'm talking about right now. In the midst of this hellish occupation, there are courageous souls who put their lives on the line every day. They are the Polish resistance. They are the home guard. They are fighters, they are couriers, they are saboteurs and they are leaders. Your father was such a man.'

"'Was?' I swallowed hard.

"Mr. Kapinski closed his eyes and nodded. 'Captain Scheinman, of blessed memory, was a leader in the resistance. With his guidance, we have caused substantial disruption to the German war effort.'

"I swiped at the tears that were dripping like a leaky faucet. I did my best to compose myself. 'I want to hear the rest.'

"'War makes strong men bold, but weak men desperate. Hunger, want, and fear easily combine to compromise a weak person's sense of honor. Nazis are very good at sniffing out these vulnerable souls and capitalizing on their weaknesses. I'm sorry to say that such a person, a member of our inner group, betrayed your father to the Nazis. That is why they came to your home.'

"'And my mother, and Milosz?'

"Again, he lowered his eyes and slowly shook his head. 'We have known them to execute entire families for much lesser crimes.' With that, I broke down. He put his arms around me and held me for quite a while. 'You may stay here as long as you like. I will stay with you.'

"'Who's the traitor? Who turned him in?'

"He hesitated, then nodded. 'You have a right to know. I believe we've identified him. I will tell you when I'm certain.'

"I spent the night curled up on the synagogue pew. My grief was overwhelming. The next morning several worshippers came for minyan. It was already daylight. I rubbed my reddened eyes, looked at the prayer group and shook my head. *To whom do you pray?* I thought.

Other than the members of your group, who the hell do you think is listening? What a waste of time and energy. I slowly left the synagogue and returned to the Shop, arriving long after my shift had started. David met me. He could tell instantly that something was wrong.

"'What happened to you? You look terrible.'

"'They killed them, David. My entire family. My father, my mother, my baby brother. All of them. The Nazis executed them in cold blood.'

"'Come with me.' He hustled me upstairs to the little room that he used for his office and his bedroom.

"'My father was betrayed by a spy for the Nazis,' I said. 'The snake! The bastard! I'll get him, David. I will have my revenge! Fucking Nazis, they will pay.' And again, I broke down.

"'Shh!' he said, wrapping his arms around me. He smoothed my hair back from my forehead and wiped the tears from my face. 'Watch your mouth. You don't want to be saying these things. Do you see what's walking around downstairs? You be careful who you talk to. What makes you think you can even talk to me?'

"I looked at him. I looked into his blue eyes. Was it possible he was also a collaborator? After all, he managed the Shop. What did he have to do to get that position? Was he also a weak link? I shook the thought from my head. No. Not David. Not possible.

"'I don't care anymore,' I said. 'I don't care who hears what I say. I'm going to get this traitor. I'm going to avenge my family. I swear it.'

"He smiled at me. 'Müller was right, you've got spunk. But uncontrolled rage is not your friend. Find your moment. It is not now. Wisdom, planning, plotting, finding your opportunity—those are your friends. You'll get your chance. Your father was a great man.'

"'You knew him? Were you part of . . . ?' He stopped me with his finger on my lips.

"'There are many others like your father. You want to honor his memory? You'll get your chance.'

"'When?'

"'Do not be impatient. Wait for your turn. The wind is shifting.'

"'How do you know that?'

"He smiled that warm, beautiful smile of his and winked at me. 'You can stay up here for a while until you feel better. I will cover for you in the Shop.' He started to leave and then turned around. 'What Mr. Kapinski said, what we we've talked about, I don't need to tell you . . .'

"'I'm not stupid, David.'

"He smiled and walked out the door. I spent the rest of the day in his room, left at dusk and returned to Yossi's basement apartment. He expected to see a happy face, but when he looked at me, he knew the worst.

"'I am so very sorry for you.' He wrapped his ancient arms around me. 'They are beasts, they are dragons, they are gargoyles and they will soon be extinct as well. It is hard to fathom such evil.' With some difficulty, he bent over and retrieved a tallith bag from under his mattress. 'Come with me.'

"'Where are we going?'

"'To the synagogue. We'll say Kaddish for your family.'"

Lena stopped and asked Catherine, "Do you know what Kaddish is?"

"Not exactly."

"It's a prayer. It praises God and yearns for the establishment of his kingdom on earth. In the strictest sense, men are obligated to say the mourner's Kaddish when a family member has died. Although not required of me, because I am a woman, Yossi felt that my parents and Milosz deserved the ritual and that I should join him in prayer. Given the times and our circumstances, prayers for peace and the establishment of God's kingdom in our world were quite relevant. But I was not receptive to prayer.

"'Kaddish?' I said to Yossi. My tone mocked him. 'To whom? To the absent God?' My voice was rising. 'Do you think someone's listening when you chant Kaddish? Face it, Yossi, if there's a God, he's long ago checked out of this hotel. Where is he when they're torturing us? Where is God Almighty when pious people are slaughtered? Where is . . .'

"'Stop!' he commanded. He grabbed my arms. 'You are a Jew. They cannot take that from you. The Nazis can take away your house, they can take away your bread, they can even take your body, but they cannot take away who you are. The Nazis seek to kill us physically and spiritually. I may not be able to stop them from killing me physically, but I am in control of my spirituality. I, and I alone, will decide when to say Kaddish, when to welcome the Sabbath, when to dance on Simchat Torah. Your father, your mother and your little brother—they were all Jews. Nazi Germany, with all its might, attacked their Jewishness, but it did not win. It did not rob them of their faith. The Nazis cannot win as long as we remain Jews. Do you understand?'

"'I admire your strength. I admire your resolve. But I cannot share your reverence. Look what they've done to you, Yossi. A learned man living minute to minute on a basement floor. No food, no water. All because you are a Jew.'

"'And I am still a Jew. And so are you. If you will not say Kaddish, will you assist me to the synagogue and I will say it for both of us? Walk with me, please. We will sanctify the name of God at a time when such sanctification seems wholly unavailing. And that is precisely why we do it. Walk with me.'

"I gave in to to him out of respect and helped him to his feet. I held the door and steadied him as we stepped out onto the stone walkways of the ghetto. 'Thank you,' I said. I looked at his kind face through watery eyes. 'How can this be happening? Tell me, Yossi, you're a man of God. How do we make rational sense out of any of this?'

"'I cannot, nor would I try. We cannot dignify such a question by trying to find a rational answer. We cannot allow that there is a sense, a reason, a rational explanation, for this nightmare. To contemplate a reason is to dishonor the victims. They were not killed for a reason, for a rational purpose. Why is there German genocide in our world? It is not a question we should ever attempt to answer. We should just defy it. No logic should ever be applied to explain this.' Hand in hand we walked to synagogue.

"The next morning I rose early, stood in the butcher's line with my ration card and walked to work. David nodded at me as I walked in the door. As down as I was, his handsome smiling face gave me a lift."

A S TIME PASSED, THE daily routines fell into place. Midmorning, we'd get a short break. The bathroom was located on the opposite side of the Shop and I'd have to dash my way quickly around the stations and through the passageways to get there and back on time. Because I was always in such a rush, I never really paid much attention to the other people working on my shift. I'd manage to wash, run some water through my hair and brush my teeth as best I could before returning to work. At lunch, we were given our portions of bread and meat. We had another break in the midafternoon and finished the shift about six P.M., unless we were assigned overtime. At night, I returned to my corner in Yossi's basement.

"In late spring, 1941, my world took a turn for the better. I was rushing around the Shop to get to the bathroom, this time taking a different route through the aisles, and I heard a girl whisper, 'Lena. Lena, is that really you?'

"I turned my head and stopped cold in my tracks. 'Karolina!' I said aloud. She winced. 'Shh,' but too late. An overseer heard us and walked over. 'No talking!' he snapped. He pushed me forward. 'Keep walking. We have many coats to sew today.'

"I couldn't believe that I had run into Karolina, and on my shift. At the end of the day, I waited for her outside. What a reunion! I wrapped my arms around her and we bawled like babies. I had reacquired a stolen piece of my life.

"Walking back to the ghetto, we caught up with what had happened. I told her all about the day my family was taken, about my time in the attic and about the Tarnowskis. When I told her about Milosz, her face flushed and she cried.

"She told me that she and her mother were evicted from their home in mid-March, displaced by a Polish family, obviously the one I'd seen. They found a tiny room in a three-story walk-up toward the back of the ghetto. Both Karolina and her mother found jobs at the Shop. They had no money and pooled their wages to buy food.

"I asked her how her mother was and she shook her head.

"'She faded away, Lena. But not what you think. Not from alcohol. She had stopped drinking, cold turkey. I was so proud of her. We'd walk to work together each day and come home together each night. She made a little apartment for us. When we had to leave our home, Mom and I packed our linens, our clothes, our dishes and even our candlesticks in a pushcart and brought them to the ghetto. Our living space was the size of large closet, but Mom made a nice home.

"'When we'd return from work, she'd make us dinner. She always told me she wasn't hungry. She'd take a few bites and say, "Here, Karolina, you eat the rest." I know now that she gave me her food so I would survive. She was told that strong, young women would be selected to work because the Nazis needed their labor. The ones who couldn't work would be discarded. She knew that the elderly were useless to the Germans. "Old people will be slaughtered," she said. My mother sacrificed herself and starved so I could live.'

"Karolina stopped walking and looked away. I tried to comfort her while she sobbed. 'I wish I'd been nicer to her during her life, Lena. Growing up, I was so quick to criticize her. I'd think, "Why can't you be like Mrs. Scheinman, instead of a frail, weak woman? Lena has these wonderful parents and I have a drunk." I always thought I was entitled to better parents. But in the end, she showed me that she was the strong one. She was solid for her daughter. And all I could do was watch her shrink and fade away. Now I live by myself in the small, unheated room that she did her best to make livable. If you don't have a nice place, you could move in with me.'

"'I'd love to. I'm sleeping on the floor of a furnace room, but I'm helping this sweet old man, Yossi. I don't think he weighs a hundred pounds. Just like your mother, he's shrinking away. He can hardly walk. I bring him food. I bring him drinks. I make sure he's covered with his blanket at night. If I move out, I'm afraid he'll die. I'm sorry.'

"'I'm sorry too, Lena, for my mother and for your family, which I always thought of as my family. I'm sorry for little Milosz. And I'm sorry for the Polish people, because we're all disposable. We exist as long as the Germans have a use for us. Use them up and throw them away like an empty jelly jar. You and I, we're alive because we can sew. Pray that the German army always needs coats. Even so, the Germans are breaking us down, piece by piece, and there's very little left. We'll be gone soon as well.'

"'Maybe not. I've heard that partisan groups are forming and that other countries are fighting the Germans.'

"She smiled. 'Lena Scheinman, always the hopeful one. Always full of sunshine. You're lucky. Your hopes can get you through the night. It's more than I've got.'

"'Well, now you have *me*,' I said with a hug. 'And I have you. We'll live for each other.'"

Catherine closed her notebook and they called it a day.

ELEVEN

...

"Cat," GLADYS SAID THROUGH Catherine's open office door, "there's a bunch of people here for your meeting this morning. Shall I tell them to have a seat in the reception area or put them in the conference room?"

Liam, sitting in a chair beside Catherine's desk, said, "What's a bunch, Gladys?"

"Four. There's a Mr. Shirley, a Miss Cooper, a Mr. Woodward and another mean-looking guy who didn't give me his name."

"All right. Tell them I'll be right out." She turned to Liam. "I thought this was just a meeting between us and Mr. Shirley."

"So did I. I suppose it's predictable that he brings an associate from his office, but he didn't say anything about bringing his client and a mean-looking guy."

Catherine stood. "It's just a power play. Let's see what they propose." They walked into the reception area, where the four stood waiting.

A short, mostly bald man in a dark blue suit, white shirt and red tie, with a black leather attaché in his left hand, stepped forward. "Good morning, Ms. Lockhart. I'm Mike Shirley." He had a broad smile, spoke with a tinge of a Southern accent and extended his right hand. "Susan Cooper is my associate, and may I introduce Mr. Arthur Woodward."

Catherine took his hand. "Good morning, nice to meet you all." Gesturing to her side, she said, "This is Liam Taggart." And then, pointing at the large man in the corner, "May I know who the third gentleman is?"

"Of course. That's Mr. Scarpini, Mr. Woodward's personal assistant."

"As I remember our phone conversation," Liam said in an annoyed tone, "you wanted to set a meeting with Catherine and me. You didn't say anything about clients or *personal assistants*."

Catherine added, "We obviously don't have Mrs. Woodward here, nor would I think it appropriate to do so before I evaluate the justification for this meeting."

"I'll tell you what the justification is, Miss Smart-mouthed Lawyer," snapped Arthur. "You're ripping off a vulnerable, senile old woman. But in this case, you picked the wrong woman, because she happens to be my mother. So you want to know why it's appropriate? It's because I say so. And if we don't have this meeting, and you don't adhere to my demands, my lawyers will file a lawsuit so fast it'll make your head spin."

Catherine just nodded. "Mr. Shirley, why don't you just turn around and head out the door. And take the rest of this group with you. Good-bye."

Shirley's smile never left his face. "Let's all calm down. Arthur, I think you should back off a little bit. You're coming on a little too strong. Let's not all quibble before we've had a chance to sit down and say our piece."

"I'm not going anywhere," Arthur said.

Liam walked to the front of the room and held the

front door open. "You heard Ms. Lockhart. Good-bye, folks."

"Nope," Arthur said. Scarpini moved in front of Arthur, opening and clenching his fists.

"One more step and I'll break you in half," Liam said. "Now get out of here."

Shirley held up his hands. "Now, now, you see, we've all gotten off on the wrong foot. Arthur, why don't you and Rico go wait outside and let me have a few words with Ms. Lockhart—that is, if Ms. Lockhart will permit me."

Catherine nodded. Arthur and Rico walked through the open door. As Arthur passed Liam, he said, "Head spin."

Liam smiled. "Well, Arthur, I don't know too much about head-spinning, but I think you're going to find out that Ms. Lockhart's really good at ass-kickin'." He closed the door after they left.

Liam, Catherine, Shirley and Ms. Cooper gathered in the conference room. "I apologize for Mr. Woodward's unseemly outburst," Shirley said. "He's very protective of his mother. She's a survivor, you know."

"I know."

Shirley continued, "May I ask what the nature of your relationship is with Mrs. Woodward?"

"Attorney-client." Catherine sat calmly and reticently, with her hands folded on the table in front of her.

"Has she formally engaged you and paid you a retainer?"

"That's none of your business."

"Well, it may very well be. You see, I have a general power of attorney in favor of Mr. Arthur Woodward."

"May I see it, please?" Catherine said. Ms. Cooper pulled a document out of her briefcase and slid it across the table. Catherine read it and slid it back.

"It expired two years ago," Catherine said. "And from

its terms, it was prepared in order for Lena to consent to the sale of her husband's business after he died. It has no application here."

"Very astute," Shirley remarked. "Except my client says he has an updated copy. I just haven't seen it yet."

"Do you have anything else to say today?" Catherine asked. "Otherwise our meeting is over."

Shirley held his hands up again. "Look, can we just be frank with one another? Arthur's mother is debilitated. In her old age, she's chasing phantoms and fairy tales. It's not just about the money, it's about helping to keep her within the boundaries of reality. You have an obligation to the profession. As a lawyer, you may not walk her down some illusory path that has no reasonable chance of a positive outcome."

"Are you finished?"

Shirley sighed and slowly shook his head. He nodded to his associate, who took another document out of her case. "I'd hoped to avoid this, but here is a Petition for the Adjudication of a Disability, to declare Mrs. Woodward disabled because of mental deterioration, and to appoint Arthur as the guardian of her person and her estate. We will file this petition Monday unless I get a call from you. I'm sure you understand me."

"You would file such a petition and strip this courageous woman of her property and her dignity just like the Nazis did seventy years ago? You'd have Arthur put her in some home? Have you no conscience?"

"I have a client who pays us very well."

Liam jumped to his feet. "Get the fuck out of this office, you slimy hack!"

"Sir! You will not address me . . ."

"Out! Either walking or flying. Now!"

Shirley looked at Catherine. "Really, Ms. Lockhart?"

She smiled. "You'd better do as he says."

Shirley gathered his papers. "You're making a big mistake."

Liam took a step around the table.

"All right, I'm leaving, I'm leaving." Shirley grabbed his coat and hurried out the door.

Catherine sat down hard. She had tears in her eyes. "Maybe I should have tried to reason with him. Now the damn thing's escalated."

"Do you honestly think that would've made a difference? He's got his marching orders from his client, who *pays very well.*"

"I feel so badly for Lena. I have to get her in and warn her." She picked up the phone and dialed. Liam sat back in his chair, gripping the armrests and shaking his head.

"Lena?" Catherine said into the phone. "I just finished a meeting with Arthur's attorney." Pause. "I know." Pause. "I agree." Pause. "No, I don't think we should ignore him. Can you come by tomorrow morning?" Pause. "Great. See you then."

TWELVE

...

L ENA HAS A TEN o'clock appointment with me this morning," Catherine said.

"Well, then, we'll have plenty of time for breakfast," Liam said, flipping three eggs over easy. Beside the stove, a plate of bacon lay covered up with a napkin.

"Actually, if you wouldn't mind, I'll just have some toast. I'm feeling a little queasy this morning."

"You need your protein. What good is a piece of toast? Dried bread? What kind of nourishment is that for my little tyke?"

"It's the only kind I'll keep down." She muffled a burp. "What did you find out about the Woodward family yesterday?"

"Much like you thought, except the investment firm of DMW Inc.—standing for D. Morris Woodward—was a lot more successful than we expected. It was sold last year for seventy-five million dollars to Progressive."

Catherine nodded. "So, there is a sizable estate involved."

"And a very good reason for Arthur to want to get his hands on Mama's money. Before the sale, he was vice-president of operations for DMW. When the business was sold, Arthur took a consulting position at Progressive, but he only lasted six months. From what I can find out, he was not well liked and was asked to resign."

"Now, there's a surprise. Were you able to find out how much of the seventy-five million sales price went to Arthur?"

Liam shook his head. "It was a privately held company. They didn't have to report the shareholders' equity, nor their distributions. I'm assuming Arthur did all right; he lives in a seven-figure house in Barrington. He also owns a seat on the exchange and trades under the name of Arthur Woodward Investments. But Lena was the sole heir to her husband's estate according to the will filed with the probate court."

"How big was the estate?"

"The probated assets were small. But that doesn't really tell us anything. I'm assuming that Lena and her husband had a sophisticated estate plan and owned everything in joint tenancy or through a trust, and the assets passed to Lena outside probate as the surviving spouse."

"So, Arthur may not have inherited anything when his father died?"

"Maybe not, but he may have received a portion of the sales price when the business was sold."

"It's puzzling. If he's living so comfortably, why would he covet his mother's money?"

"Well, two reasons come to mind." Liam slid the fried eggs onto a plate with a few pieces of bacon and walked over to the table. Catherine's hand shot up like a stop sign. "Liam, please don't set that on the table. Seriously, my stomach. Would you mind eating at the counter?" She turned her head and waved her hand. "The smell. I'm sorry." She ran out of the kitchen and down the hall.

A few minutes later Liam met her in the living room. "Are you okay?"

"Sorry. Your little tyke didn't care for bacon and eggs this morning."

Liam smiled. "So, back to Arthur. Why would he covet Mama's money? My hypotheses: first, even though he appears to be wealthy, we don't know his present financial condition. I haven't found anything negative—no lawsuits or judgments, his credit rating's good—but he may be overextended. He lives pretty large. His current investments may be risky; maybe he's in over his head on some market positions. Who knows? For all we know, he may have leveraged his expectancy. He may have convinced others to extend credit on the representation that he'll inherit his parents' estate."

"Second reason?"

"He may just be a covetous, greedy kid, who wants to control the entire Woodward fortune."

"Enough to sue his own mother?"

"Apparently so. Although the mystery is, why does he make the lawsuit contingent on Lena's abandonment of her search for Karolina's daughters? The cost of that search, even including you and me, is peanuts. It wouldn't reduce the amount of his inheritance by even one percent. Why demand that Lena stop seeing you or face a competency hearing? In other words, why are the two tied together? Makes no sense."

LENA ARRIVED AT CATHERINE'S office a little after ten A.M. Catherine handed a copy of Arthur's petition to her. Lena read it and shook her head. "Why would Arthur say these things? It's all untrue."

"I'm sorry," Catherine said. "I told you his lawyers were very aggressive."

"But Arthur signed the petition himself. It was notarized. He swore it was the truth. And it's not."

"We're going to need your medical records, Lena. They'll help us prove his allegations are unfounded." Catherine handed a HIPAA release and medical authorization form to Lena.

"When would we have to answer this petition?" Lena said.

"Well, it hasn't been filed yet. If he files it, as he's threatened, Arthur's attorney can set the matter for an initial hearing fifteen days later."

"Can he really do this? Can he take all of my property and put me in a home?"

"Could he? Not if I have anything to say about it. Arthur is the petitioner, and he has the burden of proving his case. He'll have to come to court with solid medical evidence to prove that you're disabled and lack the capacity to make personal and financial decisions."

"There won't be any medical proof. My doctors won't say I have dementia. They've known me for years."

"Unfortunately, it won't be just *your* doctors. He'll have another doctor or two, ones that he hires, who may or may not be honest. But they'll be professional testifiers and your doctors are not. Without a doubt, Arthur's doctors will review your medical records and offer their opinions that you are not capable of managing your affairs, as they have probably done dozens of times in dozens of competency cases against people they've never treated."

"A doctor who doesn't know me?"

"Correct. He will have read your medical records and information given to him by your son, and maybe some other people, and he will give his bought-and-paid-for professional opinion that . . ."

"What other people?" Lena said with a start.

"I don't know, Lena. What other people might have information about your day-to-day activities?"

"No one who would say I'm crazy."

Catherine held her hands up. "Look, at the end of the day, Arthur has to convince the court by solid evidence. Not just unsupported opinions. His doctor/witness will not carry the same evidentiary weight as your own doctor, someone who has treated you for years."

Liam interrupted. "Lena, help us make sense of this. Arthur's attorney said he would file the petition *unless* you stopped meeting with Catherine. All the theories that we've considered—Arthur's inheritance expectancy, his control of your money, possible financial trouble— would involve very large sums of money. Millions. The fees and costs of finding Karolina's daughters would be no more than a few thousand dollars. Maybe ten or fifteen thousand max. Why would Arthur launch a nuclear attack to save a few thousand dollars?"

Lena stared at her folded hands. "I think I know."

Liam and Catherine looked at each other. Neither said a word.

"It's about my will. After my husband died, I had a lawyer draw up a new will for me. Arthur knew I changed my will."

"And you excluded Arthur?" Catherine said.

"No. Not exactly."

"Does Arthur know what's in your new will? Does he know he's been partially disinherited?"

"No. He has no idea what's in my new will."

"I read your husband's will," Catherine said, "the one that's on file at the courthouse. Mr. Woodward left everything to you, and if you were not alive, then it all went to Arthur. So Arthur was in line to take the entire estate if you predeceased his father. Arthur was what we call a successor beneficiary. Before you changed your will, did it mirror your husband's?"

Lena nodded. "My husband and I had our wills drawn at the same time, years ago. They were reciprocal. Arthur was to inherit everything when my husband and I were both dead. And our trusts were pretty much the same."

Catherine leaned forward. "Lena, you don't have to tell us or anyone else what's in your most recent will or your trust. That's your private business."

"Thank you."

"I take it you did not give a copy of your new will or trust to Arthur?" Liam asked.

Lena nodded. "I did not."

"Because you didn't think he would approve?"

"Well, as you said, it's my private business."

"The lawyer who prepared this will, was he also Arthur's lawyer?"

"Of course not. There is no way that Arthur knows what's in my will or my trust. But he does know that I signed a new will."

"How does he know that?"

"He saw me take a copy of my old will out of the wall safe and he asked me where I was going. I told him I was going to the lawyer's office. When I returned, he asked me what I had done, and I told him that was an inappropriate question."

Liam looked at Catherine and shrugged. "Not hard to figure."

"Well, getting back to the petition, I will need copies of your medical records and your permission to talk with your doctors," Catherine said.

Lena picked up the petition and shook it. "The lies he asserts in this paper: I can no longer manage my affairs?

I'm confused about my day-to-day activities? My doctors have suggested that I give up my home for residential care? I have become a danger to myself and to others? Where does he get any of that?"

"Those are broad, general allegations. He'll have to provide factual proof in sufficient detail in order to win his case. The generalizations don't bother me as much as the allegations on page three, the part that reads, 'Respondent is obsessed by existence of imaginary children. She has recently devoted all of her energies and substantial sums of her savings on a quest to find beings that don't exist in the real world. No rational person would engage in such bizarre and delusional conduct.'"

Lena bowed her head, as if it had suddenly become very heavy. "Arthur, Arthur. Even though he's had a very advantaged life, Arthur's always been an insecure boy and I'm sure I share the blame. In the survivor support groups it's always an issue. Family relationships can be a struggle. I tried so hard with Arthur, believe me. But as a boy, he kept to himself a lot. Always in his room. Arthur and I . . . we could have been closer. Still, I never thought it would come to this."

Lena tapped her finger on the page. "Could a court find that I was delusional and send me to a home? I *do* believe that Karolina's children exist."

"It's not as simple as that. A delusion is a mental disorder, a belief in something that no person of sound mind would believe. But to find you incompetent or incapacitated, the court would have to find that the delusion has such a controlling influence over you that your personal and financial well-being are at risk."

"Well, isn't that what Arthur's saying?"

Catherine nodded. "Yes, it is. The petition has been artfully drawn. And I have to alert you that there's a solid line of cases in Illinois holding that a will is void and invalid if it was influenced by an insane delusion. Such a finding would mean that your new will and trust would be set aside and your old will would be probated."

"And Arthur would then take my entire estate when I died?"

"Correct."

"So, how do we defeat him?"

"With evidence. Of course, the most convincing way is to show that the girls existed."

"In fifteen days?" Liam said.

Catherine shook her head. "I'm sure I can buy us some time. But are you sure you want to proceed? This affair will be painful. And we could lose. We may not be able to find the proof that the twins are alive now or have ever been alive. Arthur could wind up appointed as your guardian. You could end up in a home."

"You should at least consider the alternative," Liam added.

"Which is?"

"I think we could probably negotiate a deal at this time," Catherine said.

"A deal to break my promise to Karolina, abandon my search and tear up my new will? No way. I won't do it. I'll fight him. Can I count on you to help me?"

"All the way," Catherine said. "I'll get to work preparing a response to Arthur's petition. I assume they will file it Monday and set it for hearing in early January." She stood and started to walk out of the room.

"Don't you have time today?" Lena said. "As long as I'm already here?"

"I'm just getting a glass of milk, Lena," she said, smiling, "but not right out of the cow. Let me get my notes."

Liam reached for his coat and said, "Cat, Lena, you'll have to excuse me. I have a little work to do outside the office. I'll catch up with you guys later."

THIRTEEN

...

W HEN LAST WE SPOKE," Catherine said, "you told me that you and Karolina had found each other."

"Right. It was May 1941. I was overjoyed reconnecting with Karolina, but I could see that, like so many of us, she had taken an emotional beating. I wished that I could move in with her. I could have helped her. We could have helped each other. But I felt responsible for Yossi. He was growing weaker by the day and had no one to look after him.

"I brought Yossi food each night. I took him to the synagogue three times a week. I brought him books from the synagogue library. When his eyes were too tired, I would read to him. Each evening I would read a section from his bible, the portion for the day. It became hard for him to walk even a few blocks. He was so bereft of energy, so frail that I thought he was going to snap like a twig. I was fighting his old age and the attritions of our oppression.

"'Tell me about your family,' I said to Yossi one night. His eyes glassed over. 'They're all gone now. My Rivka died twenty years ago. We had one son, Ephraim, who moved to Lithuania.' He shook his head.

"'Any grandchildren?'

"Yossi started crying and said, 'I cannot talk about it." So we left it and I didn't bring it up again. But for all his pain, he was usually upbeat. I attributed that to his faith and I began to realize that whether there was a God or not, He existed for Yossi. In the direst of circumstances, Yossi found hope and comfort from his religion. I could understand the measure of his devotion, but I was not capable of such beliefs.

"By the end of summer, the ghetto's population had grown significantly and now held many thousands, not just from Chrzanów but from surrounding communities. Our basic infrastructure could not support the lives of all these people. Just a simple walk around the ghetto would convince you that attrition was the Grim Reaper's major tool. His harvest was evident each day. Initially, before they built the gas chambers and crematoriums, the Nazis' principle killing machine was attrition. Death by starvation, malnutrition, parasites, disease and lack of medical care took dozens a day. In the winter, people froze to death.

"Our living conditions were unsanitary, no matter what we did. Buildings in the ghetto were old and few had indoor plumbing. The ghetto's public toilets, nothing more than outhouses, were not designed to service thousands of people. Our confined area was teeming with all sorts of diseases, lice, rodents, pestilence. It was a constant battle, and it seemed as though new deaths were reported every day.

"One night, in early September, I met Karolina on our way back from the Shop. She was carrying a paper bag.

"'I have a wonderful dinner for us tonight,' she said.

'In this magic bag, I have duck, goat cheese, bread and butter. Can you believe it?'

"'Are you serious? We could get arrested. Where did you get that?'

"She shrugged her shoulders. 'My mother's brooch.'

"I felt bad. 'I'm sorry. You should have hung onto it until the end of the war.'

"She smiled. 'I never liked it anyway. I thought it was ugly. I was able to trade it for food, and let's face it, the food is a lot prettier than the brooch.'

"We both laughed. It was true.

"'Let's picnic,' Karolina said with a lilt. It was a warm night and the sun would not set for another two hours. There was a small triangular park at the corner of the ghetto, and even a park bench to sit on.

"'I have to check on Yossi first. Can I give him a little piece of duck with his dinner?'

"'Sure. There's plenty here for the three of us,' Karolina said. 'We can certainly share with Yossi. Maybe he would like to picnic with us.'

"We stopped in front of the building and I ran down the stairs only to find Yossi curled up on his mattress, his hands on his bible. I stopped short when I saw that he had soiled himself. I bent down to wake him and quickly realized that he had passed. I sat on the floor, unable to do anything, paralyzed by despair. Yossi was a kind man who had never harmed a soul, who'd brought hope and promise into my life. It was just too damn overwhelming.

"A few minutes later, Karolina came down the stairs. 'Are you two slowpokes going to stay here all night?' Then she comprehended what had happened. 'We have to notify the Judenrat.'

"'I have to clean him up, Karolina. I can't let people see him like this.'

"'They'll prepare him for burial. They do it every day.'

"'I can't. He shouldn't look like this. He was a learned man. A good man. I need to clean him.'

"Karolina nodded. 'You're right, of course. I'll fetch the water.'

"We bathed and dressed Yossi, laid him back on the mat and crossed his hands on his chest over his bible. Then we went to see Mr. Kapinski at his apartment. He gave me a hug and thanked me for taking care of Yossi. 'I'm sure his last days were pleasant because of you, he often told me so. I'll send a group to pick up Yossi.'

"'Would you go to the synagogue with me and say Kaddish?' I said softly.

"Kapinski paused. 'Aren't you the girl who said prayers were a waste of time and energy? Didn't you mock the minyan and say, 'Who is listening?'

"'It's not for me,' I said. 'It's for Yossi.'

"He raised his eyebrows and smiled. 'Perhaps it is, and perhaps it isn't.'

"He assembled a group at the synagogue, men on the main floor and women on the balcony, and we sanctified the name of God for Yossi."

Lena stopped and looked at Catherine. "Don't you find that curious? That the first thing that came to my mind was my privilege to say Kaddish for Yossi?"

"Who am I to judge?"

"I mean, joining with other maltreated victims in prayers that praised God in such a godless setting—so flagrantly paradoxical—but it just seemed to me that Yossi would have insisted that I do so. He would have led me by the arm and directed me to say Kaddish. So I did.

"After the funeral, there was no reason that Karolina and I couldn't live together. Karolina's apartment, the one she'd shared with her mother, was small and located in a grossly overcrowded building. So many families had moved into her building and encroached upon her little corner, that her living space was insufficient for the two of us. There were so many people forced to live in such a small area, not just Jews from Chrzanów, but refugees and transferees from other towns in Upper Silesia. Karolina's floor was packed with families, many of them with young children. So we decided to look for another room. Clearly, Yossi's furnace room was too small and unhealthy. We decided to go to Mr. Kapinski, as the Judenrat was often the agency that found rooms for people.

"'There are no vacant apartments, and if I had one, I'd give it to a family with children,' Mr. Kapinski told us. 'But we have just cleaned out the old ironworks on Bozena Plaza. It's a large brick one-story warehouse with a vast open room. It'll accommodate up to fifty in little blocked-off areas. Take it quickly,' he warned. 'There are more than ten thousand people currently squeezed into our ghetto's few square blocks.'"

"Fifty people in one open room? It doesn't sound much better than the one Karolina already had," Catherine said.

"It wasn't a lot better, but Karolina's living space was too small for two. Even though the warehouse was a single room, people through their ingenuity could carve out separate living spaces. Boxes could be converted into dressers and tables. Used and abandoned furniture could be found. David smuggled out a few pieces of wool fabric for us to use as bedding. Before they were forced to abandon their home, Karolina and her mother were given sufficient time to pack their belongings. They brought bedding, dishes and a chest of drawers. Remember, all I had was what I'd stuffed into my duffel.

"The warehouse, which everyone called the 'dormitory,' had windows, high ceilings, a few bare bulbs in the hallways and a concrete floor. Unfortunately, no toilets or running water. It had a coal furnace but no coal, no kitchen, and brick walls with no insulation. Yet, by the creativity of the residents, areas were segregated and partitioned into virtual rooms. Sheets or blankets hung from the ceiling as faux walls. Pieces of furniture and boxes, strategically stacked, formed aisles. To our collective credit, virtual privacy walls were created by the respect of one family for another. Even though your neighbor was inches away, we chose not to listen or see.

"Karolina and I cordoned off a corner area of the dormitory for our sleeping and living quarters. Karolina's old chest of drawers and a wooden box that we converted into a table provided a little wall to make a border for our space. I would say that we probably had an eight-by-ten area with a window. The window was a blessing that September, but a big mistake come winter.

"During the summer, there was enough daylight for us to accomplish quite a bit before curfew. We could rise with the early sunshine and stand in the ration lines. After work we could wash our clothes. We could even take a walk, though not outside the ghetto. But by fall the hours of productivity were dwindling.

"Food was becoming scarcer. Many stores ran out of provisions by ten A.M. Nazi edicts prohibited the sale of any dairy goods or eggs to Jews. No milk, cheese or butter. This was especially hard on families with young children. Babies need milk, and a starving mother can't always provide enough. A black market developed, and prohibited products could be purchased from non-Jews, but it was dangerous and money was scarce. If one was lucky enough to buy some milk in town from a Gentile, it was usually given to the Judenrat, stored and distributed to the children. It was very risky to buy forbidden products. The Nazis would summarily shoot anyone found engaging in black market commerce.

"To further enfeeble us and prevent us from buying food on the black market, the Nazis confiscated our valuables—silver, jewelry, paintings, even nice furniture. We were required to turn in all of our jewelry at the start of the occupation, but many saved a precious piece or two. The Germans periodically searched our living quarters or our belongings and if they found cash or valuables, you were due for a beating or worse. Thus Karolina's exchange of jewelry for food was a dangerous transaction.

"At the Shop, the routine never changed. Each morning Karolina and I returned to our machines just as another woman was leaving. Three shifts operated around the clock. One right after another. Measured pieces of large, heavy black wool would periodically be laid at my station. No sooner did I finish one overcoat than Ilsa would bring another. Sometimes needles would break, I'd raise my hand, Ilsa would come and I'd catch hell for breaking a needle. Finally, after an eight-hour shift, the bell rang, and I walked back to the dormitory with Karolina.

"That was our life through the balance of 1941. Work. Eat. Sleep. We endured and, like the others, we settled into a penurious lifestyle. As long as it didn't get any worse, we felt we could outlast the occupation. Of course, we really didn't know what the Nazis or the winter had in store for us.

"Each night, as winter approached, I would curl up under my blanket, trying to keep warm in the unheated sleeping quarters. As always, I slept with Milosz's shoe in my arms, hugging it tightly like it was a teddy bear. I missed him dearly, but I had stopped crying.

"Back at the Shop, things took a turn for the better in

late fall. Siegfried, a twentysomething German enlistee, became the overseer in Karolina's section. Karolina told me that he had started hanging around her station to chat with her while she worked. He was young and lonesome, and he'd obviously taken a liking to Karolina. As I told you, she was very pretty. She had thick, black curly hair, alluring eyes, soft facial features and a knockout body. And she knew how to flirt.

"Karolina was also a deft conversationalist. No matter what you wanted to talk about, she could hold up her end of the conversation. And she was a great listener. With her sparkling eyes and seductive smile, she'd had many a boy hanging around her in high school. And now, Siegfried was interested.

"Siegfried's attention was a great boon to us. He became Karolina's protector. She was never hassled by any of the other overseers. She worked on fewer garments, but her reported production numbers never fell. Each day Siegfried would bring small portions of food wrapped in newsprint and bashfully tell Karolina that they were extras and that he would like her to have them. Cheese, meat and the most coveted of all, a piece of fruit. When no one was looking, he'd put the package into Karolina's coat pocket. Slipping a piece of fruit into Karolina's pocket and giving her a wink of his eye was a shy boy's opportunity to get close to a beautiful girl. To understand how passionate he was about Karolina, you'd have to appreciate the seriousness of his acts. Giving food to Jews was strictly prohibited.

"It was generally known to the Shop girls that getting a little friendly with a young overseer might get you an extra ration at lunch, not to mention kinder treatment in the Shop. Some of the more attractive girls secretly engaged in encounters, moonlight trysts with their overseers. Some of those developed into more serious relationships.

The girls worked fewer hours, enjoyed special treatment and were generally free from abuse.

"The Nazi hierarchy disapproved of such relationships, of course, for several reasons. Time spent flirting was time taken away from sewing. Girls who worked fewer hours finished fewer coats. Not to mention the fact that Germans were forbidden from having relations with Jews. Nevertheless, the hierarchy closed their eyes and the practice continued."

"I remember Ben telling me that his sister was captured and taken to a brothel to be used by Nazi officers," Catherine said. "The Nazi elite certainly didn't seem to mind raping and abusing young Jewish women."

"You're right. Throughout Poland, young women were seized off the streets, taken from work details, pulled out of shops and out of their homes and forced to be prostitutes or sex slaves—call it what you will. Brothels sprung up to service Nazi officers and elite Germans, like the one in Rabka, where Ben's sister was sent. But I have to tell you, little care was given to whether the abused girl was Jewish or Catholic. Brothels are now considered a substantial component of the forty-two thousand five hundred recognized Nazi persecution sites.

"At some point, most of the girls of the Shop were propositioned. 'Proposition' is probably too euphemistic a term. Many were strong-armed. Many held out, but abhorrent conditions and abject fear compelled increasing numbers to yield. Especially in the cold of winter.

"The winters in Chrzanów were cruel. The frigid temperatures penetrated the unheated buildings and thin blankets afforded little insulation. Most of us curled up as small as we could on our bedding, doubling the blanket, and even then without much relief from the bitter cold. But if a German soldier with a heated apartment showed interest in a Shop girl, she might get to spend the night in his heated bedroom. Shame is preferable to freezing to death. None of the girls passed judgment on such indiscretions."

Catherine held up her hand. "It's not necessary. You don't have to go there. And you and Karolina certainly have nothing to apologize for."

"I'm not about to apologize for anything. But you shouldn't jump to conclusions. Not everyone was so quick to climb into bed with a Nazi. Karolina was no fool. Relationships end as quickly as they begin. A long courtship was far more profitable than a burned-out flame. Siegfried was shy and Karolina was gorgeous. She kept him at a delicate distance. Sexual innuendos, but timely dismissals, kept Karolina's relationship with Siegfried in balance—on a delightfully flirtatious level.

"The winter of 1941 to 1942 was historically bitter and it began early. The December temperatures dropped well below zero. We would dress in layers—a blouse, a sweater and a coat. If you were lucky, you had a very warm coat. If you were really lucky, you had two sweaters. You have to realize, back then women did not wear pants or slacks. We wore skirts, most of them mid-calf. And if you were fortunate, you had a pair of boots that would cover your shins. A thin cotton scarf, a babushka, was all we had to cover our heads.

"Inside the Shop it was warm. Outside on the way home, it was frigid. And even when we got home, there was very little relief. The unheated apartment buildings were only a few degrees warmer than outside. Even double blankets didn't help much. Sleep was nearly impossible. There was just no way to get warm. The wind would whip through the rattling windows, even though we stuffed the seams with newsprint.

"When December settled in, and the north winds blew, it chilled me to the bone. I froze every night. I'd slide into every piece of clothing and blanket I had, and if I were lucky I'd cry myself to sleep, but an hour later I'd wake up with violent shivers. Psychologically and physically, I was losing the battle. Each day I dreaded going home. I couldn't handle anticipating another frigid eight hours. On top of that, I wasn't feeling well. I was run-down, dehydrated and malnourished. We didn't get enough vitamins or proteins to fight the cold. The meager amounts of food we had did not provide sustenance and our resistance was down. I felt like every bit of energy was sapped from my body. I began to seriously wonder if I was going to make it through another night.

"Finally, on an exceptionally bitter night in late December, as I lay curled up, doubled in my blanket, cardboard over me, shaking so hard my teeth rattled, I knew I had come to the end of my rope. I was ready to give up. I really didn't care whether I lived or died. Just take me out of this misery. And if it weren't for Karolina, right then and there, I would not have made it to the morning.

"I was lying there, shaking so badly and crying so hard, when suddenly I felt a hand tap me on my back. Karolina had come over to my bed with her blanket and her mat. 'Move over,' she said, 'You've got company.' She got under the covers and wrapped herself around me. "Don't,' I said to her, 'I think I'm getting sick and I don't want you to catch it.' 'Shut up,' she said. 'Just move over.'

"The two of us, wrapped up in each other's arms, lay on the two mats underneath two blankets. I was out of gas, ready to succumb to the nightmare. But Karolina had strength where I had none. She was determined that I should live. She brought me back from the edge. The heat of our two bodies mingled and warmed us through the night."

Lena stopped. Tears rolled down her face, her lips quivered and she took short convulsive breaths. Catherine produced a box of tissues and put her arm around Lena's shoulders to comfort her as best she could. "Do you want to stop here?" Catherine asked.

Lena shook her head. "We survived. Each ice-cold night we would curl up together, my arms around her beautiful body, our legs entwined, and we survived. Do you understand? In the cold of the Polish night, many did not. We would wake up in the morning, but some did not. Sometimes we would find little children frozen to death, their tiny bodies curled up for all eternity.

"Frostbite was common and the consequences were horrible. The ghetto clinic, with a ridiculous paucity of medical supplies, tried to treat the winter's victims, sometimes with amputation, sometimes with a bundle of bandages, but many did not survive at all. Some survived with purple fingers. But, because of the strength and willpower of Karolina, I made it."

"She kept you warm."

"It was much more than that. I told you I thought I was coming down with something. I wasn't well. Despite everything Karolina did to keep me warm, I got sick. I had a fever. I couldn't shake it. I alternated between chills and sweats. Finally it got so bad I couldn't go to work. David covered for me at the Shop. That night, Karolina came back from work with a cup of hot soup.

"'Where did you get this?' I asked. 'Don't worry about it,' she said. 'Just get better.' Of course, I knew she'd gotten the soup from Siegfried and that distressed me. Each night, she'd bring me a cup of soup, some cheese and meat. During her lunch break she'd bring me hot tea, toast with jam, even a piece of fruit. I knew where it was all coming from and I begged her not to make promises to Siegfried. I begged her not to compromise herself.

"'Shut up,' she'd say. 'Karolina can take care of herself.'

"Still, despite the food and care I was receiving, I couldn't shake the fever. I was having trouble breathing. I had a racking cough. My eyes were red. And during the day, when Karolina was at work and I had to lie in the bed alone, I shivered convulsively.

"Karolina knew I was failing. Finally, she went to the ghetto clinic, collared a doctor and brought him to see me. I was sweating badly as he examined me. When he was finished he stood, pressed his lips together and shook his head at Karolina. 'It's pneumonia,' he said in a whisper, but I heard him. 'We have no antibiotics, I'm sorry.'

"The next night Karolina didn't come home at all. She returned in the morning, stood over my bed straightening my covers and tried to sit me up. I was half-delirious.

"'Karolina, where were you?'

"'Open up. We're going to get you better.' She had a bottle of medicine and gave me a spoonful. Do you have any idea what the Nazis would do to someone who gave antibiotics to a Jew? The penalty was death. This was the risk that Siegfried took for Karolina, and I knew instantly what she'd had to do to get the medicine.

"I grabbed her wrists and cried. 'Oh, Karolina, what did you do?'

"'I'm fine. Don't concern yourself with me. Just take the medicine and get better.'

"The next night she stayed away and returned again in the early morning hours to feed me antibiotics. I cried. I said, 'Don't do this. I'm not worth it.' She hushed me.

"Karolina's sacrifices and the medicine worked. Karolina nursed me through my sickness and back to health. A week later I was well enough to return to my sewing station. Back to work, weaker but on the mend. Even after the arctic blasts had passed and the temperature moderated, and except for those nights she didn't come home, we continued to sleep together under the same blanket, our arms around each other. Karolina warmed my body, and her goodness and selflessness warmed my soul. Under the most hellish conditions of human existence, Karolina would cradle me at night and because of her, I survived."

Lena leaned forward and spoke intensely. "Now do you understand? Do you realize why I must keep my promise? I have never loved anyone in my life as deeply as I loved that woman. There was nothing she wouldn't do for me. She saved my life. I owe her and I'm going to repay her."

Catherine nodded. "We'll do it together."

"Even after spring finally arrived and the nights had warmed, it felt awkward to sleep alone. We had become so close. It was so natural for us to get into bed together. And so we did. We entered 1942 together, and that was a pivotal year for me."

Catherine put down her pen and stood to stretch.

"This would probably be a good time for us to break," Lena said. "I'm tired and I can see that you need a break as well. Can we pick up here next time?"

"Thank you."

FOURTEEN

...

I'M DYING FOR A dish of rocky road," Catherine said, sitting on the couch in her terry robe.

"And we don't have any?" Liam anticipated the worst.

"If we did, I'd get up and get it myself."

He sighed. "Cat, it's eleven P.M. There are no ice cream stores open at this hour."

"Mariano's is open till midnight."

"Mariano's is a grocery store."

"They have ice cream."

"Cat . . ."

She smiled broadly. "I have a craving."

"That's just some myth that women make up to manipulate men during pregnancy."

"How would you know? Are you a woman?"

"Women are devious. It's a proven fact."

"Do you want to carry this child?"

Liam groaned, stood, walked to the hall and put on his coat. "Mariano's is twenty minutes away," he grumbled.

"Thank you, dear."

* * *

I REVIEWED LENA'S MEDICAL RECORDS," Catherine said to Liam when he returned.

"Really, what did you learn?"

"Mmm. This ice cream is fabulous. One more little dish, please. Just a little, and then I'll tell you."

"Cat."

"I'll tell you when I get my ice cream."

Liam returned to the living room with another dish of ice cream and sat beside her. "Are you doing all right?" he said.

"What do you mean? With the pregnancy? Just because I want more ice cream?"

He shook his head. "With Lena. With her story. Is this a project we need to take on right now? I remember how depressed you became when you were interviewing Ben Solomon. He would tell you about the tragedies that occurred to him and his family during the Holocaust and you would have screaming nightmares. Don't you remember Christmas Eve, when you saw ghosts in the church vestibule? And outside the church, when you thought the chestnut salesman was an oracle?"

"The Nazis' cruelty was beyond comprehension, Liam. It's unbelievable what these people went through. But this second time around, though no less horrific, is more manageable to me. I'm in a position where I can actually help someone and make a difference. If I can help her close a chapter of her life, whether or not we ever find these children, well . . . you understand."

Liam smiled and kissed her on the cheek. "Tell me about the medical records."

"I received the records in the morning mail and followed up with a telephone conversation with Dr. Watkins late this afternoon. He's her primary-care physician and he's treated her for twenty-five years. The records themselves do not disclose any symptoms or treatments for mental deterioration. There are notes of discussions between Dr. Watkins and Lena about her mental acuity. He notes, 'Seems focused, no reports of confusion, no incidents of disorientation or poor judgment.'"

"Well, that's good. Where's Arthur going to get his medical support for a guardian petition?"

"The notes are fine. It was my conversation with the doctor that raised a couple of troublesome issues. He's noticed increased anxiety, but tends to attribute it to Lena's obsession with the two children."

Liam winced. "He said 'obsession'?"

Catherine nodded. "But not mental deterioration. He said that while one out of every three seniors will die of Alzheimer's disease, and two-thirds of them are women, he hasn't detected any of the signs in Lena. I asked him whether he ever recommended that she be evaluated for any other dementia, and he conceded that he saw no reason to do so. At her checkup he gave give her a mental-status exam that he would normally conduct on any eighty-nine-year-old woman, and she seemed fine. He saw no reason to prescribe any more extensive testing, such as brain imaging or neuropsychological testing."

Liam shrugged. "So what's your worry?"

"He was definitely concerned with her obsession with Karolina's children. Last year, she traveled alone to Poland against his advice. He had recommended that if she insisted on going, she take Arthur or a friend with her. He told her it was too dangerous for her to go alone. Lena told him she didn't want Arthur involved, and there was no one else to go with her and she was going to go alone whether he liked it or not."

Liam shook his head. "Doctors never like it when you don't follow their advice. Why didn't Dr. Watkins want her to go?"

"Physical reasons. She walks with a cane because she

has seriously arthritic hips and knees. Her balance is unstable at times. She's eighty-nine years old. According to the doctor, disregarding the obvious risks and doctor's orders, and embarking on such a strenuous journey to find these children could very well be regarded as obsessive behavior. And when I told him that Arthur alleged that she's delusional, he said that could be worrisome."

"Obsessed with a delusion?"

"Although he's not making a diagnosis, he said he couldn't rule it out. And then I got a lesson on delusional behavior. There are two types of delusions: bizarre delusions, which are strongly held beliefs in things that are realistically impossible, like Martians taking over your body, and then there are non-bizarre delusions, which are theoretically possible, but improbable and irrational, such as people who believe they are being followed by the CIA. Unless there is some basis for Lena's belief in Karolina and the two children, such a delusion that becomes the central focus of her life would amount to a psychological disorder."

"And Arthur has alleged that she is spending all of her time and her money searching for these children."

"But here's the thing, Liam, any proof, no matter how slight, of the existence of Karolina's children would negate the diagnosis of the disorder."

"So, the solution is simple: we need to get the proof. How is the ice cream?"

"Mmm."

FIFTEEN

...

A T OUR LAST SESSION, you told me a very moving story about you and Karolina, and how she saved your life. I can thoroughly appreciate why you would want to keep your promise to her. But you've never told me what you promised to do."

"I promised to come back and find her children."

"And, you also said, to give them certain information. But you've never told me what the information is."

"It's very personal, Catherine. I'm not trying to keep things from you, but do you really need to know at this point?"

"I guess not, but as your lawyer, I'm trying to develop a factual defense. In Arthur's petition, which is now set for hearing, he claims that you're delusional. If the case goes much further, I may need to submit proof that you're not."

"I understand," she said softly. "Okay. I'll tell you." She started to speak, but Catherine halted her.

"If you feel more comfortable waiting until later, then that's all right."

Lena nodded. "Good. Let's wait till later."

"I think we left off in early 1942. You told me things took a pivotal turn."

"Yes, they did. But before that, I had an incident with Rolf."

"Rolf?"

"An overseer in my section who was always making passes at me. Rolf was a corpulent, ruddy-faced redhead. Probably about twenty-eight to thirty years old. He was a big man, who stood about six foot three and weighed about three hundred pounds. He was a pompous, disagreeable punk—there's no other way to describe him. He bullied his way around the Shop thinking it was his prerogative to have his way with any woman he chose, and that included me. He started coming around my station sometime in the early part of the year, with his off-color remarks and boasts about his sexual prowess.

"I tried to ignore him the best I could. I certainly never gave him any encouragement. But he never got the hint, or wouldn't take the hint. He just kept after me, sometimes putting his hands on my shoulders, telling me how much better he could make my life, if he wanted to. I continued to shake my head and politely decline his advances. I would lift his hands off my shoulders. Then after a while, he became frustrated and angry. That's when the physical abuse started.

"As he walked his rounds, he'd purposefully bump into me, knocking me forward. Or he'd pull the garment out of my machine and throw it on the floor, saying, 'Whoops.' One day, David saw him. He pulled him aside to talk to him, but I could see Rolf was arrogantly denying any wrongdoing and dismissing any responsibility for rude behavior, all with a sardonic laugh.

"The next day, Rolf came up behind me, leaned over and said, 'Don't depend on the Jewish foreman to change my mind. I got my eyes on you. And what Rolf wants, Rolf always gets.' Then he rubbed his hand across my breast, laughed and walked away. That night, on my way out of the Shop, I told David what had happened.

"Two days later, Rolf was back harassing me. David saw him and came up from behind. He told him to come to the office. Later that day Rolf received his new orders—he was transferred to the midnight shift.

"Rolf did not take it well. He was furious. He complained to Hauptmann Richter, the Nazi officer in charge of the whole operation. As I told you, the Nazis had set up the Shop and appointed David to run it, but David was a functionary—he was always subservient to the boss, and the boss was Hauptmann Richter. Most of the time Richter was out in the cafes or the bars. He deferred to David on all operational decisions and usually left him alone, but after Rolf complained to Richter, David was asked to justify the transfer.

"That evening, David called me into his office and closed the door. 'I have something important to discuss with you.'

"'Is it about Corporal Rolf?'

"'Don't worry about him. He won't bother you anymore.'

"I looked at David skeptically. 'Right.'

"'No, seriously. I had him transferred to the night shift. He complained to Hauptmann Richter and today we had a discussion. Don't worry.'

"'What kind of discussion?'

"David smiled. 'Do you want to know how it went?'

"I nodded.

"'First, Hauptmann Richter demanded to know why Rolf's shift was changed. I told him because he was abusing one of my workers. He was trying to coerce a

Jewish woman to have sex with him. And I'd had other complaints about him as well.'

"'"Lies. Pure nonsense," Rolf said. "You take the word of this Jew? I'm only doing my job here, trying to get these lazy women to work. Sometimes I have to use a little force."

"'"With all respect, Hauptmann, I saw him rip a coat out of a woman's sewing machine and throw it on the floor," I said. "I saw him laugh when he did it. I saw him rub his hand across her chest. It's not the first time he's abused this particular worker, and she's one of my best."

"'Richter eyed Rolf disapprovingly. "Relations with Jews? That's strictly forbidden, Corporal Rolf. Do you know I could bring you up for court martial? I could have you deployed to the Eastern Front for such an offense."

"'Rolf turned white. "Relations? Me? Nothing could be further from my mind. You're making a big mistake. I would never defile myself with a Jewess. I was enforcing the edict of hard work. This woman's just trying to get me in trouble. I'm just trying to do my job here."

"'Richter nodded and said, "Well, now you will do it on the midnight shift. The transfer is approved. Let me know if there's any more trouble with this man."'

"David winked at me. 'So that was the conversation. I don't think he'll bother you anymore. But that wasn't really the reason I called you upstairs. There's something else. Sit down. Today, Mayer Kapinski said to tell you that the man who betrayed your father is Louis Feinberg.'

"I tensed. 'Is he sure?'

"David nodded. 'He's known for some time.'

"That made my blood boil. Now I was angry. 'He's known for some time? Why hasn't he done something about it? Why hasn't this man been punished?'

"'Calm down. The Judenrat found out he was a traitor

and that he was delivering secret information to the Gestapo. They began using him to send false messages. Now his usefulness has been spent. Kapinski said he would leave Feinberg's fate to you, since it was your father who was murdered. You may handle it yourself or you may decide what should be done.'

"I was stunned. How could I handle it myself? Could I play the role of executioner? I shook my head. 'I don't know what to do. I can't be responsible for the death of another person. Even if he is a traitor.'

"David smiled at me and gave me a hug. 'No one would blame you if you did. If it was me, I'd want to strangle him, but you're too damn decent to take action. If you'll permit me, I'll arrange for suitable punishment.'

"'No killing,' I said. 'I don't want the responsibility.'

"'No killing.'

"Three days later, David summoned me to his office again. 'I've arranged for Feinberg's punishment. I'd like your assistance.' Then he laid out the plan for me.

"That night, David had an anonymous note, written in German, delivered to Feinberg: *Herr Feinberg. You are directed to meet a designated messenger at the door of your building at 7:00 P.M.*"

"Promptly at seven, a chubby man in a tweed sport coat and felt Hamburg hat walked down the stairs and toward the door. He had a nose like a ferret and a pencil-thin mustache, not much more than a line across his lips. He looked puzzled—curious about the cryptic note he had received from his German handlers. He glanced from side to side.

"'Mr. Feinberg?' I said, standing at the bottom of the stairs. He looked at me and shrugged. 'Yeah, I'm Feinberg, but I have an important meeting, young lady, so please get out of my way.' He waved his hand and tried to brush past me, but I stepped in front of him.

"'I'm your meeting.'

"'You? A girl? You wrote that note?'

"I shook my head. 'I didn't write it.'

"He snorted. 'Hmph. So the Germans send a young girl to meet me and give *me* instructions? What are they thinking?' He eyed me up and down and shook his head. 'What is your name?'

"I never diverted my stare from his face. I needed to see his reaction. 'I am Lena Scheinman. I am the daughter of the man you betrayed.'

"He froze. He quickly looked around, but failed to see David standing in a darkened recess behind him. 'Captain Scheinman?'

"'You betrayed my father to the Nazis. And three other patriots. You turned them all in to the Gestapo. You knew there'd be reprisals. The Gestapo executed four families. Entire families. You condemned them all. You're a traitor and a murderer. You're no better than the Gestapo.'

"Feinberg shrugged. 'Who are you to lecture me? What do you know? You're too young. You know nothing. In case you haven't noticed, there's a war going on, and I'll do whatever it takes to stay alive. I know who's in charge around here and I'll make sure my wife and I are taken care of.'

"'What about my family? My mother and my baby brother? And the other families that were killed because of you?'

"'Unfortunate for them, but they are casualties of war. I guess they shouldn't have been spies. You wasted your time coming here. I do what I must. Someday when you're older you'll understand.'

"'I think the Judenrat and the others in our community will be most interested in what you told me.'

"'Ha! Told you what? I didn't say anything. I'll deny

it all. No one will believe your word against Louis Feinberg.'

He turned to leave, but David stepped up from behind and put a strong hand on his shoulder. 'I think you might be mistaken,' David said.

"He looked back at David. 'Look, what's done is done. Scheinman would have been caught anyway. It was only a matter of time. The Nazis knew there was a resistance group, all I did was to hasten the process a little.'

"'For favors,' I said.

"'Yes, for favors. Of course, for favors. Anyone would have.'

"'You committed treason,' David said.

"'Against who? In case you've been sleeping, we're part of Germany now. It's 1942. Wake up! There is no Poland. You talk of treason? Ha! It's Scheinman and the others who were committing treason against the Reich.'

"'Mr. Feinberg, we've heard enough,' I said. 'I thought for a moment Mr. Kapinski might be mistaken. I gave you the benefit of the doubt. More than you gave my family.' I turned and walked to the doorway. 'You are to follow me.'

"'No way,' he said with a snarl. 'You don't give me orders.'

"'Today, she does,' David said. He held Feinberg's arms tightly and pushed him out the door. There, in the middle of the street, in the January snow, stood all the members of the Judenrat and over one hundred other Jewish residents. They cursed him and pointed at him. He squirmed, but couldn't break free of David's grip.

"Mr. Kapinski approached him and said, 'You are a pariah in our community, Feinberg. A despicable traitor. You may no longer live among us. You are banished from this ghetto. Now, go!'

"'Go where? Where am I supposed to go? I'm not permitted to leave the ghetto, it's against the rules.'

"'What was it you said?' David replied. 'Unfortunate? A casualty of war?' The crowd parted and David led him toward the edge of the ghetto, toward the Chechlo River. He held out a stiff arm and a pointed finger. 'There is the bridge. Perhaps you'll find Nazis on the other side, ones who will appreciate the sacrifices you made for the Reich. Maybe they'll grant you more favors.'

"He turned around with a pleading look on his face. 'Kapinski, help me. They'll kill me. Give me a break. What can I do? Is there some penance I can pay? I have a little money.'

"Mr. Kapinski shook his head and pointed at the bridge. 'You're finished here, Louis. Go.' Feinberg crossed the bridge without looking back. We never heard from him again."

THE NEXT MORNING, I went to work as usual, but I was distracted. Much of the day I spent in a daze. The whole Feinberg incident had disturbed me. As much as I hated him, I couldn't handle the guilt knowing that his banishment would probably end in his death or transport to a labor camp. A few times during the day, David came by my station to ask if I was all right. I lied, and he knew I was lying.

"A few days after Feinberg's banishment, David summoned me to his office again. 'You have to let this go,' he said. 'Move on. Feinberg was a Nazi spy. Striking out against Feinberg was the same as striking out against any Nazi killer. Kapinski would have handled him the same way. He gave you the option because of what happened to your family.'

"'I know, but it really doesn't honor my father to send some poor, meek Jew to the slaughter, even if he is a traitor. Tell me, how do I move on? My father was a hero,

David; he never stopped fighting for Poland. But me? I sit here like a mouse and sew all day just to eat my crumbs and stay alive. And if they kill me tomorrow, what do I have to show for my life? Where are my footprints on the earth? I want to do something. I want to make my father proud.' I stood, put my hands on his shoulders and looked into his blue eyes. 'What can I do, David?'

"He stared back at me with a serious look. He pondered my question. Silent moments passed. I heard a clock tick. Then he said, 'Go back to your sewing machine. There may be something coming up. I'll call you if you can help.'

"I smiled, kissed him on the cheek and said, 'Thank you.' It was the first time I ever kissed him, but it wouldn't be the last."

Catherine raised her eyebrows and gave a modest smile.

"Enough for today," Lena said.

SIXTEEN

...

"CAT," GLADYS SAID, "THERE'S a man on the phone from the Illinois Department of Aging. He wouldn't say what it's about."

"I'm sure I know, Gladys. Just put him through."

"Attorney Lockhart, this is Agent Forrester. I'm a field investigator for the Illinois Department of Aging and we've received a report of possible elder abuse of a certain Lena Woodward of 460 East Pearson Street. I went out there to do my face-to-face, and Ms. Woodward said she wouldn't speak to me without her lawyer being present. She means you."

"Good for her," Catherine said. "I wish all my clients would have that much sense. Who reported the abuse?"

"As an attorney, you must know I can't tell you. The identity of the person making a report of elder abuse is confidential by statute."

"What's the alleged abuse?"

"Ma'am, I'm only doing my job, which is to have a face-to-face assessment with the suspected victim. If I can't do my job, I have to call in the police. And the Adult Protective Services Act makes it a crime to inter-fere with my investigation."

"Who's interfering?"

"Ma'am, unless Ms. Woodward lets me into her home, I have to file a report that refers the matter to the department for follow-up, which may include immediate protective custody. Really, all I want to do is my face-to-face assessment and she won't talk to me without you being present. So will you meet me at her residence?"

"All right, I'll be there in fifteen minutes."

A LARGE AFRICAN-AMERICAN man in a brown sport coat, white shirt, brown-and-orange-striped tie and tan pants was sitting in a leather chair in the lobby of Lena's building when Catherine arrived. He stood quickly as she entered and grabbed his black briefcase. "Miss Lockhart?"

Catherine nodded and held up her palm. "Give me a few minutes with Lena and we'll buzz you in."

He sighed. "Really, I need to see her as she is. I need to note her condition and surroundings."

"What do you think will change in five minutes, Mr. Forrester?"

He emitted a small groan and retook his seat. "I'll have to note that."

"What should I expect from this face-to-face?" Lena said to Catherine when she arrived.

"I'm sure it's just a routine home visit. He's received a report of elder abuse. He'll want to know if there's an emergency situation—is your health or safety at risk? He'll ask you a few questions, take a look around your apartment to make sure your living conditions are acceptable and then report back to his department supervisor."

"I'm not at all happy with this intrusion. I don't want to be on some caseworker's examination table. What right does a total stranger have to come into my world and pass judgment on whether my living conditions are *acceptable?*"

"I know you're not happy, but don't give him any reason to advance your case. Just answer his questions directly and politely. Don't beat him up. He's just doing his job."

Agent Forrester entered Lena's condo, looked around and let out a low whistle. Her floor-to-ceiling windows looked out onto Lake Michigan as though a living seascape were framed as art on a wall. Forrester stepped from the foyer onto the soft, dusty-blue carpeting and surveyed the furnishings. Her expansive unit was exquisitely furnished in French Provincial—rose-and-white carved chairs, tufted ottomans and occasional pieces, and a three-cushioned sofa covered in off-white linen that anchored the formal living room. Fresh flowers in crystal vases adorned the side tables. Forrester stopped abruptly and stared at an original signed oil painting hanging over a sofa table.

"Is that a . . ."

"Yes, Marc Chagall. I bought it at an auction in Lyon."

"Wow. When I got the assignment this morning, I mean, usually I go out and . . ." He paused.

"And?" Lena said, leaning forward and raising her eyebrows, waiting for him to figure out a way to finish his clumsy prelude.

"Well, I don't see Chagalls."

"Chagall speaks to me," Lena said. "We come from similar backgrounds. That particular work evokes memories of my childhood. He was . . ."

"I know, a pious Jew from a small town in Belarus. His father was a fish merchant."

Lena nodded and smiled. Her face brightened a little. "Mine owned a store in Chrzanów, Poland. Chagall was lucky that the U.S. art community smuggled him out of France before Hitler arrived. My family was not so lucky."

Forrester stood before the painting as though it were an altar. Enraptured. "I love Chagall. I suppose you've seen the ceiling at the Paris opera house?"

"You mean the Palais Garnier? The Paris opera house is now that dreadful steel thing at the Opera de la Bastille."

"Oh, right. I agree. The new house is hideous. It belongs in Houston or Phoenix. Not in Paris. Of course, I meant the Garnier."

"Did you know Chagall painted those panels right over a nineteenth-century mural?"

"I did not know that."

"Which is your favorite, Mr. Forrester? Mine is the *Pelleas and Melisande.*"

"Hmm. Gorgeous blues and pinks. I should have known, seeing your living room. I'm afraid I'm partial to *The Nutcracker.* I love ballet."

"You're testing me," Lena said with a smile. "It's *Swan Lake.*"

"You're right, of course." Then, with a twinkle in his eye, "Just doing my job."

"Will you have a cup of tea?" Lena gestured for Forrester to sit on her rose settee. "Tell me, Mr. Forrester," she said from the kitchen, putting a kettle on the stove, "why did you come over here?"

"Call me Thomas. I'm here on a routine procedure they call a face-to-face. Sometimes we get notifications that an elderly person is in distress and we have to check it out."

"You mean abuse?"

He shrugged. "That doesn't seem to be the case here."

Catherine smiled and took a seat on the other side of the room. *I am superfluous,* she thought. *Just a spectator.*

"Who complained about me?" Lena said nonchalantly.

"I'm sorry, ma'am, I'm not allowed to make that disclosure, but you probably know."

"Oh, my son, Arthur. He's very troubled, ever since my husband died."

Forrester nodded his head and accepted his cup of tea. "Perhaps, you can subtly suggest that he seek counseling, Mrs. Scheinman. I can give you references."

"Oh, call me Lena."

Forrester smiled and took out a little camera. "Is it all right if I take some pictures of your beautiful apartment? Just for the file? I promise I won't circulate them."

"Go right ahead. They appeared in *Chicago* magazine in 1993."

He walked around the unit, snapping pictures and giving a series of low whistles. "Lovely." He stopped and turned. "One more thing, please."

"Bruises? You want me to strip?" Lena said with a smug smile.

"God, no. I need to talk to you briefly about your financial situation."

"Not interested. It's not your business."

"I'm very sorry. A significant section of the Adult Protective Services Act addresses financial exploitation of the elderly. That is to say, determining whether another individual might be taking advantage of your financial resources. It's part of my evaluation."

"Nope."

His facial expression showed regret. "We do have subpoena powers."

"Then issue your subpoena. What individual, other than Arthur, is presumed to be taking advantage of my resources?"

"Apparently the report concerns an attorney and an

investigator who may be inducing you to invest your assets in a quest to locate certain individuals."

"Inducing me. Really?" She looked at Catherine. "I went to them, not the other way around. And I haven't paid her a penny. I fully expect that she will bill me for her time, as she's entitled to do, but as of this date, she hasn't used a cent of my resources."

Forrester turned his attention to Catherine, who sat in a wingback chair across the room, her legs crossed, her arms folded across her chest. "She doesn't need my help, Mr. Forrester. I have nothing to add."

Forrester stood. "Well, I won't be keeping you any longer. Thank you for your kind hospitality, Mrs. Scheinman." He smiled and set his cup down on the counter. "I mean, Lena."

SEVENTEEN

...

A WEEK AFTER FEINBERG'S banishment, during my afternoon break, David summoned me to his office again. He shut the door, arranged two chairs to face each other and invited me to sit. 'You said you wanted to do something to make your father proud. How serious are you?'

"'Serious, David. What more can I say?'

"'Serious enough to risk your life?'

"My heart beat hard against my rib cage. This was an opportunity for me to get into the fight. 'Risk, yes. Forfeit, no.'

"'Are you at all familiar with TAP, the *Tajna Armia Polska*?'

"'The Secret Polish Army?' I nodded. 'My father mentioned it to me when we talked, but I can't say I'm *familiar* with it. I think my father was involved.'

"'He most certainly was. Now it's part of the Polish Home Army, the AK. If you truly want to become involved, I mean up to your neck, then come up here tonight after work, during evening shift change.'

"I stood to leave and David said, 'Lena, I don't want anyone back at your apartment becoming alarmed at your absence. Our meeting this evening may take some time. I know you live with Karolina . . .'

"'You want me to talk to Karolina?'

"'Not about our meeting or anything we discuss. Just tell Karolina that I've invited you to have dinner with me. Can you do that? Will she believe it?'

"I blushed. 'I'm sure she'll believe it and will probably be very jealous.'

"'Is that so? Well, come back at six o'clock.' He opened the door, repeated his admonishment to disclose nothing and watched me return to work.

"At the end of the day, I met Karolina outside the building and whispered, 'David asked me if I'd have dinner with him tonight after work.' I smiled a wicked smile.

"Karolina's eyes widened and she smiled as well. 'You vamp! How'd you get so lucky? He's dreamy.'

"I shrugged. 'I guess he likes boring girls. I may be home late.' I bit my bottom lip.

"She gave me a light punch on the arm. 'You'll have to tell me all about it,' she said and left the building.

"I merged into the crowd leaving the building and slipped into the stairway. At the top of the stairs, I knocked on David's door. Another man, gaunt, tall, dressed in dark trousers, a hooded sweatshirt and a gray wind jacket, let me in. He looked me over, head to toe, and then back at David. 'This is Captain Scheinman's daughter?' he said. David nodded. 'And she can be trusted?' David nodded again. Then the man motioned for me to be seated. 'I am Jan.'

"I shook his hand.

"'We want to talk to you about a very important job, but first I want to tell you about a man,' Jan said, 'a great Polish patriot, who served at one time with your father.'

"'What's his name? Perhaps I know him.'

"Jan shook his head. 'No names—not his real name nor his code name. It's for your safety as well as his. Among us, we shall refer to him as Ares.'

"I nodded. The god of war. I was so excited, I literally sat on the edge of my chair.

"'Like your father, Ares was an Austro-Hungarian soldier in the First World War. He served valiantly as a member of the cavalry corps, though just a teenager. He entered this war as a ranked officer in the Polish Army. That's as much of his personal life as I will tell you. Should you be captured and interrogated, should you be forced to divulge everything you know, we don't want you to possess enough information to identify him.'

"'Of course.'

"'Are you familiar with the German prison camp that has been built in Oświęcim?'

"'Everyone is. It's well known. Auschwitz is only twenty kilometers from Chrzanów. Men from Chrzanów were sent to work on that prison. Has Ares been captured and sent to Auschwitz?'

"'He was not captured,' Jan said.

"Then it hit me. I sat back in my chair. 'He entered Auschwitz voluntarily? He's a prisoner by his own volition?'

"Jan nodded. 'When TAP learned about this huge prison camp being built in Oświęcim, and of the many thousands that were being sent there in 1940, they decided we needed people on the inside. A few brave members volunteered to be sent to Auschwitz for the purpose of gathering intelligence and forming an internal resistance unit.

"'On September 19, 1940, Ares walked out into the streets of Warsaw during a Nazi roundup of dissidents, intending that he be arrested and sent with the others to Auschwitz. He joined two thousand other people who were taken into custody that day. He was jailed, beaten and then shipped to Auschwitz by train.'

"I was astonished. How could anyone be that brave? 'He willingly walked into a roundup to be beaten and incarcerated in a Nazi prison camp?' I said with my jaw hanging.

"Jan nodded. 'Ares is such a man. On the inside, he makes notes, records information about who has been interned, where they are coming from, how the camp is organized and more importantly, what the Nazis are doing to the prisoners.'

"David broke in, 'They've begun mass executions, Lena. At first Auschwitz was a prisoner-of-war camp, brutal to be sure, but just a very large jail. Now it is a death camp. There have been shootings and mass executions. We know from Ares that poison gas was tested in September 1941. In locked chambers. The camp has been expanded and tens of thousands are now being imprisoned. We suspect that the Nazis intend to expand the use of poison gas to murder the prisoners. Ares has been smuggling out the truth in his reports.'

"'What do you want me to do?' I said quietly, now fully aware of the gravity of my role.

"'Ares's notes are smuggled out of the camp every couple of weeks and sent along a network,' David said. 'First here to Chrzanów, then ultimately to England. In England they are passed to the Polish Army in Exile and then given to Churchill. Presumably they also find their way to Roosevelt, now that the Americans have entered the war. It is important that the Allied leaders know exactly what is happening in Auschwitz.

"'Recently, a link in our network has broken. We lost one of our couriers. We can't be sure what happened to him, but we don't think that the Nazis have discovered the network.'

"'And you want me to take his place?' I said, excitedly. 'You want me to deliver his reports?'

"Jan nodded. 'We need to reestablish the network. We need to get those notes to England. David is too well known and too well observed to go out into the town. He rarely leaves this building. David will give you Ares's handwritten reports. We need you to take those notes and deliver them to our contact.'

"'But I'm a Jew. I have an armband and papers that identify me as *Lena Sarah Scheinman—Jüdin*. I am bound by curfew and prohibited from leaving the ghetto.'

"David and Jan looked at each other and shrugged their shoulders. 'Okay,' they said. 'We understand.' They rose from their chairs and thanked me for coming. 'Please tell no one of our discussion.'

"'Wait. You're dismissing me?'

"They nodded. 'With no hard feelings.'

"'You misread me. I only meant to say that if I'm stopped and I show them my identity card, they'll shoot me. But, I'll do it. How and when do I make the delivery? Do I go in the middle of the night? When do you want me to start? Oh, and will you give me a poison capsule to take if I'm caught? I don't want those bastards torturing me.'

"They laughed heartily and David said, 'I told you we had the right woman.' He put his arms around me. 'No poison, Lena. You won't get caught.' Then he took a bottle of wine out of his closet and set it on the table with sausage and cheese. 'We celebrate our new comrade!'"

EIGHTEEN

...

CATHERINE SIDLED SLOWLY INTO the passenger seat and grimaced a bit as she bent forward. When settled, she let out a long sigh.

"What's the matter? Are you okay? Is something wrong?"

"I wish you'd quit asking me all the time if something's wrong, Liam. Every time I grunt you want to rush me to the doctor. Pregnant women grimace, grunt, sigh, grumble and bitch. It's our Constitutional right. Leave me alone."

"It's something more. My Catherine radar picked up a troubled sigh."

Catherine grinned. "You know me too well. It's about Lena. I'm probably being overcautious, but yesterday's conversation keeps playing out in my mind and it disturbs me."

"Was it particularly terrifying?"

Catherine shook her head. "No. Actually, it was uplifting. Of course, hearing the details of her travail is horrifying, but yesterday she described a scene where she was recruited into a situation, all of which I find highly improbable. Isn't that terrible—that doubts are creeping into my mind?"

"You've always had a keen lawyer's intuition. What perked up your antennae?"

"The coming attractions, the parts of her story that I'm anticipating she'll tell me tomorrow. I don't think it can be true—at least the part that puts *her* in the middle of it. I want to believe her, but I think to myself, how is it possible that what's she's telling me all really happened to this one girl?"

"You think she's exaggerating? Maybe she's confused?"

Catherine shook her head. "Not confused. But I've heard that people who suffer from dementia, even in the initial stages, sometimes believe that the stories they read or hear about other people actually happened to them. Her own doctor told me that was a common symptom."

"He told you that she . . ."

"No, no. He was just describing symptoms of dementia in general."

"And you believe Lena shows signs of dementia?"

Catherine turned to face Liam. "No, I don't, but I'm not a doctor. I'm not competent to do a mental-status exam. What if parts of her story really belong to someone else?"

"Well, what if they do?"

"This most recent discourse . . ."

"Oh, I get it. There's a possibility that Karolina's children might just be a story she heard and not something she experienced?"

"I hate to think that. But maybe. It's certainly possible. Maybe there's some truth in Arthur's allegations. Oh God, I hope not, Liam."

"What harm is there in listening to Lena's tale? Hearing her out? What's the downside? Is it too much strain on your practice? Does she take too much time? Do you need to curtail your sessions?"

"No. Things are slow at the office right now. I can certainly find the time. The downside is my emotional investment. I just fear a grand disappointment at the end of the road. For both her and me."

"What is it about this most recent episode that triggers these doubts?"

"She's about to tell me that she embarked upon an espionage career to deliver secret notes from a spy inside Auschwitz, code-named Ares. And if that isn't bizarre enough, she says that the spy was a Polish war hero who voluntarily had himself thrown into Auschwitz so he could organize a resistance and tell the world about what was happening inside the concentration camp."

"It couldn't happen?"

"To Lena Scheinman, a person unknown to any historical accounts?"

"I admit it's questionable, but that's just it. Question her. Hell, you're the best cross-examiner I know. What is it you say: cross-examination is the crucible of truth?"

"It's not just my angst about Lena's involvement, it's about buying into the spy story itself. That she smuggled out reports of the gas chambers to the Allies? I mean there's that whole debate—why didn't we bomb Auschwitz or the rail lines when we had the chance? Why didn't we do something to stop the slaughter? As a survivor, I'm sure it's something she's rightfully pondered all of her life."

Liam nodded. "My understanding, admittedly based on minimal exposure, was that America didn't know that mass exterminations were happening until late in the war, maybe 1944 or 1945. I recall a picture of a shocked General Eisenhower at a Buchenwald sub-camp demanding that his aides take photographs and films proving to future disbelievers that the death camp really existed."

"Right. And now Lena embarks upon a story of a

Polish hero who intentionally has himself committed to Auschwitz and smuggles out diaries of the mass exterminations to Churchill and Roosevelt. Not in 1944 or 1945, but relatively early in the war. And armed with that knowledge, the Allies didn't do a damn thing to stop the genocide? For years? And Lena Scheinman's right in the middle of the mix? She's the Mata Hari who delivers the reports? Doesn't that send up credibility alerts?"

"Cat, you have the tools . . ."

"I know, I know, cross-examination is the crucible of truth. But do me a favor. Conduct some of your world-famous investigative research. See if you come across anyone like this Ares person."

"Done."

Liam slowed the car and pulled into the parking lot for Northwestern Memorial Hospital. "Let's see if those ultrasound photographers can get a good eight-by-ten glossy of the world's most beautiful baby-to-be."

"Liam, there's something else," she said, getting out of the car.

"Seriously?"

She nodded. "I've been having some pains. When I talk to the doctor, I don't want you freaking."

"Pains? What kind of pains? Where are the pains? Damn, Cat, why didn't you say something? When did you start having pains?"

"A few days ago. I'm sure it's nothing. They're very minor. They come and then they go away. I figured since we're going to the doctor anyway, I'd wait to tell him."

"Why would you wait? Where are these pains?"

"I think we'll let the doctor do the diagnosis. And there's something else."

"Something else? Something else??"

"I need more maternity clothes. We have to shop."

NINETEEN

...

Y<small>OU LOOK UNCOMFORTABLE TODAY</small>," Lena said to Catherine.

"A little back pain. Headache. Doctor says it could be a bladder infection. He's going to keep a close watch on it. Thanks for asking." She took her notes out of her file. "Last time, we were talking about your meeting with David and Jan. They told you about a secret Polish soldier who knew there were mass executions happening at Auschwitz years before anyone else in the world and he voluntarily had the Germans arrest him and send him there so that he could report it all."

Lena looked askance at Catherine. "Well, that's not exactly what I said. You obviously have some hesitations."

"Lena, I'm sure you're not purposefully fabricating any part of your story . . ."

"I'm not fabricating it purposefully or in any other way. It's true. I'm not senile. I can see it like it was yesterday."

"I'm sorry," Catherine said. "I don't mean to doubt you . . ."

"Yes, you do."

"I certainly didn't intend to offend you, Lena. Please don't get defensive. Your story is a lot for me to digest. Especially when it runs contrary to what I know."

Lena raised her eyebrows. "Exactly what do you know?"

"That the Allied leaders didn't know about the Auschwitz exterminations. It's hard for me to grasp your story that they received reports from inside the camp and then did nothing."

"And that's what you know?"

Catherine nodded. "You said you were Ben Solomon's biggest fan. Well, you weren't the only one. During our sessions, I studied with him. He taught and I learned. Probably the first time in my life that I was impelled to know historical subject matters. Ben showed me pictures of President Eisenhower at the Buchenwald death camp."

"Ohrdruf," Lena countered. "Ohrdruf was a Buchenwald sub-camp."

"In 1945 Eisenhower found naked bodies piled one on another in wooden sheds. He found thousands of starving prisoners looking like stick figures, enough that it made him sick. He never knew about it. He called upon Joseph Pulitzer and other journalists to record the scene. Pulitzer at first didn't even want to come, thinking that such a tale was preposterous. But after he arrived, he thought the reports were understated. No one knew, Lena."

"Yes, they did."

"Ben told me that General Patton was so incensed by what he saw that he ordered his military policemen to travel to the nearby town of Weimar and return with the townsfolk to show them what their leaders had done. The MPs brought back two thousand people and made them look. Many fainted. Three days later, Edward R. Murrow went on the air and broadcast from Buchenwald, and he described the horrific scene."

Catherine reached behind her and pulled a book off the shelf. She thumbed to a page and said, "Let me read this to you. Murrow said, 'I pray you to believe what I have said about Buchenwald. I have reported what I saw and heard, but only part of it. For most of it, I have no words. If I have offended you . . .'"

Lena broke in and spoke in a whisper, "'If I have offended you by this rather mild account of Buchenwald, I am not in the least sorry.'"

"Yes," Catherine said with a catch in her throat. "That's a chilling statement by one of the world's most respected reporters and someone who was certainly up to speed on what the world knew. Everyone was shocked. No one knew the extent of the Nazi genocide. And now you tell me that leaders of the free world knew all about the Final Solution, all about the crematoriums, all about the genocide and did nothing? I'm sorry, but it's a little incredible to me that a single Polish soldier volunteered to be incarcerated in Auschwitz and smuggled out reports to Churchill and Roosevelt, and they could have done something, they could have bombed the crematoria or the railroad lines, but they kept it quiet, not even telling Eisenhower . . ."

"She's right, Catherine," said Liam, walking into the conference room. "Lena's right. His name was Witold Pilecki." Liam took a seat, spread a group of papers on the table and pointed to the name. "It's spelled this way but pronounced *Vee-told Piletsky.* You asked me to do the research."

Lena hung her head. "Thank you."

Catherine was stunned. "You found the name of the spy?"

Liam nodded. "There was more than one. But I think the one Lena is talking about is Witold Pilecki. A true Polish hero. In World War I, as a teenager, he fought for the Austro-Hungarian army. He was awarded the Cross of Valor, not once, but twice. Between the wars he went to officer training school and was a second lieutenant in the Polish army when World War II started. In November 1939, when the Poles were overrun, Witold and his commanding officer formed the Polish Secret Army, the TAP. The Polish underground knew that a huge prison camp was built at Auschwitz and that tens of thousands of Poles were being interned. Using the alias Tomasz Serafinski, Pilecki volunteered to get arrested and sent to Auschwitz in order to organize a resistance unit and smuggle out information. Sometime in 1940 . . ."

"September nineteenth," Lena said.

Liam nodded and smiled. "Exactly. During a Nazi street roundup in Warsaw, Pilecki said good-bye to his two little children and his wife, merged into the group, got himself captured and transported to Auschwitz. Starting in 1941, his Auschwitz underground, called the ZOW, smuggled out detailed reports along a Polish network to the Polish Army in Exile. For a while, they even had a radio. It was Witold's hope, even though he was a prisoner, that the Allies would bomb Auschwitz."

"How did he get notes out of Auschwitz?" Catherine said.

"From time to time, prisoners escaped, believe it or not," Lena said. "There was a time in 1942 when three Polish prisoners overcame their guards, stole their uniforms and walked right out the front gate. I met one of them in David's office. Another time, a report was smuggled out in Nazi uniforms that were being taken into town to be laundered. The ZOW found different ways of smuggling out his reports."

Liam smiled and continued. "Finally, in 1943, the Nazis started to uncover the identities of the resistance leaders. One by one, members were executed. One night in April 1943, Witold managed to unlatch the back door of the bakery where he was working. He and a couple other inmates took off into the night and escaped. He made his way back to Warsaw and worked with the underground trying to get the Allies to bomb or capture Auschwitz, all to no avail."

Catherine looked astonished. "So Witold survived the war?"

"You think that's all? I'm not done. During the 1944 Warsaw Uprising, Witold commanded a unit. After a few weeks, when the uprising finally failed, Witold was captured by the Germans and sent to a POW camp. There he spent the last months of the war. In July 1945, he was liberated and went to Italy."

Catherine shook her head. "I guess he finally deserved to sit back, have a glass of Chianti and a bowl of pasta."

Liam laughed. "Think again. He returned to Poland. As you know, after the war, Poland was a puppet of the Soviet Union behind the Iron Curtain. Witold joined the Polish underground and gathered evidence of Soviet torture and atrocities carried out against Polish citizens. In 1947, he was arrested by the Communists and accused of espionage. After a make-believe trial, Witold was executed. His last words were 'Long live free Poland.' The Communists kept the information secret until 1989. He's a hero in Poland, Cat. He was awarded its highest award posthumously—the Order of the White Eagle—in 2006."

Catherine stood, walked over and hugged Lena tightly. "I'm so sorry to have doubted you. You were actually part of Witold's network?"

She shrugged. "I never met him. I knew him only as Ares."

"Tell me how you got involved."

"After my initial meeting with David and Jan, I went

back to my usual routine, if that's what you'd call it. I would sew at the Shop during the day, stand in line for food with my ration card, try to mend my worn clothing, and sleep as best I could. Other than the occasional ribbing from Karolina there was no follow-up to my dinner with David."

"Ribbing?" Liam said.

"Not your business," Catherine said.

Lena laughed and turned to Liam. "I spent the evening at David's apartment. My meeting with David and Jan was late, and I was instructed to tell Karolina that David and I had had an evening assignation. So Karolina jumped to the obvious conclusion and teased me."

Catherine pointed at Liam. "Until you've read my notes, you'd do well to listen and hold your questions."

"A thousand pardons."

Lena smiled and continued. "For several days, I wasn't called upon to do anything. Every so often, David would casually pass by my station, pretend to inspect my work, chitchat a bit and tell me to be patient.

"Daily life in the ghetto continued to deteriorate in 1942. Disease and sickness was rampant, especially among children and the elderly. But again, keep in mind that disease and disintegration were tools of the Final Solution and much cheaper than poison gas. Stronger young men were taken out and requisitioned for labor details. Sometimes just for the day, but more and more frequently, they did not return at all. Karolina maintained her relationship with Siegfried and continued to bring home provisions for us. As a result, we were healthier than most. It's very likely that without Karolina's food, I wouldn't have survived either.

"In late February of 1942, David stopped at my station, leaned over and whispered, 'At the end of your shift, come upstairs. Jan is here.'"

"Were you worried that you'd get caught in David's apartment? It was also the Shop's office, wasn't it?"

"Maybe a little. There were Nazis everywhere. Most of them were young, noncommissioned draftees, but they wore the uniform and peered distrustingly at all the girls. They had a snake's eyes, and their heads swiveled from side to side like an owl, as they hungrily looked for any infraction of their insane rules. Mainly, they were hoping to catch someone with contraband—illegal possessions, like fruit, cheese, or anything that could be used on the black market—maybe pieces of jewelry or money. Nazi eyes were everywhere, and I had concerns that I'd be discovered going up to David's room, but I trusted David and I would take risks for him.

"That evening, during the chaos of shift change—five hundred in, five hundred out—I managed to slip into the stairway and up to David's office. Jan was there in his usual dark gray outfit, sitting on the bed, smoking a cigarette. 'Are you ready to jump into the fire?' he asked.

"'Yes, I am.' I was bursting with enthusiasm.

"He unrolled white wrapping paper and took out a pair of shoes. Brown laced oxfords, service type, round toe, leather heel. I don't know what you'd call those shoes today. I don't see them anymore. If you looked at pictures from the 1940s, you'd see them, maybe on the feet of the Andrews Sisters. They were a little clunky. 'Size nine?' he said.

"'How did you know?' I asked, and then looked over at David, who was smiling.

"He handed the shoes to me and I looked them over. They were pretty and hadn't been worn, but they were all scuffed up to disguise the appearance that they were new. After all, how would a Jewish girl in the ghetto get a new pair of leather shoes?

"'Is this my reward for being a spy?' I said.

"'Try them on,' Jan said.

"I put them on my feet and they fit. 'They're fine. Very comfortable.'

"'Not too tight?'

"'No, should they be?'

"'A little. Take them off.'

"I handed them back to Jan. He pulled back the sides of a shoe to show me the inside. 'Watch.' He lifted the insole and the inner platform. Underneath the leather were three folded pieces of paper. Counting both shoes, six pieces of paper altogether. I could tell they were handwritten, though he would not show me the contents.

"'You are not to read these reports under any circumstances, Lena. They contain information about the camp and the identity of our men. So even if tortured to your death, you would not be able to reveal the contents.'

"'How reassuring,' I said. David laughed. I could always pique his humor. Jan was not amused. That was okay with me.

"'You are to deliver a load of coats to your contact tonight,' Jan said. 'When you are safely in the house, give him the papers from your shoes. If you are stopped, they may look in every stitch of clothing, but we don't think they'll take your shoes apart.'

"'Where am I supposed to get a load of coats?'

"'You work in a coat factory,' David answered.

"'But those are for the Nazis.' Then a lightbulb lit up. 'My contact is a Nazi? A Nazi's going to take these notes to Churchill?'

"'Does that bother you?' Jan said.

"'No. I think that's kind of cheeky.'

"'Good. David will wrap a load of coats for you, put them in a cart and you will wheel them to your contact tonight.'

"'Tonight? That fast? Where am I going?'

"'The address is 1403 Kościuszko. It is a redbrick house.'

"I stood as frozen as a statue. 'What's wrong?' David said.

"'That's my house.'

"'Good,' Jan said. 'So you know how to find it. And because you were a teenager in high school once, you probably know inconspicuous back ways to get home. Very good.'

"'Who . . . what Nazi pig is living in my house?'

"David put his hand on my shoulder. 'It's your old friend Colonel Müller.'

"'A Nazi colonel, who lives in my house, is my contact?'

"David nodded. 'Colonel Müller is your contact.'

"'But, when I was in the attic, I heard his wife. "I won't touch a Jew's clothes. You have to disinfect the toilets." She's a raging anti-Semite.'

"'Maybe it was an act,' Jan said.

"'Maybe? *Maybe* it was an act?'

"'And maybe not. So don't talk to the wife, just to Colonel Müller. Now you must get ready to leave. He's expecting you.'

"Then I knew. From the dispassionate way in which Jan delivered my instructions, I was just another soldier, a tool of war. I was a commodity. If I were used up, there would be another. I was being deployed.

"'I'm ready,' I said with a salute."

Catherine set her notepad down and took a deep breath. "That's enough for today. As you know, I've scheduled a motion in your case for tomorrow morning. I'm asking the court for an extension of time to file our response to Arthur's petition. I'll need a little time this evening to prepare for the hearing."

"Do you expect the judge to grant our motion? To give us adequate time?"

Catherine nodded. "Sure. It's routine. I'm certain we'll get time, but I don't know how much of an extension he'll give us. I've requested thirty days."

As Catherine walked with Lena to the front door, she said, "I'm sorry for giving you a hard time, for doubting your story. I was a little cranky today."

Lena smiled. "I'm going to attribute it to your backaches. Arthur gave me a lot of backaches before he was born." She paused. "And afterward."

TWENTY

...

O N THE EIGHTEENTH FLOOR of the Richard
J. Daley Center, in courtroom 1803, Judge Willard G. Peterson took the bench for his morning motion call. Judge Peterson had presided over his probate call with a strong fist for sixteen years. He was generally known as a fair jurist, but he'd heard it all and tolerated no nonsense.

"Good morning, Your Honor," Catherine said, handing a stapled group of papers to the judge. "This is Respondent Lena Woodward's motion for additional time to answer or otherwise plead to the petition of her son Arthur Woodward." To Catherine's right, Michael Shirley and his associate, Susan Cooper, stood with plastic smiles on their overconfident faces. Neither Arthur nor Lena was present.

The judge peered down over his reading glasses and stroked his mottled gray goatee. "I've read it." His deep voice resonated with a rumbling, grumbling sound. "Are there any objections from the petitioner?"

"I should say so," Shirley said with a bit of a twang. "This matter is set for a hearing on January twenty-first, and that's in just four days. My client's mother's well-being is in jeopardy. She suffers from severe dementia and any delay will surely inure to her detriment and perhaps the irretrievable loss of her considerable financial wealth. The petition is quite explicit. Why does the respondent need more time?"

The judge grimaced and leaned forward, staring down at Shirley. "Indeed, Mr. Shirley, why would Ms. Lockhart need more time? Since I'm sure you've already disclosed all of your documents, your entire list of witnesses and you've produced them all for their depositions, correct?"

"No, of course not, Your Honor, not yet."

"Right. And your expert medical witness? And his report? You produced them as well?"

Shirley sighed. "No."

"So, who are we kidding, Mr. Shirley?"

"Your Honor, I can produce all of the petitioner's witnesses and their reports within two weeks. Can we set the hearing on a date three weeks out?"

"No, Mr. Shirley, we cannot. I will give you a provisional date in three months. April twenty-fifth. Ms. Lockhart, you may respond to the petition within twenty-one days. I assume, like all lawyers in my courtroom, you will file a motion to dismiss, and we'll brief it, and I'll dismiss at least a part of the petition, and Mr. Shirley will refile, and you'll brief another motion and sometime in the fall we'll get around to trying this case. Am I right?"

"I do intend to file a motion, Your Honor," Catherine said.

"Surprise. Surprise," Judge Peterson said in his low gravelly voice.

From the back of the courtroom, Liam's grin stretched from ear to ear. "That's my girl," he whispered to the attorney sitting next to him. "Ass-kicker to the stars."

"Just a moment, if you please," Shirley said. "Mrs. Woodward suffers from dementia, and her condition declines and deteriorates with every passing minute. Will this court take no notice of her grievous condition? Will the record show that this court has done nothing to protect this defenseless woman from her financial predators? What will be left to preserve *sometime in the fall*?"

"Spare me the oratory, Mr. Shirley. There's no jury here."

"But, Your Honor, this is an emergency and this court is obliged to convene an interim hearing to protect the interests of the petitioner's mother. I'm not asking for your discretionary approval. The statute gives us an absolute right. She is at least entitled to the appointment of an impartial attorney."

"She has an attorney," Catherine said.

"Oh my lord," Shirley said with exaggerated hand movements. "Let's put the fox in charge of the henhouse."

Judge Peterson slammed his wooden gavel. "I demand civility in my courtroom, Mr. Shirley. You will not insult a respected member of the bar. What possible basis would you have for such a censorious comment, and it better be good."

"Most respectfully, Your Honor, the petitioner seeks to protect his mother from the fees and costs of a farcical, quixotic adventure promoted and supported by the respondent's very own attorney, the eminent Ms. Lockhart. Ms. Lockhart and her husband are the very individuals who pose the financial threat. They are the ones who abuse their fiduciary duty to Mrs. Woodward and exert undue influence over her for their financial gain."

Catherine rolled her eyes and wished at that moment

that Forrester's social services report and findings were publicly available and not confidential by statute.

Judge Peterson sat back and thought about the charges he was hearing. "These are wild charges, Mr. Shirley, and if true would require Ms. Lockhart's disbarment. If they're not true, I will have you brought up before the disciplinary commission."

"Do you think I haven't considered that, Your Honor? Do you think I would level such an accusation if I didn't have the factual support? I have a client to represent here, and even though it might be quite inconvenient for Ms. Lockhart's career, I am obliged to address this matter. Ms. Lockhart is churning fees from Mrs. Lena Woodward, a woman so beset with senile dementia that she doesn't know what's going on and cannot defend herself."

The judge pursed his lips and inhaled deeply through his nose. "Ms. Lockhart, are you representing this woman in another matter?"

"Yes, I am."

"This other matter, explain it to me."

"I cannot, Your Honor. It's confidential. I am bound by the attorney-client privilege."

"I didn't ask you what she said or you said. I only want to know what this other matter is about. Why is the subject itself confidential?"

"Because at this stage it consists entirely of confidential communications and secrets disclosed to me within the confines of my representation. Nothing has been filed or disclosed publicly."

The judge shook his head somberly. "I can order you to divulge the nature of the matter. This woman's welfare has been placed before the court."

"Respectfully, I will not obey that order. What my

client has said to me and the subject matter of our communications is strictly confidential."

"Nonsense," shouted Shirley. "She's exploiting my client's mother and draining her financial resources. And you have the power to stop her. This court must order Ms. Lockhart to fully disclose all of the details of her legal relationship with Lena Woodward, including all fees billed and paid."

"Mr. Shirley knows that such an order is improper. Your Honor would not issue such an order and if you did, I would be forced to disregard it."

The judge paused to ponder the quandary into which Shirley had maneuvered him. "Have you notes of these private conversations?"

Catherine nodded. "I do."

"I can order you to produce the notes."

"I will not obey that order. My notes of Lena's remarks are privileged."

Judge Peterson began to raise his voice. His judicial temperament, unfriendly to begin with, took a stern tone. "The privilege belongs to your client, Ms. Lockhart. Not. To. You."

Catherine remained calm. "She has not waived the privilege, nor has she authorized me to divulge any of her confidences."

"Hmm. I see. Well, let me tell you what I will do. I will give you forty-eight hours to provide me with a full description of everything you are doing on behalf of Mrs. Woodward and to produce your notes for my in-camera inspection. If you fail or refuse, I will hold you in contempt. To the extent you believe waiver is an issue, I suggest that you consult with your client and determine whether or not she will waive the privilege before you invoke it again."

"Ah," Shirley said. "In most cases that would be

proper. But here, her son has alleged that Mrs. Woodward is incompetent by reason of her weakened mental
state brought about by her advanced age. She suffers
from an all-consuming obsession to find imaginary children from a bygone era halfway around the world. And
this poor woman is now encouraged to pursue this folly
by the undue influence of her attorney and her investigator. They are the ones that are enriching themselves with
this fanciful odyssey. She does not have the mental capacity to go against her lawyer and waive the privilege."

The judge nodded. "Perhaps. And maybe I will appoint a guardian ad litem. I will consider it all next
Thursday at ten A.M. This matter is adjourned."

WHAT'S THE HARM IN having a guardian ad litem appointed as additional counsel to represent
Lena in the probate proceeding?" Liam said from the far
end of Catherine's conference table. "He'll talk to Lena
and confirm that she's sound in body and mind."

"An appointed lawyer is not my choice," Lena answered. "This is just what Arthur wants, to whittle away
at my independence. The choice of an attorney to represent me should be mine and mine alone."

"I think Judge Peterson may appoint an attorney anyway," Catherine said. "He has that authority. He'll want
an independent voice to protect the record, but you have
the right to decide what, if anything, you say to an appointed attorney. Shirley was clever to raise the issue
of undue influence, so there may even be a motion to
disqualify me as your attorney."

"What about waiving the privilege?" Liam said.
"What are you going to do Thursday morning?"

"I cannot disclose what a client says to me in private. I will give Judge Peterson a legal memorandum

on lawyer-client communication, summarizing all of the recent Illinois cases, but I think he's well aware of them. Everything that Peterson has requested is confidential, and I will continue to assert the attorney-client privilege."

"What happens if the judge finds you in contempt?" Lena said.

"He has broad powers. He can fine me or he can incarcerate me until I purge myself of the contempt."

Lena looked at Catherine and put her hand on Catherine's arm. "I don't want you to get in trouble with the judge. If you need to tell him what I've said or what we're doing, you have my permission."

"Stop!" Catherine said. "The issue is whether or not you *knowingly* and *voluntarily* approve of disclosing the content of our confidential meetings of your own free will, not under the compulsion of an illegal threat to your lawyer. And not because you want to protect me. That's not how justice works. Do you want Arthur to know everything you've said or will say in our meetings?"

Lena shook her head. "Can't we just give him a general summary, or just tell him the part where I was working in the Shop?"

"No. Once the door is open, you'll have to give full disclosure. Everything. He'll have the right to ask you anything about any of your disclosures to me. Do you want him to know everything?"

Lena shook her head. "There are some things I do not want him to know under any circumstances. Ever."

"Then this discussion is over," Catherine said. "Let's get back to Chrzanów, Poland. Tell me about your secret assignments."

"Cat," Liam interrupted. "You can't go to jail. Not even for a day. You're five months pregnant and you've got a risky pregnancy. The doctor said to keep an eye on your condition. Tell Peterson."

"I won't play the pregnancy card. He has no right to order me to divulge client confidences. Period. That's all."

"Catherine," Lena said, "I will not let you go to jail."

"This is my call. I'm in the right and Peterson knows it."

"Cat . . ." Liam said.

"Stop! This conversation is over!"

Liam stood. His face was red. "Now you listen to me. If you're going to proceed with this insane hearing, I can't stop you, but you need to be represented. You need to hire a lawyer. You cannot represent yourself."

Catherine nodded. "I'll think about it. You're probably right. Now can we get on with Lena's story?"

Lena looked at Liam and shrugged. "Okay. Back to Chrzanów and my first assignment as a courier. I was in David's apartment and I put on my new shoes and my coat. David took me to the loading dock and put a dozen coats onto a four-wheel cart. I gave a sharp nod to him, he hugged me, and I ventured out into the night. My house was eight or nine blocks away, but I had to cross a couple of busy intersections. I had only gone halfway when two SS officers in their long leather coats stopped me. One of them eyed my armband. '*Documente, Bitte.*'

"I showed him my ID and my Shop permit. He asked me where I was going. I gave him the address.

"'Why do you take coats to a residence?'

"'Because I was told to.'

"In a split second, his right hand shot out and backhanded my face. 'Do not answer me with a dismissal. I asked *why* you take these coats.'

"'Sorry,' I said, reeling from the slap. 'I have an authorization.' I reached into my pocket and pulled out a folded piece of paper. It was a delivery document, like a bill of lading, evidencing the delivery of twelve over-coats to Colonel Müller for further transfer at his direction. The SS officer read the paper and gave it back to me. Then he grabbed my cheeks between his thumb and forefinger and squeezed so hard I thought his fingers would push a hole through my flesh. 'Next time a German officer asks you a question, don't make him ask twice.'

"'No, sir.'

"He straightened the bill of his cap, brushed his hands along his coat, as though he had touched a goat, and walked away. I continued walking until I saw the lights of my house."

Lena stopped and closed her eyes. "I paused on the corner and stared at my house. For just a moment, I was thirteen. I was coming home from school. My mother and father were waiting for me. Milosz was playing with his cars in the middle of the living room. Magda was making dinner and the scent of roast beef added to the memory. I could walk right in the door and the last three years would be nothing but a dreadful nightmare and everything would be just as it was before. I closed my eyes and wished hard. I willed time to reverse itself, but the sound of a car horn brought me to my senses. It was 1942 and I was a Jew in Nazi Germany. I pushed the cart forward.

"I knocked on the door and a young girl with a shy smile opened it. Warm, well fed, safe and secure in *my* house. Is this the new Lena, I thought? Has she been chosen to take my place in the life of the girl who lives at 1403 Kościuszko? Are these just new cast members hired by the studio to play the roles of the family who lives happily at 1403 Kościuszko?

"'I'm here to see Colonel Müller,' I said to her in German. 'Just a minute,' she said and disappeared into the house. A moment later, a beautiful woman appeared at the door. She had blond hair with styled curls, red lips, a rouged face and long eyelashes. She wore a calf-length dress with padded shoulders and a deep neckline garnished with an exquisite string of pearls. She looked at me like I was trash. 'What do you want?'

"'I'm sorry to disturb, madam, but I have a delivery for Colonel Müller.'

"'Leave it on the stoop and be gone.'

"I didn't move. 'I can't. My instructions are to see him personally.'

"'Fine, then wait. He's not here.' She turned around and slammed the door. I took a seat on the concrete stoop and hoped that the colonel would get home before another SS officer came by to hassle me.

"It was dark, it was February, and I was cold. I moved around to keep warm. An hour or so later, two German soldiers, brown shirts, came walking by in animated conversation. Laughing, telling tales of conquests on a winter night. They stopped. One pointed at me. *Oh no,* I thought, *here we go again.* But they laughed again and resumed their walk. Shortly after that, a black Mercedes pulled up beside the curb, the colonel got out, locked his car and approached the door.

"'Well, if it isn't the little hitchhiker. Good evening, Miss Scheinman.' He tapped the bill of his cap and chuckled. 'So you are my new deliveryman? Very well, then, come this way.'

"He unlocked the front door, grabbed the bundle of coats from my cart and walked inside, beckoning me to follow with a tilt of his head. I stepped into the foyer and froze. Gone was the classic Polish decor so favored by my parents, with rich polished wood and traditional Polish hues of carmine, blue and gold. Gone were the soft, plush sofas in subtle woven fabrics and the stately wingback chairs. Gone were the blues and greens of the Impressionist oil paintings framed in gold leaf which had adorned the wall over the breakfront.

"Now my house was furnished in *Jugendstil,* German Art Nouveau. Cold, modern, free-form shapes. Tall pieces of glass art. Enameled vases sitting on light-grained, sculpted wood occasional tables. A steel and frosted glass dining table sat beneath a twisted bronze chandelier. Wild, provocative ink drawings, in blood oranges and browns framed in free-form chrome, lined the walls. It broke my heart. All in all, my home was unrecognizable. I stood transfixed at the sight.

"'Do you approve?' the blond woman said from her couch. 'You look as though you are passing judgment on my taste in furnishings. Does it not meet your standards? You should have seen the shit I had to throw away.'

"'I'm sorry, madam, I'm just delivering coats to Colonel Müller. I would not presume to question your exquisite taste.'

"'Ha, ha,' Colonel Müller said as he reentered the room. 'Else, are you giving this young woman a hard time?'

"Else folded her arms across her chest. 'Well, she was examining my home like she was an appraiser or something. Or maybe from the magazines? Rather than just a Jewish shop worker.' She shivered and scrunched her nose. 'Who is she to judge? I don't even like her looking at my things. She soils them with her eyes.'

"'Really, Else, she's only delivering coats from the Shop.' Then, turning to me, he said, 'I have written requisition forms in the other room. Come with me.' As I walked through the living room, Else followed me with her eyes, as though she were a leopard sitting atop a boulder.

"When I entered my father's study, the scene hit me

like a punch in the pit of my stomach. Nothing had changed. It was as if the last two years had not occurred. It was all there. My father's leather chair. The deep red Persian rug. His chestnut rolltop desk, with its little cubicles where he would hide pieces of peppermint candy for Milosz and me to find. The fringed brass lamp in the corner, a present from my grandmother, that my mother would call *chaloshes*. So many memories. So hard to take.

"The bookcase looked the same, but my father's medals and war papers were gone—stolen by some contemptible German, no doubt. Also missing were photographs of the family, especially my father's favorite—the one of Milosz and me sitting on his lap that he kept on the corner of his desk. It was all too much. I broke down.

"Colonel Müller shook his head. 'They shouldn't have sent you. I told them.'

"'I didn't know,' I cried. 'When I accepted the assignment, I didn't know where I would be sent.'

"'Well, now you know. The drops have to be made at this house. We can't do it anywhere else. Tell David he must assign some other courier.'

"I shook my head. 'No. I can handle it. I'll be all right. It was just the shock.'

"He pursed his lips. 'What happened to your face?'

"'SS. He slapped me and squeezed my face to demonstrate his racial superiority. Monsters, every one of you,' I said, glaring at him, and cried again.

"'Not everyone.' He stood looking at me for a minute and then he said, 'I don't want Else to see you like this. She'll ask me why a delivery girl should be crying in my home. We have to be careful around Else. I'm going to scream at you and make it look like I gave you a reason to cry.'

"I nodded.

"'But first, where's the report?'

"I took off my shoes, lifted the insoles and gave him the papers. He examined them and put them in a metal box, locked the box and set it into the desk drawer.

"'Are you ready?'

"I closed my eyes and nodded.

"He opened the door a crack and yelled, 'You lazy, stupid fool! Two of these coats have tears in the seams. Are you so blind you would bring me torn coats for my soldiers?' He pushed me out the door and through my living room with a stiff arm in my back. Else sat on her couch with her legs crossed, sipping her cocktail, a satisfied smile on her face. My eyes locked on her wrist and the woven gold bracelet she wore. My father gave it to my mother on their tenth wedding anniversary. Suddenly, the colonel pushed me from behind.

"'Go back and tell them to look at the damn coats before they send them,' he yelled. 'I'm tired of their incompetence.' He threw the two coats at me and shoved me hard into the foyer and against the front door. I must admit, it hurt. It wasn't hard to cry and I left the house rubbing my elbow.

"I set the coats in the cart and started pushing it back to the Shop with a grin from ear to ear. 'I did it!' I said to myself. 'I delivered my first secret report. I'm a flippin' Polish spy!' I'm sure it wasn't proper Irish style, but on the corner of Kościuszko Street, I parked my cart and danced a jig. I couldn't wait to get back to the Shop and tell David."

Liam's cell phone buzzed and he looked at the caller ID. "I apologize. I've got to take this. I'll be back in a few minutes. Sorry." He left the room and closed the door behind him.

"So, you took the two coats and reported back to David at the Shop?" Catherine said.

Lena's face lit up at the memory. "I was so proud of myself, and I wanted David to be proud of well. He was waiting for me, and I could tell he was as nervous as hell. I knew he was worried about a successful delivery of the report, of course, but I hoped that it was more. And it was. From his expression, I could tell that he was worried about *me,* about my getting back safely. It was well after midnight. He took me up to his office without a word and shut the door.

"'I delivered the papers.' I said, bursting with joy. 'I gave them to Müller. I did it, David. I did it!' I started jumping up and down. 'I did it!' He immediately put his finger to his lips. 'Shh.' But then he smiled, took me into his arms and lifted me off the floor. 'There was never a doubt,' he said. 'I knew you could.'

"I spent the night with David. It was magnificent."

Catherine smiled and nodded. "Nice. What an incredible evening."

"Oh, you have no idea."

"When was the next time you carried a report?"

"It was extremely difficult to get reports out of Auschwitz, and they came sporadically and without warning. David would be making his rounds through the Shop and he'd feign a stop by my station to examine my work. He'd lean over and say, 'We deliver tonight,' which meant I was to come by at the eleven P.M. shift change. My shoes would be waiting for me in his office.

"The second delivery, a couple of weeks later, went down without a hitch. When I knocked on the door, Colonel Müller was there to let me in. I didn't even see Else, and our exchange lasted less than five minutes. I returned with a coat, supposedly defective merchandise, which gave me an excuse to reenter the Shop after midnight and spend the night in David's office. As always, David was anxiously waiting for me."

"What was he like?"

"Kind, gentle, but solid as Gibraltar. Always deep in thought. One night, as we lay waiting for the dawn, David clasped his hands behind his head and fixed his eyes upon the ceiling. I asked him what he was thinking.

"'About when it's all over. What will our Poland be like?'

"'Or if there'll even be a Poland?'

"'Never talk like that, Lena. Never believe that, not for one minute. Because then the Nazis have won. They've conquered your mind. You've surrendered. You must continue to resist in every thought. At no time do we ever consider the battle lost.' He stared at me with those deep blue eyes. 'They won't win. I guarantee that. Nazi Germany will fail. It'll go down in flames. And people like you and I will make it happen.'"

TWENTY-ONE

...

EARLY THE NEXT MORNING, as Catherine sat at her desk drafting her memorandum to present to Judge Peterson, her concentration was interrupted by the buzz of her telephone.

"Cat, you told me to hold your calls, but Walter Jenkins is on line two."

Catherine scratched her head. "Walter Jenkins? Did he say why he's calling?"

"Nope."

"Okay, I'll take the call. Put it through."

She picked up the handset. "Good morning, Walter. To what do I owe this honor?"

"I hear you need a lawyer." She heard him chuckle.

"Maybe. How did you know?"

"Hell, Catherine, it's all over the courthouse. Peterson's going to show you who's boss."

"Bullshit. Liam told you."

"Could be."

"So, did you call me to gloat?"

"Hell, no, I called to represent you. I want to be your lawyer."

"Thanks, but I can't afford the eminent Walter Jenkins or any of his high-priced attorneys."

"Nah, this one's on the house. I never could stand Peterson and besides, I owe you one. Jack Sommers. You got us off an eighty million dollar hook."

"Thanks, anyway, Walter, but . . ."

"No buts. It's a done deal. Come on over this afternoon and we'll work on it."

She smiled and nodded, even though Walter couldn't see her. "All right, I will. And thanks, Walter. I really do need an attorney. It's very kind of you to offer. Who do you want me to see?"

"Who? Me, that's who. I'm going to handle this personally. See you at two P.M."

She put down the phone and reflected on life's intersecting circles. Walter Jenkins, her boss and public enemy number one in 2005, the time she stood up for Ben Solomon and was fired. Walter Jenkins, who came unannounced to her office in 2012, begging Catherine to represent his firm when Victor Kelsen sued them for eighty million dollars. And now the tables had turned. She needed Walter and he seemed happy to repay the favor.

She dialed Liam. "So you spilled the beans to Walter?"

"I don't want you going to jail. I'd be too lonesome. Are you going to see him today?"

"Yes, at two P.M. You didn't tell him I was pregnant, did you?"

Silence.

"Liam?"

Silence.

"Damn, Liam. I don't want Walter Jenkins knowing all my business."

"Well, I don't want you going to jail, and besides, your *business* is pretty obvious to anyone who looks at you."

"What did he say when you told him about Peterson?"

"I think he already knew. Word's getting around. I think you're going to see a courtroom full of attorneys Thursday morning. They'll be there for the show."

"Oh Christ, Liam. That's not good news. If the courtroom's packed with lawyers, Peterson's going to want to make a stand. He won't back down in the presence of the attorneys who practice before him."

"Is what it is, Cat. It's an open courtroom. Call me after you meet with Walter."

WALTER'S CORNER OFFICE HADN'T changed since Catherine worked at his firm in 2005. He still had his inlaid walnut cigar box sitting on his desk, even though he no longer smoked cigars. A putter, three golf balls and a water glass lay on a green runner next to the wall. A few pictures of his grandchildren at various stages of their development marked the passage of time. Catherine summed things up for Walter and leaned back in her chair.

"So, that's the whole story, Walter. I won't give Arthur the ammunition to stop his mother from her life's quest. If I tell Judge Peterson that I'm meeting with Lena regarding her solemn promise to find Karolina's daughters, if they're still alive, Arthur will stop at nothing to prevent her. It may be about the money, it may be about his inheritance expectancies, it may be about control—hell, he may even be right—but I have the feeling that this quest is the most important thing in Lena's life, and I'm going to fight like hell to give her the opportunity to see it through. It's my right to resist attempts to reveal client disclosures. It's Lena's privilege to have her confidential communications protected."

Walter raised his eyebrows and smiled. "As always, it's Catherine the white knight. But this time Peterson has a point. He's invoking the mental health act. He has a right to prevent a disabled adult from pursuing a financially disastrous course of conduct. Anyway, Arthur already knows about Karolina's twins. It's in his petition. I don't understand what you're hiding. You wouldn't be disclosing anything that he doesn't already know. What's the harm in telling Peterson that Lena hired you to find Karolina's daughters?"

"First of all, the harm goes to the core of the privilege—that whatever is said to an attorney in confidence shall not be disclosed without the client's consent. The mental health act doesn't do away with the privilege. In unusual circumstances, the privilege gives way only when necessary to protect against imminent danger to the client or others. There's no danger here. Arthur alleges the risk of financial dissipation.

"Second, it's about the follow-up questions. Once I reveal the subject matter of my representation, the judge will question me to reveal facts of the twins' existence. Then he'll want to know why it's so damn important for a physically challenged woman to trek halfway around the world just to tell them something. And then he'll want to know what that something is. These are things Lena does not want Arthur to know. There's some secret here, Walter. I'm sure of it."

"What's the secret?"

"If I knew, I wouldn't tell you, but I don't know. In order to serve my client, I need to keep Arthur from prying into Lena's personal business. If I give in to Peterson, I've failed. Once I answer his first question and open the door, the avalanche will start. I have to make my stand at the very first question. I'm on solid ground and you know it."

"Solid ground? Really, Catherine? You sound like one of our indignant clients. When has solid ground ever mattered when a judge wants to put his foot down? You've got yourself caught in a power struggle with the most cantankerous man on the Cook County bench. What's worse, in this particular situation, this man cares more about losing face than who's right."

"So, what's your plan?"

"You tell me, Catherine. How do you want to play it? I'm sure he'll jump at a compromise solution, one which gets him out of this standoff and allows him to keep his rigid reputation intact."

"Such as?"

"Would you agree to answer Peterson's questions privately to him in his chambers? Kind of an offer of proof, an in-camera review of your knowledge? That way, Peterson can satisfy himself that Lena's welfare is not in danger, and Arthur won't know what you've said."

Catherine shook her head. "I'd have no control over what Peterson does with the information I give him. He can and will ask me anything and everything. And if I disclose it all to him and he decides it's material, then what? He has the power to order me to put it all on the record. Then if I refuse, we're back to square one, except now I've divulged my client's confidences and they're not safe with him. I can't see how that would work."

Walter sighed. "Neither can I. Still, it would take brass balls for him to imprison a pregnant attorney on a civil contempt charge."

"I don't want you playing that card. First of all, I don't think it would work. I don't think Peterson gives a damn that I'm pregnant. Second, I'm not going to stand in front of all my peers and beg Peterson not to throw me into jail because I'm pregnant. I want him to acknowledge that the attorney-client privilege, as much as he doesn't like it, gives me the right to refuse to answer his questions. I want to stand up for my client."

Catherine reached into her attaché and pulled out a folder. "I've prepared a draft memorandum containing the points and authorities in support of my position. Use it if you think it's helpful."

Walter nodded. "I think it's a good idea to file a brief, even though it won't make any difference at the hearing. Its benefit will come when we have to appeal Peterson's order. I'll put a couple lawyers to work on this and see if they come up with anything else."

Catherine rose. "I appreciate your help very much, Walter. You're a good friend."

"So are you. See you tomorrow morning."

TWENTY-TWO

...

L IAM AND WALTER WERE right on the money; Peterson's courtroom was standing-room only on Thursday morning. Anyone who had a few minutes between court calls dropped in to see if Peterson would actually hold Catherine Lockhart in contempt and lock her up until she purged herself by answering his questions. No one doubted Peterson's resolve, just as no one had ever accused him of being sensitive or personable. Liam took a seat in the back row.

"All rise." The gavel slammed three times and Judge Peterson entered the room through the corner door. He took a step, surveyed the overflow crowd, sneered, shook his head and barked, "Don't you people have anything better to do?" He climbed the steps, took his seat and motioned for everyone else to be seated. Michael Shirley, Susan Cooper and Arthur Woodward sat at counsel table to the judge's left. Catherine and Walter were at counsel table on the right. Catherine had instructed Lena not to attend. The room grew silent.

Peterson nodded to his clerk, who announced the case. "Case number 13 P 6268, *In re: the Guardianship of Lena Woodward,* continued by previous court order for status." Shirley, Walter and Catherine stood and approached the bench.

"The record will show," Judge Peterson said, "that this matter was continued to this day following my order to Ms. Lockhart to disclose certain non-privileged information to the court and her refusal to do so. I continued this matter as a courtesy to Ms. Lockhart to enable her to see the error in her judgment and properly comply with my order." He peered down over his reading glasses at the attorneys standing before him. "I take it from the presence of Mr. Jenkins that Ms. Lockhart intends to contest my order. Is that correct, Mr. Jenkins?"

In his dark blue pinstriped suit, tailored perfectly to fit his six-foot-four frame, his monogrammed white shirt and floral Brioni tie, Walter Jenkins, past president of the bar association and founding partner of one of Chicago's leading firms, stood regally before the bench. He looked directly into the eyes of Judge Peterson and never diverted his gaze.

"That is absolutely correct," Jenkins said in sonorous tones. "Ms. Lockhart intends to abide by rule one-point-six of the Illinois Rules of Professional Conduct providing that 'A lawyer shall not reveal information relating to the representation of a client unless the client gives informed consent.' Mrs. Woodward has not given her consent and Ms. Lockhart rightfully refuses to reveal any information *relating* to her representation, which includes answering your intrusive inquiries. Your Honor well knows that the attorney-client privilege underpins the essence of the American legal system—that no one can tear down the walls of confidentiality that each and every client expects when communicating with his or her attorney. The matters entrusted to an attorney behind the closed office door are strictly and indelibly private and confidential. As such, Ms. Lockhart is simply unable to divulge confidential matters."

Peterson tapped his pencil on this desktop and swiveled his head to the left. "Do you have a response, Mr. Shirley?"

"Is a response even necessary?" Shirley said with a snort, in his Tennessee drawl. "You gave a judicial order, and Ms. Lockhart refuses to follow it. Mr. Jenkins can spout his fancy oratory all over the Daley Center, but it doesn't change the facts. Arthur alleges that his mother suffers from dementia, and, specifically, she lies in the throes of an obsessive delusion that some imaginary woman named Karolina gave birth to imaginary children seventy years ago that Mrs. Woodward, of all people, is now required to find. And my client further asserts that even if this obsession were not damaging enough to her emotional well-being, unscrupulous lawyers and investigators are willing to separate Mrs. Woodward from her considerable life savings to further this ludicrous quest to find these nonexistent children."

Shirley started to pace. "Two days ago, when I advised Your Honor that Ms. Lockhart was likely representing Mrs. Woodward in this ridiculous venture, and requested the appointment of an independent attorney, Your Honor quite rightly asked Ms. Lockhart what the nature of her representation was—not what she was told in confidence, mind you, just the nature of the matter she was handling. Such a simple request. And what did she do? She refused. Is there no more obvious admission of guilt? She wants to continue to milk this bogus case until Mrs. Woodward is out of money. But she doesn't want to tell you that, so she says, 'It's confidential.' Well, it's not. As Your Honor has quite properly noted, the nature of her engagement is not a communication, and thus it is not protected.

"So Your Honor's order is not only within legal bounds, but it's necessary to protect the interests of a poor disabled woman. In contumaciously refusing to answer, Ms. Lockhart is flagrantly violating the authority of this probate court. She thinks she's above the law and I believe this court needs to teach her a lesson. No one is above the law. We urge you to compel her to answer your proper inquiry by means of contempt sanctions, including coercive incarceration until she purges herself of her contempt and comes clean with the information."

A loud buzz of conversation began skittering among the spectators, enough so that the judge slammed his gavel several times. "Do I need to clear this courtroom?"

"May I respond, please, to the comments of Mr. Shirley, Your Honor?" Jenkins said, and took a deep breath.

Peterson waved his hand back and forth. "No. I've heard enough." He looked down at Catherine and spoke dispassionately. "This court is concerned that Mrs. Woodward may be following a path injurious to both her health and her financial well-being. That doesn't mean that I'm accepting the petitioner's unproven allegations as true, but they concern me greatly. Especially when the attorney-client privilege may be used to as a curtain to hide a lawyer's complicity in a financial scandal. I'm not saying that I believe any or all of Arthur Woodward's accusations. All I'm saying is that I deem them serious enough to invoke my responsibilities as a probate judge to conduct a further inquiry. Do you understand me, Ms. Lockhart?"

"Yes, sir, I do."

"Good. Now we're getting somewhere. Will you please comply with this court's order and inform me fully of the matter in which you represent Mrs. Woodward?"

"No, sir, I will not."

"One more time, with the knowledge that I will use

my judicial authority to sanction you, Ms. Lockhart, will you comply with this court's order?"

"No, sir, I will not."

"Regretfully, Ms. Lockhart, I hereby remand you to the custody of the Cook County sheriff to be coercively incarcerated in the Cook County Jail until you are prepared to comply with this court's orders and fully answer this court's inquiries."

Immediately, loud gasps and comments skittered through the courtroom, such that Judge Peterson again slammed his wooden gavel several times. "Silence!" he yelled. "Or she'll have company in the jail." Liam hung his head and covered his eyes with his hands.

"Motion to stay the order, if you please," Walter said. "We intend to take this matter immediately to the appellate court for an expedited review. We ask that your contempt order be stayed until the appellate court has rendered its decision."

"Denied."

The court's deputy moved from behind his desk, took out his handcuffs and approached Catherine, who stood steadfast before the bench. Judge Peterson held up his index finger. "I will not stay this order indefinitely while the appellate court takes its sweet time to consider my ruling. But I will stay the order until Monday morning at ten A.M., at which time I direct you all to return. During that time, Ms. Lockhart, I advise you to reconsider your refusal."

"Most respectfully, Your Honor," Shirley interjected, "of course I'm not happy with Your Honor's overly gracious deferment of your lawful contempt order, but during the stay may we have in place an order preventing Ms. Lockhart from meeting with Mrs. Woodward, from communicating with Mrs. Woodward, or from assessing or accepting any fees from Mrs. Woodward?"

"That's outrageous," Jenkins blared. "Mrs. Woodward has the right to consult with any attorney of her choosing at any time. This court has no right to interfere with that relationship. Such an order is *per se* reversible."

"Then reverse it, Mr. Jenkins," Judge Peterson snapped, standing and leaning far over his bench. "Take it up and see what you can do with it. Personally, I'd love to tell you what you can do with it. But the bottom line is, there are allegations raised in this courtroom that Ms. Lockhart is perverting her role as an attorney to lead a disabled woman down an indefensible path for Ms. Lockhart's own pecuniary gain. I don't know if they're true or they're false. If they're true, then there are grounds for disbarment and criminal prosecution. But they may be false, and I hope for her sake they are, and it's precisely for that reason that I ordered Ms. Lockhart to talk to me. But she won't. So the order will be to incarcerate Ms. Lockhart until she obeys. That order is stayed until Monday. In the interim, I will enter a separate order of protection strictly preventing Ms. Lockhart from accepting any fees or costs, or promises to pay any fees or costs, during the pendency of the contempt. However, I will not prevent her from meeting or communicating with whomever she chooses."

Shirley returned to counsel table, winked and smiled at Arthur, who nodded his head and pumped a fist.

"Your Honor," Walter said, "we have prepared a memorandum of law setting forth our position on the erroneous nature of this procedure and that of your order. I ask that the memorandum be filed of record at this time and considered before Monday's court hearing."

"The memorandum will be accepted. This court's adjourned."

Walter pulled Catherine aside in the hall outside the courtroom. "I'm sorry we didn't do better, but he gave you three days to change your mind. You should think about it. Before coming in here, we didn't know exactly what he would do. Now we know. He won't hesitate one second to send you to jail and keep you in jail, and the Cook County Jail is no place for you."

"What about an expedited appeal?"

"You're still looking at three, four weeks, maybe more. Do yourself a favor. Talk to Lena about waiving the privilege."

"She's not the reason. I told you, she'd waive it if I asked her to, but not because she wants the information released. She'd waive it just to protect me. I know for a fact that there are very personal issues here that she doesn't want to reveal to Arthur, and I won't be bullied into disclosing them."

"I saw a look in Peterson's eyes this morning that the rest of the courtroom didn't see," Walter said. "It was a look of fear. He's searching for a way out of this trap. None of the lawyers in that room approved of what he was doing and he knows it. The appellate court will not affirm him, he'll get a slap on the wrist, and he's pretty sure of that as well. He's bound to catch major shit one way or another. We should both think about what life-lines we can toss him. What if we could structure a limited inquiry—a specific list of questions—ones that don't divulge any more than Arthur already knows?"

Catherine nodded. "I'll think about it."

"Will you at least talk to Lena and find out what her deep dark secret is?"

Catherine nodded. "I'll see her this weekend and I'll urge her to finish her story. If she has a deep dark secret, she may reveal it to me, but I won't disclose it to anyone."

"Of course. But it may help us frame a set of questions that won't disclose her secret."

TWENTY-THREE

...

I T W A S A G L O O M Y, rainy Friday morning when Lena arrived at Catherine's office a half hour late. "What happened in court yesterday?" she said, shaking her umbrella in the office foyer.

Catherine shrugged off the question. "It wasn't very pleasant. Judge Peterson persisted in his campaign to force me to abide by his order, but he ended by continuing everything to Monday morning. Walter is very confident about our legal position and we hope to get this whole matter disposed of in the short term. We think we might be able to offer a list of questions that aren't private and won't violate your confidential disclosures. Meanwhile, I'd like to use as much time as we have over the next three days to finish your narrative. Let's you and I work really hard to get all of the background information so that Liam can start to track down the two girls."

"Of course." Lena handed her coat to Gladys and followed Catherine into the conference room.

Catherine pulled her yellow pad out of her file, flipped the pages to the end of her notes and smiled as if a thought crossed her mind.

"Something strike you as funny?" Lena said.

Catherine nodded. "We begin our sessions like a ten-part TV drama series. You know, 'Previously, on the Life of Lena Woodward . . .'"

"Lena Scheinman," she corrected with a chuckle. "*Previously,* I had completed two deliveries of the secret Auschwitz reports to Colonel Müller, the second one without a hitch. Winter was drawing to a close, but life in the ghetto continued to disintegrate. The Grim Reaper had many tools: starvation, disease, disenchantment, lack of energy, lack of purpose. Many of the elderly, or those in a weakened condition, had reached the point where they couldn't work or even forage for necessities and they lost their will to face another day. Compromised immune systems were no match for the bacteria and viruses that ran rampant throughout the ghetto. Lice, insect infestation, rats and skin diseases were more than our understaffed and unsupplied clinics could handle. Even a minor cold or the flu was life-threatening and extraordinarily contagious.

"Karolina's relationship with Siegfried kept going strong and managed to keep us well-fed. David also had access to food from the pantries at the Shop, and occasionally I'd have extra bread for us. In that regard, Karolina and I were among the privileged and we knew it. The young and healthy survived. The old and feeble expired or were sent to die.

"In late March, David tapped me on the shoulder to let me know there was a delivery to be made that night. Jan was in his room when I arrived.

"'Tonight's report is of the gravest importance,' Jan said. 'It may be the single most important message that Ares has ever sent. Be very careful, and make sure it gets to the colonel.'

"'Of course.' I put my shoes on and proceeded to the loading dock. David wrapped a dozen coats in brown paper, tied them onto the cart and put his hands on my shoulders.

"'Lena, when the information in this report hits London, it'll be a bombshell. Depending on how the Allies use the information, it could save a lot of lives—Jewish lives. Guard these reports.'

"'With my life, David.'

"He gave me a hug and off I went. That March was unusually warm, so I was dressed in a short skirt, a little below my knees, and a cotton top. The balmy spring night brought quite a social scene to the square: Wehrmacht soldiers, SS, Gestapo and assorted women laughing and partying at outdoor cafes and bars. You'd have thought you were in Berlin, in the Tiergarten or the Pariser Platz.

"My path took me directly alongside the square and pushing my cart, I drew several stares and pointed fingers. At the corner of the square, an SS officer beckoned me over with his index finger, questioned me and examined my papers. Satisfied with the written instructions, he nodded to his comrades and waved me on. I didn't notice the soldier who rose from his seat at the bar across the square and followed me into the darkened side streets.

"Once out of the lights of the square, and inasmuch as it was hours after curfew, the streets were quiet and empty. Buds were sprouting on the large bushes that bordered the residential lots like privacy fences. In the late hours, my walkway was illuminated only with occasional lights glimmering from the windows of the houses. I heard his footsteps and his breathing long before I turned around and saw the massive bulk of Corporal Rolf. He grabbed my shoulder and spun me around.

"'You little bitch. I have to be at work in an hour, on the fucking midnight shift, and you know why, don't you? Because of you! You made a fool out of me in front of my superior officer. And for what? For your sacred little body that nobody can touch? Do you think you're so much better than me? I got news. You're a fucking Jew, the lowest thing on earth.'

"He grabbed my hair and pulled my head in a circle. 'Look around, bitch. Nobody here. Nobody to rescue you tonight. Just you and me.'

"'I'm on assignment,' I said frantically. 'These coats are to go to Colonel Müller immediately. He's expecting me. Let me go and I won't say anything.'

"'I won't say anything,' he mocked. 'I won't say anything. Boo hoo. You know what I think? I think you're going to be late for your appointment.' He yanked me by my hair and pulled me backward around and behind the bushes. His other hand covered my mouth.

"'Now you're going to give me what I wanted weeks ago. Remember? Whatever Rolf wants, Rolf always gets?' I was scared to my very soul. Not only was he a savage behemoth, a snarling beast, but he was armed—a pistol on one hip and his knife on the other. I thought I'd never survive the night.

"He slid the knife out of its sheath and pointed at my skirt. 'Do you take it off or do I slice it off?'

"I stood frozen. Any other time, he would have had to kill me before I'd let him defile me. But this time Ares's report was hidden in my shoes. It could change the war. I had to get it to Colonel Müller. Never taking my eyes off him, I slid my skirt down. A salacious grin spread on his face. He threw me down on the grass and straddled over me. I watched as he loosened his belt and dropped his trousers. He started breathing hard.

"As he lowered himself onto me and bent his knees, his pistol came into my view, but not quite into my reach. I had to maneuver myself. Move to the side. Get him closer. I wrapped my arms around him and pulled him up. 'Aah,' he said. 'You like it.' His breathing was heavier now. I slid my right arm down his back, down his leg, grabbed the pistol out of its holster and shoved the barrel under his chin.

"'Get up,' I said.

"'Ha.' He laughed. 'You don't know the first thing about a gun.'

"'Don't bet on it. I'm the Captain's daughter.' I pulled the trigger and blew a hole through his head.

"I was shaking like a leaf. I had blood on my hands, on my face and on my shirt. I rolled Rolf's body off of me and under the bushes. I wiped my hands on the grass and put my skirt on. My cart was still in the street. I ran to it and quickly pushed it down the street and around the corner. I had to get to Colonel Müller, but I couldn't go into the house covered in Rolf's blood. Else would see me.

"Three blocks away, on the other side of the train tracks, the Chechlo River wound through the town. I wrung out my cotton top and washed my face and hands in the muddy water as best I could. I looked like hell, but at least most of the blood was gone.

"Finally, I made it to Colonel Müller's and knocked on the door. The colonel answered, took one look at me and stepped back in shock. 'What in the world happened to you?'

"'I was attacked.' My head was spinning. 'But I have your reports, sir.'

"He hurriedly steered me into the study and shut the door. I sat down on the leather chair, looked at him with dazed eyes and threw up.

"'Jesus Christ,' he said. 'We've got to clean you up. We're lucky Else's not here.'

"While he was out of the room, I took the reports out

of my shoes and laid them on the desk. One of the reports
unfolded. What I read there was terrifying. Insane. Totally unbelievable. As it was, I was living in a nightmare,
under the cruelest of oppressors, but Ares's notes portrayed a terror far worse than I could have imagined—a
locked, sealed chamber in Bunker 2 where naked prisoners were taken and mass-murdered by poison gas. The
report disclosed that the IG Farben factory in Monowitz
was manufacturing Zyklon B gas for the future extermination of the Jewish race.

"The report went on to describe the selection process.
Jews arriving at Auschwitz were divided into lines for
men and women. SS officers would then go through the
lines and those considered fit for labor were moved to
one side of the ramp. The others—women with children,
those under fourteen, older persons, disabled—were
taken to other barracks. A drawing of the two camps, a
layout of the barracks and cell blocks was included with
the report.

"This report was more shocking than I could have
ever imagined. No wonder Jan had stated that it was of
the gravest importance. The colonel came back into the
room while I was reading the reports. I looked at him,
grabbed the papers and shook them in his face.

"'Do you know about this? What you German monsters are doing?'

"He grabbed my shoulders. 'Shh! Not one word. You
have seen nothing. Do you understand me? This report
must get to London. If any of this leaked out, if the Gestapo got wind of it, they would find us. They would shut
down the network. And don't think for a minute they
can't find us. They are the most accomplished investigation unit in the world. Earlier this year, they found
documents in Prague that identified our best Polish intelligence agents. They tracked them down all the way to

Istanbul. If they know about Ares's reports they'll find him and all our agents, including you, me and David. You should never have read these reports.'

"'You don't have to worry about me. I won't breathe a word. All I care about is getting this information to the rest of the world.'

"He nodded. 'Tell me what happened to you tonight.'

"I narrated the attack. My jaw quivered, but not with fear. With anger. Rage.

"'Where is the body?' he said. 'We must dispose of it immediately. If the SS or the Gestapo finds out a Wehrmacht corporal has been killed, there will be a rampage of reprisals.' So, I told him to follow me and I'd take him to where I had left Rolf.

"'First we need to clean you up.' He tilted his head. 'You know where the bathroom is. Take a quick shower and we'll leave.'

"It felt odd showering in my house again. Everything was surreal. I was in my bathroom, in the shower, washing away the blood of a Nazi rapist. None of this was happening. Like one of those bizarre dreams where improbable episodes are strung together and when you wake up, you think, how could my mind have conceived of such freakish things? I finished showering and almost walked up to my bedroom.

"The colonel grabbed a shovel and we quietly left the house. We pushed my cart six or seven blocks to where I was attacked. Rolf's body, minus a large portion of his skull, lay in the bushes, his pants down around his ankles. We covered his body in coats and tried to lift him into the cart. But he weighed three hundred pounds. Dead weight. We couldn't lift him. Finally, we tipped the cart down and rolled him in.

"We dug a shallow grave by the riverbed and dumped him in. We threw the gun and his hat in after him. I stopped the colonel from pulling up his pants. 'Bury him just the way he died,' I said. 'He deserves no dignity. If someone should ever find him, they'll know why he was killed.'

"'You are one tough woman,' he said with a smile. 'I knew that the minute I met you. So, we'll bury him with his flag flying at half-mast.' We covered him up and filled in the grave.

"The colonel instructed me to take the cart back to David, and turned to walk back to his home. I should say my home. He took a step, looked back at me and said, 'Well done, Captain Scheinman's daughter. He'd be proud.'

"I reached the Shop and put the cart away. David opened his door, let me in and said, 'What in the hell happened to you?' I started to answer and collapsed into tears. I couldn't talk for several hours, except to tell him that the reports had been delivered to the colonel. As usual, I stayed with David for the rest of the night. He was so kind and understanding. He cradled me all night. Eventually, toward morning, I told him what had happened. I never did tell him I was violated.

"He told me he was proud of me. He told me I was a Polish hero. 'You don't have to carry any more reports. We'll find another courier. You did your share, more than your share.'

"'The hell you will. I read the report tonight, David. I saw what Ares wrote. It's madness. I insist on being a part of the network.' With that, he kissed me and told me how deeply he cared for me."

"Was that the night you fell in love?" Catherine said.

"I didn't tell you I fell in love with David."

"I didn't tell you I was pregnant."

Lena's smile broadened. "Well, the answer is if I hadn't already, I probably did that night. Morning came way too soon. David elbowed me. 'Shift change,' he said. 'I've got to get downstairs. You can take the day off. Go back to your apartment and sleep.'

"'Do you think I can sleep after all this?'

"'Then stay here. I'll come up later this morning.'

"So I did. Actually, I stayed for three days. It was heaven."

"Even in the direst of circumstances, love will emerge," Catherine said. "Reminds me of *Casablanca*— 'the fundamental things apply.'"

"Catherine!" Lena said sternly, but with a smile.

"Sorry, I'm a sucker for a love story. Especially a wartime love story. I feel like I'm talking to Ingrid Bergman."

"Okay. Okay. That's enough." She sat up straight, crossed her legs and smoothed her skirt. "During 1942, the Germans started their liquidation of the Polish ghettos in line with the principles adopted at the Wannsee Conference, and Chrzanów was targeted for clearance by the end of the year. As with most of the world, we were unaware of the Wannsee Conference."

"Tell me about it."

"In July 1941, Hermann Goering appointed SS Obergruppenführer Reinhard Heydrich to organize and carry out the Final Solution to the Jewish Problem. He convened a secret conference in January 1942. In that meeting, Heydrich informed the German ministry leaders that the Reich's efforts to rid Europe of its eleven million Jews by emigration, attrition and other means had proven largely unsuccessful. A new solution was necessary, a Final Solution.

"The Wannsee Protocol provided that able-bodied Jews, divided by sex, were to be sent to labor camps. All other Jews were to be gathered and deported to transit camps and from there to death camps, where mass exterminations would rid the continent of its remaining ten million Jews. Accordingly, in 1942 the Germans began transports from the Chrzanów ghetto."

"So Germany began mass executions following the Wannsee Conference?"

Lena shook her head. "Mass murders were already taking place throughout Poland and the Soviet territories. Death camps, like Treblinka, had already been built and Nazis were already executing Jews. Even before the conference, the death camp at Belzec was under construction. The thrust of the Wannsee Conference was to make the deportations and transports more efficient, and to leave no uncertainty of the fate of Europe's Jews. To that end, ghettos in Polish cities were being cleared out and towns were being made *judenfrei* one at a time.

"In May, the Nazi command demanded that the Chrzanów Judenrat supply fifteen hundred names for immediate transport, comprised of children under the age of ten and adults over sixty. The professed reason, the one given to us through the Judenrat, was that the ghetto was too crowded and workers needed to be resettled. Young children cannot work and older people couldn't do the heavy work the Germans wanted. The official Nazi explanation was that the babies and young children would be sent to a children's camp to be trained and reeducated. The seniors would be sent to camps where labor was much less strenuous.

"That order went through the ghetto like a thunderbolt. Parents were not about to send their children away. Mothers clung to their babies and begged the Judenrat to do something. Some tried to escape, but all roads had checkpoints and the attempts were futile. The Nazis were quick to inform us of the runaways they captured and executed.

"Immediately, the Judenrat filed its objections with

the Nazi command: you can't tear young children away from their parents. But the Germans said the children's camp had playgrounds, hospitals, nurses and matrons, a place where they could go to school, where they would be with other children and where they would be taught skills useful in the workplace. 'Our children's camps are much healthier than living in your squalid ghettos,' they said.

"Many of the parents refused to believe the Nazis and tried to hide their children, but soldiers came through the ghetto and physically grabbed the little children. Parents who resisted were shot. Some parents begged to go with their children, but the Germans told them it was only a children's camp—no parents allowed. The Nazis promised that all parents would be reunited with their children after the war. Ultimately, over twelve hundred children were gathered at the Chrzanów train station. At the railroad embarkation point, the Nazis gave each child a piece of bread with marmalade to show them how much fun it was going to be. They waved good-bye to wailing parents and innocently climbed into the boxcars. We know now that they did not survive; there were no children's camps.

"That day, when I returned to our apartment, I saw that the children's deportation was especially hard on Karolina. Not that it didn't dishearten everyone; anyone with a human heart was disconsolate, but to Karolina, it was as if she were personally affected. She cried for nights and nights, and then I finally understood why. We were in the middle of bathing and washing our clothes in a bucket we'd filled from the fountain when Karolina saw me staring at her naked body. We locked eyes.

"'Oh, damn, Karolina. How far along?'

"She bit her lip. 'Three months.'

"'Siegfried?'

"'I haven't been with anyone else, Lena,' she said indignantly.

"'Does he know?'

"'I don't think so. It's always pretty dark when we're together.'

"'Are you going to tell him?'

"'I'm not sure, but unless I abort this baby, I can't keep it from him much longer.'

"'Is that what you're planning? Are you thinking of terminating your pregnancy?'

"Her jaw quivered and her eyes filled with tears. She grabbed hold of my shoulders and shook them. 'I don't know, Lena. I don't know. I don't want to. I don't know. What should I do?'

"'What can I say? How do you two feel about each other?'

"'He says he loves me. He says it all the time.'

"'If you think he loves you, I mean really loves you, and he's not just saying that in the heat of the night, then you need to tell him. If you're not going to tell him, then you need to break off your relationship.'

"'I don't want to break up with Siegfried. I don't want to hurt him. He wouldn't understand. We have these long conversations about our life together when the war is over. He has a family home in Bavaria.'

"That sounded so improbable to me. 'He knows you're Jewish?'

"She nodded. 'Of course. He says he doesn't care. He loves me. He said his parents would love me, too.'

"I was shocked by the whole thing. Wrong time, wrong place, wrong person, wrong everything. 'Do you love him, Karolina?'

"'I think so. I mean, he's a nice guy. He's kind. He's gentle. He's very good to me. But damn, Lena, how's this ever going to work? It's against the law for him to have relations with a Jewish girl. We could get caught any day. He could be convicted of a crime. Sent to the Russian front. Who knows what?'

"I had no answers. I knew she needed counseling and advice, but I was just too dumbfounded by the whole thing. All I could do was hug her. We stood that way for quite a while, both of us crying.

"'I could ask Dr. Gold for an abortion. I know he's already done a few at the clinic.'

"'Is that what you want?'

"She pitifully shook her head. 'No.'

"I thought to myself, how foolish of her to want to keep this baby. They just tore twelve hundred children away from their parents. Even if they didn't deport any more, how could she raise a baby under these conditions? Then it occurred to me that in the midst of this dehumanizing war, she had found something beautiful, something very human. Something to love. Something to hang onto.

"'There's a terrible risk of infection with any surgeries at the clinic,' I said firmly. 'I wouldn't recommend it. Leah Gruenberg died after she had her abortion. They don't have any medicines. If it were me, I'd probably keep the baby too. Besides, in another six months things could be different. The war could be over.'

"She wiped a tear from her eye. 'Thanks, Lena.'

"I patted her bump. 'You're already showing a little. You either have to break off the relationship or tell him.'

"She nodded. 'You're right. I'll tell him.'"

TWENTY-FOUR

...

IN APRIL AND MAY we saw several deportations, but none that were limited to children. Because the ghetto was ordered to systematically empty, the Judenrat was charged with supplying additional lists of names for 'resettlement.' The inclusion of your name on the list meant that your entire family was to show up at the market square to be transported.

"The official explanation from the Nazis was that other work camps were being constructed with new housing and ample room for all who were willing to work. People were told to take their nicest clothes and pack as much as they could in one suitcase per person. They gave each family a white marker to write their names and home addresses on the sides of each piece of luggage. That was to ensure that they could find their luggage when they got to the resettlement camp, and if it got lost, it would be forwarded to them."

Lena shook her head. "Deep down, it sounded like a lie, but even a morsel of hope was enough to induce people to pack, line up and board the trains for resettlement without resistance.

"The Shop continued to manufacture coats and jackets,

and those working at the Shop were generally immune from deportation lists, but in June rumors started circulating that the Shop would be closing by the end of the year. I don't know if one of the girls overheard something or if our workloads were decreasing, but fear of the shutdown created anxiety among all of us. It was the only job left for Jews and the only thing saving us from the resettlement lists.

"I told you about winters in the ghetto, how harsh and deadly they were. Well, summers brought their own torments. Imagine thousands of people crammed into tiny living spaces in blistering temperatures with no way to cool off. Clean water was scarce. The Germans posted warnings about using the central fountain and erected a sign declaring it was contaminated with typhus. Some drank it anyway, believing it was just a German tactic to prevent us from getting water. Karolina and I found a well at a house on the other side of the tracks, outside the ghetto. We would fill bottles in the middle of the night.

"Insects—mosquitoes, flies, bugs of all sorts— flourished in the summer heat. People who chose to sleep outside and find respite from the heat were attacked by insects. Small pests—rats, mice—infested our area and our living quarters, especially the dormitory. The Shop, with its fifteen hundred workers, was a pressure cooker. A few fans were installed to bolster production, but they afforded little relief."

"Wait a minute, Lena," Catherine said. "You never told me what happened when Karolina told Siegfried that she was pregnant. What did he do?"

"I'm trying to keep this chronological. Siegfried was sent on a delivery detail, taking finished coats in a convoy up north. He was gone and didn't return for a few weeks. The day he returned, Karolina was sitting at her station, and he came over to tell her he was back and that he wanted to see her. She didn't come home that night.

"I saw her at the break the next afternoon. She winked at me. Because there were other women around, all she could say was, 'It's good. Tell you later.'

"She didn't come back to our apartment to sleep for a few days. When she did, she filled me in. Siegfried had stopped at his home on his way back and told his mother that he had fallen in love with a German girl. He wanted to get married as soon as possible."

"A German girl?"

"Well, technically he was correct. Chrzanów had been annexed into Germany along with the Upper Silesian towns in 1939 after the Blitzkrieg. So she really was a German girl in 1942. And she could speak German. He figured he could get away with it."

"She was a Jew, not a German citizen."

"Details, details. He figured with the progress the Germans were making, the war would soon be over and he'd return to Bavaria with Karolina, his German girlfriend. But Karolina wasn't quite as optimistic. She related the conversation to me.

"'Did your mother ask you about my religion?' Karolina had said.

"He hemmed and hawed, and finally said, 'Well, she didn't ask me. I guess she just made her assumptions. She only asked me what kind of a person you were—and I told her beautiful, exciting, sweet and lovely.'

"'What's she going to do when she finds out who I really am?'

"'Why would she find out? Who would tell her?'

"'Siegfried, I think you're being naïve. The Germans trace everybody's bloodlines. They'll want to know who my parents and grandparents were.'

"'Don't worry,' Siegfried said. 'We'll cross that bridge when we come to it. After the war no one will care.'

"So, that's how Karolina and Siegfried left it. They would take it day by day. For the moment they were both at the Shop. He would make sure she was well taken care of, with food, clothing and special treatment."

"Pretty risky, if you ask me," Catherine said. "What if Siegfried were transferred? There was a war going on."

"What were her alternatives? We were prisoners in a ghetto, under awful circumstances. We had learned that the ghetto was to be cleared out, that we would be sent somewhere else. What did the future hold for us? Karolina's plan, no matter how improbable, was at least a plan.

"From then on, Karolina would spend an occasional night away and I didn't question her. I came to understand that it wasn't all for food and privilege. She had genuine feelings for her German soldier. I was not about to sit in judgment on my best friend."

TWENTY-FIVE

...

THROUGH THE SPRING OF 1942, Karolina and I stayed locked in a routine. We went to work every day at the Shop. I would occasionally carry reports to the colonel, though they were coming much less frequently. Karolina would spend time with Siegfried and I was increasing my time with David. But routines are so deceiving. They make you believe in constancy. In Chrzanów, the only constant was unpredictability. Chrzanów was changing. Deportations were on the increase. More names were posted every day.

"To some extent, productive workers at the Shop were spared from transports. David made sure that Karolina and I were known to be among the best coat producers, so we were sure to be left off the lists. But the writing was on the wall. The ghetto was shrinking. Soon there would be no more Jews in Chrzanów.

"Changes were also taking place at the Shop. New German managers were arriving and David was training and delegating some of his responsibilities to younger German soldiers. One night in May, as we lay together in David's room, he told me that he had heard about a new garment factory at a sub-camp in Germany. He was asked to participate in a meeting where the organization of the camp was discussed.

"'I may have to go there to set up the factory.'

"'When?'

"'They didn't say. If it happens, it'll probably be next year sometime.'

"'Can you take us with you?'

"'You mean you and Karolina?'

"'Of course.'

"He thought about it for a while and then said, 'I can train you as a shop foreman. But not Karolina too.'

"I nodded. 'It'll be okay. Siegfried will take care of her. He's going to marry her and take her to live on his parents' farm in Bavaria.'

"David shook his head. 'Are you kidding?'

"'Why?'

"'We're in the middle of a war. Siegfried is a young enlisted man, a *schütze,* an infantryman. How is he going to take Karolina as his wife and go to live in Bavaria? He's stationed here. He could be sent anywhere. Right now, Germany has almost four million troops fighting on the Eastern Front. Every infantryman I've talked to is afraid he'll be shipped there tomorrow. Siegfried has no rank, no seniority.'

"'He's told Karolina that when he gets the chance he'll take her to stay with his mother until the war is over.'

"'I hope for her sake that it works out, but I'm skeptical.' He rolled over and kissed me. 'But you—I don't want to lose you. I can train you as my shop foreman and try to bring you along.'

"'What does a shop foreman do?'

"He smiled. 'Whatever I tell her to do.'

"'Is that so? Well, I don't know if I like this job.'"

Lena stopped and took a deep breath. "It's funny—in the middle of the horrors of the occupation, we found moments to be happy. Life could be sweet and laying with David was the sweetest of all. I knew he'd do everything he could to protect me. I felt certain we'd survive and be together forever."

"But?"

"He was sent away a week later. It was all sudden and shocking. I came to work and a German officer was introduced to the Shop workers as the new foreman. Siegfried told Karolina that David had been transferred to a new location deep in Germany. I was devastated. We didn't even get a chance to say good-bye."

"That must have been awful. The two of you had become so close."

"We were intimate one night and separated the next. I had no idea when or if I would ever see him again. My protector was gone, my lover was gone, and I had no idea what my role in the network would be. No matter which way you turned, the war would punch you in the face. I decided to go see the colonel.

"I had no assignment to take coats and no written authority to leave the ghetto. I couldn't push the cart full of coats as I had in the past. If I were stopped on the way to or from Colonel Müller's, I would have no excuse. But I went anyway. I knocked on the door and the colonel's daughter answered. She turned and yelled, 'Daddy, the girl from the coat factory is here again.'

"Colonel Müller came to the door with a puzzled look on his face. We stood on the stoop. 'What are you doing here?'

"'David has been sent away.'

"'I know that. He's been transferred to Gross-Rosen. There's a textile factory up there.'

"'When is he coming back?'

"He shook his head. 'There are no plans to bring him back.'

"'But what about the Shop?'

"'Major Fahlstein is now in charge. I'm sure you've seen him. But it doesn't matter. The Shop will be closed within eight months.'

"For me, it was like getting hit in the gut with a series of punches. One right after another. 'What about the network?'

"'You've never heard about a network, remember?'

"I was dazed. 'I want to be sent to Gross-Rosen. Can you arrange it?'

"He shook his head. 'You don't want to go there, it's a concentration camp. The conditions are terrible.'

"'They're terrible in Chrzanów.'

"'They're much worse at Gross-Rosen. Now go home, little hitchhiker. Stay in Chrzanów as long as you can. Survival. It's all about survival.'

"He went into the house, came back with an authorization for me to be on the street and told me it would be best if I didn't come around anymore. He wouldn't be able to explain it."

TWENTY-SIX

...

SUMMER PASSED AND THE crisp autumn nights returned. Life at the Shop went on, but all around us the ghetto was deflating. Each week, the names of families were posted on the town kiosk. They were instructed to appear at the square with their suitcases. On the appointed day, German soldiers, many with dogs, took roll call and marched them off to the train station for their so-called resettlement. Some of the transports were going north to labor camps at Mauthausen and Gross-Rosen, but as the fall progressed, the majority of the trains were going straight to Auschwitz. I watched in horror as families walked with their young children and babies, knowing from the secret reports that they were destined to be separated on arrival and sent to die. Fourteen years old was the cutoff for survival at Auschwitz.

"By November, Karolina was getting as big as a house. Major Fahlstein would look at her and shake his head, but Siegfried lobbied for her and convinced the major that she was producing better than most of the girls at the Shop. After all, it was the production numbers that mattered. If you produced, you stayed. If your numbers fell, you were shipped out. With the transports, the number of seamstresses was declining significantly and the major needed all of his good workers. So Karolina had a job as long as she could sit up.

"Without David, news of the war consisted only of scattered rumors, mostly untrue: the British had retaken France, Berlin had been bombed, Hitler was dead. All nonsense. Through Siegfried, we heard the other side, the Nazi propaganda: German troops were on the steps of Moscow, America had surrendered to the Japanese, London had been bombed to smithereens. In Chrzanów, we were truly on an information island, isolated from the rest of the world.

"One day turned into the next. We continued with our daily routines even though the ghetto's fate was preordained—all Jews were to be resettled. By December, more than half our population had packed a suitcase and boarded the trains to other camps. I was told that the Shop would be closed within weeks and that the manufacture of coats and uniforms was being relocated to labor camps. It made sense. In Chrzanów, workers were still receiving wages, even Jews. But a shop that paid wages could not compete with the concentration camps that had slave labor. Manufacturing Economics 101.

"December also saw the return of the winter freeze. Once again we stuffed newsprint in the window seams. We slept in our coats. But this time around, it was hard for Karolina and me to sleep together under the same blankets. She was so uncomfortable, she couldn't sleep anyway. She'd get up in the middle of the night and roll her back over a soccer ball. She'd have to stretch to take deep breaths. She was always apologizing for all the grunts and groans that came with every movement.

"With the end of the ghetto patently in sight, Karolina decided to raise the issue of going to live with Siegfried's mother in Bavaria. Wouldn't it be wiser to have the baby there, in a clean and warm environment? When could we go? But Siegfried said the timing was bad. He couldn't get leave to travel and he hadn't figured out how he'd get Karolina out of the ghetto just yet. But he told her not to worry."

"That bastard never intended to marry her, did he?" Catherine said.

"You're wrong. He loved her very much. I know that now. I suppose, given the time and circumstances, they were just fools in love. She believed they'd make a home together and raise a family, just as he was foolish enough to think he could accomplish it all during the war. But he loved her and he continued to provide us with food, fruit, milk, cheese and meat. As a result, we were the healthiest two girls in the ghetto.

"Karolina's contractions started in the first week of January. After work, we asked Muriel Bernstein to come and have a look at her. Muriel was a student nurse in Kraków before the war, and thank God she was still working at the clinic. The Judenrat had been able to keep two doctors and three nurses in the Chrzanów clinic and off the deportation list.

"'She's dilating,' Muriel said. 'It won't be long now. Get yourselves some clean sheets and clean water. Come get me when the contractions are ten minutes apart.'

"Muriel wasn't wrong. At six the next morning I ran to the clinic. 'Where's Muriel Bernstein?'

"'She hasn't come in yet. She's probably still at home. At number fourteen Sosna Street.'

"I ran there as fast as I could, but found that Muriel had gone to the bakery to stand in line for bread and rolls. Off I ran again. When I got to the bakery, I found her near the back of the line. 'She's having her baby,' I said, totally out of breath. 'She says her contractions are three minutes.'

"'Three minutes? I told you to get me at ten minutes.'

"'I know, but I was sleeping and she didn't want to wake me.'

"The two of us took off and ran back to the building to find Karolina lying on her back, her hands clenching the sides of the mattress with all her might. 'Oh my God, it hurts,' she cried.

"Muriel bent down, spread Karolina's knees and said, 'Oh, mercy, not a minute to spare. I see the crown.' She spread the clean sheet underneath and washed her hands. 'Okay, it's time. You're going to have your baby now, Karolina. Give her a push. Harder, Karolina. C'mon, girl.'

"Karolina screamed and Rachel entered the world, a beautiful little six-pound girl. Muriel handed the baby to me. 'Hold her,' she said. 'Karolina's not finished yet.' Muriel kneeled back down on the floor. 'Karolina, you've got another one coming. You're going to have to give me another big push. C'mon, honey. Push hard.' The second little girl was born two minutes later. She named her Leah. The three of us sat there looking at these two lovely babies and cried. There they were. Karolina's twins.

"I carry that image in my mind as clearly as if it were this morning. Karolina lying on her bed, a baby on each arm. The sweetest smile you ever saw on my best friend's face. Muriel stood washing her hands. Me? I just stood there crying.

"'May God bless the three of you,' Muriel said. 'May we all survive this war in health and love.'"

Catherine set down her notepad, stood and stretched. "That's lovely, Lena. A beautiful story. Now we need to break. It's late, it's Friday night and I'm tired. Let's pick this up first thing tomorrow morning."

TWENTY-SEVEN

...

L
IAM MET CATHERINE AT the door, helped her with her coat and gave her his welcome-home kiss. "How'd it go today?"

"Remember when I said that listening to Lena's narrative didn't disturb me as much as when I sat with Ben?"

"Right. You said it was no less horrific, but more manageable because you thought you could help her."

Catherine nodded. "I could be wrong."

"About helping her?"

"About being more manageable. It's unsettling, Liam. It disturbs me to the core. I'm angry. I want revenge. I want retribution. I want to parade every one of those Nazi monsters to their ultimate roll call and watch as judgment is pronounced."

"It was seventy years ago, Cat. They lost the war, many stood trial before a war crimes tribunal, and most of them went to jail or were executed. Germany paid billions in retribution."

"And the lives that they took, were they restored as well, Liam? The moms, the dads, the babies—did they give them back their lives?"

"I understand. How is Lena taking all this, reliving the story day-by-day?"

Catherine shook her head. "Cool as a cucumber. Oh, every once in a while she'll pause, take a deep breath and plow forward. Sometimes she'll weep, but she keeps it all under control."

"She's a woman on a mission. How far did you get today?"

"Karolina had her babies. Rachel and Leah. The story was beautiful, heartwarming. I wanted to cheer. Except there's no way those babies survived."

"Lena thinks they did."

"I know. I was tempted to go all night just to find out how she thinks they survived, but all my instincts tell me it would have been impossible. Siegfried's never going to take those two Jewish babies to his mother's home deep in Germany. Karolina's a fool to think that. Winter is coming to Chrzanów and the buildings are unheated. Food is scarce. How are newborns going to survive? And then, of course, there is the Final Solution. The ghetto is being deconstructed, due to be cleared of all Jews within months. The buildings will be razed. The ghetto torn down. Whoever is left will board trains for transport to other camps, and most will go to Auschwitz. Babies, children under fourteen, disabled, the elderly— they won't be resettled. They'll be murdered as soon as they arrive at a camp. Only the young and strong have a chance at survival. We know now that almost all of Poland's three million Jews were murdered."

"But Lena believes the twins survived?"

Catherine shrugged. "Apparently."

"Do you still believe there is a hidden secret yet to be revealed?"

"Without a doubt. Every bone in my lawyer's being senses a deep, dark secret. But I don't know if she'll ever willingly reveal it. I might sniff it out, but maybe not."

"Delusional?"

"I don't think so. She'd have to have one hell of an imagination. She tells the story in such detail. But do me a favor. See if Nazi records show the existence of a Colonel Müller. If so, was he assigned to Chrzanów? And if so, what happened to him?"

"Okay. I should be able to do that. But I have to tell you, I'm more than a little concerned about you. In your condition, you know, experiencing the details, bit by bit, of . . ."

"In my condition, huh? In my delicate condition?"

"Hold on. I didn't mean . . ."

"The hell you didn't."

"You're pregnant, you're hearing stories about babies dying, you're emotional . . ."

"Emotional! Are you insane? Are you saying that I should be indifferent, ambivalent, unaffected? Is that how you would be? Because I don't think so. As a father-to-be, as a human being, you'd be just as disturbed as I am. Disturbed and furious."

"Take it easy, Cat. I'm not trying to upset you, I'm . . ."

"Forget it." She turned and left the room.

Liam sat in silence on the couch for several minutes and then went to look for her. He found her in the bedroom, sobbing into her pillow. He sat down and gently rubbed her back. "I'm sorry, Cat."

"It's not your fault. Karolina's twins—there's no way they survived."

TWENTY-EIGHT

...

SATURDAY MORNING IN CATHERINE'S office.
A pot of coffee, a few croissants. Lena was pensive.
She stood at the window, sipped her coffee and
gazed into the ether. "That January morning," she said
softly, "the miracle of birth, our belief in the future." She
turned and faced Catherine. "How naïve we were."

"We have two more days to finish your story, Lena. I
want to know the whole story, everything, before I go to
court on Monday morning. Can we do that?"

"I don't see why not. I remember it all like it was yesterday."

Catherine picked up her notepad. "Good. Full speed
ahead."

"Karolina held the babies to her breasts. 'Are they
beautiful, Lena? Who do they look like? Do they look
like their father? I think I see a little of my mother.'

"'They're the prettiest babies I've ever seen,' Muriel
said. 'They look like two beautiful Polish babies. Two
strong Jewish girls.' We laughed.

"'Lena, when you go to work today, be sure to tell
Siegfried,' Karolina said. 'And write a letter to David.
He'll want to know.'

"I stood there taking in the incongruity of it all. The warm glow of this new mother joyfully introducing her new babies to the world, standing in stark contrast to her bleak surroundings—a corner of a converted warehouse, separated from the other residents by only a few boxes and hanging sheets.

"The January temperatures were unforgiving and the daylight was minimal. I bundled a few blankets and set them by Karolina along with fresh water and our little cache of food. Muriel and I helped her with her personal needs and changed the babies, but neither of us could stay with her during the day. The clinic was a few blocks away, and Muriel promised to check up on Karolina as often as she could. I couldn't leave the shop until the end of my shift.

"As we left the apartment, Muriel pulled me aside. 'We must get them to someplace warm. Those babies won't survive the bitter cold.'

"'What about the clinic?' I said. 'The clinic is warm.'

"Muriel shook her head. 'Typhus. Diphtheria. Influenza. Even lice. There's disease at the clinic every day. She'll have to find some other place. Can Siegfried help us? He's a German officer.'

"'He's not an officer, just an enlisted man, but I'll talk to him this morning.'

"When we took our morning break, I found Siegfried and asked him to walk over and talk to me in the corner of the Shop. 'The babies were born last night.'

"'Babies?'

"'Yep. Twins. Their names are Rachel and Leah, and they're beautiful.'

"'That is very wonderful. I will pack extra provisions for you today. Let me know every way I can help.'

"'Here's how you can help. Right now we need a warm place for the babies to live. The apartment we share is unheated and unhealthy.'

"'Aren't they all that way in the ghetto?'

"'Of course, but the babies won't survive unless we get them to a heated room. Maybe this is the time to get them to your mother's.'

"'That's not possible. There's no way I can leave.'

"I put my hands on my hips. 'Siegfried!'

"'I can't take her now. I'll try to think of something. Tell her.'

"'Tell her yourself. Why don't you come visit after work?'

"He quickly shook his head. 'No, no. I can't do that. They watch everyone very closely. I can't go into the ghetto. They'll ask why.'

"'You're a German. You can go anywhere you want.'

"'No.' He became extremely nervous. 'N-not tonight. There is a detail. I am required to attend. Not tonight.'

"'Well, then, I'll tell her you'll come by tomorrow.'

"'Um, yes, tomorrow.' He nodded his head up and down in quick jerks and looked around the Shop to see if anyone was watching.

"At the end of the day, Siegfried brought a large package to me at my station. 'I don't think tomorrow will work,' he said. 'But I will find a way to see her sometime. We'll talk tomorrow.'

"I was disgusted with Siegfried, but Karolina was unfazed. 'Don't worry, Lena,' she said when I returned that evening. 'Siegfried has to plan it all very carefully. He just can't pick up and go. I'm sure he's making arrangements to send me to his mother, but it must all be very secretive. He must hide it from his superiors, you know. He cares very deeply about us. Look at the wonderful provisions he sent today.'

"On that note, she was right. There was a week's worth of milk, cheese, meat and bread. And even some fruit. Enough to send Siegfried to the Stalingrad front.

Muriel came by that evening. She did her physical examination and pronounced that mother and babies were doing just fine. Karolina's milk was coming in and the babies had a strong appetite. But she took me aside.

"'What did Siegfried say about moving her?'

"I shook my head. 'We can't count on him. He won't go to Bavaria now. I asked about a warm apartment, but I'm not hopeful. I tried to persuade him to come visit, and that's where the conversation ended.'

"'You need to be more direct. Confront him. It's too damn cold to stay in this drafty, unheated building. Those babies won't make it through January.'

"'What about the other buildings? Many families are now gone. Are any of their apartments heated?'

"Muriel shook her head. 'As far as I know, there is no fuel anywhere in the ghetto. It's not allowed. None of the apartments have heat. Do you remember last winter? The ones who froze to death? Do you remember how many babies died?'

"'I do. I almost froze to death myself.' I pointed at Karolina. 'She saved my life.'

"'If our babies have any chance, they need to get to a heated room.'

"I knew what I had to do. 'I'll take care of it,' I said. 'I'll talk to Siegfried tomorrow. Like it or not, he's going to help. He loves Karolina.' Muriel thanked me and left. That night, the four of us—Karolina, Rachel, Leah and I—all slept together under layers of blankets. Maybe I shouldn't say slept. Still, even with all of us, it wasn't really warm and I resolved that something had to be done.

"The next day at morning break, I went to confront Siegfried but I couldn't find him. At the afternoon break, one of the other overseers told me that Siegfried hadn't come in. He'd reported sick.

"Then I got an idea. That night I took Muriel to Yossi's

basement. 'There's a furnace down here, and the room's pretty well insulated. If we can clean it up, it'll be much warmer than the drafty dormitory. And if we can get some coal, it can be quite livable.'

"Muriel looked around and scrunched her nose. 'It's filthy down here. I see mouse feces. And besides, where do you think you're going to get coal? There's not a lump in the whole ghetto.'

"'Leave that to me.'

"Early the next morning, I arrived at the Shop and cornered Siegfried. 'We found a room with a furnace. A coal furnace.'

"He bit his lip and nodded. 'So Karolina wants me to get coal?'

"'Right.'

"'It's strictly verboten. There is a written order. If I got caught doing that I'd be court-martialed.'

"'Siegfried, we're in the middle of coal mining country. There's coal everywhere you look. We'll all freeze unless you get us a supply of coal. And we need it now.'

"He shook his head. 'It's very dangerous. For you too. If you're found with coal, you'll be punished.'

"I snarled. 'Do it!'

"He rubbed his hand on his forehead. 'I could try.'

"'Try? You've taken on a responsibility here. You've made commitments to Karolina. She's your fiancée.'

"'Shh.' He put his finger to his lips. 'You can't say that around here.'

"'Karolina wants to know when you're going to take her and the babies to your mother's house. The ghetto's coming down piece by piece.'

"He started to twitch and he tensed up, clenching his fists. 'I can't do it right now. I can't do it right now. I told Karolina that's our plan for the future, when the war is over and everything settles down.'

"'That's not the way she heard it.'

"'How would I get her to Bavaria? I can't even get there myself.'

"'You have ways. There are always ways. You're a German. You have to get us out, all of us: Karolina, Muriel, me, and the babies.'

"'I can't. Stop making demands on me. You'll all just have to make do for now, like all the other Jews in the ghetto.'

"That infuriated me. I clenched my teeth. 'Like all the other Jews? Listen, Siegfried, I'm not making a casual request. This is a demand. You'll have a supply of coal, in a bucket, here tonight. Understand? Otherwise, I'm going to bring those babies to the Shop tomorrow morning to get warm and I'm going to tell everyone that you said it was okay.'

"'I didn't say it was okay.'

"'Really? And I'm going to tell everyone that they're *your* babies.'

"'*My* babies? Why would you do that? I'll be sent straight to the Eastern Front. Are you crazy?'

"'Maybe I am. But those babies will die if we don't get coal. And maybe Karolina will die too. And I'm not going to let that happen. So, you bring a bucket of coal to the shop tonight. Are we on the same page here, Siegfried?'

"He gulped hard. 'You are definitely crazy. You'll get us all killed.'

"'I'm not going to watch those babies freeze to death. You get the coal or I'll bring them all here tomorrow, so help me God.'

"He sighed and nodded. 'I'll have it for you after work.'

"I don't know where I found the courage, but I pointed my index finger and popped it on his chest. 'And you find a way to get Karolina to your mother's. I know you care for her, or at least you said you did at one time. I don't know why, but she cares for you, Siegfried. Don't disappoint her.'

"He nodded. 'I *do* care for her. What you say, it's unfair. This is a war and I'm a soldier. If I were discovered, it would be disastrous for both of us. I'll get coal and food for you to take back to her, but that may be all I can do right now.'

"That night, Muriel and I scrubbed down Yossi's basement and disinfected it as best we could. We found an abandoned dresser in an empty apartment and converted two of the drawers into cribs. Siegfried delivered on his promise. After work there was a bucket full of coal and another bag of provisions. All it took was a few pieces of coal and the little room warmed nicely. Later that night we moved Karolina, the two babies, all of our things and me into that little furnace room. With the bed, the cribs, a dresser and our few possessions, you might think the room was quite crowded. We considered it cozy.

"Karolina was overcome with emotion. She couldn't thank us enough. Lying there in that little room, tears in her eyes, a baby on each arm, that was all the thanks we needed. We told her that Siegfried had supplied the coal and food at great risk to himself, and that he was elated to hear the news.

"'Does Siegfried want to come and see the babies?' she asked.

"I shook my head. 'He thinks it's too risky at this time and doesn't want to put you in danger. But he still plans to bring you to his mother's.'

"Karolina smiled. 'You don't have to lie for me,' she said gently. 'I don't expect him to keep his word. Maybe if times were different, we could've made a nice life together. He's not really a Nazi, you know. He was conscripted. He's just a farm boy. He doesn't know a Jew from a lamppost.'"

TWENTY-NINE

...

T HE NEW SHOP FOREMAN, Major Fahlstein, was an older man with gray hair and large, round eyeglasses. He came by my station a few days after the twins were born and asked me about Karolina and why she wasn't coming to work. 'I need her,' he said. 'She's one of my best.'

"I stopped short of telling him about the babies. Families with babies were the first ones on the list. I'm sure he knew Karolina was pregnant, but he probably didn't know when she was due. 'She has a bit of the croup,' I said, 'but she's recovering nicely and I expect her back to work within a few days,' even though I didn't know if she'd ever come back to work. Who would care for the two newborns? Who would feed the babies?

"Another deportation came and fourteen hundred more Jews were lined up and marched to the trains. There were very few children left in the ghetto. Families with little children had already been put on the list for deportation and sent out. By February, the only people immune from deportation were the members of the Judenrat, the doctors and nurses of the clinic, and the most productive seamstresses at the Shop. Everyone else checked the board each week, praying that their names would not be on the list.

"The winter of 1942 to 1943 brought major changes to Chrzanów. Orders came down to clear out and destroy the ghetto, orders in compliance with Reinhard Heydrich's implementation of the Final Solution: strong and healthy Jews living in ghettos were to be sent to slave labor camps. The rest were to be sent to one of the six extermination camps: Sobibór, Chelmno, Belzec, Treblinka, Majdanek, and Auschwitz-Birkenau. Transports were to begin immediately. Of course, deportations had been going on in Chrzanów for months. Now there was an observable increase.

"The winter of 1942 to 1943 also impacted the German presence in Chrzanów. Before the winter, our town was crawling with German soldiers, SS officers, and Gestapo, filling the square, the restaurants and the bars, and harassing us on every corner. Now there were noticeably fewer Germans in the square. We didn't know it at the time, but it was due to the carnage in the eastern campaign.

"Hitler's Russian strategy was a disaster, which most historians regard as the turning point in the war. The Wehrmacht suffered over a million casualties in 1941 to 1942 in their unsuccessful drive to take Moscow. After the army's retreat, Hitler changed his strategy and in 1942 sent his armies south to take Stalingrad and the rich oil fields of the Caucasus.

"The Battle of Stalingrad was the bloodiest of the war. One million Russians died. Eight hundred and fifty thousand Axis troops died and what was left of the German Sixth Army surrendered. The city of Stalingrad was bombed to rubble. Total lives lost in the battle exceeded two million. When news of Germany's defeat and surrender at Stalingrad spread across the world it had an emotional effect. To the Allies it was a sign that Russia was a powerful and competent ally and that Germany could be defeated. To the Germans it was demoralizing.

"For us, totally uninformed about the progress of the war, the winter brought an increased demand for wool coats and a sharp reduction in the German presence in Chrzanów. Week by week we'd see the number of young German soldiers in our shop decrease. Rumors spread that things were going badly on the Eastern Front and that's why enlisted men, especially those who worked in the Shop, were being redeployed.

"Because of the need for coats, Major Fahlstein received permission to keep one hundred Jewish women free from transports to work in the Shop. I went to him and asked if he intended to keep Karolina and me.

"'Where is Karolina?' he said. 'I would keep her if she'd return to work. She's one of my best. But she's been out for almost a month.'

"'She'll be back in a week or two.'

"'Not good enough. Either she comes back on Friday or I'm releasing her name for resettlement.' I started to object, but he turned and walked away.

"Friday was just two days away. Karolina was healthy enough, but what about the babies? She couldn't leave them alone. There was certainly no day care in the Chrzanów ghetto, and no babysitters. In fact, it had been strongly against Judenrat policy to conceive any children since 1940. That night, I asked Muriel to meet with Karolina and me in the basement apartment. I had a plan.

"'Major Fahlstein says that he'll only keep Karolina if she returns by Friday,' I said. 'We know we can't leave the babies. The only solution is to juggle our shifts. I can stay on the day shift. If we can get Karolina assigned to the evening shift, I can watch the babies until she comes home.'

"'What about shift change?' Karolina asked. 'There's an hour when neither one of us will be here.'

"I looked at Muriel. She nodded. 'I'll cover the hour.'

"The next day at the Shop I informed Major Fahlstein that Karolina would be back and that she preferred the evening shift. He was delighted. He was getting one of his best seamstresses back, and one who even volunteered to work the evening shift.

"Muriel was a godsend. Not only did she help us with the babies, but she found baby supplies in the abandoned apartments. She brought over several one-piece outfits, little pink bodysuits, baby blankets, hand-knit sweaters and two coats. She also found three baby bottles and an assortment of nipples to feed the babies when Karolina was at work.

"'Where did you get all this stuff?' Karolina said.

"Muriel smiled, but it was a smile tinged with regret. 'They were left behind.'

"That realization made Karolina cry. 'How can I take these? They were given to other little children with love, children who were rounded up and sent off on the trains. These clothes belong to those children.'

"'They're not here anymore,' Muriel said in a consoling tone. 'I'm sure the parents would want you to have them rather than see the Nazis throw them away.'

"Karolina nodded. She hugged the clothes. 'I'm sure you're right. I'll treat them with love and care.'

"As we entered March, we felt reasonably secure for the time being. The basement apartment was warm, we were well stocked with food, drink, clothing and coal, and we had solved the day care dilemma. After all, as Colonel Müller had said, it's all about survival. One day to the next. Little did we know what would happen within the next thirty days."

told her that my wife would be coming to live with her but I didn't know when. I told her we wanted to live on the farm and make a family. Tell Karolina, if I die in battle, she should go to my mother's and tell her that we were married. That this is now my family. I hope my letter will get to my mother, but the war . . .'

"As he turned to leave, I put my hand on his shoulder. 'Come and say hello to Muriel and the babies that you've been keeping alive. They're beautiful.'

"Siegfried shook his head. 'I can't.'

"I pulled on his sleeve. 'Yes, you can.'

"The two of us entered the ghetto and walked down the stairs to the basement, where Muriel was holding the babies. At first he was afraid, but when Muriel handed them to him, his mouth dropped open and he got all teary-eyed. 'They're beautiful.'

"'They're alive because of you, Siegfried,' Muriel said. 'They're beautiful and strong because a caring German soldier provided for them.'

"Through his sobs, he made attempts at speech with phrases that were totally incomprehensible. The only thing I understood was 'Damn this ungodly war.' He hugged them tightly and sat on the bed.

"'Which is which?' he asked.

"'This one's Rachel. This one's Leah.'

"He kissed each one. 'Good-bye Rachel; good-bye, Leah. I hope to see you again soon.' He handed the babies back to Muriel, bowed slightly and quickly left the room. That was the last we ever heard from Siegfried. I put the paper with his mother's address safely away in my duffel.

"That night, when Karolina came home, we told her about Siegfried's visit.

"She walked over to look at her sleeping babies. 'I told you he loved me. I told you he cared about all of us.

He's kind, Lena. He's done whatever he could to keep us and the babies alive. It hasn't been easy for him.'

"Two weeks later, Major Fahlstein called a meeting and addressed all of the shop workers. 'We have received orders to close the Shop on April fifteenth. All material will be shipped to other centers. All Jews will be sent for resettlement. There will be trains to take you to other work centers. The ghetto area in the northeast section will be demolished. I have given each of you a strong recommendation.' He swallowed hard. 'Of course, I do not have so much influence, but I requested that each of you be sent to a work center where your sewing skills will be valuable. I am sorry. Truly so.'

"All I could think about was the babies. How could we protect them? I already knew the fate of Jewish babies sent for resettlement. I knew what awaited them when they disembarked from the train cars. That night, we gathered in the basement.

"'We only have days,' I said. 'We need to find a home for Rachel and Leah.'

"'Why do we need to find a home?' Karolina said. 'I'm a top seamstress. Fahlstein will recommend me. I'll take the girls with me to wherever they send me. You'll come too, Lena, and we'll work the shifts just like we do here. We'll all be together.'

"I shook my head. 'They won't let you take the babies to a labor camp.'

"'What will they let me do with them?' Her voice was cracking.

"All I could do was shake my head.

"'Oh no. They can't take my babies from me. I'll hide from them here in the ghetto.'

"Again, I shook my head sadly. 'They'll sweep the ghetto. You've seen them on roll calls. They'll search every room.'

"'They've never searched the basement.'

"'I'm sure this time there'll be no room left unsearched. Besides, Karolina, they've made plans to destroy the ghetto. They'll bulldoze these buildings.'

"'I can't let them take my babies.' Karolina became agitated. She paced quickly back and forth, her muscles twitching. 'They can't have my babies!' she shrieked.

"I picked up my duffel and took out the folded paper. 'This is the address of Siegfried's mother in Germany. He has written to her and told her to expect you.'

"'What good does that do us? How am I supposed to get to Bavaria?'

"I took a deep breath. 'I have an idea. Would you trust Colonel Müller to take you and the twins to Siegfried's mother's house?'

"'A Nazi colonel? Absolutely not. What kind of idea is that? The Nazis murder Jewish babies.'

"'I trust Colonel Müller.'

"'Why would you trust him? Do you think he got to be a colonel by befriending Jews?'

"'I can't tell you why. I just do. And I think you can depend on my judgment here.'

"Muriel walked over to Karolina and put her arm around her. 'I don't think we have much choice.'

"The three of us stood together in a group embrace. I said, 'Let me talk to the colonel tomorrow night.'"

THIRTY-ONE

...

T HE NEXT NIGHT, AFTER work, I left the
twins with Muriel and made my way to Colonel
Müller's. The evening was unusually warm for a
spring night and the square had seen many such nights
filled with German partiers. But it was April 1943 and
Chrzanów was quiet. Most of the Germans had left. The
ghetto was almost vacant. I didn't see a soul on the way
to my house.

"It was nine o'clock when I arrived. The lights were
on in the living room. If only time could reverse itself
and I could open the door and walk into 1938. I stood at
the door a few minutes before I knocked.

"Else opened the door and stared at me. She had
a martini glass in her hand and was dressed in a full-
length, black sequined party dress. Her blond hair was
pulled back tightly and clasped with a pearl ring. She
looked at me and made a face, like she had encountered
a slug in the middle of her sidewalk.

"'I suppose you want to see my husband?'

"'Yes, please, if I may.'

"'Ach. I am so happy to be getting out of this Polish

shithole and back to Berlin. Wait here.' She turned and walked inside, slamming the door.

"*They're sending Colonel Müller back to Germany,* I thought. *That's perfect. He can find a way to take our babies to Regensburg.*

"He came to the door, fully decked out in his dress grays, braids hanging from his shoulder boards, and rows of medals sat above his breast pocket. He motioned for me to step back onto the sidewalk. 'What are you doing here? Are you crazy? I told you not to come here anymore.'

"'I need a favor.'

"'From *me*?'

"I explained about the babies and our need to get them to Regensburg. 'I think Karolina and I will be sent to a labor camp, but the two girls . . .'

"He shook his head. 'Impossible. They won't survive.'

"'That's why I need you to take them to Bavaria.'

"He laughed out loud. 'And how am I supposed to do that? In ten days I'm driving my car to Berlin. Shall I just make a five-hundred-mile side trip to Regensburg? And perhaps you'd like to explain this whole scenario to Else. I'm sure she'd love to help. She loves Jewish babies.'

"'You're our only hope.'

"'Please. This conversation is going nowhere.'

"'What are we supposed to do with the two little girls?'

"'Put them on the train.'

"'They'll die.'

"'Yes, they will.'

"'If you won't take them to Regensburg, help me drive them out to the Tarnowskis.'

"'Herr farmer? Hmph. Herr farmer and Herr farmer's wife are long gone. They took off in the middle of the night long ago for parts unknown. I guess they were the smart ones.'

"Just then, I remembered Mr. Tarnowski telling me that they had a plan. And I could have gone with them. But that was water under the bridge. I stared directly at the colonel. 'You have to find a way to help us. I know you are a good man. You're not one of them.'

"'You're wrong. I am a colonel in the Wehrmacht. I have stayed alive knowing what I can do and what I can't. If what I've done with the network brings an end to the war, saves millions of lives, then the risk was justified. For these two little babies, whose odds of growing up are next to none, I'm sorry, little hitchhiker, but there's nothing I can do. Good night.' He turned, walked into the house and left me standing on the sidewalk.

"Muriel and Karolina were anxiously waiting for me when I returned, but when she saw my expression, Karolina started to cry.

"'We'll figure something out,' I said.

"We debated going to work for the next few days, but although the Shop was closing, we were required to go. Major Fahlstein's recommendation could mean the difference between being sent to a work camp or being sent to Auschwitz. So, once again, I worked the day shift, Karolina worked the night shift and Muriel stayed with the twins.

"It was eerie at the Shop, just a handful of workers, most of them busy packing up supplies for transport north. The German overseers were gone. Only Major Fahlstein and two guards remained.

"Two days before the Shop was set to close, Major Fahlstein said, 'There will not be a night shift today. If you know any of the night shift workers, go get them, we could use them now.'

"I walked back to the apartment. Karolina was playing with the babies and humming a lullaby. She shook her head. 'I'm not going in. I'm going to spend my time with our babies. Every minute we have left.'

"'But Major Fahlstein's recommendations—you don't want to be left off the list.'

"'I don't care.'

"I nodded. Who could blame her? I returned to work. Major Fahlstein noted that Karolina was a no-show.

"After work that night we caucused again. I was out of ideas. I wished David were there; he'd always had a plan. I missed David.

"Finally, Karolina stood. 'Let's make a run for it,' she said. 'I think we can make our way to the country. There aren't that many Germans left. We'll find a family that will take us in and hide us till the war is over.'

"'You're dreaming,' I said. 'First of all, you'd never make the country; you'd be shot leaving the city. There are still guards here. Second, even if you could get to the country, where are you going to find a family that'll take in three Jewish women and two babies?'

"'We'll have to take that chance. Maybe they'll just take in the babies. We'll keep walking until we find someone. What's our choice, Lena? Hand the babies over to the Nazis?'

"'She's right,' Muriel said. 'What are we supposed to do? If we board a train with the twins, they'll be taken from us on arrival. And you know what they'll do.' She walked over and put her arm around Karolina. 'Don't you worry, honey. I'll go with you.'

"'You're both nuts,' I said. 'There's an excellent chance that we can all get assigned to a work camp. We can sew clothes and survive the war.'

"'Not the babies.'

"I nodded. 'Not the babies.' I walked over and joined them in a hug. 'I must be as crazy as you two, but count me in.'"

THIRTY-TWO

...

COLONEL KARL HEINZ MÜLLER, decorated at the battle of Galicia in World War I, was assigned to Chrzanów in the Upper Silesia district in 1941," Liam said. "He was transferred to Berlin in 1943, where he was stationed at the Bendlerstrasse and attached to General Friedrich Olbricht. While working there he was introduced to Oberstlieutenant Klaus von Stauffenberg. Both Olbricht and von Stauffenberg were members of the secret German Resistance."

"Why do I know the name von Stauffenberg?" Catherine said.

"From the plot to kill Hitler in the bunker."

"Right. The failed coup."

"Müller himself was actually part of the German Resistance going back several years, but he became a serious conspirator with von Stauffenberg in 1944. He was present at the Wolfsschanze on July 20, 1944, when the bomb exploded and failed to kill Hitler. Von Stauffenberg was executed on July twenty-first. Müller was shot by a firing squad for high treason on August first."

"So, there actually was a Colonel Müller who was a

member of the German underground? Lena wasn't lying and she wasn't delusional."

"Not as concerns Colonel Müller. Her story about the network is very believable. And about his aloofness when it came to helping Lena hide the babies. My research disclosed that while many of the German high command despised Hitler and his ambition, they were still German loyalists. They deplored Hitler's genocide, but they were the German elite. They liked the political structure and their social privileges. They enjoyed their status. Many of them were fascistic.

"Müller may have spearheaded underground resistance groups, and died trying to overthrow Hitler and the Nazi Party, but he was no Thomas Jefferson. He cut his teeth on authoritarianism."

Catherine cleared the breakfast dishes. "It's good to have Lena's story corroborated. Thanks for the research."

"But you still think she's holding back?"

Catherine nodded. "There's no doubt in my mind. There's a story beneath the surface here, I just don't know what it is. I don't know why, I just know that there's a part that's locked away, that we may never find out."

Liam's cell phone buzzed. He saw the caller ID, raised his eyebrows and motioned for Catherine to come close.

"Liam Taggart . . . Hello, Arthur . . . This morning? . . . I don't know, I'll have to run it by Ms. Lockhart. Why don't I call you back in a while . . . Good-bye."

Catherine stood with her hands on her hips. "Arthur Woodward? What the hell did he want?"

"He wants to meet with me later this morning."

"Did he say why?"

"Nope."

"Fascinating."

"Do you want me to meet with him?"

"Sure. Why not?"

At eleven o'clock, Arthur and his personal assistant, Rico, arrived at Liam's one-room office. Liam stood at the door and shook Arthur's hand. "Can we leave the muscle outside?"

"Of course." Arthur turned to Rico. "Why don't you wait in the car?"

Liam walked over to his credenza. "I'm brewing a pot. Can I offer you a cup?"

Arthur nodded. "Just black."

"So, what brings you out today?"

"Are we off the record, Liam? Just you and me?"

Liam nodded.

Arthur took a sip of coffee. "Look, I'm not a bad guy, no matter what you may think. Maybe I'm overprotective of my mother, but she's eighty-nine and I'm her only relative. I've seen her go from a socialite, very involved in civic matters, serving on the boards of substantial charitable foundations, to a woman obsessed with finding two girls for which no evidence exists or has ever existed. Do you understand? She's Sir Galahad in search of the Holy Grail. The only thing on her mind is this Karolina matter.

"In her den, the room where my father and I watched basketball games, where he read at night and listened to his music, she's got maps of Europe spread out all over the place. There must be twenty history books on the war in Poland. My father never read a single one of them. They're all hers. There are dozens of printouts of Polish train schedules from the 1940s. Seriously? I mean, what the hell? It's all she cares about. She's trapped in a lost decade. Whatever you think my motives are, I'm only concerned about my mother. I have no interest in seeing your wife go to jail in some misguided effort to protect the attorney-client privilege. I'm willing to call the whole thing off."

"In exchange for what?"

"Not much, really. I'm not asking Catherine to withdraw. Let her do her thing. Let her charge her fees, make her money. I understand she's got a small office and my mother is a big-time client for her. I get it. No problem."

Liam stood. "Well, thank you very much, Arthur. I'll tell Catherine you're dismissing your petition."

Arthur held up his finger. "Not quite so fast. I said I wouldn't stop Catherine from representing my mother. But only under certain conditions. Just between you and me, right? I want to know exactly what's going on, what she's telling Catherine and what they're going to do. I want to be kept in the loop. That way I can make sure that nothing bad is going to happen to her. You get me? I only care about my mother. You don't even have to tell my mother or Catherine that we made this arrangement. Just let me know, from time to time, what's going on. What has she done, what has she learned. That's all. And I'll take your word for it. We don't even need to put it in writing."

"You didn't really expect me to accept that offer, did you, Arthur? I mean, you didn't drive all the way over here with Gonzo to make that stupid offer. Go behind my wife's back and violate the attorney-client privilege? What's really on your mind?"

Arthur chuckled. "You're a tough guy, Liam. But okay. I'll tell you what worries me. I think someone in the old country is trying to run a number on my mother. Rip her off. There's something going on back there in Poland or Germany. I mean, why would she all of a sudden pick this up now at age eighty-nine? She could have searched for Karolina's babies for sixty years. Now all of a sudden she's compelled to find them? When they're probably dead, if they ever existed?"

"I suppose she'd say it's none of your business."

"She probably would. But I'm not going to let some con artist in Poland grab all my father's money. Ain't gonna happen. Look, you're the great investigator. Have you found any evidence that Karolina Neuman ever lived or died? What proof did you uncover in all your sleuthing that someone named Karolina Neuman ever gave birth to any children? Did you come across any birth certificates? Any little Neumans? You know, if you had them and showed them to the judge, this case would be over."

"I can't tell you anything about my work in this case. You know that."

Arthur nodded. "Okay, so you answered my question. Just what I figured. Let me tell you, I'm a man of considerable means. I can get things done. As you may have imagined, I've had my people researching this Karolina and they've all come up with nothing. Nothing at all. So if all my money can't produce a shred of evidence, then the evidence doesn't exist. And that's a fact. So here's the deal: you keep me in the loop, provide me with a day-by-day rundown on what my mother's doing and who she's talking to and I'll back off. Otherwise, I'll crush you and your wife like a bug. Depend on it."

"Oh, stop with childish threats."

Arthur stood. "Thanks for the coffee, Liam. Think about what I said. You want to keep your wife out of jail? Play ball. Let me know by Sunday night, give me the thumbs-up and we'll all be BFFs. Otherwise? . . ." He stamped his foot on the floor like he was crushing out a cigarette.

"Gosh, I thought we were already BFFs. I guess I'll just have to unfriend you. Get the fuck out of my office."

Arthur stopped at the door. "Think about it, funny man. It's your wife."

THIRTY-THREE

...

"HE SOUNDS DESPERATE TO me," Catherine said, holding her phone to her ear and rocking back in her desk chair. "I still can't figure out why he's so passionate about stopping Lena from finding these girls."

"It's the inheritance. What else could it be? I'm sure he believes that she changed her will to cut him out of part of her estate and share it with Karolina's daughters, if they're still alive, or if not, then maybe their descendants. If Lena can't find the twins, then it all goes to Arthur."

"It makes sense. Lena's due here in a few minutes. I have one more day before the hearing to learn the whole story. Lena and I are on a parallel course. In her story, she has one more day to figure out how to save the babies, and I have one more day to figure out how to stay out of jail. I'll talk to you later."

"See you at home."

Just then, Gladys poked her head in the doorway and announced that Lena had arrived.

"Well, we have a lot of ground to cover today," Catherine said. "So let's roll up our sleeves and get to work."

Lena smiled. She sat proud and tall, a silver turtleneck sweater complemented by a strand of cultured pearls. "Muriel, Karolina and I had mutually decided to make a run for it, to escape from Chrzanów in advance of the transports that were due to take place in a couple of days. We bundled up the babies, each of us took a duffel, we packed whatever food and milk we could carry, and in the middle of that April night, we ventured out to find a savior.

"From my night excursions, I knew which streets were the darkest, which houses were vacant and which route was the safest. We skirted around the square and headed east across the railroad tracks and through the field. Our goal was the rural road and the Tarnowski farm. I wasn't sure that the colonel had been truthful or accurate when he told me about the Tarnowskis. Maybe they were still there. Maybe a new family was there, another kind family of farmers that would want to save the babies. Maybe the Tarnowskis' son had returned.

"The night was warm and stars were out, and fortune favored us with a new moon. We stayed out of sight and reached a wooded area on the outskirts of Chrzanów. We traveled a kilometer or two through the woods, but in the dark found passage too precarious. Twigs, fallen trees, and uneven ground made travel with the infants too dangerous. We had to get back to the road.

"The Tarnowski farm was ten kilometers out Slaska Street, a long way to carry the twins. We hadn't even made it halfway when the night began to give way to predawn glows. There was a grove of ash trees off to the left and we decided to make camp there for a few hours to rest and feed the babies. The early April foliage was thin and poor cover for us, so we had to go deep into the woods to be hidden from the road.

"I remember the three of us, sitting on our duffels, so proud we had made it out of Chrzanów without detection and confident that we could actually escape the fate of the transports. When the babies had finished, they fell asleep and off we marched again. Back to the road and out into the country.

"The midmorning sun was bright and we followed the road through rolling fields of nascent wheat. The washed-out, bleached-out remnants of winter were slowly being replaced by the greens, yellows and golds that would once again color the land. Stands of budding trees were responding to spring's rejuvenation.

"'Stop!' Muriel suddenly said. 'There's a car coming.'

"Sure enough, in the distance there was a black sedan. We hustled into the field and laid down in the winter grass. The occupants of the car, not expecting to see anyone in the fields, kept right on going until they were out of sight. We smiled at each other and resumed our trek. This was almost too easy. Soon the Tarnowski farm came into view.

"There was a car in the drive and that was a bad sign. I knew that the Tarnowskis didn't own a car. I knew that the Nazis had confiscated every car owned by a Chrzanów resident. If there was a car, it probably meant there were Germans inside. We decided to keep on going. The next farmhouse was several kilometers away and it was just past sundown when we approached. There were no cars, no wagons and no lights on in the farmhouse. If we were lucky, it was abandoned. Who knew how long we could stay there?

"As we walked up the drive, a woman stuck her head out of the farmhouse door. 'What are you doing here? This is my property.'

"'We don't mean any harm, ma'am. We're just walking up the road. We thought maybe we could get some water, or spend the night in your barn? We'd be gone in the morning.'

"'Just keep on walkin'. You got no business here. We don't want no trouble, so you just turn around and get yourself off the property.'

"'Yes, ma'am. We don't want any trouble either. Sorry to have bothered you.'

"By this time we had traveled twenty kilometers carrying duffels and two babies. We were bushed. But we had to keep walking. The sun had set and it was getting cool. We saw a farm in the distance and headed toward it with the hope that we'd find a place to sleep.

"It was dark when we reached the farmhouse. There were lights on in the windows. There were no cars, no signs of Germans. 'Should we knock on the door?' Karolina asked.

"'I vote to head straight for the barn,' Muriel said. 'Maybe they won't find us till morning and by then we will have rested and the babies will have been fed. Besides, it's getting cold and the barn will be warm.'

"I agreed. We quietly opened the barn door. There was a swayback brown horse in a stall. Lots of hay. A great place to sleep. Karolina fed the babies, sang them a lullaby and we all slept—how should I say this—like babies. Except Rachel and Leah would only sleep for a few hours. Then they'd wake up and cry for their breakfast.

"At sunrise, the barn door opened and an old man— blue overalls, flannel shirt, wiry white hair and a carbine in his hand—walked forward and said, 'What are you all doing in my barn?'

"'Resting,' I said. 'We have two little babies and we're trying to stay alive.'

"'Running from them Nazis?'

"'Yes, sir, we are.'

"'They're all over this territory, you best be careful. They catch you, they'll kill you.'

"'Yes, sir. We know.'

"'You all stay here and I'll fetch you some breakfast. Then you have to be on your way.'

"'Thank you, sir. God bless you, sir.'

"He and his wife brought us a tray with scrambled eggs, cheese and three glasses of milk. She was a plump lady with a flowered housedress and a big smile. 'Let me see those babies,' she said. 'I heard them all night long.' Karolina handed Leah to her, and the woman rocked her in her arms. 'My lord, she's so sweet. Just like my Eva.'

"'We'd love to have you stay,' the farmer said, 'but they come by all the time and they'll kill us if we harbor you.'

"'We understand, and thank you for the generous breakfast. We'll be on our way.'

"They packed us a little more food and off we went. Once again, keeping out of sight as much as we could. Two or three kilometers farther and we came upon another farmhouse. There were chickens in the yard and a milk cow in the pasture. A middle-age woman, thin, with unkempt rust-colored hair, was tilling a vegetable garden. She beckoned us over.

"'Where you headed?'

"'We're not sure. Away from Chrzanów is all we know.'

"'Well, you're about to hit the village of Olkusz. There's not much there.'

"'Germans?'

"The woman shook her head. Not many. Some, though. You folks look tired. Been walking long?'

"'Yes. All the way from Chrzanów,' Karolina said.

"'Did you have breakfast?'

"'We did, thank you. Your kind neighbors down the road let us sleep in their barn and fed us this morning.'

"'Must have been the Kloskys. Well, come on in and rest your feet and have a glass of fresh milk.'

"She brought us into her kitchen, took out a pitcher of milk and some cookies and said, 'I have to run an errand. You folks make yourself at home. I'll be back shortly.'

"She climbed into her wagon, gave the horse a nudge and off she went. We sat in the kitchen and shared a little milk, so grateful for the hospitality. About fifteen minutes later, a canvas-covered truck rolled into her drive and four soldiers got out, weapons drawn. They ran up into the house and yelled, '*Herauskommen, herauskommen.*' Karolina began to cry.

"As the Nazis walked us out of the farmhouse, the woman flashed a wicked, broken-tooth smile at us. 'You get back to where you belong. You stay the hell away from my house.' Then she yelled at the soldiers. 'Don't forget to pick up the Kloskys. They helped to hide these runaways.'

"We sat in the back of the truck, so dejected, so sorry we'd trusted that woman. Karolina sat on one side holding Rachel, I sat on the other side holding Leah. Muriel sat next to an expressionless Nazi soldier, automatic weapon in his hand. He stared straight ahead with no emotion. He could have been made of plastic. As we rolled past the Kloskys, we saw a German truck in their driveway. Their generosity had condemned them.

"In one hour, the truck had covered our two-day walk and took us directly back to Chrzanów, where the remaining Jews were being gathered in the town square. All of them were dressed in their best clothes, with one suitcase, ready for transport to the lovely work camp the Germans had promised.

"The square was a vista of chaos; a thousand or more families standing with their belongings—suitcases or bundled up sheets—many wearing two or more layers of clothes. People holding on to their children, their

suitcases and boxes, and several carrying their belongings bundled up in a sheet, like a peddler with his bag.
There were also a dozen weaponized soldiers, some with
growling, barking dogs, prodding people with batons
and rifles. There were SS men in long wool trench coats,
and the ice-cold Gestapo, in their leather coats, were
overseeing the whole affair.

"A megaphone blasted, 'Line up in groups of five.
Check the lists for your name. Those of you on the first
train will stand on the far south end of the square. Those
of you on the second train will stand on the north end of
the square. This is the final Chrzanów resettlement. You
are all being sent to new work camps. Much nicer and
cleaner than the filthy ghetto where you live. All will be
given the opportunity to work and earn your freedom.
Everyone who works will be well fed and taken care of
in clean, healthy surroundings. Check the lists, find your
names and line up.' The message was repeated over and
over.

"We walked over to the board and searched for our
names. My name was on the list for the second train.
I looked at the north end and I recognized many of the
other women as workers in the Shop. My train was obviously going to another textile plant. But Karolina and
Muriel were on the list for the first train. I looked to the
south end, to the other group, and saw a large number of
older people, children, and those who looked weak and
unhealthy. I knew instantly that the first train would be
going to Auschwitz.

"I started to panic. How could my friends be on the
first train? They were young and healthy. How could
they be going to Auschwitz? We looked at each other and
I started to cry. This wasn't supposed to happen.

"The Nazis were starting to prod the people in the
first line. Megaphones were ordering those on the first

train to move forward. A long train with several redbrick-colored boxcars had pulled into the station. I ran over to my friends.

"'This has to be a mistake,' I said.

"Muriel smiled a gentle but sad smile. She knew what was going on. 'We're both on the list for the first train. You go stand with your group. Don't worry about us, we'll be okay.'

"'Oh no,' I said. 'Major Fahlstein was supposed to put you on the other list. You need to tell someone. You're supposed to go to the north end. You're not supposed to be on this train.'

"Karolina hugged me. 'We gave it a damn good try, didn't we, Lena? I actually thought we were going to make it. And we almost did.' She looked wistful and smiled. 'You know, sitting in that woman's kitchen, the three of us with our babies, I thought to myself, how lucky can a girl get? I've found the two best friends anyone ever had and we're all going to survive this night-mare. We're going to be all right. That feeling, Lena, that feeling of freedom, if only for just a day, was worth it. It lifted my heart. Thank you, Lena. Thank you for every-thing.' She kissed me. 'You need to go now. They're go-ing to be boarding us.'

"I was filled with panic. There had to be something I could do. I looked around the square. There, standing in the middle, heads above the others, was Colonel Müller. 'Stay here,' I shouted. 'Stay here and hang on to those babies. Don't move yet.' I dashed over to the colonel.

"He pretended he didn't know me. He grabbed me by the arm and said, 'Where do you belong, young woman?'

"'On the north end.'

"'I'll walk you there and make sure you get in the right line.'

"As we walked out of earshot of the other soldiers,

he said, 'You are such a troublemaker, little hitchhiker. Make sure you get in the line on the north end of the square. It's going to Gross-Rosen. The other line goes to Auschwitz.'

"I could barely hold it together. 'Karolina and Muriel. They're standing over there. It's a mistake. Their names are on the wrong list. You have to get them. Please. Put them on the list for the second train.'

"'I can't do that. The lists are final.'

"'You have to. I risked my life to help your network, and all I'm asking you to do is to switch two women.'

"'And two babies.'

"'Yes. Please switch Karolina and Muriel.'

"He shook his head. 'The lists are all final. They know who's supposed to be on each train.'

"'Change the lists. You can do it. You're a colonel.'

"'A colonel who knows how to stay alive. A colonel who knows how to take risks when they're for the greater good, not for two girlfriends.'

"I couldn't accept that for an answer. I looked around the square. 'If you don't switch them, I'll expose you right here and now in this square. I'll run over to the Gestapo and tell them who you really are.'

"Colonel Müller laughed hard. I thought his sides would split. 'You are the bravest little imp I ever met. Go get in the north line before I shoot you.'

"'Please. Please,' I begged.

"He shook his head in exasperation. 'Stand here. I'll see if anything can be done.'

"The lines had formed and we stood for hours waiting for the trains to load. Finally the line for Auschwitz started to board the train. Soldiers were packing people into the boxcars. I broke into tears. I was ready to sprint over to the Auschwitz line, join my friends and the babies, and face whatever fate awaited us, when I saw Colonel Müller walking toward me, Karolina on one side and Muriel on the other. Each one held a baby. Colonel Müller looked at me and winked. 'Good-bye, little hitchhiker. See you when the war's over.'"

"Wow. He was a stand-up guy after all."

"Yes, he was, and that was the death knell for him. He ended up in front of a firing squad for treason. He was a good man, Catherine. And he was right. When he took risks, they were for the greater good. His group almost killed Hitler in 1944."

"So, the three of you boarded the train for Gross-Rosen?"

"The three of us and our twins."

THIRTY-FOUR

...

WE STOOD IN LINE for hours. No water, no food. We watched the group bound for Auschwitz as they were loaded into the boxcars. So many stuffed into each car. There would be no room for people to sit. We watched the Nazis push them in, pack them in, slide the doors shut and flip the locks. The train pulled out of the station with noisy jerks and slowly moved out of sight. When the train had left, our group was marched across the square to the platform.

"Again, we waited. Evening settled in. Muriel and I sheltered Karolina so she could feed the twins. They were the only babies in our group, which was mostly composed of women, young and strong. Although many looked kindly upon Karolina and the babies, some were resentful.

"Finally, we saw the lights of a train. It wasn't a train of boxcars like the one that had gone to Auschwitz. It was a passenger train."

"A passenger train?" Catherine said. "All the pictures of Jewish prisoners that I've ever seen were in boxcars and cattle cars."

"Most were, but the Nazis would commandeer other

trains whenever necessary. Cattle cars, open freight cars and even passenger trains. We were loaded onto a passenger train with comfortable seats, windows, even bathrooms. Compared to the horrors of the boxcars, our passenger train was a luxury. There were more seats than passengers and the windows could be lowered. There were guards on each car, but they hardly paid any attention.

"The boarding was uneventful. Muriel and I sat in one seat. Karolina and the twins sat in the seat facing us. I still had some food in my duffel, so we had nourishment. Gross-Rosen was about two hundred miles away from Chrzanów. Ordinarily, the trip wouldn't take more than four or five hours. But we were a deportation train, the lowest of priorities, and our train gave way to the needs of the German military. We traveled slowly and would be switched to a siding whenever an army transport or a supply train needed the main track.

"As the train rocked along, we took turns hugging the babies. Karolina rubbed her hand gently over their heads, sung lullabies to them and sobbed intermittently. We all did. Their fate was unknown, but we all feared the worst. Still, we had come this far, and as long as we were all still here together, maybe we'd find a way.

"The train poked along and the night was warm. Most of the passengers had lowered their windows down and had fallen asleep. I don't think the Germans worried about any of us jumping out of the windows of a moving train. After all, we were the privileged workers who were being reassigned because of our skills. We were needed and we would surely survive the war. Whenever we pulled onto a side track and stopped, the guards would disembark and stand on the platform with their rifles just in case some foolish girl harbored thoughts of freedom.

"Dawn broke on another sunny, warm day. Our train came to a stop again on a siding. Karolina was feeding the twins when an older woman, bony and unkempt, walked up the aisle and stopped at our seats. She shook her head. 'I've been to Gross-Rosen,' she said in a raspy voice. 'Before I was transferred to the Shop, I labored at Gross-Rosen. It's no picnic, let me tell you. Women are treated like slaves. Worse than slaves. We slept four together on a wooden plank covered with a few pieces of straw. Soup twice a day. Bread once.' Then she pointed at the babies. 'They won't let you have those babies, you know. There's no babies there.'

"'That's enough,' Muriel said.

"The old woman wouldn't shut up. 'The SS. They'll take those babies from you the minute you arrive. They won't let you have them. No one has babies.'

"Muriel stood. 'I said, that's enough. Now just keep walking.'

"The old woman's voice rose. In a raspy, high-pitched tone she said, 'They'll kill your babies. I've seen them do it. Those babies are as good as dead.'

"Karolina's eyes grew wide. She scooped up the twins and held them tight to her chest.

"Muriel stepped out into the aisle. 'I told you to keep walking, now get out of here.'

"The old woman shook her head and moved toward the end of the car. After a few steps, she turned around. 'I've seen them. The SS. I know. Those babies. They're dead.'

"'Don't listen to her,' I said. 'She's just a crazy old hag. We need to hold on to hope.'

"Karolina fixed her gaze upon the babies. 'She's right,' she said softly. She lifted her head and stared at me. 'She's right. They are condemned. They're as good as dead.'

"'Stop saying that, Karolina.' But she started to shake. Her jaw quivered. She gazed out of the window and her eyes glassed over, as if she had fallen into a stupor. I lifted both of the babies out of her lap. I motioned for Muriel.

"'Karolina,' Muriel said, loudly. 'Look at me. We're going to do our best to take care of our babies. Don't listen to that old woman. We got this far, didn't we?'

"Karolina just sat in her seat, unresponsive, staring out the window, twitching, as though she were catatonic. Muriel sat right next to her and put her arm around her. 'Talk to me, Karolina.' But she didn't respond. Muriel looked at me and shook her head. 'Let's give her some time. She'll come around.'

"The train jerked hard. We pulled back onto the main track and started rolling slowly again, moving along at a snail's pace through Poland's farm country. The wheat fields on each side of the tracks were speckled with greens and golds, new shafts waking up, sprouting green through the brown winter grass. Rarely did we see a village, and when we did, we slowly rolled straight through. Karolina sat in a daze and seemed unaware of her surroundings. From time to time she would mumble. I thought I heard her say 'Madeleine' and I wondered what made her think about her dog at a time like this.

"Two or three hours later, in the heat of the midday, right after we had pulled back onto the main tracks from yet another sidetrack, Karolina looked at me and reached for Leah. We were facing each other, sitting in the window seats. I was glad to see her more alert and coming out of her stupor. 'She's just a little bundle of joy,' I said as I handed the child to her. I continued to hold Rachel and rock her in my arms.

"After a moment, Karolina leaned forward. 'I'm not going to let the Nazis kill our babies. I'm going to save them, Lena, and I want your help.'

"I was worried. She wasn't thinking straight. 'What do you have in mind?'

"'Where is that paper with Siegfried's mother's address?'

"I reached into my duffel. 'It's right here.'

"'Give it to me. Do you have something to write with?'

"I shook my head. She tore a blank piece from the bottom of Siegfried's paper, took a pin from Leah's diaper and poked it into her finger. With her blood, she copied the address onto the torn piece of paper. 'Here,' she told me. 'Pin this paper onto Rachel's diaper.' I took Rachel out of her rolled-up blanket and pinned the address like I was told. Karolina pinned the top portion of Siegfried's paper with the handwritten address onto Leah's diaper. Then we each rolled the babies back into their blankets. I had no idea what she had in mind or what person she figured was going to take these babies to the address on Siegfried's papers. I started to ask, 'Who is going to carry these twins . . .'

"'Shh,' she commanded as we pulled onto another side track. A streamlined passenger train rushed past us, rattling and shaking our car. She continued to stare out the window until we started slowly pulling away from the siding. Then suddenly she stood and from the bottom of her soul said, 'Lord, forgive me,' and she heaved Leah out the window and into the field. 'Good-bye, my precious.'

"Then she looked at me. 'Throw Rachel. Now!'

"I looked down at the baby. Her eyes were bright and clear. So beautiful. So trusting. And at that moment Rachel locked eyes with me and smiled sweetly. It tore my heart out. 'No, Karolina, I can't.'

"'We can't let them kill her, Lena. Throw Rachel as far as you can. Do it now.'

"'I can't. I . . . I can't.'

"Like a madwoman she stood over me. 'Throw her,' she screamed at the top of her lungs. 'Now!! Throw Rachel!! It's her only chance!'

"I stood up and flung Rachel as far as I could. I watched her little body windmill out into the field and roll down a hill. Shocked at what I had done, I sat down and burst into tears. Karolina grabbed me and pulled me close to her. Her fingernails dug into my flesh. 'They're going to live, Lena. They're not going to die. Do you hear me?'

"I nodded.

"'When this war is over and we are freed, we're coming back to find them. Understand?'

"I nodded. I was in total disbelief at what we had done. Our beautiful babies.

"'If I don't make it, Lena, promise me that you'll come back and find the babies.'

"I swallowed hard.

"'Promise me,' she yelled and shook my shoulders.

"'I promise. So help me God, I promise.'

"'We'll tell them, Lena. We'll tell the babies about us, how much we loved them. How we would never have abandoned them ever, except to save their lives. Promise me.'

"'I promise.'

"Karolina sat back in her seat and didn't say another word until the train pulled into the Gross-Rosen concentration camp. Muriel, who'd sat frozen, dumbfounded, through the entire episode, just stared at the two of us. Nothing further was said."

Catherine put her pen down. She stood and took a deep breath. She teetered and placed her hands on the table to steady herself.

"I'm sorry," Lena said. "Are you all right?"

Catherine shook her head. "No, not really. Not this minute." She reached out and hugged Lena, and the two of them cried together. "I don't know what to say."

"I understand. I don't know how we had the strength. They would have died at the camp, you know. I see it in my mind every day and I still can't process it. Karolina found the strength and the resolve. It really was the only possible way to save their lives. But Rachel's smile, that smile she gave to me right before she left us, has stayed with me ever since. Do you want to stop for the day?"

"I do. I think that's all I can handle today."

"I'm very sorry. Are you still going to be my lawyer?"

"Lena, I'm honored to be your lawyer."

THIRTY-FIVE

...

L IAM ENTERED THE FOYER and saw Catherine's coat hanging on the hook. He checked his watch. Three-thirty. He walked into the living room and saw Catherine lying on the couch.

"Are you all right? I thought you were working all day? Do we need to rush you to the hospital?"

"Will you stop doing that every time I have a headache or runny nose? I've had a rough day."

"Lena?"

She nodded. "You have no idea."

"Did you get the whole story?"

"I got enough."

"But you stopped?"

"Had to. And don't think it's just because I'm pregnant, although I'm sure that has something to do with it. Liam, they threw them out of the window of a moving train. The twins. Lena and Karolina threw them off of a moving fucking train. They flung their babies out the window."

Liam sat down hard. "Oh, Jesus. How terrible. I feel so badly for them all." He shook his head, slid over and put his arms around a weeping Catherine.

"Liam, they thought they were saving the babies'

lives. They knew that the Nazis would kill the babies as soon as the train got to the camp. Dead on arrival. They did the only thing they could think of. Who would have that strength? Not me."

"Me neither. I couldn't throw my child out of a train. A helpless baby? I would go mad."

"I have an inkling that one or more of them did."

"What does this do to our assignment? How are we supposed to find out about two persons who died as babies seventy years ago?"

"Obviously, Lena thinks they survived. Either way, she wants closure. Can't we do that for her? She bore the responsibility for the fate of one of those babies. She took Rachel and threw her into a field. She loved that child. Hell, Liam, the way she tells the story, it's like the babies were hers as well. She calls them *our* babies."

"I'm starting to think Arthur might be correct. Maybe Lena has talked herself into a scenario, deluded herself into thinking that the babies had a chance at survival and that belief consumes her. Is that delusional behavior? Is it irrational? Jesus, Cat, I don't know."

"Don't, Liam. She's not delusional. She's a hero. Every inch of her story rings true. I can't find a flaw. Could there be embellishments after so many years? Confusion of dates? Times? The way particular details actually played out? There could be, but I don't think there are. She's got every detail and one follows the other. Bizarre? Yes. But we're talking about the Holocaust. What's more unbelievable than that?"

"More unbelievable? Two rational people who thought it was a good idea to throw two babies out of a window of a moving train and expect them to survive."

"It was done to save their lives. It was the only chance they had. They would have been killed a few hours later. Everyone knew that. She pinned an address on both babies and threw them into a field from a slow-moving train. They had a chance at life. Slim, but a chance. They had no chance if they took them to the concentration camp."

"That's what Karolina did with her dog, Madeleine. Abandoned him in a field."

Catherine nodded. "Rather than turn him over to the Nazis to be killed. You're right. Lena told me that Karolina went into a dazed state and mumbled 'Madeleine' before she abandoned her babies. Now you're getting it."

"I don't know if I'm getting it. She didn't abandon them, she threw them out of a window of a moving train."

"Will you stop saying that?"

"No, follow me here. Karolina throws the babies out of a train window in 1943 somewhere in rural Poland. For whatever reason, Lena feels compelled to find them, but she waits seventy years before hiring me. Do I have that right?"

"No. Lena threw one of the babies herself. She bears the guilt. And she promised Karolina she'd come back and find them and tell them that they were loved and not abandoned. She swore to God."

"Where was the train when they threw the babies?"

Catherine shook her head. "She doesn't know. Somewhere between Chrzanów and Gross-Rosen, which is now Rogoznica, Poland. A few hundred miles."

Liam threw his hands up. "A few hundred miles? And why now? Lena survived. She could have looked for them in 1945 at the end of the war. And anytime thereafter. And what happened to Karolina?"

"I don't know yet what happened to Karolina, but my guess is that she didn't make it. As to why she's so compelled to find them now—that's the jackpot question. There's a reason, Liam. That's the undisclosed secret I'm always talking about."

Liam shook his head. "Without some kind of proof of her story, you're going to have a hell of a time defeating Arthur. Maybe she's not delusional, but I certainly think Lena evidences signs of an obsessive behavior disorder. Didn't the doctor tell you that it could be a psychological disorder if it consumes one's life?"

Catherine nodded. "Yes."

"What are you going to do tomorrow morning before Judge Peterson?" Liam asked.

"I'm going to stand my ground. He has no right to force me to reveal client confidences."

"Lena wouldn't waive them?"

"I wouldn't ask her. She's on the up-and-up, Liam. I know it."

Liam closed his eyes and shook his head. "I don't know how she expects me to find those kids. Even if her story's all true. Without proof, it's an unwinnable defense. This case could wind up as a disaster for Lena. And what makes it all the worse is that you're preparing to go to jail."

"I know you're upset, but don't give up. Please. See if you can find out anything about a woman named Muriel Bernstein. She was a student nurse in Kraków in 1939 and was on the transport to Gross-Rosen. She was sitting with them. Also, see if you can find a family named Schultz in Regensburg, Germany. That may be where the babies ended up. That was Siegfried's family name. Either one of those people could corroborate Lena's story."

"Siegfried? Like the opera? There must be a million Siegfrieds in Germany. And Schultz? Could he have a more common last name? That's like tracking down a man named Smith in America. Not to mention that Muriel Bernstein is a pretty common name as well."

"Too hard for the great Taggart?"

"I didn't say that."

THIRTY-SIX

...

CATHERINE TOSSED AND TURNED all night and finally rose before sunrise. Liam was brewing a pot of coffee when she entered the kitchen.

"Sorry to wake you. I couldn't sleep last night," she said.

"I noticed. What's in your hand?"

"It's an overnight bag. A toothbrush, some toiletries. My medicine."

"Seriously? Cat, I can't let you do this. You're a high-risk pregnant woman. You are not going to spend time in the nasty confines of the Cook County Jail."

"First of all, I'm not high risk. Second, it's not a decision for you to make. I'm meeting Walter at seven-thirty. He still believes that Peterson will back down. Walter can't remember the last time they locked up a lawyer for refusing to reveal a confidence. Anyway, he's sure that it won't stand up on appeal."

"An appeal could take weeks, even months."

"Liam, why are we arguing about this? You're not telling me anything I don't know. I understand that you're worried, and I'm sorry to cause you stress, but I really believe in what I'm doing and I need you to support me."

She put her arms around his neck. "This might be the most important thing I've ever done. People like Lena, they had more courage in their little fingers than I'll ever have. I'm standing up for what I believe. I have to do my part, and if protecting her means confronting Judge Peterson, then I'm going to do it. I won't give Arthur the ammunition to take away Lena's independence and put her in a home. She will not be locked up again."

A S BEFORE, JUDGE PETERSON'S courtroom was standing-room only when Walter and Catherine entered. Earlier that morning she stood before her closet trying to decide on her outfit for judgment day. What does one wear to go to jail? She finally selected her navy suit, a white blouse and a red, white and blue silk scarf. Very American. No jewelry.

She and Walter had met that morning. She told him not to play the pregnancy card. She didn't want mercy, she wanted justice.

"We need to make a clear record this morning," Walter had said. "If we're going to ask the appellate court for an expedited review, we need to put it all on the record."

"Do you think he'll actually lock me up?"

"Yes, I do. Shirley has skillfully backed Peterson into a corner. He won't hesitate unless you consent to follow his order."

"Well, that's not going to happen. Let's go."

Catherine and Walter took their seats at counsel table. Across the room, Arthur sat next to Shirley. An arrogant grin stretched across Arthur's face, as if to say, "You're about to get yours." He tried to catch Catherine's attention and lock eyes, but she wouldn't give him the satisfaction. Liam sat in the front row, wishing it were possible to resolve the dispute by knocking Arthur into next week.

The corner door opened, the crowd hushed and Judge Peterson followed his court personnel into the room, the duck behind the ducklings. "All rise." Catherine stood tall and confident. Arthur leaned forward and craned his neck trying to catch her attention. His pompous smile never left his lips.

"Case number 13 P 6268, *In re: the Guardianship of Lena Woodward,* continued by previous court order for status," announced the clerk.

Walter, Catherine, Shirley and Arthur rose and approached the bench. The judge motioned for the overflow courtroom to be seated. In a quiet voice, he said, "The record will show that this matter has been continued by me for a third time to allow Ms. Lockhart to bring herself within compliance of this court's orders, which heretofore she has intentionally resisted. Since she is represented, I will address my remarks to Mr. Jenkins. Does Ms. Lockhart understand the terms of my order?"

"She does, Your Honor."

"Does she have any questions at all about what this court requires of her?"

"She does not, Your Honor."

The judge took off his reading glasses. He leaned forward. "It is not my desire to sanction anyone, especially such a committed attorney as Ms. Lockhart, but I have a duty, a responsibility as a probate judge, to protect the elderly members of our society who come before me. Does Ms. Lockhart understand that?"

"She understands what you articulate as your duty."

"So that my record is absolutely clear, the petitioner, Arthur Woodward, has, under oath, alleged that his mother, Lena Woodward, is a disabled adult by reason of her senile dementia. Specifically, he has asserted that her mental state has deteriorated to the point where she now suffers from an obsessive-compulsive disorder to locate people who do not exist and who never did exist." He turned to Shirley. "Is that essentially correct, Mr. Shirley?"

Arthur vigorously nodded his head up and down, stepped in front of his attorney and interjected, "That's right, Your Honor. She's got some crazy delusion that a woman named Karolina had two girls during the war and that she's got to go find them. Ridiculous. And this lawyer here, Lockhart, is leading her on, trying to get her hands on all my mother's money."

Judge Peterson slammed his gavel. "I did not address you, sir. I addressed your attorney. When I want you to speak, I'll let you know. Right now, you turn around, go back to counsel table, take a seat and keep quiet." Arthur tilted forward to look at Catherine, put a satisfied grin on his face, turned and strutted to counsel table.

Shirley answered the judge's question by saying, "Your Honor is correct in briefly summarizing the allegations of the petition. We are concerned about the conflicting position in which Ms. Lockhart has placed herself."

The judge nodded. "As am I. Mr. Jenkins, Ms. Lockhart herself has stated in open court that she is representing the alleged disabled person in a matter separate and distinct from this probate case. It may very well be an entirely proper representation. But the petitioner has alleged otherwise. It is my responsibility as a probate judge to inquire. It is also my judgment that by entering an appearance on behalf of Mrs. Woodward in this probate case, and by declaring to me in open court that she does represent Mrs. Woodward in a secondary matter, Ms. Lockhart has thrust herself into this controversy. If there is nothing untoward about the attorney-client relationship in the secondary matter, then let her tell me and this proceeding is over."

Walter turned to face Catherine, who shook her head. "Your Honor," Walter said, "divulging the information you seek would require her to betray the confidence that Mrs. Woodward has justifiably placed in the sanctity of the attorney-client relationship. It would broadcast to the public that private, privileged communications from a client to an attorney are confidential and protected from disclosure only until some judge or litigant decides he wants to know them. Ms. Lockhart intends to stand firm and is quite certain that the appellate court will see it that way as well."

"Well, she's going to get a chance to find out. Ms. Lockhart, I put it to you one last time. Will you comply with this court's order and advise me fully about the subject matter of your representation of Mrs. Woodward in the separate matter?"

"No, sir, I will not."

"Then you have left me with no choice. Given my responsibility to Mrs. Woodward, the alleged disabled person, I hereby confirm my finding of direct contempt and remand you to the custody of the Cook County sheriff to be held in the Cook County Jail, from day to day, from week to week, until you are prepared . . ."

"You'll do no such thing," bellowed a voice from the back of the courtroom. A tall woman, with glaring eyes and a determined look on her face, pushed back the swinging gate and with the assistance of her cane confidently strode directly toward the bench.

"Lena!" Catherine said.

"Who is this woman?" Judge Peterson demanded.

"Mother, what are you doing here?" Arthur said, popping to his feet.

Lena turned and stiffly pointed at her son. "Arthur, sit down and shut up." Which he did.

Shirley was startled. "Apparently, she is the respondent, Lena Woodward, Your Honor."

"That's correct. I'm Lena Scheinman Woodward, and the accusations of my irresponsible son are pure poppycock."

The judge raised his eyebrows. "Any layperson who comes before me to testify must be sworn in."

"She's not here to testify, Your Honor," Catherine said. "Lena, you're not required to say one word."

"I'm not going to let you go to jail. That's my choice, not yours. I'll answer any questions this judge wants to know. I have nothing to hide."

Judge Peterson looked to Catherine. "She's apparently overruled you."

Lena raised her hand and swore to tell the truth.

"Is Catherine Lockhart your attorney in this probate matter?"

"Yes."

"Is she also your attorney in another matter?"

Lena paused. She tilted her head this way and that. "I believe that's a technical question. I have not signed any papers. I have not formally engaged her. I haven't paid her any money. But I consider her to be my attorney. I've sat in her office for several days and talked her ears off. She's a very good listener."

The judge wrinkled his forehead. "And you haven't paid her? Have you agreed to pay her anything?"

Lena shook her head. "No, we've never even discussed fees, but if I had, don't you think that's my business and not Arthur's? I'm taking up quite a bit of this attorney's valuable time. Why should I expect her to work for free?"

"Can you tell me what these talking sessions are all

about? Without disclosing the actual conversations, can you tell me, in general, what is the subject matter of your discussions? And before you answer, I will give you time to consult with Ms. Lockhart or Mr. Jenkins."

"I don't need time."

"You don't have to answer those questions," Catherine said. "And I advise you not to. He could ask follow-up questions. Once you open the door, you can't limit his inquiry."

"I understand that. It's okay. I'm proud of what I'm doing." Lena looked directly into the eyes of Judge Peterson. "In 1943, on a Nazi transport train to the Gross-Rosen concentration camp, two beautiful little girls were abandoned and lost. Intentionally. It was my fault. I take the responsibility for the decision to abandon them in an effort to save them from certain death at the hands of the Nazis. When we did that, I gave my solemn promise to go back and try to find them. They may not be alive, Your Honor. I know that. But they did exist and I held those babies in my arms. After all these years, I've finally found the courage to fulfill that promise. I can't do it alone. I've asked Catherine Lockhart and her husband to help me. Have I done something illegal?"

Judge Peterson exhaled a grateful sigh. "No, ma'am, you have not." He sat back. "Since the court's basic inquiry of Ms. Lockhart has now been satisfied, and since I'm also satisfied that Mrs. Woodward's financial estate has not been depleted or placed at risk, and, most importantly, based upon my observations of the witness this morning, this contempt hearing is dismissed. Ms. Lockhart, any findings of contempt are stricken from the record. You are free to go."

"Just a minute," Shirley interjected. "I have questions. I want my right of cross-examination."

"Denied."

"But, Your Honor, all you've done today is to complete the contempt hearing. This case isn't over. My client, Arthur Woodward, still maintains that his mother is suffering from an obsessive-compulsive disorder to find children that do not exist. We've done our homework and we strongly believe there is no proof they exist or were ever born. Just because this woman comes to court, puts on a good show and says they existed doesn't make it true. Arthur's petition is pending, and we insist upon keeping our trial date of April twenty-fifth."

Lena turned around and looked sternly at Arthur, who hid his face.

"Is that correct, Mr. Woodard?" Judge Peterson said. "Do you still wish to proceed to trial on your petition to declare your mother a disabled person?"

Arthur nodded. "I do."

"He does, he most definitely does," Shirley said.

"Very well. This matter is continued to April twenty-fifth for trial on Mr. Woodward's petition to declare Mrs. Woodward a disabled person. We'll consider the proofs on that date. This hearing is adjourned."

Outside of the courtroom, in the busy halls of the courthouse, Lena, Liam and Catherine gathered. "Did you tell her to come today?" Catherine said to Liam.

"I'd be revealing a confidence, wouldn't I?"

"I did it of my own accord," Lena said. "I called Liam. I couldn't allow your loyalty to subject you to punishment. I'm sorry if I stepped on your legal toes."

Just then Shirley and Arthur walked out of the courtroom. Arthur looked sheepishly at Lena. "I'm sorry, Mother, but I have to do what I have to do."

"No, you're not sorry. Not in the least. Arthur, I'm ashamed of you. This is an entirely selfish pursuit."

"Well, you're wrong. I'm doing it for your own good, to protect you. I just can't see you throwing all Dad's

money away on some preposterous quest for two Polish children. If such children ever existed. Perhaps you
believe in your mind they're the daughters you always
wanted. Maybe that's it, huh? Maybe it was never very
satisfying just having a son, was it? You'd rather chase
after imaginary daughters."

With tears in her eyes, Lena took a quick step and
slapped Arthur's face.

"Did you see that? Did you see that?" Arthur said to
Shirley. "Didn't I tell you she's out of control?"

Shirley tugged at Arthur's sleeve and pulled him toward the elevator. "C'mon, Arthur. Don't make a scene
here. You'll have your day on April twenty-fifth."

"Damn right I will."

Lena shook her head and blotted her eyes with her
handkerchief. "He was never like that before my husband died. He never forgave me for selling the business.
He wanted it for himself. To tell the truth, I didn't think
he was capable of running my husband's business, but it
didn't really matter because the business had to be sold
to pay the estate taxes. It's what my husband wanted anyway."

THIRTY-SEVEN

...

"MURIEL, KAROLINA AND I arrived at Gross-Rosen concentration camp in a state of total shock," Lena said as she started another session in Catherine's office. "The main entrance was similar to the entrance to Auschwitz. It was a large brick façade. The entrance to the camp was through a tall archway flanked by two one-story buildings, like wings on either side. ARBEIT MACHT FREI was stenciled over the archway beneath three windows. 'Work makes you free.' History's most cruel joke.

"We disembarked from the passenger cars and were pushed into two lines, one for men and one for women. I held Karolina close to me. She was still in a stunned state. Truthfully, I wasn't much better. We clung to each other, staggered by what we had done, wondering how we could possibly carry on. All the women were led into a room and told to disrobe. We were being cleaned, disinfected. Jews were known to have lice and other dirty diseases, they told us. Each of us was handed a tiny piece of soap.

"We showered and were led into a large empty room. No towels. The door was locked and we were kept in the room for hours. About a hundred naked women. From time to time, a guard or two would come in. They'd tell us to stand and be counted. They'd call our names. They had a list. Sometimes the guards were women. Sometimes they were men who would look us over, point and make snide remarks. They subjected us to cavity searches twice. Often they would stare and comment about which ones looked strong. They asked us what we did before we got there." She shook her head. "I was in bad shape mentally. All I remember was the room was cold and we had no clothes.

"Finally, guards came in and separated us. Half of the women were given uniforms and marched out. Karolina and I were in the other half. We were given our uniforms and marched back to the train tracks. We were told that our group was going to a sub-camp. To our good fortune, it was a production sub-camp, not a construction sub-camp."

"I don't think I understand," Catherine said.

"Construction sub-camps were hard labor. Work in the quarry, work in the mines. Bomb shelter construction, removing rubble, underground construction—many of the manufacturing facilities were underground, like tire manufacturing and weapons manufacturing. Prisoners assigned to construction sub-camps had a short lifespan. Because of malnutrition and hard labor, prisoners became emaciated, they lost muscle mass, their immune systems were weakened. Many died within six months. There was a term used in the camps—*müselmanner*—to define someone who had lost more than a third of her body weight. At that stage the body begins to consume itself and mental acuity fails. People become zombielike, apathetic, and it's only a matter of time.

"My group headed back to the train. Muriel was not with us. I guess it's because she told them she was a nurse and was sent somewhere else. My group was going to a textile plant."

"You didn't stay at Gross-Rosen?"

"Gross-Rosen was a huge conglomerate, a concentration camp with over one hundred sub-camps spread all over Poland, Germany and Czechoslovakia. At its peak, Gross-Rosen held over one hundred thousand prisoners. Some were sent to be slave laborers for Blaupunkt, some for IG Farben, some for Mercedes-Benz; others worked for other German corporations, like Bosch, Bayer, and Audi. Our train headed south to Parschnitz, a sub-camp just over the Czechoslovakian border.

"We boarded the same train that had brought us to the main camp. When Karolina saw the train she began to shake. Almost as though she had palsy. As she boarded, she let out a deep moan that came from the bottom of her soul. 'Aaahhhh.' It frightened the women. The guards came running over telling her to shut up. But she kept moaning. One of the guards swatted her with his rifle stock and knocked her down. She bruised on the side of her face.

"'Don't, please,' I yelled. 'I'll take care of her. She'll be all right. Please, don't hurt her.' I wrapped my arms around her and tried to cover her mouth. I put her in the seat and talked to her, telling her it would be okay. I told her to stay strong, we needed to survive, come back and find the girls, but I could see that Karolina was slipping away.

"The train pulled out of Gross-Rosen and started its slow journey toward Parschnitz. Karolina remained distant and lethargic. It was like she had snapped. From time to time she'd call out the names of our babies. She'd moan, she'd cry. She'd tell me how sorry she was. I did all I could to comfort her.

"When the train arrived at Parschnitz, we were

marched to large barracks where the workers slept in wooden partitions. We were given new uniforms—short-sleeve, calf-length smocks with three or four buttons. They were made of a scratchy material, like a mixture of cotton and linen. Each woman was also given a scarf or bonnet to wear over her hair. I would soon learn that the uniforms were made in the camp's sewing shops. We were allowed to keep our own shoes. Each of us had a little locker where we'd keep our cups, bowls and the week's portion of bread.

"I guided Karolina to a sleeping area and held her through the night. The next morning we marched to the textile factory. Hundreds of women worked a variety of textile machines. Some unloaded cotton bales. Some operated spinning machines, the machines to make threads and yarn. Other women sat at sewing machines. Karolina was placed at a large cotton-spinning machine. She didn't move.

"'Get to work! What's wrong with you?' yelled a female guard, but Karolina could not respond. 'Do you talk?' the guard yelled in her face.

"I rushed over and told the guard that she was the best seamstress at the Shop in Chrzanów, and that she had just lost her children but she would be okay, I would see to it. I offered to watch over her if she could be assigned to a sewing station. At first the guard pushed me away and prodded Karolina with a baton. But she didn't respond. Then the guard swung the baton, hit Karolina in the ribs and knocked her to the floor. I covered her and held my hands over her head. 'Please, don't. Tell them, Karolina, tell them you will work.' But she sat with a blank stare, holding her ribs.

"'I can take care of her,' I cried. 'Please.' The guard looked at us on the floor, shook her head with a disgusted look, and said, 'Take her to a sewing station, but I tell you both, if she doesn't produce, I will have no more patience.'

"I pulled her to her feet, took her to the station next to me and sat her down at the machine. 'Please, Karolina. Why won't you work? They'll kill you if you don't start working.'

"There were tears rolling down her cheeks. 'I don't care. I don't want to live anymore, Lena. It's all too much.'

"'Yes, you do. Of course you do. You need to survive. If not for yourself, then for the babies. We're going to get our babies. Together. You and me. Please, Karolina.'"

"She started to sew, but was moving in slow motion. I knew she wouldn't get any garments made so I doubled up my efforts and placed completed garments on her table. By the end of the day, the guard came by and commented, 'This is not acceptable production. You two have to do better tomorrow.'

"We walked slowly back to the barracks. I could see that Karolina was wincing from the pain in her ribs. Bowls of soup and a third of a loaf of bread and some butter were provided. The bread had to last for three days. Karolina wouldn't eat.

"I tried to feed her. 'Eat, Karolina.' But she shook her head. 'You take mine,' she said.

"I begged her, but to no avail. Karolina looked at me with defeat in her eyes and said, 'I can't do this. I can't sit here like nothing has happened and make clothes for the Germans. I miss our babies. I want the little ones. I need to hold them. They need us, Lena, and I need them. I have to go to them.'

"'We will,' I answered. 'As soon as we're freed, we'll come back and find them. No matter where they are.'

"She didn't sleep at all that night. Every time I looked at her, she was staring wide-eyed into space. Her lips were moving and I could tell she was planning something. I saw that look on her face.

"At dawn we were awakened by the guards and told to line up. They took us out into the yard for roll call. When they had finished they marched us in groups of five across the yard toward the factory. Suddenly, Karolina bolted out of line and ran for the gate.

"'Halt! Halt!' But Karolina was running at full speed. I broke out of the line and took off after her. I was stronger, faster. I could catch her. 'Stop, Karolina. Please.'

"'Halt!'

"'Don't shoot!' I yelled in German, wildly waving my arms. *Nicht schießen! Nicht schießen!* I'll stop her. Don't shoot her.'

"A volley of shots rang out and Karolina tumbled to the ground. I ran up to her and wrapped my arms around her. She had been hit several times and she was barely breathing. 'Oh, my dear Karolina. Why? Why? You could have survived.' I held her tightly. 'Damn it, Karolina! I love you so much. We could have made it.'

"She coughed and lightly shook her head. 'I'm not a survivor, Lena. I never had your strength,' she said weakly. 'You were always my hero. You'll survive and find our babies. I know you will. Tell them I loved them. Find them, Lena. I love you.' Those were her last words. I closed her eyes for her."

Lena balled her hands into fists and held them hard against her cheeks. "She knew they would shoot her. That's the way she wanted to go out. Running after our babies. Life had become too hard for her. I saw it, I knew it, but I couldn't save her from her despair."

"I'm so sorry," Catherine said.

"They pried me off of her and dragged her lifeless body away. I was pushed back into line and marched to the factory." Lena buried her face in her hands and sobbed. "I lost my best friend."

The room was quiet for a few moments, and Lena finally said, "Could we take a walk? Would you mind?"

"Sure," Catherine said. She retrieved their coats and the two proceeded down Webster toward the Lincoln Park Conservatory. It was a mild spring day and they found a bench beside the dormant flower gardens in front of the conservatory. A park district worker was tilling a flowerbed for planting. In a few weeks, the gardens would be ablaze in color.

"Through the years, I never told a soul what really happened. Not even my husband. No one knew the details. Once the war was over, I closed the door. And locked it. Now, as painful as it is, I must open it. I'm grateful that I found you to open it with me."

"Thank you. I feel privileged."

THIRTY-EIGHT

...

A MILD SPRING DAY along the shores of Lake Michigan still carries a healthy dose of wind chill. Lena wrapped her scarf around her neck. "After Karolina died, I felt like I had nothing left. What more could happen? Was it even worthwhile going through the motions? Yet, for some unknown reason, I rose in the morning and put one foot in front of the other. I marched in line with the other women, slaves in a textile factory. Somewhere I found an inner drive to survive.

"Life at Parschnitz was hard in every way. Soup in the morning and at night. Bread twice a week. You could eat it all at once or portion it out. It was a pretty tough decision for a starving woman. At night we were packed into sleeping quarters in our barracks. Four women to a partitioned space.

"For months I was severely depressed. I had lost everyone. My family, Karolina, Muriel, the babies. Every day I woke up and every night I went to sleep, and every day was just the same. The only variation was in the garments we were required to sew. Sometimes they were camp uniforms, sometimes Wehrmacht uniforms, sometimes clothes for civilians—shirts, dresses, skirts.

"There was a barbed wire fence surrounding the camp, separating it from the road, and guard towers stood at intervals. We were free to roam inside the camp outside our barracks, even near the fencing. From time to time, Czechoslovakians would pass by on the adjoining road. Sometimes kids on bicycles. And they'd stop and talk to us. The townsfolk were very nice and on occasion they'd bring a piece of fruit, a bunch of bananas, a hunk of cheese and throw it over the fence.

"Some of us still had a little money. I came into the camp with some money I'd hidden in the lining of my shoe. If the guards weren't paying attention, it was possible to buy a piece of meat from some of the kids, who became quite adroit at black market sales. You'd be surprised how your body would benefit from an occasional piece of fruit or some protein, both of which were missing from the camp diet.

"Perhaps just as important as the occasional piece of food was the news that the townsfolk would give us about the war. They knew the Russians had repulsed the German attack. They knew that the German army had suffered defeats in North Africa. Most encouraging were the reports about the Allied bombing campaigns.

"It seemed like one woman or another would always get encouraging war information from a townie, and the word spread throughout the camp like ripples on a pond. Throughout 1943, the Allied bombing was far from us, so we could never actually hear it for ourselves. Nevertheless, the townsfolk encouraged us. It didn't take much.

"I had reichsmarks. I told you that when Germany occupied Chrzanów and annexed the city, it abolished our currency, the zloty, and required everyone to exchange zlotys for reichsmarks. The same was true for Czechoslovakia. Korunas were abolished and exchanged for reichsmarks. Therefore, I had official currency hidden in my shoes. I learned quickly how to bargain on the black market. My chief contact was Dŭsan, a lanky sixteen-year-old, who would come by the fence on his blue bike.

"As long as my reichsmarks held out, I could stay healthy. Malnutrition was a slippery slope. If your health declined, you were weakened and susceptible to disease. If you were weak, you were unproductive. If you were unproductive, you were sent to the death camps. Dŭsan would bring eggs. Such a small item, so packed with protein, could keep you healthy.

"In the factory, many of the girls sewed pockets into their smocks. I learned that trick the first week. Dŭsan would bring eggs, slip them through the fence and I'd hide them in my pockets.

"Dŭsan was also the Edward R. Murrow of Parschnitz. His family obviously had access to a radio, and he'd delight in telling me the progress of the war. In July, he hung around the fence until late at night to tell me that the Allies had bombed Rome and the king of Italy had arrested Mussolini. 'If that fat duce can fall, so can the Austrian Paper Hanger,' Dŭsan said with a grin. That night he gave me three eggs as a present. I liked that kid a lot.

"The winter of 1943 to 1944 was harsh, and the frozen nights and days were a melancholy reminder of the nights Karolina and I slept together. In retrospect, our times in the little basement, the three of us and the babies, were sweet, wonderful memories, and I missed them all deeply.

"Dŭsan had relatives in Ukraine. They kept him informed on the Soviet progress through Ukraine in 1943. By the following April, the Russians had advanced to Romania, less than five hundred miles away. As much as Dŭsan's hard-boiled eggs nourished me physically, his information was nourishment for my soul.

"In late May, Dŭsan stopped by and told me that the

American army was marching up Italy. It wouldn't be long now. I was starving that day and I asked him if he could get me a chicken. He smiled. 'You want me to cook it?'

"'Oh, yes. How much?'

"'Two reichsmarks'

"'I don't have that much left. I'm about out of money.'

"'How much do you have?'

"'Ten reichspfennigs.'

"'Ten reichspfennigs? That's nothing. How about fifty?'

"'Truly, Dušan, ten is all I have.'

"'Okay. For you, it's a deal. I'll be back tomorrow.'

"The next evening, I stood by the fence waiting for Dušan. Soon I saw his bike roll up. He got off, reached into his back pack and prepared to throw the sack over the fence when a man shouted, *'Hör auf!*—Freeze!'

"Two Parschnitz police officers got out of the car and grabbed Dušan. I turned and ran as fast as I could into the barracks and quickly slid into my bunk. A few minutes later, several camp guards came in and yelled at us all to line up. It didn't take long for the police officers to recognize me. I was taken out of the camp and put in the back of a police van.

"They drove into town and took me to the district jail. I had committed a criminal offense in the town of Parschnitz, so I was sent to jail. I was locked up to await further orders."

"How awful," Catherine said.

"You'd think so, but the conditions at the jail were a vast improvement over the camp. The jail had showers and indoor bathrooms. The jail had two meals a day, many of them home cooked. Marek, the jailer, was a kind, roly-poly Czech who treated everyone with respect."

"What happened to Dŭsan?"

"I don't know. I never saw him again. But the Czechs I met in jail were impressive. Two men and a woman were brought into the jail by the town police on a charge of drunk and disorderly conduct. They only spent a few days, but we got to know each other. They told me they were partisans, members of the Czechoslovak Forces of the Interior, the resistance movement. They told me about the Normandy invasion that took place on June sixth, two weeks earlier. Their movement was getting ready to launch its operations as well. 'It's only a matter of time until Germany falls,' they said. 'If you can last six months, you'll go home.'

"I felt uplifted. Life in the jail was tolerable. Six months seemed easy. When the Czechs were released, they winked at me and said, 'Stay strong. Stay positive. Germany will soon be history.'"

"Did you ever find out what happened to the Czech resistance? Was their movement successful?"

Lena shook her head from side to side. "Define success. They battled the German army, caused a significant obstruction, and helped the Russians advance into Poland. But, from what I read, the Russian army abandoned them and they were slaughtered. Stalin pulled his troops out of Czechoslovakia at a critical moment and sent them to Hungary. Without the Soviet support, the resistance was crushed. That was typical of the Russians."

Catherine nodded. "That reminds me of the 1944 Warsaw Uprising."

"You're exactly right. Both uprisings were crushed by the Nazis, and both of them occurred because the Soviet army stalled and did not support the resistance. In Warsaw, the Russians camped on the east side of the Vistula River and watched the Nazis level the city. In each case, the absence of Russian support condemned the uprising, and it was no accident. Both the uprisings were late in the war, and Stalin delayed his armies intentionally to weaken the Polish and Czechoslovakian resistance movements and make it easier for the Soviets to occupy the countries after the war.

"I remained in jail for a few weeks. On July 1, 1944, a few days after my Czech friends were released, Marek came into my cell, handcuffed me and took me outside. We started walking down the streets of the little town when I asked him, 'Why did you come for me? Where are we going?'

"'I have orders to take you to the train.'

"I figured I was headed back to Gross-Rosen. I was sure they needed help in the textile camp. I was excited. Maybe this time I'd be able to reconnect with David. I thought about him a lot. This was a great opportunity for me.

"'Where is the train going?' I asked.

"'Auschwitz.'

"I froze in my steps and started crying.

"Marek looked at me and shook his head. 'Why are you crying? You're getting out of jail.'

"'Why? Because Auschwitz is a death camp. Because I know what's happening there. I've known since 1942.'

"To his credit, Marek expressed genuine concern. He stopped and leaned his head toward me, speaking softly. 'Not everybody dies. Many are chosen to work. You are young and you are strong. You have kept yourself healthy. When you get there, they will look you over. Stand up straight and tall. Do not look them in the eyes or confront them or plead with them. But look like the powerful woman you are. Do whatever they tell you. You can survive.' He paused and then said, 'I hear the Russians are not far. Maybe next year. Keep your head down and survive.'"

A strong gust of wind blew and Lena shivered a bit. "I'm getting a little chilly sitting on this park bench, Catherine. The lake knows it's not summer yet. Would you mind if we returned to your office?"

"Shall we stop for lunch?"

Lena nodded. "I'll buy. Is that considered paying you a fee?" She laughed.

"Could be. My rates are getting cheap."

THIRTY-NINE

...

A BLACK ENGINE PULLING eleven blood-red boxcars stood poised to leave at the Parschnitz train station when Marek and I arrived. The first nine cars were locked, and German soldiers were loading the tenth car with Czechoslovakians and fifty or so families heavily dressed in mountain clothing. 'They're Roma—Gypsies,' Marek whispered. 'From the Carpathians.' He shook his head. 'They will be treated harshly. They will die. I have seen it before. There is a special camp at Auschwitz where they put the Gypsies.'

"When we got closer, I was taken aback by the noise. There were moans and screams coming from several of the forward cars. Marek walked me directly to an SS officer and presented my transit order. The officer directed me to stand with a group of women at the far end of the platform. I recognized some of them from the Parschnitz workshop.

"Marek talked to the officer for a few minutes and then returned to me. 'You will be in the last car with people from Parschnitz. There are only forty.' He pointed at the first section of the train. 'In those cars are Hungarian Jews from Budapest. Maybe three to four thousand.

They have been on the train for many hours, maybe days. They have not been fed. It is hot and there is no ventilation. I suspect some, maybe many, have died. That is why you hear screams.'

"'For days?'

"'Regrettably so. But for you, there are only fifty miles to go and only forty people in your car. Remember, when you get there, look strong and do not cause trouble. Survival, it's all about survival.'"

"Just as Colonel Müller had said," noted Catherine.

Lena lifted her eyebrows and nodded. "You have to keep telling yourself; you can get through this. You can do it. It became my mantra. 'You can do this.' You claw, you fight. If you give up, you become another statistic.

"When the time came, my group was loaded into the last car. It was an empty wooden boxcar with no openings. There were two buckets inside, which a guard removed. Forty of us filed into the car and the guard returned with the two buckets. One of them had cloudy water and a ladle. The other was quite distinctly the receptacle for human waste. It had been emptied but not cleaned. The door was shut and locked, leaving us all in a dark, humid container.

"With a jerk and a snap, the car lurched forward, knocking some us off our feet and spilling some of the drinking water through the cracks in the floor. The excrement bucket tipped over, but no one had used it yet. There was very little air in the car. I quickly got the sense of why the people in the forward cars were screaming.

"The trip to Auschwitz-Birkenau took less than three hours. Thankfully, none of us needed to drink the remaining foul water or relieve ourselves in the bucket. We had ample room to sit on the floor. No one died and no one convulsed. We rode in silence. Compared to the other cars on our train, we were the fortunate ones. The trip was dark, quiet and relatively peaceful. The arrival at Auschwitz-Birkenau was anything but.

"The doors were pulled open and bright sunlight poured in, temporarily blinding us. The scene on the platform below was a frontal assault on all of our senses. Two trains, sitting side by side on parallel tracks, were unloading passengers simultaneously. Thousands of prisoners alighting from dozens of boxcars. Soldiers were screaming, dogs were barking, people whose legs were unsteady from the cramped trip were falling down and were being trampled. The *sonderkommandos*—inmates in blue-and-gray-striped uniforms who served as lackeys to the SS—were herding people into two lines, kicking and swinging sticks and batons. '*Raus, raus,*' they shouted, pulling people, dead and alive, from the boxcars. Dozens of armed guards—the rank and file *Schutzstaffel*—stood on the perimeter with rifles at the ready.

"Women were shoved into one line and men into another. Loose children were running, looking for their parents. Women shouted for their separated sons, men shouted for their wives. Names. I heard so many yell names. 'Selma, where are you?' 'Nina.' 'Maurice.'

"People kept trying to hold onto their suitcases and their duffels, but the *sonderkommandos* kept telling them that all the luggage would be sorted and delivered to them later that night. 'Don't worry about your belongings, just get into line and we'll bring your bags to you later.'

"'Men to the left, women to the right. Five across. Men to the left, women to the right. March straight ahead. Keep moving.'

"It was perfectly orchestrated chaos. If it wasn't the blinding sunlight, or the abusive *sonderkommandos,* or the shouting, or the dogs, then it was the stench. As soon as you stepped down from the boxcar, this horrible, rancid smell overpowered you. I'd never smelled anything like that before, and I can't even give you a comparison. But it was obviously coming from the four chimneys.

"At the front of each line were the SS officers. They were elegantly dressed in their uniforms. Shiny black boots and belts. Hats square upon their heads. They were the selectors. They'd look at you and point. You go this way, you go that way. You go to the right, you to the left. Dispassionate, indifferent, impassive SS officers, occasionally joking among themselves. Passing the time until their shift was done. Each person was examined for a few seconds, like a grocery shopper looking through a bin for the best head of lettuce. Point to the left, point to the right. No discussion. No appeal. They were sorting people as if they were sorting mail, and with just as little emotion.

"As we shuffled forward, the woman in front of me, thin and sickly, kept pinching her cheeks, hard, twisting, trying to get color into them. When she arrived at the front, she smiled and puffed out her chest. '*Links!*' the SS officer barked, meaning you go to the left. Then he looked at me. '*Rechts.*' You go to the right. There were fewer women on the right; most of the women in line went to the left. My group headed south toward the women's barracks. The line on the left headed west toward the chimneys. Almost all of the Hungarians who came on the train were sent to the left and were immediately taken to buildings I later learned were gas chambers."

Catherine looked confused. "All the Hungarians?"

"Hungary, as you may know, was an ally of Germany, but all during the war, Hungary's prime minister refused to deport their Jews to the camps. It wasn't until the spring of 1944, when German troops occupied Hungary, that transports of Jews to Auschwitz began. The week

I arrived, eighteen trains of Hungarian Jews were unloaded, and nine out of ten prisoners were sent directly to the gas chambers. They weren't registered, they weren't numbered. They filed directly into disrobing rooms and then to the gas chambers. Over four hundred thousand Hungarian Jews were murdered by poison gas between May and July, 1944.

"As for me, Marek was right, I was selected for labor and marched with other women to be processed. We were each issued a card with our camp registration number. Then we were taken to the barbers, who cut off our hair and shaved our heads and our bodies. All body hair was removed. No lotion, of course. All of us suffered razor burn, nicks and cuts. Naked, we were marched to the showers and sprayed with some stinging disinfectant that burned everywhere that the sharp razors had been. Next, we were all issued striped uniforms and headscarves. My uniform had a yellow triangle stitched on the left pocket pointing down, and a red triangle on top of it pointing up. When they were layered, they looked like a Jewish star. Yellow signified I was a Jewish prisoner; red signified a political prisoner.

"Next, they took us to be photographed. We were asked for our names, our addresses and our next of kin. At that point, I broke down, because I had to answer 'none.' Finally, we stood in a line and stepped forward to a table, where my left arm was painfully tattooed with a needle and some black liquid. From then on, my forearm would identify me as a numbered piece of German inventory. I ceased being a human being with a name. With my insignia uniform, my shaven head and my numbered tattoo, I had officially been dehumanized."

Lena pulled back the sleeve on her left arm. There, on the outside of her forearm was the identification—A18943. Catherine swallowed hard.

"After registration, we were all taken to barracks. When I first stepped off the train and looked at Auschwitz-Birkenau, I saw rows and rows of long, wooden barracks over acres of property. As far as the eye could see. Birkenau's barracks were all identical, patterned after horse stables, and shipped prefabricated from Germany. Inside, against each long wall, were three levels of wooden shelving—three-tiered sleeping bunks where seven to eight hundred inmates slept. Eight to a bunk. At its height, Birkenau housed ninety thousand prisoners.

"But that's not where they put me. There was an older section to the left with brick barracks, known as sector B1, and that's where I was assigned. Inside my building there were sixty partitions, each with three levels, for a total of one hundred and eighty sleeping spaces. Nothing more than cubbyholes. Each one was about five feet wide. In each cubbyhole, four women squeezed in on a bed of loose straw. A total of seven hundred and twenty women were housed in my building. One toilet.

"I entered the building and looked around for an available sleeping place, a partition with only three women. As I walked down the aisle, I received unwelcome stares. If I stopped before a space that had only three women, they glared at me defiantly and shook their heads, and I kept walking. I walked up and down the same aisles two or three times. Nobody wanted me. As much as I had told myself, 'Keep going, you can do this,' I was ready to throw in the towel. I cried. Enough was enough. What more could be heaped on my back? My own people had turned against me and didn't want me. I was truly at the end of the road. Finally, a young woman said, 'We have room for you.'

"I climbed into the bottom tier, with a concrete floor, and tried to make myself as small as possible, but as you can see, I am not a small woman. 'I'm Chaya,' said the young woman. 'Don't think unkindly of the others; most of them are very nice. It's just that they would rather sleep three rather than four in their bunk. I'll help you get acquainted.'" Lena paused and wiped a tear. "Chaya was a beautiful woman."

Catherine smiled sympathetically and set a box of tissues on the table. "Tell me about Chaya. What was her full name? What did she look like?"

"Ha. What did any of us look like? Heads shaven, skin and bones, no makeup, pasty white complexions, sores from biting bugs. Some of us had lost teeth; the rest were yellowed. We saw beauty in a different way. A deeper way. Chaya Aronovich was a beautiful person. She took the time to befriend me and teach me the ropes.

"I must admit that I was a bit standoffish at first. I didn't want to get close to her. I didn't think I could handle the loss of another emotional connection. In the last three years I had lost so many people I cared about. My mother, my father, Milosz, Yossi, Karolina, Muriel, David and our babies. I didn't think I could do it again—get close to somebody and have her ripped out of my life. I didn't think I could give away another piece of my heart. But you know what, I was wrong. The heart regenerates. It always manufactures another piece to give away.

"Auschwitz was frightening. The first day had been overwhelming. Chaya took me under her wing and gave me the emotional support to keep going. She introduced me to the girls in the barracks. Once I wasn't a threat to their sleeping arrangements, they were friendly. Chaya helped me to settle into my routine.

"Every morning at four-thirty, a loud metal gong woke us up. We'd rush to stand in line to use the toilet, and then hurry to stand out in the yard waiting for an SS officer to come and count us. Sometimes he'd get there by six. Sometimes later. After he counted us, a kapo would bring the morning's meal—a cup of ersatz coffee. No food. From there we'd separate into our work squads to be marched to our job locations. I worked in the Birkenau kitchen.

"I helped prepare lunch for the inmates, which consisted of soup, usually just vegetable, but occasionally there were tiny scraps of meat. Soup was delivered throughout the camp in large barrels. For supper, I'd help prepare a four-inch loaf of bread with either an ounce of meat or a pat of butter or jam. The total caloric value was less than a thousand, carefully designed by the Nazis to result in malnutrition and ultimately debilitation. Remember, Birkenau was built as an extermination camp—to kill people. The kitchens were feeding over seventy thousand people, but they were only expected to live three months. By then, malnutrition, weakness, exposure, hypothermia, or some other cause would end your Birkenau tenancy and make room for the next occupant.

"Besides the horrendous knowledge that thousands of people were being murdered every day, right where you lived and slept and ate, it was torture for us to bear witness to the senseless cruelties that were dished out right before our eyes by the kapos, the *blockführers,* and the SS. Although the men were victimized more than the women, it was not unusual to see flogging, beating, humiliation, or even a random execution. The SS had the authority to deliver any punishment they saw fit, including death on the impulse of the moment. Throughout the summer, trains pulled in and new arrivals were marched straight to the gas chambers. The crematoriums ran twenty-four hours a day. Auschwitz-Birkenau at its peak was killing two thousand an hour.

"Chaya was an observant woman. She would pray every morning. She told me she kept the Sabbath every week. She urged me to pray with her, but I scoffed. How did she even know when it was Friday? All the days were the same in Auschwitz.

"'How can you still believe in God, Chaya, while our people suffer in concentration camps? Where is he? Where is God Almighty? Show him to me. Where is God in Auschwitz?'

"She answered me calmly. 'He's right here, Lena. You just have to bring him in. That's what's most important. In this most evil of places, God is pure goodness and I bring him in, right into these barracks. Right into the face of every Nazi. Every woman in this building is a Jew, and the Nazis have made every possible effort to eradicate Judaism. But as long as we stay true to our faith, they fail. They can take everything I have, but they can't take my Jewishness. So, in the depths of this camp, I defy them. I defeat them.'

"I thought of Yossi and said, 'I knew a man in Chrzanów who you would have liked very much.'

"'Tomorrow is Shabbat,' she said. 'I hope you'll join me.'

"The following night, when we had all bedded down, Chaya got up and went to the middle of the cell block. She pretended to light candles. She had no candles, she had no matches, but we could see them in our mind. She said the hamotzi over a piece of bread that she had saved. She drank a cup of water like it was wine. One by one, the other inmates in our building got up and stood behind her. Not all of them, but many. They joined her in the prayers. Chaya passed around small crumbs of the bread she had blessed. Then they all joined her in softly singing *Lecha Dodi,* the ancient liturgical poem sung to greet the Sabbath bride. It was moving, Catherine. She had brought God into the camp, right into our barracks. From then on, every Friday, with the other women, I would join her.

"In the fall, things began to change. We started to notice the bombing. U.S. army air force planes flying from
their base in Italy could now reach our area. Installations
and strategic targets, like the IG Farben plant, were within
a few miles and planes flew over Auschwitz all the time."

"Were you frightened by the sound of the bombing?"
Catherine said. "Didn't you worry that Auschwitz would
be bombed?"

"We would have welcomed it. You get to a point where
you no longer fear death. You don't want to die, but you
know it's a possibility and you're not afraid. If the Allies
were to bomb Auschwitz, I would have cheered. There's
nothing I would have rather seen than a bomb fall on
the crematoriums and the gas chambers and take out
the Nazi killing machines. If it took out the SS and the
sonderkommandos as well, then I would have thought it
was a very good day."

"Even if it meant that some of you would die?"

"Yes."

"There's still quite a controversy over whether the Allies should have bombed Auschwitz, isn't there?"

"Well, they chose not to. They knew about Auschwitz;
they had reports and aerial photographs. They wavered
on whether they should or shouldn't. They even made
plans. But in the end they set the plans aside. There are
lots of theories on why they didn't. Some say that in
1944 the planes weren't capable of surgical strikes. They
couldn't bomb with sufficient accuracy to take out just
the gas chambers and crematoriums without risking the
death of seventy thousand inmates.

"Others argue that the Allies were committed to use
their air raids for military and strategic targets only, not
to save prisoners. In 1944, the U.S. air force command
said it couldn't do raids over Auschwitz without diverting
substantial air support from other venues. That wasn't

true. The U.S. was already bombing in the Auschwitz area—IG Farben was five miles away.

"For me, the explanation that makes the most sense is that no military branch wanted to take responsibility for killing tens of thousands of Jews. Germany was the guilty party for killing Jews. Germany was running death camps. Germany would be solely responsible for the deaths of millions of civilians, not bombs from Allied planes. The plan finally adopted by the Allies was to liberate the Jews by ground forces. After all, the Russians were very close to Auschwitz and had already liberated the Majdanek death camp east of Lublin.

"As the air raids increased and the Russians closed in, the Nazis began to dismantle the camp. Their plan was to destroy the camp and all evidence of the genocide. In September and October, the *sonderkommandos,* who served the Nazis by clearing out the bodies from the gas chambers and taking them to the crematoriums, were all gathered and executed. The Nazis wanted no witnesses, no one left behind to tell the story. They expected all the Auschwitz-Birkenau inmates to die or to be transferred to other camps to die.

"All but one of the crematoriums and one gas chamber were shut down by the end of the year. Instead of trains bringing in prisoners, we now saw blocks of inmates being loaded onto trains to go to other camps deep inside Germany. Half the prison population was gone by the end of 1944.

"Every day, every night, we heard the sounds of bombs and gunfire. It was music. It was the Allied air force orchestra's percussion section. Boom boom. The Russians were just a few miles from our camp and we heard their gunfire. Boom. The Germans hastily began to destroy what was left of Auschwitz-Birkenau, trying to leave no trace of the camp and its horrors. They set fire to wooden barracks, they burned buildings to the ground. They blew up the crematoriums. But they weren't about to let the prisoners go. They weren't done with us.

"On the night of January 18, 1945, my building was rousted from sleep about three A.M. Everybody was ordered to stand outside for roll call. It was snowing and very cold. The snow on the ground was at least a foot deep. We stood outside in our dresses, thin hooded overcoats and wooden shoes. No socks. Finally, we were counted and told to line up in groups of five. This was to be the Auschwitz death march.

"The plan was to have us walk through several villages to the Wodzislaw train station for transport to Buchenwald, Mauthausen or other camps deep in Germany. The march was expected to take less than a week and cover thirty-five miles. They gave us each a loaf of bread, a slab of butter and told us to make it last.

"Many could not endure such a hardship. The Nazis made it quite clear what our choices were. Those who were unable to walk on such a journey and wanted to stay behind could do so and they would be shot. As hard as it is to believe, some chose not to go and went back into the barracks. The rest of us walked out through the front gate into the bitter Polish night. Snow was up to my shins and in my shoes. Chaya and I walked side by side. I kept telling myself, 'Lena, you can do this. You're a survivor. You can do this.'

"So we walked. Anyone who fell behind, anyone who stumbled, anyone who couldn't stay in line, was shot and left by the side of the road. We marched during the night and rested during the day. The SS guards had warm coats compared to our threadbare coats, but they were cold as well. After several hours of walking, they would try to find a barn or an empty building for us, and for them, to get shelter from the snow and to rest.

"We were into our second day, somewhere in Silesia, and the blowing snow would not quit. 'Keep going, Chaya,' I said to her. 'You can do this.' And she said the same to me, even though I could not feel my feet. They were mostly numb, except it felt like I was walking on needles. Finally, the SS found a large empty barn and told us we'd have three hours to rest. Chaya and I laid down in the corner of a horse stall and covered ourselves with hay and straw to get warm.

"The sound of gunfire, machine guns and tank cannons grew louder. The Russians were a stone's throw away. Finally, a large boom sent vibrations through the barn. I thought the walls would break apart. Even the guards themselves were frightened. 'Get up! Get up!' they yelled. 'Everybody out. Now! *Raus, raus. Schnell. Macht schnell.*' The inmates scrambled to their feet, the guards collected them and prodded them and they all rushed out of the barn. But not me. I slid under the hay. I covered myself up with hay and straw and did not move.

"The guards kept yelling, hustling the inmates to get in line, and I tried not to breathe. 'Move, move, hurry up,' they yelled. '*Schnell. Macht schnell.*' But now their voices were fading, farther away, down the road. They hadn't stopped to count. No roll call. The sound grew thinner and thinner. I didn't move a muscle. I didn't move a single straw or piece of hay. An hour or so later I poked my head up, brushed the hay from my face and looked around the barn. Nothing. Everyone was gone. Even Chaya. And then it came to me.

"I was free!

"I was free for the first time in four years. My tormentors had rushed away in fear, heading deep into Germany. They herded their captives, pushing the women through the snow, to trains, to boxcars, to other concentration camps far inside Germany, where they would be starved and abused and worked until they died. But I had escaped. I was free. And the first thing I did was to drop to my knees and pray for those women. I prayed for Chaya. Isn't that funny? I never prayed for myself. Never believed in prayer, never gave it a second thought. But at that moment, when I stood alone in the barn, a free person, I prayed to God to protect those Jewish women, to strike those Nazis down and free those women. I knew there was a God, because I was free, and now I urged him to free the others. 'Do it, God.' Crazy, wasn't I?"

"Not at all."

FORTY

...

A NY LUCK RESEARCHING KAROLINA or her babies?" Catherine asked. Liam sat at the dining room table with papers spread about, his laptop opened to the database of "Gross-Rosen in Rogoznica" Web site and a Guinness on a coaster. Catherine hung her coat and walked into the dining room.

"Not so far. Right now I'm trying to find the records that reflect registration for Lena after her stop at the main Gross-Rosen camp. I haven't found any specific databases for Parschnitz."

"Are you doubting her story?"

"No, no. I'm just tying up all the dates, making sure she got her dates right. I want them to coincide with Muriel Bernstein."

Catherine looked shocked. "You found Muriel?"

"Sure did. I mean, I found the record of her stays at the concentration camps, yes."

"Did she survive? Can we talk to her?"

Liam shrugged. "I know she survived the war, but I don't know what happened after the war ended. Gross-Rosen's main camp, where Muriel worked as a nurse, was evacuated as the Russian army was advancing. The inmates were marched to a train and transferred to Bergen-Belsen, Buchenwald, Mauthausen, and other camps."

"What happened to Muriel?"

"Muriel Bernstein, if that's *our* Muriel Bernstein—there's more than one—arrived at the Mauthausen concentration camp in February 1945, coincidentally about the same time as Simon Wiesenthal arrived there from Auschwitz. That might have been where Lena would have gone had she not escaped. On May 5, 1945, the U.S. 11th Armored Division liberated the camp. Muriel's listed as a survivor. That's as far as I got."

"That's great. If Muriel's still alive, she'd make a great witness. She knew Karolina and the babies. She was there when the babies were born and when they were thrown from the train. Eyewitness proof. So, keep after it."

"I know."

"What records have you uncovered for Lena?"

"Well, she was enrolled at Gross-Rosen along with Muriel but transferred to the Parschnitz sub-camp, and as I've said, I have no records from there."

"Any records from the Parschnitz jail?"

"Forget about it."

"Lena went to Auschwitz on July first."

"I know, but many of the Auschwitz records were destroyed."

"I have someone else for you to look up. Chaya Aronovich. She was with Lena in Auschwitz and left on the death march on January 18, 1945."

Liam nodded. "What are your thoughts with regard to Chaya?"

"She wasn't in Chrzanów and didn't know Karolina, but she was close to Lena for six months in Auschwitz.

Lena may have had conversations with Chaya about Karolina and the babies as early as 1944."

"How does that help?"

"It goes to the issue of whether those are recent delusions brought about by senility. If Lena discussed Karolina and the babies with Chaya in 1944, then her current beliefs aren't a product of a deteriorating mental state. She believed them seventy years ago. Either Muriel or Chaya would dispel the notion that her so-called delusional obsession was caused by senile dementia. That might be enough to win our probate case even if we can't prove that Karolina's babies survived."

"I get it. I've also made requests through the Yad Vashem Museum's Central Database of Shoah Victims' Names. It's the most comprehensive identity search available, but I haven't heard back yet."

"Well, add Chaya Aronovich. Does Yad Vashem keep current information on survivors?"

"Some. And they store millions of pages of testimony, video and audio remembrances. I've made contact with a staff member in the archives and she's agreed to meet with me next week."

"Next week? You're going to Israel next week?"

"Yep."

"Liam, you didn't tell me."

"Oh, sorry, I was going to, I just forgot. May I have permission to go to Israel next week to meet with a staff member at Yad Vashem?"

"Well, maybe I wanted to go too."

"Then buy a ticket."

"Liam. You know I'm not flying."

He hugged her. "Actually, it's better for you to stay and finish up with Lena. I'm going to find out what I can in Israel and then swing by Poland. Maybe I can turn up something useful."

"Okay. Good idea."

"Where do you stand in finishing up with Lena?"

Catherine stared longingly at Liam. "God, I wish I could have a beer. Or a stiff drink. Lena's narrative today was about as tough as it gets."

Liam smiled and put his palm on her considerable baby bump. "My guy doesn't drink yet."

Catherine covered his hand with hers. "He's kicking. Do you feel it?"

"So you agree it's a he?"

Catherine laughed. "Do you really want to know?"

"Nope."

FORTY-ONE

...

"YOU WERE FREE," CATHERINE said. "After all those years of enslavement, you were free."

"Yes, I was. But freedom is a relative term. The SS had left and I stayed behind, but I was in a barn, in a prison uniform, with wooden shoes. I hadn't eaten in a day. I wasn't sure where I was or where I could go. I had no money, no family, and I was scared to death of the German army and the Russian army.

"But, as you say, I was free. I stood up, brushed the hay off my body and took stock of my surroundings. I called out, 'Anyone here? Chaya?' But there was no answer."

"Can I stop you for a moment?" Catherine said. "Have you spoken with Chaya since that day in the barn?"

Lena shook her head.

"How about Muriel?"

"No, I'm afraid not. After the war, as I'm about to tell you, things became chaotic. All of Europe was in shambles. Millions of people were wandering around with no place to go. There was no way of contacting anyone. By the time things settled down, it was several years later. I was in Chicago. I don't know where Muriel and Chaya went."

"But I understand there's a database. You contributed testimony to the Yad Vashem database, didn't you?"

Lena nodded. "Certainly. I gave them a video statement. They have all my information on file."

"Isn't it reasonable to assume that Muriel and Chaya, if they survived, would have done the same, or that others might have provided Yad Vashem with information about them?"

"I don't know. Maybe."

"I'm a little surprised. Why didn't you look up Muriel and Chaya? And what about David?"

Lena shrugged. "Life became too complicated and I just wanted to move on. I didn't want to think about the Holocaust anymore. I wanted to put it all behind me."

"I hate to be so lawyery, but that's not entirely true. You voluntarily sat for a video statement with Yad Vashem *after* the Holocaust. You've been very active in survivor organizations for years. You were a leader in the protest against the Neo-Nazis' plan to march in Skokie, Illinois, in 1978, holding a placard on the street. You didn't exactly move on."

"How did you know about Skokie?"

"Liam. He's pretty damn good at what he does."

Lena sat for a moment biting on her bottom lip. "Well, the answer is I didn't search for Muriel or Chaya."

"What about David?"

"That's a different story. May I just proceed with my narrative now?"

Catherine picked up her notepad. "Of course. Please do."

"Everyone had left. I peeked out of the door of the barn. There wasn't a soul in sight. I saw a farmhouse a few hundred yards away, but I'd been there and done that with a woman that turned me in. I wasn't about to trust some stranger again and end up in a Nazi truck. I knew what direction the march had gone—west, into Czechoslovakia, running away from the Russians, who were coming from the east. I knew where Oświęcim was on the map. It was almost due east, and from there Chrzanów was only thirteen miles northeast. I knew I would have to circle around Auschwitz, going straight north from where I was and then east. I didn't want to take a chance on going anywhere near Auschwitz again, so I headed north.

"The road was empty. I saw no pedestrians or wagons, which was understandable because I was in the middle of a battle zone and no civilian in his right mind would be out and about. Rapid bursts of machine gun fire filled the air to the west. I was pretty sure the next town, Kobiór, was about three miles due north, but that's not where the road went. It went west toward the Nazis. Standing between Kobiór and me was a thick forest. There were no trails and the snow was fresh, but I had no choice. I would go north through the woods.

"I was exhausted, famished and thirsty. I tried to melt the snow in my hands and drink it, but it was too cold and the snow was too dry. In many places the snow was knee deep and, underneath my smock and coat, my legs were bare. My lower extremities were frozen.

"I talked to myself in the third person. 'Keep moving, Lena. You can do it. One step after the next. Keep moving, Lena. Take another step. One more step. You're a survivor.' Encouraging words, but in truth, I didn't have much left.

"Finally, I exited the forest and when I did, I ran smack into the Soviet brigade. I came around a tree and found myself staring straight into the barrel of a cannon on a Russian T-25 tank. My legs wobbled and I passed out.

"The next thing I knew I was lying in a booth in a

Kobiór coffee shop. A Russian soldier and a woman in a bakery apron were standing over me. An olive-green Russian jeep with a white star on its hood was sitting by the curb. The woman tried to offer me a cup of hot tea.

"'Are you okay, honey?'

"'How did I get here?'

"The Russian soldier raised his hand. I sat up, took a sip of tea and a bite of cookie. Oh my God, a cookie. My taste buds didn't know what to think. How long had it been?

"'You were in the camp? The very large one to the south?' the soldier asked. I nodded. 'You're very brave,' he said, and he kissed me on the forehead. 'My troops have now taken the camp and freed a few thousand of your people. It was just the same as we saw at Majdanek.' He shook his head. 'Where will you go now?'

"I shrugged. 'Chrzanów, I guess. That's my home. Are there any Nazis still there?'

"He shook his head and smiled. 'There are no more Nazis in Poland. They ran like rats.'

"'Thank you for bringing me here. I don't think I could have taken another step.' I started to get up. 'I better be going now.'

"The shop owner looked at my body of skin and bones, shook her head and wagged her finger. 'You sit right here. Let me get you some food and dry clothes.'

"I didn't know how to respond. For four years I struggled, I fought just to subsist through the meanest of human conditions, under the boot of the most sadistic, savage monsters the earth had ever known. No one cared whether I lived or died. Actually, they hoped I would die. And now a total stranger was insisting that I accept her caring offer to give me nourishment and warm clothes. I couldn't hold it together. I fell apart.

"I didn't know who to hug first. It had been such a long

time. The soldier—his name was Yuri—said he had to leave; he had a war to fight. He was proud to have helped me. The bakery shop owner—her name was Alicja— brought me hot pierogies and steamed vegetables. She told me she had a room over the shop. I could stay there as long as I wanted. How do you repay such kindness? She didn't want anything. She was repaid by the opportunity to do good. She didn't care if I was Jewish. I was a human in need.

"In the little apartment upstairs there was a bathtub. I hadn't had a bath for four years. Alicja filled the tub with hot water and laid out a sweater, a long wool skirt, boots and warm socks. That night I slept on a feather bed for the first time since the Nazis broke into my home and seized my family. You can't imagine what that felt like. When I woke up the next morning, it took a while for me to realize that I hadn't died and gone to heaven.

"I dressed and walked down the stairs into the bakery, where Alicja dished up a hot breakfast. My stomach had shrunk, so I couldn't eat much. But it was delicious. Afterward, I took a cup of coffee and walked outside to look at the market square. The sun was shining and reflecting off the freshly fallen snow. The world was so bright, I had to squint. The air was fresh and smelled so clean. There were no chimneys, no Germans, no roll calls, no marches. No SS with rifles. People strolled through the snow with their children, going anywhere they pleased, without fear.

"I stayed with Alicja and accepted her generous care. Finally, on the sixth day at breakfast, when I had regained some of my strength, I said, 'I have to get back to my home. I am forever grateful to you, but I need to know if anyone survived.' Maybe some of my friends had returned. Maybe David had returned. God, I longed to see David. Alicja arranged for her neighbor to take me back to Chrzanów. She gave me a warm coat and a duffel that she filled with rolls, fruit, sausages and a bottle of milk. I promised to come back and visit.

"Alicja's friend dropped me at the Chrzanów town square and I looked around trying to assimilate the present. I wasn't wearing an armband, I had no papers and I wasn't subject to arrest. So different from the last time I stood in that spot, when there was a megaphone shouting commands and there were lines forming to march groups to the railroad tracks and we were holding our babies. The Nazis were gone, as was more than half of my town. But I was free and I had returned.

"A few of the shops had reopened, but the square was quiet. I don't know how to explain it to you, but as I stood there looking at my town, now free of Germans, I didn't see the memories of my childhood, of the happy, bustling village I knew. I didn't see my classmates heading home from school. I didn't see my friends and myself running through the square, or eating ice cream in the summertime. I didn't see my parents, or Milosz, or Karolina or any of the things I remembered from my childhood. The square only held visions of SS officers sitting in cafes and bars, laughing and drinking, while Jews with their heads down quietly tried to slip by without abuse. My mind saw German officers stopping and bullying elderly men. I saw me, pushing a cartload of coats.

"I walked slowly northeast to where the ghetto once stood. The Shop was an empty shell. Most of the ghetto buildings had been torn down or bulldozed, presumably when the Nazis cleared it out in the spring of 1943. I returned to the building where Yossi had his basement apartment. Half of the building had been obliterated, most likely by a tank, and it lay open like a gaping wound. What remained was mostly rubble—bricks and twisted metal—but I was able to pull some bricks away, find the entrance and walk down the stairs to the furnace room. There, still sitting on the floor, were the two drawers we used for baby cribs. Soft wool blankets still lined the drawers. I sat on the mat that had been my bed and cried until I had no more tears.

"I rose from the mat and reached behind the furnace. There, where I had hidden it in the dark corner in 1943, was Milosz's shoe. I kissed it and put it in my duffel. I still had my piece of Milosz. When I reached into the bag, I saw that Alicja had not only given me food and extra clothes, she had generously given me money. Taking stock of where I was and what had happened, I wondered why I was chosen to be the lucky one. The only survivor. I certainly did not feel worthy.

"It was still late in January, but the day was sunny and relatively warm, and I set out to see what was left of Chrzanów. As you might expect, my steps led me directly to 1403 Kościuszko, my parents' house."

Gladys poked her head in the conference room door, interrupted Lena and said, "Cat, your other is here."

Catherine glanced over at Lena and said, "Gladys refuses to call him my *significant* other or my husband. He's just my *other*. Gladys and Liam are engaged in eternal banter. Send him back, Gladys."

Liam walked into the room, kissed his wife, shook Lena's hand and said, "I just stopped by on my way to the airport. I wanted to tell you I have a line on Siegfried Schultz. The Nazi army records list his address in Scharmassing, Germany."

"That was the town," Lena said. "I can't remember the street, but the paper we pinned on the babies gave Siegfried's mother's address in Scharmassing."

"Dorfstrasse is the name of the street. It's about sixty miles north of the Munich airport."

"Are you going there?"

Liam nodded. "I'm going there after I go to Jerusalem. I don't expect to meet up with Siegfried, but if those babies made their way into Germany, I might be able to find out something."

Lena shook her head. "No wonder Ben raved about you two."

"One more thing," Liam said. "The babies were tossed into the wheat fields on the way from Chrzanów to Gross-Rosen, correct?"

Lena nodded.

"And as I remember the story, the train was moving slowly, right?"

Lena nodded again. "Very slowly. We had just pulled out of a side track and were starting up again."

"Can you estimate how far you'd gone on your journey from Chrzanów to Gross-Rosen?"

Lena shook her head. "I don't think so."

"Think hard, Lena. Had you gone halfway?"

"Yes, more than halfway. We had gone a day and a night, we had that confrontation with the woman, Karolina sat and stared into space for quite a while and then we dressed the babies. Maybe two-thirds of the way."

"Okay. Good work. I'll see you guys in a few days." Liam left and closed the door.

"Do you think he'll find them?" Lena said excitedly.

"He's really good at what he does. Nobody better."

FORTY-TWO

...

I DECIDED TO GO home and started walking through the square toward Kościuszko Street. When I was a child, Jews owned most of the stores in the square. We were shopkeepers. When the Nazis invaded, they took the stores away from us and gave most of them to Gentiles. Now, as I walked through the market square, many of those stores were shuttered.

"I continued down the residential streets and noticed that many of the houses were vacant as well. It felt like Chrzanów had been ravaged. I guess it had. Sixteen thousand Jews had been killed or transported out of Chrzanów. More than half the population was gone. The Nazis who had confiscated our homes, like Colonel Müller, were also gone.

"I stood in front of my house wondering if I wanted to go inside. The way the Müllers had changed my house had upset me so much when I was bringing the reports to the colonel. I didn't want to walk in and see Else's ghost sitting on the couch, her nose in the air, my mother's bracelet on her arm. I wanted to remember my home the way it was when I lived there.

"Nevertheless, I walked up to the door. It occurred

to me that the last time I stood here I was begging the colonel to save the babies. So long ago. Something urged me to just open the door and go inside. If the house were vacant, could I move in? Could I live here again?

"I tried the door, but it was locked. I knocked. No one answered. I walked around to the back door and it was locked as well. I looked for a window to open, but it was winter and they were shut. I peered in through the living room windows and was about to leave when the front door opened and a man said, 'What are you doing here?'

"'I should ask what *you* are doing here. This is my house.'

"'To hell with you. I bought it, I paid good money for it, now get out of here.'

"'Who did you pay money to? No one had the right to sell my house to you. This house belongs to my father, Captain Scheinman.'

"The man stormed belligerently into the yard. 'Yeah, well, it's mine now. Jews forfeited their property. That was the German law. Since we were part of Germany, it was all legal. I bought it, so it's mine. Now leave or I'll get my gun.'

"I stood my ground. 'You don't have a gun, the Nazis took all the guns. Jewish forfeiture was an illegal act. And I don't believe you paid anybody. You're a squatter.'

"'Look, lady, whoever you are, my family is now living in this house. My wife and my three kids. And we're not moving. I'm not giving it to you. Since you're obviously Jewish, why do you want to be here? There are no Jews in Chrzanów anymore.'

"'Well, there's at least one now.'

"He just shook his head. 'Just go away. I'm not moving, and no Polish authority will force me to move.' He went back into the house and locked the door. He was probably right. What was I going to do?

"Closer to the square there were several empty houses. I was cold and I entered one to sit down and eat my lunch. The house was furnished but abandoned. I surmised that some SS officer or ranking German soldier had been living in the house when the Russians approached and left in a hurry. I had just criticized a man for being a squatter in my house, but that's what I was about to do, except if the real owner showed up, I would have gladly returned the house to him. Unfortunately, very few Chrzanów Jews lived to come back. That was the sad truth.

"I unwrapped some of the sausage Alicja had packed for me and drank some of my milk. Then I headed back to the square to see if any of my friends had returned. In front of the bakery, I saw Frank Wolczinski, a Catholic classmate who I knew from my short tenure in the public high school. He told me that a few Jewish residents were starting to straggle back and that Eva Fishman had returned. She was two years older, and a friend from the Kraków Gymnasium. Frank offered to buy me a beer and we went into the bar.

"He asked me to tell him where I had been for the last four years and I just shook my head. 'I don't think I could and you don't want to know.'

"He nodded. 'I heard some things. I hoped that they weren't true. Listen, some of the younger crowd gathers at the Kryjówka Bar each night after ten. Will you join me tonight? I'll buy?' It was an offer I gladly accepted.

"I asked him if he'd heard anything about David or any more of the Jewish students. He shook his head. Only Eva. He gave me her address and told me he'd see me later at the Kryjówka.

"I tracked Eva down later that afternoon. I had always known her as a stocky girl, but she'd lost a lot of weight and her dress hung on her like she was a wire hanger. We briefly shared our experiences. She had been at a

Gross-Rosen sub-camp as well, an underground camp in northern Poland that made munitions. She saw a few Chrzanów people there, but then she said that most everyone had been tortured and killed, and she broke into tears. She didn't know anything about David. I stayed a little while longer and went back to my new home.

"February came, and while it was quiet in Chrzanów, the war wasn't over by any means. We'd see and hear planes flying over Chrzanów every day. The Nazis were gone from our area, but they were hunkering down in Germany, hoping for the development of Hitler's super-weapon. Blasts from Russian bombs continued west of us. Russian troops would come through Chrzanów on their way into Germany. Sometimes they were cordial, but we encountered plenty of boisterous, rude and even brutal Russian soldiers.

"The Russians didn't give a damn if we were Jewish or Christian, they would just occupy the town for a few days, bully their way around and continue on their military advance into Germany. On the one hand, you could get angry at the belligerent way they made their presence known, but on the other hand, they were our liberators. Still, reports of sexual abuse circulated among the women and we knew not to go out alone, only in groups.

"I tried to look for a job, but there wasn't anything available in Chrzanów. I was frugal with my food and my money, so for the time being, I was okay. Through March and into April, stragglers would return from the camps, the lucky ones, with stories that no one wanted to tell and no one wanted to hear. Bit by bit, the Jewish population increased, but only minimally.

"Sometime in late April, I was invited to a wedding. Sarah Sternberg was getting married to a man she met in the Płaszów camp outside of Kraków. His ears had been boxed, and for all intents and purposes, he was deaf. The

ceremony and reception were held at one of the Chrzanów synagogues. During the occupation, the Nazis had
used the synagogue as an arms depot. Although battered
and defaced, the synagogue was being restored and the
hundred or so Jews that had returned to Chrzanów were
trying to reconstruct a Jewish community.

"A rabbi came in from Kraków and the families had
built a chuppah, which they had decorated with early
spring flowers. Our little community gathered for what
was to be the first Jewish ceremony since the Nazi occupation. It felt good to openly celebrate such a positive,
affirming event. I went with a group of girls and was
standing with a glass of wine when someone tapped me
on the shoulder and said, 'Hey, spunky one.'

"I spun around and there he was. David Woodward. I
couldn't believe it and I threw my arms around him and
cried like a baby."

"Did you say Woodward?"

"Of course. Didn't you know? I married David."

Catherine was shocked and dropped her pen. "No,
you never said your husband's name was David. Believe
me, I'd have picked up on that. The business—it was
called D. Morris Woodward Investments."

"Right. David Morris Woodward. David called the
business D. Morris Woodward because he liked the way
it sounded, and Morris was also his father's name."

Catherine shook her head. "I never would have
thought. You are so full of surprises."

Lena smiled mischievously. "Oh, you have no idea.
David and I reconnected at Sarah Sternberg's wedding.
He had lost a lot of weight, like the rest of us, and there
were wrinkles on his face that hadn't been there before.
His left arm was a little misshapen from a beating he
received. As with many of us, he had scars that were vis-
ible and scars that were not.

"The years had taken away some of his boyish exuberance, but not his spirit. Or his smile. His eyes were as blue and as kind as ever. He stood there in a dark blue sport coat with an open collar shirt and gray slacks, neatly pressed. And I was just as entranced as I had ever been. Maybe more so.

"'You made it,' he said. 'I always knew you would.'

"'Oh, my God, I've asked everyone about you. Everywhere I went. Colonel Müller said you were transferred to Gross-Rosen, and when I was sent there, I thought I'd join up with you, but I was immediately shipped out to Parschnitz. I worked in the textile factory and I figured you might be there too, but I never saw you and no one had heard of you. Were you in Czechoslovakia?'

"David shook his head. 'I was in the Neusalz subcamp in western Poland, running a textile mill. I had hoped they would send you there, but Neusalz was a terrible place.'

"'Let's not talk about the camps. Only the future.'

"He looked at me and I could see water in his eyes and he said, 'All these months, all these years, I dreamed we'd meet again and we would talk about our future.' With that, David put his arm around me, raised his glass and his voice and said, 'Ladies and gentlemen, may I invite you to another wedding. In one month, in this synagogue, God willing, Lena Scheinman and I will be married.'

"I was floored. People were clapping and cheering. I looked at David and said, 'You didn't ask me to marry you and I didn't say yes.'

"'Will you marry me, Lena Scheinman?'

"'Oh, yes!'

"The wedding was planned for Sunday, May 13, 1945. In the interim, on May seventh, Germany surrendered and the war was officially over."

"That's such a coincidence," Catherine said. "That's my due date. May thirteenth."

"It's getting close now, isn't it?"

Catherine smiled and nodded. "He's an active little guy. So, you married David on May thirteenth?"

"There were celebrations in Chrzanów all through the month of May, including the wedding of Mr. and Mrs. David Woodward. All the survivors, those who had made it back to Chrzanów, attended. Alicja came from Kobiór. It was a lovely May night and our wedding was outside under the stars. For us on that night, the Holocaust had never existed.

"We settled into the little house that I had occupied and tried, with the others, to rejuvenate our Jewish community. But it was not to be. The sad fact was that the Chrzanów Jews had been slaughtered. Eliminated. Those few that had survived and returned found the town unrecognizable. What was left of a once-vibrant Chrzanów was now a handful of townsfolk, battered and bruised by the war. Chrzanów's economy had been decimated. The Russians were now in command and taking over the town. Administrators had been appointed. Poland would be Communist."

Catherine closed her notebook. "Enough for today, Lena. Can we pick up next week?"

"Catherine, I'd like you to come to my apartment next Tuesday. There's something I'd like you to see."

FORTY-THREE

...

CATHERINE SAT IN HER bedroom with her feet raised, rubbing vitamin E lotion on her abdomen with her right hand, holding her phone in her left. Liam was in Israel.

"Cat, I met with Ruth Abrams today. She's a curator in the archives here at Yad Vashem. Lena is well documented here. As you know, she gave a video history. It's about an hour long and she gives quite a detailed narrative about prewar Chrzanów and her time in the camps. But she doesn't mention Karolina or the babies. Totally omitted. Doesn't that trouble you?"

"A little, but I can understand it. Why would she want to relive the story of the twins, and permanently record how she threw them out of the window? She's never told this story before. She told me that after the war she closed and locked that door. Did she talk about Milosz and her time in the attic?"

"Oh, yes. And her time at the Tarnowski farm. Obviously the hours she spent with you provide much greater detail than the one-hour videotape she made. But the chronology is the same. She summarizes her time in the Shop, her time in the Parschnitz concentration camp and her captivity in Auschwitz. She talks about her escape from the death march and her return to Chrzanów. She even mentioned that while she worked in the Shop, she lived in a furnace room in the ghetto. But she totally omits Karolina and the twins."

"I don't find that inconsistent. It's just too painful."

"I also researched Karolina Neuman. She's listed here as a Shoah victim, killed at the Parschnitz sub-camp. Born in 1922, died in 1943. No survivors."

"No mention of her twins?"

"Nope."

"Well, think about it, Liam. Who would know about the twins?"

"Are you kidding? Lena would know. She may have been the very person who gave the information about Karolina to the museum. But she didn't say anything about the twins."

"And you find that disturbing?"

"Well, yeah."

"Any luck finding Muriel or Chaya?"

"Chaya is deceased. She died in 1945. Probably on the death march. But I had better luck with Muriel. She's still alive. I was given an address in New York and I believe she still lives there. I've tried to contact her, but so far I've had no luck."

"So now what?"

"I'm going first to Scharmassing, Germany. I'm going to try to track down the Schultz family. That would seem to be the logical starting point to finding the twins. If they survived being cast into a field from a moving train. If somebody found them and rescued them, then they would have seen the address. I'm going there first."

"I agree. That makes sense."

"How's my little tyke doing? Growing fast?"

"Kicking the stuffings out of me and keeping me up at night."

"Then it's probably a boy, and with legs like that, the Chicago Bears will want to take a look at him."

"It could be a girl, you know."

"Well, then, she'll be kicking ass in some courtroom like her mother."

"Do you want to know?"

"Nope."

"So when do you leave for Germany?"

"Tomorrow. Tonight I'm having dinner with Kayla Cummings."

"Kayla? Seriously? Do I have to worry about you two again?"

"Again? What's that supposed to mean?"

"It means I worried about the two of you before. Tell me you're not having dinner in Hebron. You know she's a reckless intelligence agent. She's pulled you into the battlefields before."

"Do I sense a return of Cat jealousy?"

"No. Maybe I was last year when you were spending so much time with a gorgeous spy on the beaches of Hawaii and chasing after Sophie Sommers."

"On the beaches of Hawaii? I think it was me and a suspicious jealous woman named Catherine on the beaches of Hawaii, whose unreasonable suspicions were proven to be false. And besides, we were chasing after Arif al-Zahani, a terrorist in Israel."

"Right. Through Hebron, the most dangerous city in the world. You tell her that you can't be entering any danger zones, you're about to be a father."

"I'll be sure to do that."

"Okay. Tell Kayla I said hello and I'm happy that's she's doing well."

"I will."

"And just mention that Liam Taggart is now a *married* man with a family."

"Ha, ha. I'll do that. I love you, good-bye."

FORTY-FOUR

• • •

L IAM LANDED AT THE Munich airport, rented a car and drove north toward Regensburg through the rolling farmlands of Bavaria, a patchwork of greens and golds. Arriving in Regensburg late in the afternoon, he booked a room at the Muencher Hof, on the main square near the Danube. A dinner of schnitzel, a couple steins of Erdinger weissbier, a walk around the old city and Liam retired for the night.

After breakfast, Liam drove south to the little rural village of Scharmassing and 155 Dorfstrasse, the last known address for Siegfried Schultz. The white stone two-story house with a red tiled roof had been well cared for. Liam, carrying a German-English dictionary in his hand, rang the doorbell and an older man in gray slacks and blue cotton shirt, buttoned at the neck, came to the door.

"Ja, was wollen Sie?"

"Do you speak English? *Sprechen Sie Englisch?"*

"Ja. A little." He pinched his thumb and index finger to show how little he spoke.

"Thank you. My name is Liam Taggart and I'm looking for the family of Siegfried Schultz."

"Siegfried Schultz?" He shook his head. "*Ich weiß nicht,* I don't know Siegfried Schultz."

"He used to live here. In 1941."

"1941? Ach. Seventy years." He shrugged. "I'm here for only forty. The man before me, his name was Burger. Not Schultz."

"Siegfried Schultz was a soldier. His mother lived here. I think she may have taken in two little babies in 1943."

"Two babies?"

Liam nodded.

"Why do you need to know?"

"The two babies were lost during the war. I'm working for the mother who lost them."

He shrugged. "I come from Pfaffenberg in 1963. I would not know anything about babies."

Liam turned to leave and the man called, "Excuse me, please, Herr Taggart. Fräu Strauss, she is eighty-six, but she knows of everybody in Scharmassing. Go to her. Twenty-two Rosenstrasse in Oberhinkofen. It's just down the road. Tell her Werner sent you." He smiled and nodded. "She speaks Englisch, *ja.*"

"Thank you very much. *Danke,*" Liam said.

The Strauss townhome was just a few miles away. She answered the door in a formless blue-and-pink-patterned housedress and pink fur-lined moccasins. Her hair was silver-gray and rolled into a bun. She squinted at Liam.

"Fräu Strauss, Werner sent me to you."

"Werner Hoffman?"

"I think so. On Dorfstrasse."

She pursed her lips, thought a minute, nodded, stepped back from the door and said, "Come in."

She walked into her living room and gestured for him to follow with a quick brushing flip of her hand. "Sit."

Her living room was furnished with large overstuffed pieces covered in floral fabrics. And white doilies. Doilies sat on the tables, on the arms of the chairs and on the backs of the couch cushions. Liam sat gently on the edge of the couch.

"I'm looking for the family of Siegfried Schultz. He used to live at 155 Dorfstrasse."

"Yes. Of course. Helga Schultz."

Liam smiled broadly. "Wonderful. Did Helga have any children besides Siegfried? Did she have two little girls?"

Fräu Strauss tilted her head back and stared with one eye. "Why are you wanting to know? Is this legitimate?"

Liam laughed. "Absolutely. I'm an investigator tracking down the story of two little babies that were left behind and lost during the war. I believe they may have been taken to Fräu Schultz. In fact, her son Siegfried may have been the father. I'm working for a friend of their mother who now lives in America."

"Hmm. Helga never said anything about Siegfried having children. And she would have. She wanted grandchildren. I didn't have any, and Helga would have bragged. Oh my, she would have bragged." She shook her head. "Siegfried was killed during the war, you know. In Ukraine."

"Siegfried may not have wanted to tell his mother about the babies until he could see her in person."

"*Ja,* that would make sense. But he never came back from the front."

"And the babies? Did anyone bring two babies to Fräu Schultz?"

Fräu Strauss shook her head. "No. No babies. Siegfried was Helga's only child. She would have loved to have two babies. She would have told me for sure. When Siegfried died, Helga had no use for the farm. She sold her farm in 1950 and moved into town. She passed in 1974. She didn't have much when she died, and what she had she left to the church. She had no surviving relatives."

Liam sighed and stood to leave. "Thank you for your time, Fräu Strauss."

"Sorry I could not be much help to you in your investigation."

"Actually, you did help. You crossed a possibility off the list. Thanks again."

Liam called Catherine from the Munich airport and gave her a report.

"Are you coming home?" Catherine asked.

"Not yet. I'm flying to Kraków in an hour. I'm going to trace the route of the train and make inquiries for a couple of days. Maybe someone will come forward."

"Liam, we're running out of time. The court date is approaching and if we don't have some proof of Karolina or the twins, I'll have a hard time countering Arthur's argument that they don't exist. Especially now that we know she never mentioned them at Yad Vashem. You've got to find some evidence."

"That deadline's unreasonable. It's possible someone will have a memory of two babies being found by the railroad tracks, or maybe Muriel Bernstein will surface to confirm Lena's story, but we need more time. I think you should move for a continuance, maybe a couple months."

"I don't think Peterson will give it to me. I'm not his favorite lawyer, you know."

"It can't hurt to try. Hell, just sixty days. What's the rush?"

"You heard Peterson. He's protecting the vulnerable elderly who are mercifully brought under his wings in the probate division."

"Lena didn't look so vulnerable when she was there. She scared the crap out of Arthur."

"Yes, she did. I'll file the motion. Maybe he'll give us sixty days. Good luck in Poland."

FORTY-FIVE

...

O N TUESDAY MORNING, CATHERINE arrived
at Lena's home on Pearson Street. She entered
the condominium, handed her coat to Lena and
strolled to the windows to gaze at Lake Michigan. The
wind was churning up the lake and eight-foot whitecaps
were crashing against the retaining wall, spraying water
onto Lake Shore Drive.

"I wanted you to see something special to me," Lena
said. She walked over to her breakfront and opened the
glass door. She pointed to a little pedestal sitting on a
shelf all by itself. A treasured centerpiece in her cabinet.
"Do you see that? Do you know what it is?"

Catherine nodded. "I do. It's Milosz's shoe."

"Arthur thinks I'm silly for displaying it like that.
A battered child's shoe placed so prominently when I
could display my fine china and silver pieces. But it's
all I have left of my family in Chrzanów. It's the only
thing to show that they ever existed. If something happens to me, Catherine, or when my time is finished, I
want you to have it."

Catherine swallowed hard. "Oh no, I can't. It belongs
to your family."

Lena smiled and hugged Catherine. "That is how I think of you. To Arthur it will mean nothing."

"It will mean something to me, Lena. I'd be proud to have it."

"Good. Then let me finish my story and together we shall try to find the twins."

"I have to tell you, so far, Liam has had no luck. The twins weren't taken to Siegfried's mother. She died without any surviving family. Liam intends to make inquiries of people along the train route. Yad Vashem has no record of the twins."

"I know that, but no one at Yad Vashem would have known their names. We didn't pin the names on the children for fear they would be identified as Jewish. I was at Yad Vashem and when I gave my history, I asked whether any Polish citizens reported finding two young babies by a railroad track. They had no record of any such reports from our area. They told me that many orphaned children were saved by the Allies when they overran Germany and Poland, but many of them were in camps or were found in orphanages."

"But you didn't tell the historians at Yad Vashem about Rachel and Leah, did you?"

Lena shook her head. "I did not. I could not."

"The twins could certainly have been among those rescued, Lena. That should make you feel a little more at ease. Even if we can't locate them, it's possible that they were rescued."

"I want to believe that. But unless Liam is successful, I'll never know. I'm so pleased he's making inquiries."

"I have to be honest with you. Without some proof of Karolina's twins, we'll have a tough time with Arthur's petition. He'll tell the story of how you've become fixated on them—your maps, your research, the train schedules.

That's evidence that the quest has taken a prominent place in your life. He'll try to create a presumption."

"A presumption of what?"

"That you suffer from an all-consuming obsession. And if we have no proof of their birth or their existence, he'll assert it's all a delusion."

"How does a presumption affect us?"

"It means that the burden of going forward with the evidence would shift. Arthur claims it's all imaginary—Karolina and the babies–and it would become your obligation to produce evidence to prove that they existed. So far, Liam can't find any. A failure to rebut the presumption could result in a conclusion that your compulsive search for the babies is a product of mental deterioration."

Lena nodded.

"Judge Peterson's not required to reach that conclusion. He can view all the evidence, including your testimony, and decide that you're just fine. I think you make a very good witness. You certainly acquitted yourself nicely when you were last in court."

"But he could, right? He could find me to be delusional and put me in a home?"

Catherine shrugged. "He could. But we'll fight like hell to prevent that from happening. And don't count out Liam."

"Thank you."

"All right, then, let's get back to the story."

"As I told you, David and I married and settled into the house where I was a squatter. David tried to set up a little tailor shop in the square. He somehow managed to obtain a sewing machine and cleaned out a storefront. He put up signs and we passed out flyers, but he couldn't make a go of it."

"Strange. He was such a good tailor. He managed the

Shop and ran the textile operation at Gross-Rosen. How come he couldn't make it work?"

"I could say because of the postwar economy, but that wouldn't be entirely accurate. Our community, the forty percent of Chrzanów that we grew up with, was gone. Like all the other small towns in Poland, the Jewish community had been eradicated. Deported. Shipped out to the camps. And remember, for years the Nazis ran a huge propaganda campaign telling everyone that Jews were the anti-Christ. People were told not to do business with Jews. Posters depicted Jews as ugly, sneaky, dirty monsters that spread disease.

"The few of us that returned after the war faced a town that had been subjected to and even tolerated Nazi propaganda for over ten years. Many blamed the Jews for the war. After all, they saw the war as Hitler's campaign to rid Europe of the Jewish scourge. Goebbels ran a very effective propaganda machine. I'm not saying everybody harbored these feelings, and there are always exceptions, but generally Polish towns were unfriendly to returning survivors. It was obvious to David and me that we were unwelcome and unable to integrate into the non-Jewish fabric of Chrzanów.

"David had a tailor shop, but he couldn't compete with the tailor shop owned by a Catholic on the other side of the square. Money was very tight and I don't know how he did it, and I guess I didn't want to know, but David began to make money by smuggling cigarettes."

"Seriously? He was a smuggler?"

Lena laughed and held her hand to her mouth in jocular embarrassment. "He was. My husband the pirate. He'd go off in the middle of the night, meet up with people and come back with cartons of cigarettes. He'd sell them to the Russians and throughout the town. He made enough money for us to live comfortably, but we knew we couldn't make a life in Chrzanów.

"Poland was becoming a Soviet satellite, behind the Iron Curtain, and Stalin was appointing ministers to run the government. They weren't friendly to Jews either. Communism, and the anti-Semitism that lay beneath the surface, was forcing us to consider immigrating to other lands. David's brother had immigrated to New York before the war and he now lived in Chicago. We decided to join him, but we needed a visa, and in 1945 that was impossible.

"For several years, Western countries had established strict quotas on immigration, especially for Jews. After the war, Great Britain, Canada and the U.S. were still enforcing tight immigration quotas for European refugees and they were reluctant to relax them. David figured the best way to get to America was to enter an American Displaced Persons Camp and apply for a visa."

"I can't believe the two of you wanted to live in another camp."

"It was how we would get to America. If we stayed in Chrzanów, we would have been stuck behind the Iron Curtain in an unfriendly town. We didn't have any other choice. This was also a conclusion reached by two hundred and fifty thousand other Jews.

"At the end of the war, in May 1945, there were seven to eight million displaced persons wandering around Europe. A million and a half of them were German soldiers. By July, the number of DPs had been reduced to four million. By September, all but a million had been repatriated to their home countries. But of the million that remained, two hundred and fifty thousand were Jews that had no place to go, for the reasons I've just explained. We were the unrepatriables. We called ourselves the *She'erit ha-Pletah*, the surviving remnant.

"To address the refugee problem, the Allied countries set up camps in Allied-occupied Germany, Austria and Italy. They were little towns, little communities for us to live in until we could find a home. There were British, French and American camps. David researched the camps and decided we would go to Foehrenwald, in the U.S. zone. It was south of Munich in the foothills of the Austrian Alps. We would take a train to Vienna, then to Munich and make our way down to Foehrenwald, but before we left, I had one more thing I had to do.

"I told David to borrow a horse and wagon and take me to Auschwitz. 'Are you crazy?' he said. 'Why would you want to return to the gates of hell?'

"'Take me to Auschwitz. I want to stand there and see it through liberated eyes.'

"It was October, the leaves were turning and we traveled south thirteen miles to Oświęcim. The Silesian hills were bathed in oranges, yellows, reds and browns. Clip-clopping along with no fear of capture or death, it was hard to believe this pastoral setting was a theater of war just nine months earlier. We entered Auschwitz's buffered area along the railroad tracks. The barbed wire fences were still in place and we followed the tracks right up to the main gate. The iron sign, ARBEIT MACHT FREI, still arched above the entrance.

"I got out of the wagon and walked into the vacant camp. It was surreal. It held no terror for me any longer. In many ways it was satisfying, knowing the Germans had been defeated, that their vicious reign of evil had been vanquished. It was divine closure. I walked slowly through Auschwitz and then to Birkenau. The grounds of torment and depravity were now empty. Of the vast execution chambers, only four brick chimneys remained, reminding society of the wickedness that once lived here. I showed David the barracks where I slept and where

Chaya befriended me. I showed him the kitchen where I worked. I said all my good-byes. I closed the book and I have not been back since.

"We packed our bags and left for Foehrenwald the next day."

FORTY-SIX

...

L IAM BOARDED THE TRAIN in Chrzanów for the trip to Rogoznica, the very same route that Karolina took with Lena, Muriel and the two babies. He sat on the right-hand side, by the windows, just as Karolina and Lena had. On his lap was an iPad that would tell him the precise GPS coordinates as the train proceeded north. Agnesa, a twenty-year-old college student with long brown hair, a checkered blouse and blue jeans, sat beside Liam chatting with him and telling him about the towns they passed. Liam had hired Agnesa in Kraków to be his interpreter. He knew he'd be traveling through rural communities where he couldn't depend on everyone to speak English, and he'd quickly come to terms with his limitations—Polish was too tough a language to traverse with a pocket dictionary.

Liam kept a careful lookout for track sidings. Lena had said the babies were thrown soon after they left a siding. In seventy years, one could expect a railroad line to change somewhat, but Liam was confident he could mark the likely spots. Thankfully, the Communists hadn't wanted to spend a lot of money on infrastructure and the railroad lines appeared to be unchanged.

The trip covered one hundred seventy miles and took about three hours. Unlike Karolina's trip, which took days, the train traveled quickly with few stops. Liam had to be quick to click and save the GPS coordinates at the precise moments, but he thought he covered it pretty well. Each time there was a railroad siding, he'd save the location.

When he arrived in Rogoznica, he and Agnesa rented a car and retraced the path, stopping at each GPS point to survey the area. Forests covered a substantial part of the journey, and Liam knew that the babies weren't thrown into a forest. Railroad sidings in those areas were crossed off the list.

Farmlands that sat just beyond a railroad siding, the kind described by Lena, where the babies could have been deposited, were whittled down to four. Only four possible areas to canvass where someone might have found an abandoned baby. In each of the four locations, Liam and Agnesa stopped to knock on doors. How long has your family been living here? Do you know the name of the family that lived here in 1943? Have you ever heard a story about a baby that was found out in the meadow by the train tracks? Do you know of someone in town who would know what went on in 1943?

In the town of Domaniów, in the rural administrative district called Gmina Domaniów, they hit the bull's-eye. A very old man, the keeper of the town's post office, nodded his head. "There were *two* little babies, not just one. One was found over there." He pointed south, toward the tracks. "One over there." He pointed north.

Liam's heart was pounding hard against his chest. "The babies, were they found alive?"

The old man nodded. "Oh, yes. Both of them. No one knew where they came from, but we figured they would have come off of a train. Crazy things happened during the war." He leaned forward. "Especially to Jews, you know." Liam nodded. He knew.

"The babies were each wrapped up nice and warm. They even had an address pinned to them, an address somewhere in the middle of Germany. Nobody around here was going to take any baby hundreds of miles into the middle of Germany during the war. No sir."

"What happened? Who raised those babies?"

"Well, they were found by Ena Wolczyk, but she didn't keep them. She was getting up there in age. She asked around and, it being the war and all, it was hard to find a family that wanted to take the responsibility of raising two little ones."

"What did Ena do with the babies?"

"Not really sure. I just know that no one in Domanióv raised them."

Liam sighed. "How can we find out what happened to them?"

The old man shrugged. "Ena's long gone. Her daughter's passed as well. I don't know."

"If I write out a notice, like a little sign, one that says if you have any information about the two babies found by Ena Wolczyk in 1943, would you please call the following, could you hang it here in the post office?"

"Sure. Happy to help."

Liam turned to Agnesa. "Would you make a sign for me, please? Attach a few of my cards to the bottom."

Liam handed the paper to the old man and said, "I really appreciate your help. You have no idea how happy this is going to make a woman back in Chicago. Those babies were born to a very close friend of hers. A girl named Karolina. Knowledge that the babies survived will set her mind at ease."

"Karolina, huh? Well, I'm happy to help. If anyone has any information about these babies, I'll be sure to get ahold of you."

"One more thing. Is there an orphanage nearby?"

The man nodded. "I think there's one run by the church in Wroclaw. About an hour straight east. Might not be such a bad idea. Pretty sharp thinking."

IN AN OFFICE, IN a two-hundred-year-old gothic church in Wroclaw, Poland, Sister Maria looked through her file cabinet and her stack of note cards. "There were many Jewish children hidden by orphanages during the war,' she said in perfect English. 'Including here at St. Stanislaus, all at great risk to the sisters, I might add. From time to time, the SS would barge through here and demand IDs for the children. They'd want to know the ancestry for each of our wards. We forged papers and forged birth certificates for every Jewish child we took in. A child old enough to understand was given a Christian name and told to never speak his Jewish name. Sometimes we were able to place children with a Polish family. At the end of the war, the remaining Jewish children were sent to DP camps. I have the records for 1943 right here."

She thumbed through the index cards and shook her head. "I don't see any twins being admitted. There were baby girls that were dropped off, especially in 1942 and 1943, when the ghettos were being cleared out, but none that are noted to be twins. Of course, I wasn't here back then, so I don't know all the stories. And though we're taught never to lie"—she winked—"the index cards didn't always tell the truth."

"This would have been in mid-April," Liam said. "I believe they were brought here by Ena Wolczyk from the village of Domaniów. She wasn't Jewish."

Sister Maria nodded and thumbed through the cards again. "There were two babies brought here in April 1943. The notes reflect that neither one was brought in by the mother."

"That's it!" Liam said.

Sister Maria continued to shake her head. "They weren't twins."

"How do you know?"

"One was five months old and the other was three months old."

"Do your records show who adopted the children?"

"Certainly."

"May I know their names?"

"Certainly not. That would be strictly against our adoption rules and Poland's adoption laws."

Liam leaned forward in his chair, crossed his hands on the desk as he had in his catechism days, and said, "Sister, may I tell you the story about the woman who hired me?"

When he had finished telling Sister Maria about Lena, he said, "I have a gut feeling that these babies were really twins and when the church drafted forged IDs, they wrote them down as being from two different families, of two different ages. Lena Scheinman made a promise to their mother to find them. How could it possibly hurt to bend the rules just a little bit? It isn't like Lena would interfere with their upbringing or harm the relationship with their adoptive parents. If these women are still alive, they're seventy-two years old."

"I'm afraid it's quite impossible. Under no circumstances can I *voluntarily* give you private information protected by law." Sister Maria looked directly into Liam's eyes. "Do you understand me?"

"Perfectly."

"Good. I will take your name and number and let you

know if anything turns up. But if you will please excuse me for just a minute, I need to check and see when Mass is served today."

With that, Sister Maria pushed the two cards to the middle of the desk, left the room and closed the door. Liam quickly copied the information from the cards and replaced them on the desk.

CAT, THEY SURVIVED! THE twins! They survived and were rescued by a woman in Domaniów, Poland."

"Liam, I can't believe it. Are they still alive?"

"I don't know. Actually, there's a lot I don't know, but I'm much further along than when I started. If Ena Wolczyk took them to the Wroclaw orphanage in April 1943, then I know their last names."

"I don't understand."

"Ena Wolczyk, long since dead, lived in Domaniów. She found the two babies alive in the wheat fields by the tracks. She wasn't able to raise them and she didn't keep them. No one in Domaniów today knows what she did with them. I figured she might have given them to an orphanage, so I visited St. Stanislaus Catholic Church in a nearby city. Sure enough, the sisters ran an orphanage during the war. Their records show that they took in two babies in April 1943, but the records also say they were different ages. The index cards reflect that one was three months and the other was five months. That might have just been their way of deceiving the Nazis. Anyway, I have the names of the families that adopted the babies after the war and their addresses."

"How did you learn that? Adoption agencies don't disclose that information."

"Ah, it's me Irish charm."

"It always worked on me. So what are you doing now? We don't have much more time. And what about Muriel Bernstein?"

"I have two families and two addresses, albeit from the forties, but I'm going tracking. And Muriel still hasn't returned my calls. I'll keep trying."

"Lena will be thrilled to hear about your discoveries. Do you think I should tell her before we know for sure?"

"We *do* know for sure. Karolina's twins survived. They were thrown out of the window of a moving train by two desperate women and they lived. The Domaniów postman even told me they had addresses pinned to them when they were found. I'm just not certain what happened to them afterward. I'll bet they went to the orphanage, and that's the lead I'm going to follow. But, Cat, it's going to take time. My information is seventy years old. You've got to get that continuance."

"I filed the motion. It'll be heard tomorrow morning."

"Good luck. Love you. Take care of the little tyke-to-be."

FORTY-SEVEN

...

JUDGE PETERSON READ THE motion as Catherine and Shirley stood silently before the bench.

"Why do you need sixty days?" Judge Peterson said, peering over his reading glasses.

"Because our investigator has established evidence that the twins existed and survived the war," Catherine answered. "He is presently in Poland endeavoring to contact them."

"Why is that important to me?"

"We are here in your courtroom because the petitioner has alleged that Lena Woodward suffers from an obsession to find two girls who never existed. We know now that they did exist and were alive in 1943."

"For my purposes as a judge of the probate division, does that resolve all of the issues in the petition? Mr. Woodward has alleged there is mental deterioration based on dementia. He's alleged she is consumed by an obsessive desire to find two children, whether they existed or not, and that the obsession is a psychological disorder brought on by her age, isn't all that so?"

"Yes, Your Honor, but the entire factual basis for that assertion is flawed because—"

"Factual basis, Ms. Lockhart? Aren't we now talking about what goes on in a trial? I mean, one lawyer introduces facts, then the other lawyer introduces facts, and then some judge, in this case me, decides which facts will carry the day. Have I described a trial correctly, Ms. Lockhart?"

"Yes, but the entire factual foundation for Mr. Woodward's petition is that the twins are imaginary, that they never existed, which he won't be able to prove. . . ."

"Then he will lose, won't he?"

"But, Your Honor, I just need an additional sixty days to secure my evidence."

Judge Peterson curled his lips. "I'm out of patience. Motion denied."

"May I have two more weeks? Just two more weeks?"

Peterson snarled and said, "Very well. Two weeks. Period. Trial starts May ninth. I will only continue it again in the event of a death. Yours. Call the next case."

B EFORE WE START TODAY, Lena, I have some wonderful news. But first you have to sit down."

"The judge granted our motion to continue the case?" Lena said as she took her seat.

"Yes, for only two weeks, but that's not the really good news. Did you take your heart medicine today?"

Lena glared in mock annoyance. "I don't take heart medicine. There's nothing wrong with my heart or my brain."

"Okay. Take a deep breath, Lena. The babies lived. They survived. Liam has learned that the babies survived. A woman in Domaniów, Poland, found them laying in the wheat fields, right by the train tracks. They had Siegfried's address pinned to their diapers."

Lena froze. Her body stiffened and she stared straight

ahead. "They lived," she whispered without moving. "They lived after all."

"Lena? Lena, look at me. Are you all right"

Lena slumped down in her chair, her hand covering her eyes and mouth. She sobbed loudly and profoundly. She cried, she laughed. Pure hysteria. Catherine quickly came to her side. "Lena, Lena, are you okay?"

"Karolina was right. She was right all along. At the cost of her sanity and her life, she saved those babies. We threw our babies out of a train to save them from certain death and she was right. They lived. Karolina, wherever you are, know that our babies lived. Thank the Lord." She looked up into Catherine's eyes, which were also filled with tears, and said, "Thank you, and thanks to Liam."

"You're all right?"

She nodded. "I don't know how to tell you this, but the pain I've carried for all these years has been lifted from my soul." She shook her head and sobbed. "Can you imagine how it feels to believe you may have heaved a lovely child to her death? Had I known this fifty, sixty years ago, I would have . . . Never mind. It doesn't matter."

"Liam believes they were taken to an orphanage and he has their adoptive names. If anyone can track them down, it's Liam. He says he has a lead. I wish I could tell you more."

"You told me they survived, and now I know Karolina and I saved their lives. You have to understand what it was like. They were the children that were never meant to be. The Judenrat, the elders, all our friends—everyone warned girls not to get pregnant. Never bring a baby into this troubled world. If a girl was so reckless, so thoughtless as to give birth, then the baby was doomed—bound to starve, be tortured or slaughtered. Can you possibly imagine the conflict of emotions that comes with giving birth during the Holocaust—the joy, the guilt, the fear, the love?" She sniffed and wiped her eyes. "But we saved our babies. Our babies lived."

Catherine waited until Lena was able to compose herself. "Do you want to go on with the story? We can talk another day."

"No, I'm all right. I'm more than all right. Let's finish up. There's not much left. David and I were on our way to the Foehrenwald DP Camp, a large camp set up by the U.S. army in a residential complex that previously housed workers for the IG Farben plant. The units were pretty nice, among the nicest of all the DP camps. They were small, but they had running water, kitchens and central heat.

"Foehrenwald's community quickly established schools, health centers and a variety of cultural activities. By the time we arrived, Foehrenwald had over four thousand residents. The United Nations Relief and Rehabilitation Agency provided food, medicine, clothing and occupational training.

"All in all, it wasn't a bad place to live, but it was a temporary solution. All the families had made applications for visas and were just waiting for their immigration papers to be processed. Most of the residents wanted to immigrate to Israel, but in 1945, Israel was not a state. That area of the Middle East was administered by Britain as British Mandatory Palestine. Neville Chamberlain's prewar strict quotas were still in effect and there was violent Arab resistance to Jewish immigration, spearheaded by the mufti of Jerusalem, Amin al-Husseini. In fact, it was the mufti's position that all Jews presently in Palestine should be forced to leave. Of course, the situation changed in 1948, when Israel became a state.

"Actually, 1948 was a pivotal year for us as well. The United States Congress passed the Displaced Persons Act, allowing for up to two hundred thousand war refugees to enter the U.S. Still, it wasn't easy, especially for Jews. You had to have a sponsor and an ability to earn a living. We were lucky because David's brother was already living on the West Side of Chicago and he sponsored us. We got our visa and arrived in January 1949."

Catherine's phone buzzed and she picked up the receiver. Gladys said, "Cat, Liam's on the other line and he wants to talk to you, but he doesn't want you to take the call in front of Lena."

Catherine stood. "Lena, I have to take an important call in my office. Please excuse me for a few minutes. Let Gladys know if you want some coffee or need anything."

With the door closed, Catherine answered the call. "What's up? Tell me you found the twins."

"Not yet. I'm closing in on one, but that's not why I called. I just got off the phone with Muriel Bernstein. Let me play you the recording."

"You recorded the telephone call?"

"Yep."

"Liam, did you get her permission to record the call?"

"Oh, it must have slipped my mind. Would you please just listen?

"Okay."

"Hello. This is Muriel."

"Muriel, my name is Liam Taggart. I'm a private investigator and I've been hired by Lena Scheinman."

"Lena? Oh, my word. She's alive? I haven't spoken to her since the middle of the war. Is she all right?"

"She's fine. More than fine—she's as healthy as can be. Her name is now Lena Woodward."

"Woodward? She married David Woodward?"

"Sure did. They were happily married for over sixty years. He died two years ago."

"You have no idea how that warms my heart. I would love to see Lena. Where does she live?"

"In Chicago. Just a two-hour plane ride away from you. Maybe I can arrange it. Can I tell you about my assignment?"

"By all means. How can I help you?"

"During the war, as I'm sure you must remember, Lena made a solemn vow to Karolina that she would return and find Karolina's twins."

"Karolina's twins?"

"Right."

"Karolina Neuman?"

"Yes. Of course."

<Silence>

"Muriel?"

"Mr. Taggart, exactly what did Lena tell you?"

"You don't remember the promise?"

"Why don't you refresh my memory?"

"On the train to Gross-Rosen, the three of you were sitting together, is that right?"

"Oh, yes. We boarded the train in Chrzanów. It was actually a passenger train."

"Exactly. And Karolina was holding her twins when a woman came by and told her that the Nazis would kill her babies as soon as they arrived at the camp. Karolina then threw one baby out of the window and Lena threw the other one. Lena and Karolina vowed to come back and find Karolina's babies."

<Silence>

"Muriel?"

"What is it that you want from me, Mr. Taggart?"

"A few months ago, Lena hired me to try to find Karolina's babies and I'm very close to doing just that. I'm pleased to tell you that both of them survived and were taken to a nearby orphanage. But Lena's son has initiated a legal proceeding to declare Lena incompetent and stop her from keeping her promise to find Karolina's twins. He's alleged in court that Karolina's babies never existed and that his mother is delusional."

"How awful for Lena. Oh my goodness, by her own son? But you haven't answered my question, Mr. Taggart. What do you want from me?"

"Well, if you were so disposed, I'd like you to come to Chicago and testify in court that Karolina had twins, that they actually existed and that Lena promised to come back and find them. Lena can defeat her son's petition with your testimony."

"How about Karolina? Do you know what became of Karolina Neuman?"

"Unfortunately, she died at the Parschnitz concentration camp. According to Lena, she was so distraught about losing her babies that she tried to escape and was shot by the guards."

"How terribly sad. Well, I don't travel much anymore. I'm afraid I can't come to Chicago."

"That's all right, Muriel. Lena's attorney can take your testimony with a video deposition in New York. We can come to you."

"You don't want to do that, Mr. Taggart."

"Yes, we do. I haven't found those girls yet, and without your testimony Lena may lose her case."

"My testimony won't help Lena."

"Why not? You were the nurse who delivered the twins in the Chrzanów ghetto, weren't you?"

"Yes, I was."

"Lena needs to prove that Karolina's twins really existed. Why is that so hard for you?"

"Talk to Lena. Good-bye."

Liam turned off the recorder. "Did you hear that, Cat? Can you believe she won't testify?"

"Yes. And I think I know why."

"I'm listening."

"Karolina Neuman never had twins. She never had any babies. Muriel won't give a video deposition to support Lena's story because it isn't true. Muriel delivered the babies all right, but they weren't Karolina's. They were Lena's. Lena had the twins."

"Holy shit. And the whole story about Karolina's babies?"

"Was a cover-up. Lena Scheinman loved David Woodward and they spent nights together in his room. Lena got pregnant. David was sent away a few weeks later and never knew. They were David's babies."

"Oh, my God."

"I've had my suspicions all along, but when you told me about Fräu Strauss and what she said about Helga Schultz, that started me to thinking. You know, I always told you I suspected there was a deep, dark secret. Over the past few days, I went back through my notes and there they were—all the clues. Now that you've told me about Muriel, I'm certain. When Lena was describing the birth of the babies, she was talking about herself. If you reverse Lena and Karolina, the relationship, the story, it all fits together."

"What about the conversation they had when they were bathing, when Lena first noticed that Karolina was pregnant?" Liam said. "And they discussed abortion."

"Reverse it."

"But what about Siegfried? Lena asked Karolina whether she could live in Bavaria as Siegfried's wife. Didn't they talk about raising Siegfried's Jewish babies in Germany?"

"No. The talk was about whether Karolina and Siegfried could make a life together in Germany. When he wrote to his mother, he told her about falling in love with a German girl. He never told her about children. Even when Siegfried wrote down his address, he did it so that Karolina could live with his mother. Nothing on the paper alerts his mother to children. Think about it. Fräu Strauss told you she never heard of Siegfried fathering any children, and she would have because Helga Schultz would have bragged about them.

"When they needed coal from Siegfried, they twisted his arm by threatening to bring the babies to the Shop and tell everyone that they were *his* babies. The way Lena describes it, Siegfried was shocked and said, '*My* babies? Why would you do that?' He was shocked because they weren't his.

"Ninety percent of Lena's narration was true. Karolina had an affair with Siegfried. She slept with him to save Lena's life, but she didn't get pregnant. Karolina didn't have the twins—Muriel practically told you that. Lena was the one who gave birth. Karolina, Muriel and Lena lived in Yossi's basement apartment with *Lena's* twins. They shared the babysitting duties by alternating shifts.

"The rest of the story, Lena's involvement in the network, was all true. Through your research you verified the identities of Colonel Müller and Witold Pilecki. I'm sure it's true that the colonel arranged for her to be sent to Gross-Rosen rather than Auschwitz. I'm equally certain that a woman on the train warned them about the Nazis, and confirmed what they already knew, that the Nazis would take the babies when they arrived. The story about throwing the babies out of the window is absolutely true, you've proven it. They were rescued in Domaniów, Poland. Whether it was Karolina's idea or Lena's, I don't know. I tend to think it was Karolina's. She seemed to be the stronger of the two—that is, until they arrived at Gross-Rosen, but it really doesn't matter. For seventy years, Lena has concealed the fact that she was the mother of those twins.

"The clues were all there, Liam. I just didn't see them. She continually referred to the babies as *our* babies. Even Karolina's last words were 'You'll survive and find *our* babies.' Not *my* babies. It all makes sense, Liam. She waited all these years to begin her search because she couldn't tell David that she had killed his daughters. She told me that she refused to discuss the Holocaust or any part of it with David or anyone else for many years.

"David never knew he had daughters. Don't you remember her saying that David wanted daughters? Do you remember how Arthur derided her in court, saying she only wanted a daughter, not a son? She couldn't do it, Liam. She couldn't tell David that he *did* have daughters and that she'd heaved them out of the window of a moving train and probably killed them.

"Lena was crippled with guilt, but she was too afraid to find out about the babies while David was still alive. It was all bottled up inside of her, and a few years ago it was just too much. She's in her eighties, and if she's ever going to keep that promise, she'd better do it now. So, she made up the story about Karolina and a desire to return to Poland to find out what happened to Karolina's twins. It was all a cover-up.

"When I gave her your news, that the babies had survived, she became hysterical like nothing I'd ever seen. She reacted as only a mother could. Now we have confirmation from Muriel. What possible reason would there be for Muriel to refuse to help her friend? Think about it. Because she'd have to reveal the truth and she feared that telling the truth would hurt Lena."

"Are you going to tell Lena that you know?"

"Not right now. There's no reason to do that, and I think she's too vulnerable, too susceptible to a breakdown.

For the time being, let's just say you found out that Karolina's twins survived."

"How are you going to handle the trial?"

"That's a good question. I haven't figured that one out yet. Peterson wouldn't give me more than two weeks, so I'll have to be ready. I've subpoenaed Lena's doctor; he'll be a good witness. I have her medical records. I've subpoenaed Mr. Forrester, the IDA agent. I'll do the best I can. How close are you to finding out anything more about the children?"

"Pretty damn close on one. The other one is a dead end—the family originally lived in Wroclaw but moved in the early fifties with no forwarding address. At least, not one I can find. Remember, Poland was behind the Iron Curtain, a Communist puppet, and all of its official records were secret. They were only released within the last twenty years. Digging through these archives is impossible."

"But you're close on one of the girls, right? If you find one, that's all we need."

"Well, maybe. If she's still alive, if the woman would be cooperative, if she would agree to testify, if she knew she was adopted, if she knew she was tossed from a railroad train, if she was the right age, and if their DNA matched. There's a lot of 'ifs.' I'm zeroing in, but you're not giving me very much time."

"I'm giving you all I have."

"Okay. Talk to you later. Love you."

Catherine returned to the conference room, where Lena and Gladys were engaged in an animated conversation.

"Lena, are you ready to finish up?"

"There's not much more. I've told you almost everything I know. When we got to Chicago, David opened up a tailor shop. What else would he do? But, as I told you, David was an entrepreneur."

"Don't tell me he smuggled cigarettes."

Lena laughed. "No. But he bought a couple little grocery stores in the neighborhood, and he invested his money wisely. He and I studied the financial markets together, and we became quite astute on market movements. Together we formed D. Morris Woodward Investments. Sixty-two years ago, we had Arthur."

Catherine held up her hand. "Let me stop you for a minute. When did you first start talking to David about Karolina's twins?"

"Why does that matter?"

Catherine shrugged. "It could come up in the hearing."

"Maybe four years ago."

"Never before that? Are you saying that you never told David about the babies until four years ago?"

"That's right. I told you that I wanted to move on and not talk about what happened during the war. It's true that I gave a history to Yad Vashem and I've been involved with survivors' groups, but I never wanted to talk about my personal experiences until I came to you. David and I did not share all of our wartime experiences with each other. It was too painful for each of us. Too personal. David never knew what happened with Rolf. He never knew about my experiences in Auschwitz."

"But four years ago you brought up Karolina for the first time."

"I only said that my friend Karolina had twins. David was gone when she gave birth. He asked what happened to them and I told him Karolina abandoned them in a field. Nothing about the train. I told him that I made a promise to try to find them, but that I didn't think it was possible, so I had never tried. That's as much as he ever knew."

"When we first started our sessions, you told me that David urged you to keep your promise and find Karolina's twins."

"Did I say that?"

"Yes, it's right in my notes."

"Well, I don't understand why any of this is very important. I didn't try to do anything for sixty years because I couldn't deal with it. It was all too traumatic. I could not face trying to find a baby that I threw out of a window. I couldn't face the memories of Karolina. Surely you can appreciate that." She wiped a tear with her fingertips.

Catherine reached over and placed her hand on Lena's shoulder. "Of course, I do. I'm sorry to be so adversarial. I guess it's just my nature as a lawyer."

Lena stood to leave. "Just knowing that the babies didn't die, that they survived the ordeal and were later adopted, that's really more than I could have ever hoped to learn. You know, I really don't care what happens in court in two weeks. It doesn't matter anymore. You and Liam have fulfilled my promise. The babies lived. Karolina and I, we made the right decision when we threw them into the fields."

"Who made the decision, Lena? Was it you or Karolina?"

"Oh, it was Karolina. After all, they were her babies."

FORTY-EIGHT

...

WHEN LIAM RETURNED TO Chicago, he received a text message from Arthur. It read, "Please meet with me in advance of the court hearing. Just you and me. No lawyers."

"What do you suppose he wants?" Catherine said.

"No idea. Maybe he would like to pitch a deal."

"The only deal Lena would accept is a total withdrawal of the petition."

"I think if that's what he had in mind it wouldn't be necessary to meet. My guess is that he wants financial control, and for that, he'd give up an appointment as guardian of the person."

Catherine nodded. "Could be. Did you set up a meeting?"

"Not without talking to you."

"Go ahead. See what he wants."

IN A WICKER PARK coffee shop, Arthur sat alone, his hands around a cup of cappuccino. He stood when Liam walked in.

"Thanks for coming," Arthur said. "I know there's a lot

of animosity between our two offices, but I hope to have a little powwow and smoke a peace pipe, if you know what I mean. I really don't want to hurt my mother."

"Seriously? Maybe you never read the memo, but filing a petition to declare your mother incompetent isn't going to get you nominated for son of the year."

"Peace pipe, Liam."

"What's on your mind, Arthur?"

"Until just a few years ago, my mother and I never had any problems. Until this Karolina thing, we were close, sort of. I mean, as close as you can get to someone who has been through as much as my mother. I know she's telling her life history to Catherine, which was more than she ever did with me, but any person who suffered like my mother has horrors locked up inside her head. She never spoke about the Holocaust with me. Ever. Her trials and hardships were never open to discussion in our home. But I knew they were always present in her memory. Anyone who lives with a survivor knows that.

"A couple of years before my father died, she brought up a story about her childhood friend, Karolina. It came out of the blue. For whatever reason, she started telling us that she needed to honor a promise she made seventy years ago. My father—he loved her and went along with it. He even encouraged her, but before my father died, it was just talk. Now my mother wants to go find them, no matter what the financial or emotional cost.

"This Karolina thing has become a fixation. An obsession. I've talked to psychiatrists. They tell me there's serious psychological risk that emotional damage can occur when the object of someone's fixation turns out to be nothing but thin air. And believe me, this is nothing but thin air. She's living with this obsession. What happens when she finds out it's bogus? Have you thought about that? It would be very bad for her."

"It's not bogus. The children survived."

"Right. What are their names today?"

"I don't know yet."

"Look, even if Karolina's twins were real, she's never going to find them and besides, that doesn't end the case. It's about her obsession. I want to make a deal."

"It has nothing to do with the money, your inheritance?"

"Fuck, no. I don't need her inheritance. I only care about her well-being. But I don't want her spending all my dad's money or giving it away to some fictitious person or to children she never met."

"I'm sure."

"Well, whether you believe me or not really doesn't matter to me. Money squandered on lawyers and investigators to travel around the world chasing rumors and fairy tales in a wild goose chase is one thing. Giving it away to strangers is yet another. If I'm controlling the money, well, you understand."

"What's your proposition?"

"Appoint me irrevocable guardian of her estate, give me control of her finances, and I'll drop the rest. I won't put her in a home."

Liam shook his head and stood to leave. "You're an asshole."

Arthur picked up his check and threw a twenty-dollar bill on the table. "Think about it. We have court in a few days."

SHE'D PROBABLY TAKE THAT deal, Liam. I don't think she cares about fighting him anymore. She's learned the babies survived and that was the most important thing to her. She knows that a trial would be very hard on her. She doesn't want to give her personal history in an open courtroom. I'm the only one she's ever confided in. I'm afraid she'll refuse to testify. I can't imagine her taking the stand and being cross-examined by Michael Shirley. And as of today, we have no proof of the existence of the twins. What are your thoughts?"

"I know it might make sense to take the deal, but I'd like you to hold off. I'm playing a long shot. I've got something cooking. I'm pretty sure I can come through and it won't be necessary for her to testify."

"What is it?"

"I'll tell you when I come home tonight. I'm still working on it. Trust me. We still have a few days."

"Okay."

"Besides, you're the best ass-kicker I know. Don't sell yourself short. You can probably win this case in your sleep without my help or Lena's testimony."

"What have you been drinking?"

FORTY-NINE

•••

JUDGE PETERSON TOOK HIS seat at the raised bench and nodded to his clerk. She slammed the wooden gavel three times and announced, "Case number 13 P 6268, *In re: the Guardianship of Lena Woodward*. Cause on trial."

"Are both sides answering ready for trial?" Judge Peterson said.

Shirley snapped to his feet. "Petitioner is ready, Your Honor."

"Is respondent ready?"

Catherine stood and looked nervously around the courtroom. She looked at her watch. She looked at the door. "Respondent renews her motion for a short continuance."

"Denied. Is respondent ready for trial?"

"Very shortly, Your Honor. Can we start tomorrow?"

"No."

"This afternoon?"

"No."

Catherine reluctantly nodded. "Then respondent is ready." Catherine kept turning her head to check the door. Liam had promised he'd get there before the trial started, but he'd had a stop to make. He'd told her to stall.

"Your Honor," Catherine said. "Before we commence testimony this morning, we've received an offer from the petitioner which we would like to discuss. May we have a one-hour break to negotiate?"

"No. Discussions are over. You've had months to do your negotiations. Mr. Shirley, call your first witness."

Catherine remained standing. "Your Honor, may I have a short break to use the ladies' room. As you can see, I'm very pregnant." She smiled.

Peterson sighed loudly. "Five minutes. And then we're starting."

Lena leaned over and whispered, "Catherine, what's going on?"

"You'll find out. I hope."

Ten minutes later, Catherine returned to the courtroom and took her seat. Still no Liam. Judge Peterson said, "Finally. Mr. Shirley, call your first witness."

"Petitioner calls Mr. Arthur Woodward to the stand."

Arthur stood, looked at Catherine and Lena, shook his head, and walked to the witness stand. He swore to tell the truth and sat straight and confident. Shirley led him through a brief history of his childhood and his relationship with his mother and father. Then, after fifteen minutes, he got to the heart of the matter.

"It all began four years ago," Arthur said. "She started having these visions of someone named Karolina. I'd never heard about her before. My mother would cry. She'd tell my father that Karolina's babies are gone, someone needs to find them. She kept saying, 'I need to go to Poland and find Karolina's babies.' Babies, Your Honor, who would now be in their seventies, if they were still alive and if they ever existed. But she still calls them babies."

Arthur continued. "After my father died, it became all-consuming. She'd sit in front of the cocktail table with maps of Poland spread out everywhere. Travel brochures. Train schedules. She'd send away for information on train travel in the 1940s. She had shelves and shelves filled with GPS photos of farmland and railroad tracks. She didn't seem to want to do anything but focus on this obsession."

Lena's eyes were tearing and she sat with her handkerchief, dabbing her eyes. "I can't do this," she mumbled.

"I'd come over at night to see my mother and she'd be staring at her computer, trying to find out about people in little cities in Poland and Germany. She searched online archives and printed out small-town European newspaper clippings from the late forties. I'd tell her to give up on it. Move on. We'd have shouting matches where she'd tell me to mind my own business. I'd tell her, 'This *is* my business. Do you know how ridiculous you are, looking at a computer to find people who don't exist, who don't—"

"Stop!" Lena shouted, jumping to her feet and banging her fist on the table. "Stop this hearing! Stop it right now! I concede. Give him whatever he wants. I'll hear no more of this."

Catherine stood, put her hands on Lena's shoulders and tried to calm her. "Don't do this, Lena," she whispered. "Let's be patient. Liam told us to wait. Besides, we didn't get the chance to tell our side of the story yet. If it comes down to it, I think I can win this hearing."

"It's over, Catherine. I can't fight anymore. I can't endure this and I won't testify. I will not get on that witness stand."

"Your Honor, may we have a short recess? As you can see, my client is very upset."

"Request denied. Does Mrs. Woodward wish to admit

the allegations of the petition? Does she now agree to judgment in favor of the petitioner?"

"She does not!" yelled Liam from the back of the courtroom. "Lena, don't say another word. Catherine, I need to see you immediately."

Catherine turned to the judge. "I'm very sorry, Your Honor, but my investigator has just arrived with information that will bear on the balance of this trial. I need a few minutes, please."

Judge Peterson shook his head. "There's a witness on the stand. Your client has just confessed judgment on the pleadings . . ."

"Your Honor, just a quick moment, please? Let the record show that you were fair. If my investigator has nothing, then I won't stand in Lena's way and the case will be over. But I have the feeling that Mr. Taggart has brought us very important information that will change the course of this hearing."

"I most strenuously object," Shirley said.

"I weary of all this drama, Ms. Lockhart," Judge Peterson said. "It better be good. The court will allow you a fifteen-minute recess."

Liam turned and left the courtroom.

"What the hell is this all about?" Arthur said. "Another showboat tactic, Ms. Lockhart? Putting off the inevitable? You heard my mother. She concedes."

Catherine leaned over and whispered, "Lena, come with me."

Tears rolled out of Lena's eyes and dropped onto the courtroom table. She shook her head. "Let's just get this over with."

"Not yet. Come with me."

Catherine handed Lena her cane and helped her to her feet. They slowly walked toward the courtroom door.

"Fifteen minutes," Arthur yelled. "After that, I'm calling the shots. No more Lockhart. No more Karolina."

Lena and Catherine walked into the hall and toward Liam, who stood by the windows with two women. Catherine looked at them and smiled broadly. The women were tall, poised and stylishly dressed. They smiled warmly at Lena.

"Come on, Lena," Catherine said, prodding her forward. But Lena stood still and wouldn't move. Liam brought the two women across the hall and directly to Lena. "I'd like to introduce you to Sofia Stachiewicz and Aniela Lersky," he said, "otherwise known to you as Rachel and Leah."

Lena's face flushed, her mouth quivered, her hands shook. Catherine put her arm around her shoulders to steady her. Lena looked into Catherine's eyes.

"Karolina," Lena said softly. "They're her twins."

"No," Catherine said with a gentle smile. "Tell them the truth, Lena. It's all right."

She took a deep breath and swallowed hard. "I can't."

"Yes, you can. They already know."

Lena broke into sobs as she reached out for her babies. "I'm so sorry."

"Sorry? You gave us our lives," Sofia said. "However you did it, you had the courage to save both of our lives. Thank you. Mother."

They stood together, the three of them, warmly embracing each other for several minutes.

With her arms wrapped around Aniela, Lena said, "The last moment I held you, you had a twinkle in your eye and you smiled at me. I've held that smile in my eyes every day since 1943. You still have the same smile."

Liam whispered to Catherine, "Sorry I didn't get here earlier. Their plane was late."

"We have so much to tell you," Aniela said. "All about our lives. Liam has arranged for us to stay for the entire week."

"We want to know all about our mother and father," Sofia added.

"Oh, I wish you had known your father," Lena said. "David was a wonderful man and he would have loved to know you. If I had been stronger, maybe I'd have found you years ago and you would have known him. But I wasn't. I do have many pictures to show you."

Shirley pushed the courtroom door open, poked his head out and said, "The judge is back, Ms. Lockhart."

The five walked into the courtroom and straight up to the bench.

"Your Honor, I would like to introduce Mrs. Woodward's twin daughters, who have just arrived from Europe."

"What?" Arthur said, jumping to his feet. "It's true? This crazy story? There really are twins? And they're not Karolina's? You're telling me these are *my* sisters?"

Lena nodded tearfully. A satisfied smile was on her face. "You are all the children of David and Lena Woodward. Arthur, I'm sorry to have deceived you. I'm sorry I wasn't able to tell you or your father. That's my fault. But these lovely women are your blood sisters."

Arthur looked sharply at Shirley. "You told me you had the evidence. You told me you could prove that my mother was delusional. There was no doubt. What about Dr. Sullivan, the expert who was coming to court to give his opinion that my mother suffered from an obsessive delusion brought about by dementia?"

Shirley flippantly sat tapping his pen on his notepad. "The best opinion money can buy."

Arthur turned to face his mother. "I can't believe this. This is a shock."

"Do you want to wait for the DNA?" Liam said.

Arthur shook his head. "No. There's no point." He looked at his lawyer with disgust and then back at Lena. "What is there to say? If it makes any difference, I always thought . . ."

"It doesn't matter," Lena said. "It doesn't matter what you always thought, or what you did. It doesn't matter, because you're my son and I will always love you."

Arthur picked up his briefcase, put on his coat and said, "Dismiss the case, Mike."

"But, Arthur," Shirley responded, "she won't take the stand. She's afraid to testify. I can win this case in my sleep."

"Dismiss it." He started walking toward the door when Lena said, "Don't you want to meet your sisters?"

He stopped, thought for a minute, and said, "Are you sure they want to meet me?"

Lena nodded. "Come and meet your sisters. They've traveled a long way."

As the Woodward children shook hands and greeted each other for the first time, Liam turned to Catherine and elbowed her. "Chokes me all up."

"How did you ever find them both?"

"I found Sofia. I had an address in Warsaw. I had no clue about Aniela. When I met with Sofia, she told me that she and Aniela have known they were sisters for more than forty years. They're very close."

"How did they know?"

"Each of their parents told them they were adopted from the St. Stanislaus orphanage. The nuns in the 1970s all knew the story about the two babies that were found by the railroad tracks, wrapped up and thrown off a train during the war. The nuns knew they were twins when they were brought in, but they fudged the information on the IDs. When Sofia came to St. Stanislaus to inquire about her adoption, the nuns put her in touch with Aniela. When I found Sofia and told her all about Lena, she said, 'Oh, you need to meet my sister. She lives in Paris.' We flew there together. As I'm sure they'll tell you, both of them have had extraordinary careers. Sofia is a pediatrician. Aniela is a publisher of a French fashion magazine. They were so eager to come to Chicago to meet their mother and defend her in this lawsuit. They dropped everything and flew out last night."

Judge Peterson, who had been leaning back and watching the whole scene, said, "Mr. Shirley? Are you moving to dismiss?"

"I guess so. That's what my client wants."

Judge Peterson slammed his gavel. "So ordered."

FIFTY

...

I N A PRIVATE DINING room in a Streeterville
steakhouse, Lena, Sofia, and Aniela sat at a large
round table with Catherine and Liam, celebrating the
grand reunion. There was so much information to share,
and so much urgency to share it, that it was difficult to
complete an entire sentence without interruption. Seventy years was a lot of catch-up.

Pictures of Lena's four grandchildren and ten great-grandchildren lay on the table. Sofia tapped her finger on
the pictures. "They are your legacy."

"I want to meet them all," Lena said.

Just then the door to the dining room opened and Arthur walked in. Catherine quickly glanced at Lena.

"I insisted that he come," Lena said. "I intend to repair this broken relationship."

"And Arthur? Is that his intent as well?"

She shrugged. "Well, he's here."

Arthur took a seat at the opposite side of the table and
immediately ordered a martini. He nodded at his mother.
"Thank you for including me."

"Thank you for telling your lawyer to dismiss the
case," Lena said.

"Don't give me too much credit, it wasn't that charitable of a gesture. You were right and I was wrong."

"But I wouldn't have testified. You could have won."

"It was the wrong thing to do."

Aniela pulled a wrinkled piece of paper out of her purse and set it on the table. "I saved something. For all these years. I don't know why. When I was found in the field, this paper was pinned to my diaper. It had an address in Sharmassing, Germany. Later in life, I went to look for Helga Schultz, thinking she might have been my mother, but by then she was dead and the folks in town told me she didn't have any girls. We finally figured that someone wanted to us to be sent there to hide during the war, and that maybe she had agreed to hide us."

"Pinning the address to your diaper, that was Karolina's idea," Lena said.

"We both had the same addresses pinned to our diapers, and that's how the orphanage knew we were twins."

Lena was suddenly on the verge of tears. She covered her eyes.

"What's wrong, Mama?" Sofia said.

"For so many years, I didn't look for you. I wish I had. I wish David had met you. I could have searched, but I didn't. I never even told David. I never told Arthur. No one knew I had these two lovely babies. You were sealed behind closed doors, deep, deep inside of me. I couldn't face the shame that I had thrown my babies away."

"Mama, you did the only thing possible," Aniela said. "How many mothers would have had that courage? We weren't thrown away, we were packaged for delivery. We're all here today because you took the bold step to rescue us from slaughter."

"Still, I wish I would have found you earlier."

"I doubt you could have located them much before now," Liam said. "For almost fifty years Poland was locked behind the Iron Curtain. Searches would have been next to impossible."

Arthur lifted his glass. "If you'll permit me, with a dose of humility, I lift my glass to my mother"—he shrugged—"*our* mother, the most determined woman I know. She never gives up." He looked at his sisters and nodded.

Lena smiled. "Thank you, Arthur."

"What is our actual birthday, Mama?" Aniela asked. "We never knew for sure."

"January fifth. I remember it like yesterday. With the help of Muriel and Karolina, I brought you into the world with all our hopes for a brighter future. They were two strong women who loved you both very much. They loved you and fed you and would have done anything for you." She shook her head and wiped a tear. "None of us would have made it without them."

The waiter brought in a bottle of champagne. Liam held it up. "This bottle is a gift from a very special person. It comes with an e-mail." He took a piece of paper out of his pocket. "It reads, 'To my dear friend Lena and the Woodward family. I'm sorry I couldn't make it to your celebration tonight. I'm there in spirit. I wish you all the very best. Lena, God bless you, you kept your promise. All my love, Muriel Bernstein.'"

The spirited celebration continued well into the night. A little after midnight, without warning, Catherine reached out, grabbed Liam's arm and squeezed. Hard. "Liam! Liam!"

"What?" What!!!"

She arched her back and held her abdomen. "Liam!"

"Oh, my God! Oh, my God. It's time. Holy shit. I gotta go. We gotta go. Damn, Catherine, we don't have our car."

Arthur stood. "My car's outside. I'll have Rico drive you."

"Rico? Thanks all the same, I think we'll take a cab."

"Liam!!!" Catherine said through clenched teeth, "Let. Rico. Drive!"

"Okay, okay, let's go. Rico drives! It's been a lot of fun, Woodwards. We'll catch up with you later."

Before Catherine could leave, Lena reached out and squeezed her hand. "God bless you!" she whispered. Then she smiled a knowing smile. "It's a boy, isn't it?"

Catherine put her finger to her lips and winked.

ACKNOWLEDGMENTS

Karolina's Twins is a work of fiction. The story was inspired by the life of Fay Scharf Waldman, a woman of extraordinary courage, determination, and wisdom. However, *Karolina's Twins* is not intended to be a biographical account of Fay's life. Lena Woodward is a fictional character who experienced many of the travails described to me by Fay but, in the process of creating a work of fiction, some of the episodes, though authentic in their occurrence to others, did not involve Fay. I have endeavored to portray the history of World War II Poland, the town of Chrzanów, the Gross-Rosen subcamps, the Auschwitz-Birkenau death camps and postwar Europe as accurately as possible. To that end, I drew upon the accounts of courageous survivors, many of which may be found in memoirs, Yizkor Books, museum archives and in the personal stories conveyed to me over the past few years. Except for the court drama, which is entirely a product of my imagination, I believe the events described in *Karolina's Twins* are genuine.

I am eternally grateful to Fay, for sharing her story with me, and to her daughter, Hannah, who kindly gave me an enormous portion of her time to fill in the details. Sincere thanks go out to Fay's loving son, Fred Waldman—who, I must tell you, bears absolutely no resemblance in any way to my fictional character Arthur Woodward, a person who did not exist in real life. Thanks as well to Barbara Waldman and Carol Chaikin. The memories of the Waldman family and the wealth of materials available to me gives me confidence that the environment in which the characters play their roles is authentic.

I am also grateful to my editor, Jennifer Weis, my tireless agent, Maura Teitelbaum, and the staff at St. Martin's Press, for their assistance and wise guidance. Thanks to my readers for their suggestions, among them Katie Lang Lawrence, Kathleen Smith, David and Cindy Pogrund and Linda Waldman. And, as always, my deepest gratitude to my wife, Monica, who read the pages as they came off the printer and provided invaluable feedback. *Karolina's Twins* would not have been possible without her continuing support, encouragement and wise edits.

How the Story of *Karolina's Twins* Found Me

by Ron Balson

I was inspired to write *Karolina's Twins* by a remarkable and courageous woman named Fay.

While on tour supporting *Once We Were Brothers* in 2012, a woman called me and introduced herself. "I am a survivor," she said, "and I've read many books on the Holocaust. Your book got it just right. I thought I was reading about my family." I asked her to lunch and we found a nearby cafe where, over a sandwich (for me) and a salad (for her) and many cups of coffee, she told me her story.

When the Nazis occupied Fay's town, Fay's father made arrangements for Fay to stay with a farm family and money was sewn into her clothing. She was later arrested by the SS when she left the farm and was forced to sew uniforms at the Shop, sent to Gross-Rosen Concentration Camp when the Shop closed, and was arrested and sent to Auschwitz when she tried to buy a chicken. Fay luckily escaped while on the Auschwitz death march.

I based my character Lena Scheinman on Fay. In my novel, Lena engages Liam Taggart as her investigator and his wife, Catherine Lockhart, as her attorney to help her fulfill her sacred promise to her best friend, Karolina, to go back to Poland and find Karolina's twin babies lost and abandoned during the Holocaust. The novel traces the lives of Lena and Karolina from their childhood in Chrzanów, Poland, through the Nazi occupation, the forced labor camps, the concentration camps, and eventually to the escape from the Auschwitz death march.

My fictional account is based on these true events, with Fay's permission. I am grateful to her for seeking me out, sharing her story, and entrusting me to bring it to you.

I did my best to be faithful to the facts, and my research was extensive. I traveled back to Chrzanów and walked in her footsteps, to her house, to the market square, and to the Chrzanów ghetto where she lived while she was forced to work sewing German uniforms at the Shop. I located her high school in Krakow. I went to Auschwitz and to the brick barracks, known as Sector B1, where Fay slept in the lower concrete bunk. I studied numerous historical accounts of Chrzanów and the camps where she was sent. I did additional research through the Holocaust museums in Washington and Skokie, and in Yad Vashem in Jerusalem. Though it is a novel, a fictional account, it mirrors Fay's life, including the heartwarming story of how she met her husband after her liberation.

I hope Lena's story has touched you as deeply as Fay's touched me that first afternoon.

—*Ron Balson*